LONA HANSON

Drumlummon
Montana Literary Masters Series

Vol. 1 *Food of Gods and Starvelings:*
The Selected Poems of Grace Stone Coates (2007),
edited by Lee Rostad & Rick Newby

Vol. 2 *Notes for a Novel:*
The Selected Poems of Frieda Fligelman (2008),
edited by Alexandra Swaney & Rick Newby

Vol. 3 *The Pass: A Novel* (2009),
by Thomas Savage, with an
introduction by O. Alan Weltzien
(in collaboration with Riverbend Publishing)

Vol. 4 *Lona Hanson: A Novel* (2011),
by Thomas Savage, with an
introduction by O. Alan Weltzien
(in collaboration with Riverbend Publishing)

LONA HANSON

A NOVEL

THOMAS SAVAGE

With an Introduction by O. Alan Weltzien

DRUMLUMMON
INSTITUTE

RIVERBEND
PUBLISHING

Riverbend Publishing
P.O. Box 5833
Helena, MT 59604
riverbendpublishing.com

Drumlummon Institute
info@drumlummon.org
www.drumlummon.org

Lona Hanson: An Introduction

O. Alan Weltzien

AFTER THE PUBLICATION OF HIS FIRST NOVEL *The Pass* (1944), Thomas Savage switched publishers, and in 1948 Simon & Schuster brought out *Lona Hanson*, which sold much better than his debut novel. In fact, Savage's second novel, which he subsequently judged "too sentimental," proved, along with his strikingly different third novel, *A Bargain With God* (1953), his greatest commercial successes. *Lona Hanson*, published four years after *The Pass*, completed Savage's initial literary survey of the American West and set up the primary themes and characters of his six subsequent Western novels. If *The Pass* insists that a ranch dynasty always "spoils something," *Lona Hanson* memorably elaborates the theme of a dysfunctional ranch family and the various forms of loss it exacts. In addition, it sardonically scrutinizes the cattle-driven local economy and "Sentinel," Savage's first name and version of the far-off county seat of Dillon. To define old Dillon in her article, "Dillon at the Divide" (*Greater Yellowstone*, Summer 2005), historian Liza Nicholas quotes more than once from *Lona Hanson*. An unsigned reviewer in the *New World Herald Tribune Weekly Book Review* (October 17, 1948) remarked, "Mr. Savage does not believe in happy endings." The melodramatic ending of *Lona Hanson* does not undercut the grim, relentless logic of the plot preceding it. Savage's resistance to, even revulsion from, hack Western plots in film or print stamped his own independence as he set about writing the Rocky Mountain West he knew first hand, from the inside.

Published the year after A. B. Guthrie's foundational *The Big Sky* (1947), *Lona Hanson* is also a foundational text and, more than Guthrie's tale, a negative anatomy of empire. *The Pass* covers eleven years, 1913–24, as Jess Bentley establishes a cattle ranch, in the process losing both his newborn son and, later, his wife; *Lona Hanson* assesses the cattle ranch from the vantage of the third generation though, in historical time, it picks up where *The Pass* leaves off. It covers five years, opening in mid-1928 and concluding in the spring following Roosevelt's arrival in the White House. The fierce grip of the Depression and its effects upon cattle ranchers is felt in the novel's second half, above all on the title character. The Depression's grip is exceeded by the land's, however, as the 20,000 acres of the Bart Ranch serve as both a refrain and a tyrannical credo. This is Jane Smiley's *One Thousand Acres*, written decades earlier and on a far larger scale, one appropriate to the arid realities of the Northern Rockies, and one with similarly disastrous effects upon family. Savage demonstrates the land's unyielding hold over young Lona, who goes to any lengths to preserve it and, in the process, grows increasingly isolated and alone. She becomes her first name.

Her last name is a misnomer, as her father, a ranchhand (Jim Hanson) who married into the family then ran off with a cook, is a non-entity. Lona is a Bart, her great-grandfather, patriarch Bert Bart's worthy descendant who inherits and tries to run the ranch that sprawls across the "Lost Horse Valley," a thinly disguised Horse Prairie—Savage's first extended use of the Brenner Ranch that belonged to his stepfather's family. The fancy-but-worn home place is modeled upon the Dutch colonial-style ranch house of the Yearians, Savage's mother's family (p. 42), eight miles south of Tendoy, Idaho. Lona will return the ranch to solvency no matter the cost, just when the Depression crashes the cattle market. Modeled upon domineering women including Emma Russell Yearian, Savage's maternal grandmother and the Sheep Queen of Idaho, and Isabel Brenner James, Savage's younger half-sister, Lona wears the pants, and the novel enacts a generational role reversal as she bosses her mother, Ruth Bart; her effete husband, struggling novelist Clyde Barrows; and others. Savage unflinchingly turns up the focus upon the painful burden of the Bart Ranch: upon the "fancy" ranch house's cold rooms and silence and myriad signs of shabbiness, as well as Bert Bart's heavy, black walnut bedroom suite and forbidding portrait—a presence in the novel worthy of Nathaniel Hawthorne (e.g. *House of the Seven Gables*)—and big Pierce Arrow, which Lona drives. As conditions become more straitened in the early 1930s, and Lona more desperate, Savage increasingly exposes squalid details in the ostensibly fancy house and car, and the loud silences that mark the tragic distances between family members.

Savage masterfully crescendos the silence swirling through the "great old house." An outsider and, as it turns out, temporary resident, Clyde Barrows, "felt there had never been any gaiety in that room, no one had ever laughed or been foolish. There had been piano music, but always serious, longing. The room might be shaken by anger, but there had never been gentleness there, or generosity. The old man in the portrait probably had seen to that" (p. 167). Lona worries that his mother, a briefer visitor with "a streak of cruelty" (p. 181), will "notice the old house getting shabby, the worn carpet on the stairs, the plumbing, the heating, the outbuildings needing paint, the age of the car. She might be shrewd enough to know that twenty thousand acres can suck you dry. She might sense the breath of decay" (p. 171). Obviously the reader, also a temporary visitor, misses no clues that something is rotten in the state of Lost Horse Valley. Later, in the "funny quiet in ranch houses after noon" (p. 270), Lona moves like a wraith, disconnected: "Strange how often you have looked at the pendulum of the big clock. Because it is the only moving thing in the room. Nothing in the room ever moves, not even the people who sit there, for they sit still as statues, looking at something outside, watching" (p. 271). It's not Poe's House of Usher, but in the House of Bart, hermetic and worn, little life remains and silence replaces voices, let alone laughter.

In Chapter 28, Savage has Lona and her mismatched husband pay a rare social call upon poor neighbors, the Irwins, whom Lona's grandfather, Tom Bart, had befriended. They discuss Theodore Dreiser's big influential novel, *An American Tragedy* (1925), in which another Clyde, Clyde Griffiths, is caught between two women, ultimately drowning his pregnant, lower-class, first girl friend. Savage's Clyde, an easterner who was the only "dude" who responded to Tom Bart's advertisement (*"Come to a real ranch,"* p. 113), finds himself caught between his mannish, brusque young wife, who thought she was marrying into money that would save the Bart Ranch, and his mother-in-law, Ruth, his soulmate. (Barrows will inherit no money, Lona learns after the wedding.) Savage glosses Dreiser's plot (p. 209) in a way that references the American tragedy he is writing. After all, Clyde declares, "'it's a good study of what blood and background can do'," which accurately glosses the achievement of *Lona Hanson.* The Dreiser reference, appearing in a novel one short generation later, becomes a sly mirror through which we judge a species of Western, rural tragedy Savage knew intimately. Lona declares, "'You know I never read anything,'" which, apart from stock reports or the occasional pop magazine story (also consumed by the hands in the bunkhouse), is true. With great irony, Savage has Clyde, a cultured and bookish man, hand Lona the copy of *An American Tragedy,* encouraging and teaching her: "'Go ahead, Lona. There's a lot more to living than working" (p. 209). Clyde fingers a fundamental American dilemma, one that the twenty-first-century United States still wrestles with. Wife and husband voice their respective identities which disclose an unbridgeable chasm between them. Lona's tragedy consists in her life buried inside work because she can imagine no self apart from the Bart legacy, the 20,000 acres.

In this ranch dynasty, the patriarch proves one tough act to follow. Bert Bart's weight and implacability are measured by his explosive, monosyllabic names. Dead for fifteen years at the novel's outset, his presence pervades the novel, from the Bart Block in distant Sentinel to that ponderous walnut furniture in his bedroom and the massive, grandfather clock in the living room. Savage compares his portrait in the hall to that of Kaiser Wilhelm II: "There is the same finely chiseled nose, the imperious chin, the upward tilt of the mustache. The eyes were colder than the Kaiser's, greenish. They followed you up the hall, never relaxing the watchfulness that had made the Bart Ranch one of the largest and richest in the state" (p. 42). Savage forces the reader to feel what his descendants live with daily, hourly: "See the massive gold chain across the vest, and the fob, the profile of a golden steer with a ruby for an eye. The cold eyes watch still and judge, ruling the house, and the twenty thousand acres" (p. 43). Neither his son, Tom, nor his granddaughter, Ruth, fit this man and legacy (though Tom wears his fob chain). Instead, in Savage's allegorical genealogy, he re-appears in his green-eyed great-granddaughter, an unmistakable avatar in the novel's very first scene: "There was something angular about her, square shoulders, a firm full mouth that might be cruel, as if some Bart had been a Viking" (pp. 1–2). Later, she usually carries and slaps her quirt, emblem of male power. To sustain Bert's legacy, Lona boxes herself into a corner wherein she might keep the acreage, but she has lost family and potential friends. In *The Pass* Jess Bentley loses his family as he builds his ranch; now, Lona Hanson loses hers, and her humanity, as she struggles to keep it.

In another respect, the genealogy sustains the oldest cliché of antiphonal generations as father (Bert) and son (Tom), and mother (Ruth) and daughter (Lona), prove opposites. Tom Bart, who dies halfway through the novel, is a friendly and generous man but a business failure. Savage borrowed his geniality from his maternal grandfather of the same name, Thomas Yearian, and his expensive tastes in horses and finery (and ability to drain a fortune) from his paternal grandfather, John C. Brenner, both of whom founded ranches. Tom Bart knows he doesn't measure up as he sits in his father's office: "He felt a helpless amusement that his own affairs were in such a mess. But it was worth it. His father was known in the state as a fine gentleman. His father had earned that. He himself was known as a good fellow. That was worth it, too" (p. 44).

Part of *Lona Hanson's* irony comes from the gap between ruthlessness and generosity; between Bert's reputation and Tom's. The sentimental plot of the Irwins, small-hold neighbors and dependents upon the Barts, attests to Tom's open-handedness, but the novel proposes antitheses rather than some blend of "fine gentleman" and "good fellow." In the *business* of a ranch dynasty, "good fellow" counts for little, in fact may be a huge liability. In terms of his inheritance, Tom remains a fool, and "the gentle, dreamy old man" dies (p. 134) after the onset of the Depression, Ruth being "left a shabby, tottering kingdom" (p. 135).

Savage deftly introduces the October 1929 stock market crash: some casual bar talk in "Cross-Roads"—his first use of Armstead, the small town that got inundated in 1964 under the Clark Canyon Dam reservoir—includes speculation that even Tom Bart must sell cattle. The narrator comments, "[old Bert Bart] had built well. The foundation was solid. But the walls were rotten" (p. 111). This symbolic gloss of the House (and Ranch) That Bert Built defines both Tom's failure and Lona's challenge. Part of the novel's achievement consists in its sympathetic brushstrokes around Lona, who emerges as more than a hard-hearted slave to her legacy. She is also a victim of bad luck and bad timing, confused by her suppressed femininity and subject to twinges of guilt about a range of hypocritical or immoral actions that hurt others. For example, she chastises Ruth like an angry mother after discovering she stole Lona's stash of money to buy and wear a new green dress on her Sentinel "date" with Clyde (pp. 219–20), yet in Butte Lona blows a wad transforming herself into an attractive woman (pp. 225–56). She fires old Art after his pledge of loyalty (p. 246) and plays an implicit role (the Bart "blackmail") in hastening consumptive Dan Irwin's death and the Irwins' dispossession. Those twinges do not retard her self-destructive course, as Lona "had never been neighborly" and is always "fighting alone" (p. 258). More than in *The Pass*, Savage introduces four character types who surround his protagonist and whom he will re-use, subject to variations, in later Western-set novels, notably his finest, *The Power of the Dog* (1967).

THE OPENING ARC OF FOUR CHAPTERS, set in the flats of Butte during rodeo, introduce us to Eddie Rohn, Lona's subsequent lover and natural partner: a wannabe rodeo star who has quit his Mormon past and the family potato farm near Idaho Falls. Eddie remains honest, kind, a capable rancher, of unquestioned integrity and but limited intelligence or articulateness beyond the worlds of ranch or rodeo. For Lona, he's always handsome and sexual, and always awakens her female desire. This arc also strips away any hint of rodeo glamour (cf. the Bonnie and Steve Earl story) and sets the Lona-Eddie relationship, as she rides and wins the $50 purse, pays for new clothes and drinks, offers him a job and herself, yet hides her Bart identity. Subsequently, Eddie walks a tightrope between the bunkhouse and the big house, between being a hand and the owner's intended, as the pair reverse gender stereotypes. His soft-spokenness and gentleness (e.g. regards the Irwins; or the month-old starving calf, Chapter 11) offsets her hard-headed manipulation of him vis-à-vis Tom Martin. Lona remains intensely attracted to Eddie even after fatally pledging herself to Clyde Barrows under the mistaken belief that his family money will pay the $15,000 bank note held on the ranch, a "chattel mortgage" poised over Lona like a guillotine blade.

If Clyde finds himself caught between Lona, a wife who hardly respects him and physically avoids him (including their bed, at times), and Ruth, a confidante only five years older, Lona finds herself caught between Eddie, Clyde, and Joe Martin. Eddie quits the ranch following the marriage, but Lona tracks his string of increasing rodeo successes and eventually, after the marriage's collapse, prevails upon him to return. Savage typically devotes a chapter to the backstory of his characters surrounding Lona. We read Eddie's story first (Chapter 3), then Ruth's (Chapter 7), then Joe Martin's (Chapters 10 and 12), and finally Clyde Barrows' (Chapter 15). Barrows, thin and delicate, arrives as a thirty-year-old self-defined failure, with a 400–500-page novel manuscript in his suitcase. But he is transformed by Lona and the Ranch, he cowboys up, and he revises and completes his novel—encouraged by Ruth, not Lona. Ruth, a beauty and a quiet alcoholic, is drawn in some respects from Savage's mother, Elizabeth Yearian Savage Brenner. Both are born the same year (1892) and both play the piano. For Ruth, Mozart—Savage's favorite composer—has little place in the ranch world, and she feels a failure until, having drawn close to Clyde (e.g. their "date" in Sentinel, Chapter 29), and despite it being "a kind of incest" (and despite half-hearted and imperfectly imagined suicide attempts), the two of them leave as a couple, Clyde asking Lona for a divorce. Clyde and Ruth can't cook or help keep the Ranch going with its reduced crew. With Clyde, Savage has fictionalized, for the first time, aspects of himself (e.g. he spent seven years working on *The Pass*), and with Ruth he borrowed other facets of his mother than those used in *The Pass's* Beth Bentley. Certainly Savage, a ranch native, never felt at home in such a world as Bert Bart's, concluding there was no room for French composers Cesar Franck and Ernest Chausson, both of whom are mentioned in *Lona Hanson*. Ruth is the first draft of Rose Gordon in *Power of the Dog* just as Clyde re-appears, in younger form, as her son, Peter Gordon, and as Gerry Sawyer, protagonist of *The Liar* (1969).

Joe Martin, loosely based upon Savage's eccentric, bachelor uncle, William Brenner, becomes the first draft of one of Savage's most memorable characters, Phil Burbank (*Power of the Dog*) and Ed Brewer (*I Heard My Sister Speak My Name* [1977]). Savage stresses his white eyebrows and eyelashes, his fastidiousness and secrecy and expertise. He has a "stiff walk" opposite Eddie's easy, rolling gait. When Tom Bart first meets and hires him, he is braiding a watch chain like an artist, just as Burbank later braids. Joe has roughed up the young new whore in Sentinel's "Dixie Rooms" (Chapter 10), just as he later rapes a drunk Lona in her Butte hotel room (pp. 242–43). Martin keeps his own counsel and money, and the other hands, excepting Eddie, defer to him: "They hated him, but he never worried about things. He didn't give a damn whether he had a job or not" (p. 180). He proves himself indispensable and smart. His silent calculation controls others, including, increasingly, Lona, and like the later Phil Burbank and Ed Brewer, "his hands were narrow and ugly, his wrists, bony, long arms" (p. 241). He keeps his suitcase clean and locked, though Lona has pried it open and discovered his unopened whiskey and .32—and is caught in the act by Tom (Chapter 10). The novel becomes a contest of wills as he exercises increasing control over the reduced ranch operation and Lona, right up through the implausible, overheated final chapter. Lona is blackmailed by this mean bastard whom she earlier controlled.

In one fascinating instance, a spring branding scene, Savage closely anticipates the taut opening of *Power of the Dog*: "Then the castration, the scrotum held with the thumb and first two fingers, the knife, and then the blood oozing down the leg. Joe Martin castrated, and he threw the testicles into the fire where they roasted and burst, white and puffy" (p. 210). The opening paragraph of *Power* echoes this passage designed to make us wince. Martin thus clearly anticipates Phil Burbank whom Annie Proulx, in her Afterword to the paperback re-issue of *Power* (2001), famously calls a "vicious bitch."

In addition to major characters, Savage convincingly draws a series of minor characters including Bonnie Earl, disillusioned rodeo star; Betty Irwin, pillar of support for her consumptive husband; Mrs. Dean, competent Ranch cook, long a widow; old Art, garrulous senior in the bunkhouse (with his dog, Toots, hated by Joe) modeled upon *The Pass's* Old Billy; poor Miss Julia Avery in Sentinel, cautionary tale for Ruth (Chapter 7); or even Alma, proprietress of Sentinel's Dixie Rooms whorehouse. In another respect, both Cross-Roads (Armstead) and Sentinel (Dillon) emerge as composite characters. Savage does not bother fictionalizing some features, as he names Highway 91 twice and Dillon's Cabbage Patch with its "rickety little cabins and tarpaper shacks of the poor, of the drunks, of the old men and women too proud to go on the county" (p. 39). Though Sentinel features the Bart Block and Street with its 1888 bank that closes one winter early in the Depression (p. 258), as well as thinly fictionalized fixtures such as Rodney's Store, the Arrow Grocery (p. 175), and the Hartwig Theatre (p. 213), Savage's panoptic gaze focuses as closely upon the Dixie Rooms as anywhere. He sketches the whores with the sympathy of a Toulouse-Lautrec in his favorite Paris brothels. Savage is masterful in evoking the power and opulence of ranchers and their wives in hotels, or bar conversations in Cross-Roads, or bunkhouse chatter at the Ranch with its sundry forms of male longing. His sardonic commentary extends beyond the town whorehouse to, for example, the decline of domestic piano culture in Lost Horse Valley, or Horse Prairie (pp. 116–18).

In addition, Savage is an able lyricist, limning the Lost Horse Valley and Bart Ranch in four seasons, pulling us in close to admire the kinds of details Lona loves in this high, lonesome landscape. Whether it's the play of slanting sunlight across hay stubble in snowy December, or the surge of water and splash of green in the late spring, Savage captures the landscape in its sundry hues with the sure touch of an insider. Those poetic evocations enable the reader to more easily sense, if not accept, the unbreakable bond between protagonist and land. Savage suggests a chthonic basis to Lona's attachment to the ranch, for she has known no other world, nor can she imagine one apart from the Bart legacy. She cannot conceive selling the ranch, as many Montana families have chosen, or been forced, to do in the sundry climatic and economic cycles of the past century. After all, *Lona Hanson* treats a quintessentially Western, and Montanan, subject. Lona's identity is eroding, as the narrator glosses the novel's primary theme after Lona has discovered the $15,000 debt incurred by Tom Bart, in addition to other overdrawn accounts: "If you are beginning to doubt your position in the world when you've got twenty thousand acres, what are you going to think when even the acres are not secure?" (p. 183). Apart from her proprietary inheritance, Lona is nothing.

And in Savage's grimly deterministic view, the whole proprietary relationship is as rotten as the walls of "the great old house" (pp. 110–11) In the scene with Sentinel banker Peter Barton, midway through the novel, when Lona discovers the $15,000 debt accrued from Tom's re-purchase of "'a piece of wasteland from a wild-cat mining company. Where the gold camp was'" (p. 150), she alleges her grandfather's insanity, for the moment advancing that claim as a defense. Savage alludes to the first gold camp scene:

> She sat down and leaned forward, seeing it all. "I found him one night in front of the old cabins, on this land he bought. I wondered why he was there. I see it now. He was sitting in a chair. He looked like he'd been crying." She hesitated. "He was talking to himself" (p. 152).

Near the climax, pregnant and vulnerable and desperate, Lona has accepted her grandfather's purchase of the "bad land" as she stands above it. The narrator's second-person gloss links reader with protagonist: "When you lost a part of you you were crippled, deformed. You had lost something that wouldn't grow back. Or in its place grew something strange and ugly that you had to hide. She was glad, fiercely glad that he had bought it back" (pp. 290–91). Savage implies that Lona finally realizes the relation of "bad land" to "the good land to the west"—the productive 20,000 acres—and understands "the smile that was not a smile but a sadness," accepting Tom's profligacy and recognizing that "[h]e was half alive. . . . Making the most out of half a life" (p. 291).

While Lona fathoms her grandfather in ways she had not earlier, she has trapped herself in a corner, alone except for the ruthless Joe Martin. Or rather, the legacy has trapped her. She neither fully comprehends nor endorses the novel's originating scene when she discovers her grandfather in the gold camp ruins: the first of the three gold camp scenes or references, an intertextual strand that structures *Lona Hanson*. Ruth knows why Tom Bart returns periodically to the gold camp (p. 67), but Lona, torn between her irreconcilable desires to be Eddie's lover and Bart Ranch boss, female and male, cannot accept what she overhears:

> He sat at a table, and there was a candle, a candle throwing a feeble nervous light. A small light, and his face was pale and sickly as he spoke directly into the corner of the cabin. His lips moved slowly, but his voice was flat and sank into the rotten logs. He said, "I wish you'd never bought the God-damned ranch."
>
> Her eyes followed his voice across the room to the corner, vague in a thin pool of light. He said, "We're all afraid. Afraid of everything. And afraid to leave."
>
> She moved closer, eyes hungry for someone real in the corner.
>
> But there was no one there, only the thin pool of light.
>
> She started toward him, then stopped. For in his face she saw what her mother saw in hers, what she saw in her mother's: loneliness that sickened and twisted. She turned away, began to walk away, afraid. Afraid of deformity (pp. 69–70).

The homily of this scene, based upon the placer gold mining in Jefferson Davis Gulch that financed the Yearian ranch, is unambiguous. In Savage's version of the archetypal discovery and extraction of gold and its aftermath, a ranch leads to moral ruination. Savage has Tom voice the novel's cautionary tale, one Lona is doomed to enact. Tom rues the day, cursing the inheritance as though a cattle empire, and the energy required to retain the appearance of wealth, is a fundamental mistake, one that destroys the inheritors. In this first place, the son weakly rebels against the father as Tom talks back to the portrait and presence that otherwise rule the ranch. In Savage's Hawthornian rewrite, the Primal Sin of the Great-Grandfather is visited upon the subsequent generations. And Lona, supreme emblem of the social, even human, deformity she earlier feared, is left with the bleakest of consolations: "She guessed it was better than nothing—nothing at all" (p. 306). In Savage's impressive allegory of empire, land wealth proves as relentless and corrupting as gold or other modes of wealth. Of course it isn't always as deterministic or fatal, but in my experience and reading, ranches most always exact a high toll upon the families owned by them. *Lona Hanson*, appearing fairly early in the gathering flood of Montana literature, deserves to be much better known for its exacting treatment of decline and fall.

To Louise Franchot Munson,
a very great lady

CHAPTER 1 Already a few townspeople had gathered to see the train pull in, and they stood near the door of the station and around the express truck, talking softly. In a few minutes the headlight of the Union Pacific would loom up down the track, pale in the late summer dusk. The faint smoke of distant fires hung in the air, and the gentle hiss of a lazy spray forever turning, playing on the station lawn and on the neat pattern of white rocks that spelled out SENTINEL, MONTANA.

A telegraph key clicked inside the station as the old Pierce-Arrow touring car drew up beside the curb.

Tom Bart got out, a man about seventy, lean and bronze and gentle in a big Stetson hat, California riding pants, tan gabardine shirt and pearl buttons, a belt of hand-carved leather. He wore no vest; only a few links of the heavy watch chain showed above his pants pocket, but the fob was visible, a small steer in profile, made from hammered gold. The eye was a good ruby.

"Well, darling," he said. "Here we are, Lona."

He walked around the car to help his granddaughter out but she was already on the sidewalk, the traveling case in her hand, the expensive pigskin case—her mother's. He stood awkwardly a moment, smiling.

She was tall, but no more than eighteen. Her big Stetson hat was almost as big as her grandfather's, but worn. Her riding skirt of blue denim was clean and neat, but a little shabby. Her polished boots were scarred. Her blonde hair was dutch-cut, faded from the sun where the ends came below her hat. There was

1

something angular about her, square shoulders, a firm full mouth that might be cruel, as if some Bart had been a Viking.

But she was nervous. Her green eyes darted out toward the track.

Tom Bart said, "I'll wait with you till the train comes."

Her glance was quick. "No. Don't bother, Grandpa. I don't need you."

The old man looked as though he would speak, but he shrugged, then grinned. "Don't know why you want to see the rodeo. You ride better than—" She wasn't listening. He said, "I suppose I'll worry. There's only one hotel in Butte—only one hotel where you can *stay*."

"You told me, Grandpa."

"Butte Hotel."

"Yes, Grandpa." She had no intention of staying at the Butte Hotel during a rodeo. The rodeo crowd stayed at a place called the Commercial.

He wished she wouldn't keep saying "grandpa." It reminded him of his years and his importance and—he guessed—his failure. He looked sheepish.

"You left the ranch—on good terms with your mother, Lona?"

"Yes, Grandpa."

He said, "I was afraid—" His eyes were gentle, worried. "You know your mother—loves you, Lona?" Even he could see it was stupid to talk like this to her.

She said, "I'd better get my ticket. So—"

She watched him hesitate again. "You've got plenty of money?" He reached toward his pocket.

"Enough, Grandpa."

She waited until the car was gone. Then she walked swiftly across to the drugstore and bought the lipstick. The first one she had ever had.

The train pulled into Butte long after midnight. Somewhere off in the darkness, somewhere across the dark railroad yards (see that swinging blob of light, a brakeman's lantern) a clock struck once for some half hour.

The others had gone now; she stood still beside the darkened coach, the traveling case at her feet. She started at the soft sound of escaping air beneath the coach and the dull clanking of a brake released. She picked up the case and moved toward the dark station.

Butte was sleeping as silent and aloof as the country she knew. Butte was ugly. The station was in the old part of town. Above it there ran a block of dirty brick buildings, ghostly in a weak street light, buildings of the eighties sagging under granite cornices. At the street level was a fruit store with oranges piled in pyramids, and a cat sleeping in the window. Far at the back of the store an electric light glimmered weak and unshaded over the cash register. There was a saloon next door, and on the dirty window in chipped gilt letters she read THE CLUB.

The second floor was a lodging house. The dark windows showed flimsy curtains and potted plants. Two windows were shaded, but around one of the shades and through the lacelike holes in it bright white light shone.

You got to the second floor, she saw, by a deep, narrow entrance beside the saloon, through a door with a breast-high window. Behind it rose ladderlike stairs to a landing where a tiny night light showed a small white sign. From somewhere above came the muffled blare of jazz.

The saloon door opened. A man stood in the street, his face hidden by the shadow of a telephone pole. She knew he watched her. She stood still. The man moved a few feet, then went in the entrance of the lodging house. Only when he had reached the landing where the night light burned and turned to a second flight of stairs did she breathe again.

The silence was deeper for the muffled jazz. *You gotta see mama every night or you can't see mama at all.* The drawn shade over the window fluttered as if a door were opened and closed.

Her grandfather had said, "Take a taxi. Say, Butte Hotel."

There was no taxi. She began to walk, her riding boots loud on the sidewalk, her hat hiding her face. She didn't look back to the station, at the lodging house. She wanted to wash her hands.

The street was steep and the houses flush with it. Rubbish was sodden in gutters and drains.

"So and so," her grandfather had said, "lived on the Hill."

It had sounded like the right place to live. She was going, she hoped, to the Hill, but block after block of the street crossed dingy alleys where dark shapes of trucks and ashcans loomed.

Dawn broke suddenly, and ahead was a business section, familiar-looking, like a larger Sentinel, fresh in the early morning.

Parked just ahead was a big black sedan, and a sign hung in the back window: TAXI. And then she saw the clear, sharp lines of the Butte Hotel, a big "B" glowing palely above it.

She paused, breathed deep, and the air on the Hill was as fresh as home.

The driver of the big sedan, slumped and dozing behind the wheel, was alert as she spoke. He was young, hard-looking, but his smile was genial.

"Where to?" he asked, and saw her bag, the expensive, good pigskin bag. "Where to—lady?"

She climbed inside with dignity and moved her booted feet as he shoved in the traveling case. She paused. Then, "Commercial Hotel."

The young hard driver looked at her, at her cool young face, at the faded blond hair hanging under the big hat, and her eyes.

"Commercial?"

She nodded. The young man hesitated.

"O.K." he said.

The big car purred, climbed for a minute up the Hill, then swung left and left again.

She had closed her eyes, the car seemed to coast. She smiled, relaxed. She was going to the rodeo. She was going to find companionship and laughter. She was going to see Bonnie Earl in person, World's Champion Cowgirl, whose likeness on a cheap postcard was stuck between the mirror and frame of her bureau.

Bonnie Earl . . .

Lona opened her eyes, started. She had seen these squalid houses before, these grimy stores, and the station, vague in the half-light.

She leaned forward in the seat and touched the driver's shoulder. "Where is it—the Commercial Hotel?"

The big car stopped smoothly. The young man reached over the seat and flicked the door handle. "Right here, babe."

She climbed out clumsily, hesitated, and took out the traveling case herself. She handed the driver a dollar, and waited for the change.

The young man looked at her. "What you waiting for?"

She said, "My change."

"Ain't no change."

"Oh."

The young man grinned. "Course," he added, "if you need cash."

She turned away. There was the fruit store. There was the electric light, feeble. The cat still slept.

There was The Club, and the narrow entrance to the lodging house. To the Commercial Hotel, rates 75¢-up.

CHAPTER 2   The little sign beneath the night light on the first landing said "night bell." She rang it, and heard it tinkle weakly somewhere in the silence between one jazz record and another.

Now she stood in the narrow hall beside a shallow alcove, a kind of bay where a window opened on the close black wall of another building. There were two straight chairs, a spittoon, a sick fern, a rickety side table with spool legs, and a battered open notebook filled with scrawled names and numbers. A pencil on a string dangled beside it, and over it a second sign was penned crudely on cardboard: *Register here.*

There was no one in the hall; she stood, uneasy, beside the table, waiting, her proud face relaxed a moment. She put down the traveling case. Then, suddenly, she stooped and picked up the case.

The station was just across the street. As her mind raced ahead she saw herself buying a ticket, taking the next train home. Swept by nostalgia for the little town of Sentinel, the safe little town of Sentinel, she saw herself standing in the telephone booth there, calling the ranch. "I'm in Sentinel," she would say. "Come and get me."

Now she was moving toward the stairs, hurrying as a sense of filth swept over her again.

"Hello, dearie."

She froze, then turned. A figure hurried down the dim hall. "I heard you. But I was tied up."

The old woman wore an old woman's felt slippers; they scuffed and whispered as she walked, but she was spry, and her thin gray hair was in tight little curls. She wore a short dress; her thin bony legs were blotched with tangled veins, her powder was dead white in the weak light.

The old woman hovered near, steering Lona back to the rickety table and the notebook, grinning with even false teeth. She spoke thickly, drunk, but not unsteady. "I got several nice rooms," the old lady said elegantly. She watched Lona. "Alone, dearie?"

Lona nodded, "Yes."

The old lady smiled archly. "You won't be, for long. Come in after, and join the party." She winked and jerked a small thumb down the hall to the room with the light under the door. "We're going it in there."

"Thanks, no," Lona said coldly, and the old woman looked away from her eyes. "I'd like to wash and go to bed."

The old woman grew formal again, hand on her hip. "There's a toilet and bowl next to No. 6. Just write your name here."

Lona hesitated. "I don't think—" But she was tired.

"Here in the notebook," the old lady smiled, peering over Lona's shoulder. "Oh. Lona Bart Hanson. Three names!" The old lady tittered. "Some is lucky to have two." The formality came over her again. "I guess you must be one of those contestants? You got riding boots on. One of the lady bronc-riders? I always notice things—"

Lona said, "Do I pay now?"

The old lady's eyes went to the traveling case. "No, dearie. You got a bag." She grew more elegant. "Pleasant dreams." She watched as Lona went down the hall.

Lona locked herself in No. 6, exhausted now, but conscious of the things in her bag, the pretty new cotton dress, the new silk stockings and the lipstick.

No one had been surprised at her going to the rodeo. She supposed both her mother and her grandfather understood her feeling for Bonnie Earl. It was exactly the kind of thing they would under-

stand. It made her self-conscious, but they would understand her
wanting to see Bonnie Earl in person, the World's Champion Cowgirl. Only her mother suspected there was something beyond Bonnie Earl and the rodeo that required silk stockings and a lipstick.

A question of her mother's had brought on a scene.

But do you know what it is to have always been a wallflower?
To doubt you have anything to attract a man? To wonder if
there's something wrong—something ugly about you?

She had never had a date. In Sentinel High School, no boy had
ever asked her to dance, and what she had learned of dancing
was at her boarding place in town. The family there had a daughter, a pretty girl, and a phonograph.

"Here, this is good, Lona. Now, you lead."

*I can't give you anything but love, baby. That's the only thing
I've plenty of, baby.*

"Cute words, Lona. You lead."

There was a picture in a magazine, and it said, "Be popular,
learn to dance." There was a couple dancing in the picture, and
as they danced by they smiled at a girl who sat alone because
she could not dance. Maybe there was something ugly about the
girl.

There were times when nothing mattered but someday to know
what a boy said to you in the back seat of a parked car, to know
longing and fear.

The bed in No. 6 was cheap and iron, covered with a tattered
pink rayon cover. She lay down for a minute, just to rest, just to
rest. . . .

She awoke, confused. The room was pale with daylight, and
the bulb overhead still burned, the filament weak and red. The
ceiling was cracked and stained by a leaky roof or faulty plumbing. The wallpaper was dingy brown, with faded purple flowers
at regular intervals, and edged with a border that buckled and
curled. The one window faced another building, and outside the
dusty glass traffic surged and ebbed.

Silent inside.

The sharp creak of the bed was real. She knew what she would
do. She would take a streetcar to the rodeo grounds, be able to

tell her grandfather that she had seen it, come back, pick up her bag, pay the bill, and take the next train home.

She opened the door and peered down the long hall, flanked with closed doors. Now she was going down the hall, strong-feeling, and ahead she saw the stairs of the first landing. She passed the last closed door, and the dingy silence was behind her when she passed the bay, the shabby furniture vague in the gray light, the rickety table, the dog-eared notebook, the pencil on the string. She wanted to rub out her name.

Now, the stairs down—

"Yes?"

She took a second step down, refusing to hear the door click behind her and creak open. "Yes?" The hoarse voice again. Lona stopped and turned.

The old lady stood in the half-open door, leaning out, her old bejeweled fingers tight on the knob. "Where you think you're going?" The make-up on the old face was smeared, the tight little curls tangled, and beneath the eyes the flesh sagged in brown pockets.

"I'm going—" Guilt flooded over her.

"Trying to sneak out?"

"What—do you mean?"

"Trying to sneak out without paying." The old lady moved down the hall toward her, modestly clutching the padded blue wrapper.

"You can see I haven't my traveling case."

"Oh dear me!" The old lady snickered. "Your traveling case! You ain't got no bag. You ain't got a pot—"

Lona's hands shook. "You saw it. You said I needn't pay until I left. And I don't intend to pay—"

"Oh!" The old lady drew back in mock fear. "A tough one! Well, I've dealt with tough ones." She moved proudly toward the telephone.

Lona spoke suddenly, afraid of the woman, afraid of the strange gray light, afraid of the closed doors, and the telephone. "Look—in my room. See if it's there."

"Well—" The old lady stopped, and looked back. "Well—all right." She began to move sideways down the hall. "You'll sneak out. Try to sneak out. If you do, I'll call the police. I know the police. I know you people." She smiled shrewdly, nodding her head, sidling down the hall. She opened the door of No. 6 and glanced inside. "Well," she said.

Lona looked at her. "You're satisfied?"

The old lady shrugged. "I guess so." Her eyes lit up. "Just remember. I got your number."

Lona walked down the stairs, clutching her small purse, but walking as though she carried her quirt.

Butte was not a town, not a Sentinel grown big, but a city, and you would call it that without your tongue in your cheek. Visitors from the East were surprised when they stood before the station, looking up toward the business section where the great modern Butte Hotel loomed above lesser brick buildings, and where, in the distance, the tall, gaunt hoists like huge black skeletons lifted the tons of copper ore from the earth.

"A mile high and a mile deep," they said, and travelers, remembering the power and the strength of the hoists and the crowded hilly streets, took up the phrase and repeated it sagely.

"A wicked city, too," they repeated, where gambling was open, where men and women crowded near roulette wheels, where rich ranchers scorned chips and played with silver dollars, where genial bums begged dimes to gamble. And there was Silver Street.

In Butte, people winked slyly and said, "Silver Street."

For late in the evenings even high-school boys crowded in their fathers' sedans and drove slowly along Silver Street, past the dingy little cubicles, cribs, they called them, snickering at the women inside who tapped invitations on the windows.

"Tap-tap-tap." With a ring on the finger. "Tap-tap-tap."

The bold young men, the big strapping boys with narrow waists and broad supple-muscled shoulders who played football, walked up to the girls and insulted them, as a man would, and maybe went inside, as a man would, and told stories about it later, sitting on benches in the high-school gym.

That was the everyday Butte.

Now Butte went wild. Rodeo was in the air. Automobiles roared up the steep streets, great gaudy banners fluttered, red-white-and-blue banners stretched on taut ropes over the steep crooked streets.

In the Butte Hotel crowds jostled potted palms, the big men from the little towns, bankers and druggists from Sentinel, undertakers and dentists from Missoula, lofty and self-conscious with men they knew quite well, their wives polite in new clothes.

Masons, Rotarians, Elks and Eagles had reservations to dine in the Copper Bowl of the Butte Hotel. "Well, Tom," they said. "Going to take in the big show?" They grew lofty in the ornate lobby of the great hotel, there where the spruce bellboys moved so quickly and silently.

At the cigar counter the handsome young woman with white skin and sleek black hair done in a Spanish way sold cigarettes and accepted tips with a husky thank you.

The governor was registered there, and his black Cadillac and uniformed chauffeur waited in front. Rush and excitement everywhere, and the cars roared up and down, disputing with clanging, lurching streetcars whose bright new signs said "Rodeo Grounds."

The rodeo grounds were on the flat below the town. The arena stretched bare and hot at the base of the hill, and even there the acrid fumes from the smelters killed every green growing thing.

From the cupola of the grandstand a flag fluttered in the hot breeze over a maze of corrals and alleys and chutes, high, short narrow boxes big enough for a horse and rider, a gate that swung, leaving horse and rider in the open—a bronc chute.

Color and movement there, where riders strode about in red satin shirts, tight at the cuff and full in the arms, collars open to the second button showing manly hair. They wore handmade boots of white leather or blue, elaborately inlaid with hearts or diamonds, spades or clubs. They were rough, hard dandies, striding, or perched on fences, rolling cigarettes and letting them hang from their lower lips.

The cowboy's life was every man's dream, a drifting, roving life of muscle and cunning against brute horseflesh. Men riding high and proud in red silk shirts.

But there were the cowgirls, the professionals.

They were not the followers of these primitive men, but their equals. They wore short riding skirts of white buckskin and short fringed jackets. They were slight, thin women, and men shuddered when they climbed on a bucking horse and came out fighting, fighting these thin, pretty women with hard eyes. Rose. Pearl. Ruby.

Mary Pickford curls.

When a horse bucked, you thought of their stomachs, the pounding, and of their wombs. It made you sick.

There was Bonnie Earl.

She was the top; she photographed well, and her wide generous smile on the front pages drew thousands. She was tiny, too.

"Jesus," you thought. "Think of a little woman like that. . . ."

The courage of her. You thought of pioneer women, of a vanishing race of brave proud women, and you got a little sad.

You were proud of Bonnie Earl.

She had married—and for love—the World's Champion Cowboy. There were photographs of the two of them on handsome horses, sitting straight, smiling, and pictures of them facing the camera, hand-in-hand, Bonnie with her curls and big eyes shy, just a little behind that strapping lean handsome redhead. Few women today, you thought, had such respect for a man.

Bonnie could sing the ballads, the "Strawberry Roan," the "Santa Fe Trail," the "Red River Valley," and some she made up herself, sing them in a high, thin plain voice that went straight to the heart. And—Bonnie Earl was the World's Champion Cowgirl. Almost hidden beneath her big hat she could bulldog a steer in seconds, and she rode a bronc with a man's ease. "Queen of the West," they called her, and they should have, too; but you knew the title embarrassed her.

You only had to look at her picture.

Her star had risen suddenly. No paper published the fact that she was thirty, that she had been riding in third-string rodeos for ten years before the public knew her, that she had jostled and pushed her way forward, smiling her smile. Her photographs were retouched; the skin was tight over her small bony face; her tiny, thin arms and legs were strong and supple as a cat's. Her eyes were wide and innocent only when it paid. She married Steve Earl because it paid.

Bonnie Earl, who had been Gertrude Peterson, felt awful. Her head ached; her stomach trembled; she hated her husband. The night before he had humiliated her before a bunch of chippies.

Her pleasure at riding in Butte had gone flat. She had not, in the first place, wanted to put up at that dingy dump, the Commercial. It wasn't as if they couldn't afford something better—she and Steve had had a good season, and what was the use of having money if you couldn't blow it? But Steve—well, Steve.

"It'd look funny, Bon."

There was quite a row.

She despised the other women of the show. Only a few of them were bronc-riders like herself. The others—trick riders, parade women, calf-ropers. Young women, running after Steve.

"Chippies," she whispered.

The sun was hot on the flat at noon; heat waves rose, and Butte was a mirage on the hill behind. A few cars of curious townspeople had already come to the grounds, staring at the riders. One car had stopped near the corral gate where Steve stood, hatless, the sun bright on his red head, and around him grouped a swarm of little boys, a couple of them dressed up in play-cowboy outfits. He was laughing and talking to them.

"Faker," whispered Bonnie Earl, and went on examining her saddle, tying up the strings so they'd be out of the way when she rode.

She had not felt like a party. The train had been late into Butte, and when she and Steve had seen to their horses, it had been well past midnight. They had taken a taxi from the grounds to the Commercial—in spite of what she wanted. She had decided, then, to go right to bed. Well, old Mae had a party going. There must have been twenty in that room, thick with smoke and stinking with whiskey. Steve had donated two quarts; they had had a couple of drinks, and she had wanted to go. But Steve had lingered.

Several riders she knew had come up from the Soda Springs show, and over and over again they said, "Remember, Bonnie, when you used to ride down there?" Days, they remembered, when she had half-died for a ten-spot. They wouldn't forget, wouldn't forget she had been one of them.

"You been lucky, Bonnie girl," they said.

Lucky, hell! She could ride, and they couldn't.

She had cornered Steve. "I'm dog-tired," she said. "The show tomorrow—and it's late."

He put her off. "Have another drink, Bonnie."

Well, she'd had several, pouring them herself, for she seldom let anyone wait on her; she had made a point of pouring her own drinks.

She knew Steve: it made her sick how he waited on the girls, pouring them drinks and handing them cigarettes and lighting them, hurrying to pull out a match and light it with his thumb. He had a way of bowing over them—a regular fine gentleman.

"No thank you," she had said. "I'll pour my own."

There was damned little air, and a damned phonograph and a lot of scratchy jazz, played over and over, and one of the girls sang.

"Listen, Steve, I'm going to bed. You stay here, if you want to. You wait on the ladies, pour their drinks, light their smokes." Her voice had risen, and she hadn't given a damn. Not one damn.

He had looked stupidly at her; he always looked stupid, dumb, when he drank.

"You want to be waited on?" he asked. "Well, all right."

The hot sun beat down as she tied up the strings of her saddle, but she shivered, remembering. "Have a drink, Queenie," he had said. "Have a cigarette." She couldn't shut him up. She wanted to fly at him, hit him, shut his mouth, hurt him. "Let me help you into bed, Queenie. Let me help little Queenie." He bowed, like an idiot, and had crooked his arm to her.

Then the girls began to titter. "Damn you," she had cried. "Damn you, damn you to *hell!*"

But it wasn't Steve, it wasn't the girls, it wasn't the Commercial Hotel that made her sick now. She thought she was going to vomit, thinking of what it really was, and she kept swallowing, and feeling the saddle strings in her hands.

Right now she was standing close to a raw little pine-board shack there on the grounds, close to the corrals, and in a few minutes she was going to smile at the Rodeo Association official, step forward and draw a piece of paper from a hat, a little folded slip of paper.

The name of a horse was going to be on it, the horse she would ride that day, and she was sick, because of a horse she might draw.

She hadn't always felt this way; she used to take what came. But good God, when you'd been with the game ten years, when you'd heard the awful quiet in the stands, the sort of sucking in of a thousand breaths at once, when you'd seen stretchers, and blood, and broken, zigzagged arms . . .

And then the collections they took up, money clinking into a hat somebody passed around, and some women crying, or just standing there, slumped.

It was the *name* of the damned horse. Lady Killer.

Lady Killer.

A jinx horse. Lady Killer had killed a woman, thrown a woman against a fence. Bonnie Earl had known that the girl was sick before that ride, had spoken to the girl, seen the girl take white pills. For her stomach, the girl said. But Bonnie knew, and remembered the fuzzy way the girl talked.

Somewhere in that hat, Lady Killer was on a slip of paper.

She felt herself moving forward; she heard the official call, and she drew herself up, and began to smile her smile. There was the hat, right in the center of the table.

The creaky old orange streetcar lurched and swayed along the tracks, and Lona sat straight on the hard braided straw seat. Now she knew the keen embarrassment of waiting for a streetcar on the wrong side of the street, of running after it before it stopped, conscious now of the oddness of her clothes in a city.

Hers was not a gaudy buckskin riding skirt of the professional, not the bright silk shirt and white hat. Her boots were good, but worn, her skirt clean, but drab, and her white shirt was as tailored as a boy's. She sat, clutching her small purse, starting when the car slowed to a stop to pick up passengers, hating to ask the motorman where to get off. She shook off her uneasiness, for her confidence that she was going to be among her own kind was childishly strong. She glanced once behind, at Butte, even uglier in daylight, sprawling beneath its haze of choking smoke.

But on the flat the sun shone fiercely, and the car, lonely on that vast glaring expanse, stopped. People got out and moved toward the high-arched wood gate of the grandstand, gabbling of prices and tickets and seats.

". . . them bleachers. Hotter than hell."

She pressed along with the crowd, jostled and pushed. The sun glared, and through it an old man walked with inflated balloons on strings and celluloid birds attached to strings on sticks that whirred and fluttered when you twirled them.

The crowd pushed. Inside the gate the gaudy painted canvas of concession stands flapped and bulged in the heat, human figures painted there to mammoth size writhed, paint chipping from grotesquely grinning faces of sword-swallowers and human skeletons. Hawkers cried: for a dime, a thin dime you could gaze on a creature half man, half woman, or watch a woman's naked stomach wriggle and squirm.

Here you are, folks.

Hawkers singled out someone. "Hey, good lookin'! You with the green hat with the chicken feathers. Take a look at the man who has no boooooones!"

Lona pushed on, sidling, elbowing. No grandstand for her. She would see the show from the chutes, talk with the riders, with *her kind of people.* Behind her a voice grated over a wheezing calliope. ". . . dances the hootchie-kootchie and no holds barred, eh, boys?" Ahead of her she saw a little canvas-covered concession, open at the front with a new pine counter exposed to the sun so the reddish knots oozed pitch. There was a square black griddle with kerosene burners underneath, and on it a thin, pale old man with a gray beard-stubble fried frankfurts that curled. The old man wiped his hands on his gray apron, and sadly pressed the curling frankfurts down with a long-handled fork until they hissed and squirmed. His voice was sad. "Come and get your hot dawgs! Come on, lady." Hot grease sizzled and mingled with the kerosene fumes. "Only one thin dime."

The beads of sweat on the old man's brow couldn't kill her hunger; she felt a little faint from it. The all-night lunch counter across from the Commercial was dirty, and there had been only men in there, leaning against the counter.

"Come on, lady."

The old man sliced a bun neatly without looking up, one wicked slash with the big knife. He shoved the long sharp fork-tines under a sizzling frankfurt and flipped it on the bun. "Mustard?" The small mustard pot had a wooden spoon, and mustard crust was dark around the edges. He said, "Hot enough for you?"

Lona nodded and swallowed a bite.

He said, "You a contestant?"

She nodded. Why must she lie—why must she be ashamed she was not a contestant, that she did not ride as well as those she mimicked?

"Trick?"

"No," she said easily. "Bronc."

If she moved away, she wouldn't have to lie; she began to move away.

The old man spoke softly. "Hey, lady."

She stopped, her eyes questioning, poised.

The old man said, "Ain't you forgot something?"

"Forgot?"

"Paying. You didn't pay."

Her face broke into a smile. "I forgot."

The old man watched her quietly.

And she was looking stupidly at her empty hands, still smiling. She opened her mouth to speak, shut it, her tongue hard and dry. "I had my purse," she said thickly, stupidly. "Why, I had my purse."

The old man was sad. "You ain't got it now."

Her eyes swept the ground; guilt surged over and chained her. "I had it. When I came in, I had it."

The old man said, "You had about a million dollars in it." His thin voice rose.

She glanced quickly at the crowd near her. "It's all the money I had."

The old man spoke tiredly. "Why'd you do it? Why'd you have to cheat for a thin dime. Just a kid, and cheating for a dime."

She glanced at her hands. She hadn't even a ring for security—nothing, and now he was saying, ". . . kid like you. End in a whorehouse. Kid like you'd cheat in a whorehouse."

She couldn't shed the guilt. "I'll pay you. I'll come back. I'll get the money."

"Steal it," he said. "Pick a pocket. Roll a fellow, sneak and cheat."
It was hot, and his voice was shrill. "Now," he said softly, "get
out. Now get out." His small eyes were hard. He sliced a frankfurt neatly, and pressed it hard against the griddle.

Her pale skin was flushed and burning. Lona Bart Hanson
licking an old man's boots because she hadn't a dime. Sick, she
had to sit down, had to think—but she couldn't sit in the grandstand, couldn't go where you had to have money. Her steps were
faster. She could feel herself running from a thin voice, from hard
small knowing eyes.

"Cheat in a whorehouse. Now get out."

It was all before her, a montage, the narrow hall in the Commercial, the sick fern and the window that opened on a blank
wall, and the old woman with hard knowing eyes.

"I got your number. I'll call police. Sneaking . . ."

She moved on, eyes straight ahead. She bit her lip hard, and
made a swift decision: she would borrow money—she would borrow it from people she understood. Why, she even felt a little
proud to know what it was to be broke in the middle of a rodeo
crowd, broke as the rodeo crowd knew and understood being
broke. She recalled stories of riders killed in shows, pounded to
pulp by a horse's hooves, thrown against fences, and a rider's
stepping forward, passing his hat. Then a widow had money to
bury her husband, a child would not go hungry.

They were good people. Her kind of people.

She walked swiftly down to the chutes.

Old cars were parked near the chutes, old secondhand cars,
touring cars and broken-down sedans. If you take out the back
seat, there is room for your saddle and bedroll and your wife and
her saddle. There were stubby old Overlands with gastanks under
the dash, Maxwells, cut-down old cars from every western state,
covered with Wyoming mud, red Texas dust. Skimpy camp equipment was set out in the narrow shade of the cars, pots and pans,
and the ashes of a fire, light as a feather, stirred in the hot breeze.
Saddles were turned carefully on their sides to keep the skirts
straight.

Lona walked down among the cars, sniffing the odor of the sun on old paint and cracked leather upholstery. It was strangely silent beyond the cars, down near the chutes, and through the stillness the noise of the crowd surged. Just on the other side there, near the heavy gates, cowboys moved silently to the chutes, the hot wind tugging at the fullness of their bright silk sleeves, and sweat showed through in streaks and patches. They dragged their saddles to the chutes into the shade, and they did not speak.

Bonnie Earl leaned forward with folded arms against one chute, squinting a little, looking through the opening at the horse standing inside, head down a little, standing quietly. He would stand just as quietly in a few minutes when she dragged her saddle out of the sun and looked on critically while Steve cinched it for her.

No, damn him. She'd cinch it herself.

She watched the coal black horse stand quietly, a black, sleek horse. A pretty bucker—a horse for the crowd, but not tough. Midnight, his name was.

She was calm, now, and she let her eyes move to her hands, folded on the plank of the chute, and felt the calmness surge proudly through her. She had made no fuss about drawing, and she could have, and could have gotten away with it, too. For she was Bonnie Earl. And when she saw she hadn't drawn Lady Killer —when her heart stopped beating and weak relief came, she had smiled and done a generous thing.

"Take Lady Killer's name out of that hat," she said. "These kids here—" And she had smiled her smile. They had loved her in that moment.

She hadn't been *afraid* to draw, and God or luck or something— well, she had drawn Midnight, and she could smell his hide there. The other cowgirls stood at a distance from her, talking among themselves. They watched her light a cigarette and smoke it down with steady hands. Yes, they loved her. Bonnie Earl—Bon's all right.

The shout from the crowd seemed far away, and the silence that came, then the bawling of a horse. She knew the program; the rodeo had started. The cowboys were riding.

That silence was strange to Lona. She had imagined the movement and the noise around the chutes would be like that at the ranch on Sundays when a few riders ran in a bunch of horses and rode them out, shouting and laughing and joking.

Here, it wasn't like that. Two men sat on the fence, looking into the arena; their faces were serious, and once, when they turned to glance at her, she smiled. But they had looked back into the arena; their glance, their silence raised a curious barrier. She watched their backs, embarrassed, awkward, and then looked helplessly about her down to the chutes where the dust rose.

The words she had to speak mocked her.

"I lost my purse. I lost my purse. I want to borrow . . ."

Get out of here. You cheat.

Five dollars was a lot of money. The cowboys on the fence were not the free, open-handed breed she knew, but strange, serious men. And five dollars was a lot of money.

She began to walk slowly, self-consciously along the outside of the nearest chute toward the group of pretty cowgirls, and before she mingled with them she straightened her hat and brushed her sleeves. She stopped among them and leaned easily against the chute, as they did. Pretty girls, made up with rouge, lipstick, and their hair was soft and pretty under their big white hats.

". . . in Soda Springs," one said. "I told her either to lay off him, or I'd . . ."

"What did she say?"

The pretty girl in the buckskin skirt shrugged. "What could she say?" They moved away as Lona looked at them, a half-friendly, eager smile on her lips, ready to break into something more if they glanced at her.

She heard, ". . . will ride. Steven Earl. World's Champeen Cowboy!" Heard the roar from the crowd, heard the waiting— then the squeak of a heavy gate, then the pounding of hoofs, and the hot-smelling dust was choking. Her eyes moved back to the chute.

Bonnie Earl was there.

Bonnie Earl was there.

Small and frail, Bonnie Earl stood there quietly, looking into the chute at a black horse. She wore a big hat, and her face was tiny, frank, alone and cool and *good.* She was not like the others;

she was real, generous, understanding—the girl on the picture postcard.

Lona's heart sang.

With a sudden movement Bonnie Earl walked into the sun, stooped toward the ground and began to struggle with the heavy saddle, tugging at it, pulling at straps. It was then that Lona saw Bonnie's face close, tired and drawn. Bonnie Earl needed help.

Lona didn't hesitate. Her heart still singing, her shame gone, she walked swift and straight to Bonnie Earl.

She said, "Let me help you."

The small body of Bonnie Earl stiffened as she stooped there; she turned her head slowly, stiff-necked; the big eyes were narrow now, her voice soft. "Steve sent you over, didn't he? Steve said come help me."

The smile on Lona's face was puzzled. "No. No, I—"

"He's got to have his joke. Got to send his chippies over." Bonnie Earl glanced around her at the other women, close and listening, pretending not to hear. Then, suddenly, Bonnie saw that this plain girl was not one of them: to this moonstruck, stagestruck girl she had laid herself open.

Now she stood up, drew herself up and stood spraddle-legged, her cigarette dangling carelessly from her lips, her hands on her hips. Slowly her narrowed eyes went over Lona, took in the worn boots, the clean worn riding skirt, the white shirt, the slightly battered hat with the thong under the chin. Somebody's cast-off clothes on this moonstruck-stagestruck girl. Stagestruck while the band blared.

The lines around Bonnie Earl's mouth crinkled to a grin, and she began to nod her head like a wise, mischievous doll. "Say," she said, half wondering, half amused, and her voice carried. "What do you think you are, anyway—a cowgirl?" Bonnie turned to grin at the pretty girls. They took her cue. They saw the plain face of Lona Bart Hanson, no powder, no lipstick, sun-bleached hair under a worn hat, and they saw her strong shoulders and hands.

One said, "Maybe she thinks she's a cowboy—more like."

They began to laugh, chattering like sparrows, and Bonnie Earl laughed, and stooped over her saddle again.

Lona stood there a moment, her face crimson, shamed, as if touched by some ugliness. Not until she turned did her green eyes blaze, when it was too late, when there was no one to see— and almost tripped over the long legs of a young man.

C H A P T E R   His name was Edward Hiram Rohn. It was his father's idea, that name: Edward after an uncle, long dead. But, old-fashioned, his father always called him "son."

"Edward was a fine man, son. Always did right and he had a real good hardware business. He was respected by all."

And he was called Hiram because a Hiram was a great man in the Mormon Church.

His father, a stooped, wondering man, raised potatoes, toiled for his family, and always under his nails was the black soil of southern Idaho, a reminder of the potatoes, and the stoop, too, was a reminder. You stooped over the long, long rows, straddling them, and your back ached and your head swam in the Idaho sun.

His old man: his old man's neck was thin, leathery, and he buttoned up the last button of his shirt, but wore no tie, ever. It looked funny to button up the last button and wear no tie—like a man wanting to be a gentleman but not daring to go whole hog. The other farmers around Idaho Falls did not bother with the top button: but then, they had no Edwards in their families, and no sisters who had taught school.

Edward Hiram Rohn, but the fellows of thirteen called him Eddie: they would have no Edward Hirams. They came from the little potato farms around the bustling little city, and their lives were his. In that country they closed school for a week in November so the boys could pick potatoes, and the girls could sort and help with the canning—plain little girls who sometimes went to high school in the town, and learned to use a little powder, and to want clothes.

"All the time you want pretty dresses and shoes with high heels."

But no fellow went to high school—a fellow helped his dad. His dad got old, and maybe began to drink, and then a fellow took over. He was younger than his dad, and could drink without it hurting the place so much. Then men came to the son to be hired, salesmen asked for the son, and the father slipped into the old days, and the son began to stoop from the potatoes.

That life was not for Eddie Rohn; he thought and thought.

He knew Saturday nights.

When the chores were done after supper, all the young men like himself had carried the frothy milk in buckets to the house and separated it, and split the wood and carried it in. Then they stripped off their shirts and leaned over tin washbasins and scrubbed their faces and necks hard. The older ones shaved carefully and used bay rum, as a man will, who shaves.

"Smell pretty for the girls."

Some young farmer had a tin-lizzy. He drove by the small farms in the cool of the evening when the killdeers chirped in the tall rank grass along the sloughs where the night mist rose. Rattle-rattle, the old cars went, and the horns went *oooo-gah*.

Remember?

Screen doors slammed, the spring whined taut behind young farmers coming out red-faced in store clothing, blue serge, a little short of arm and leg; they wore cheap, serious middle-aged men's hats, and heavy black shoes. For work or dress, the catalog said.

Saturday night was almost more than a fellow could stand.

There was the wonder of having friends, of riding in the flivver, with dusk falling, and then night, as the old car putted along to the Roseland just outside of town, a low, sprawling raw-pine building where you danced, where the orchestra played *What do we do, what do we do, on a dew-dew-dewy day* . . . with a lilt that made you hump your shoulders at that part.

And there was the wonder of the light dancing of the girls, fragile and delicate, good girls who had seemed so plain in their mothers' kitchens. And the other girls—their voices were different, those other girls. They looked at you different. You felt funny in your chest and stomach. You said, "Let's go out in the car."

Eddie had had them; but after he'd had them the music was ugly in the distance, and the lights brassy in the hall, and the girl watched him closely over the shoulder of somebody else, or quar-

reled with him. And he could never talk about them in the poolrooms, or in the men's room.

He guessed he was funny.

In the winter when the back roads were snowy and you went
in sleighs, when blankets of soft snow hung over the straw stacks
and potato cellars, there were no dances. Saturday nights you
went to the Broadway Club, in the city. A long, old narrow building with five pooltables: green shaded lights hung above them and
tobacco smoke was good and thick.

You played call-shot, or a game called shit-house, an easy game.
Billiards were too fancy, but sometimes businessmen came in and
played, arching their fingers delicately, pausing before they made
a hard shot with the long slick cue sticks.

Or you sat in the chairs alongside and smoked, and talked to the
gentle, wicked old men who spent their days and nights there because it was like the old saloons, and their stories were of whiskey,
and of women seduced in a wonderful past that would never live
again.

They never spoke of the land they had farmed.

Eddie Rohn noticed that. Guiltily, he hated the flat little farm
and the moist black soil, and the little farms that bordered it. The
little farms were in a valley with a flat floor, but around it the
mountains were lofty, and far in the hazy distance were the three
peaks, standing blue, misty, remote—the Three Sisters, they called
them.

He would look up from straddling the rows of potatoes, his
back aching, and see the blue range. Before he was born, before
the farmers came, the country was cow country, great ranches
sprawled in the valley and up the foothills; beef cattle ranged in
the hills.

That life he felt: knew it inside. Knew the names of the big
ranches beyond the Three Sisters, and their locations—knew their
brands: Hash-Knife, Straddle-Bug, Square & Compass. He knew
cowboy songs, and hummed them in secret. He had two dog-eared
saddle and boot catalogs, and he knew what saddle he'd buy.

And once . . .

Once there were banners in the streets of Idaho Falls, flying
high in the hot breeze; the cattlemen held their convention at the

Bonneville Hotel. Big, genial, swaggering men from another world, big men in trim high-heeled boots inlaid with colored leather. They had ten-gallon hats worth thirty-five dollars, Stetsons, and tight-fitting California pants.

He remembered the back-slapping, the loud loud laughter before the Bonneville Hotel. He had watched, ashamed of his bib-overalls, of his flat-heeled shoes, and he spoke reverently to his chum. "Oh, Jesus. How'd you like to be a fellow like them?"

But the chum was no dreamer. "I'd be one in a pig's eye, same as you. Shoot a game of pool, cowboy?"

What the cowboy had said to him in the Broadway Club one Saturday night was fate, and fate was big.

Sometimes cowboys drifted into town, hopping off freights at night, hoping for a job, for at night the neat farm fences were hidden, the country looked big and wild, like cow country.

They were quick to see what the country really was: they saw it in the Broadway Club.

The cowboy was tall and rangy, boots scuffed from cinders, big hat battered and dusty, but he lounged, idle and proud, against the bar where they sold soft drinks, root beers and cherry flips.

Now Eddie Rohn lounged, too, and drank a root beer. His legs were as lean and long as the cowboys, his hips as narrow, his shoulders as broad. And he didn't stoop.

The cowboy winked at him, and looked out into the Broadway Club. "Farmers," the cowboy drawled.

Eddie nodded wisely, heart bumping.

The cowboy looked at him. "Get the hell out of here, kid. You look like you could ride."

He was silent with his friends that night, and his girl was puzzled and angry. "You never open your mouth," she said. "You're a regular stick."

Maybe the only selfish thing he ever did was leave the farm. He wished his father hadn't given him the gold watch, for in the gift was a strangeness: he knew young men shouldn't get gold watches until their dads died, at a ceremony where the women in the house cried, and the end of it was giving the son the gold watch of his father.

It was too fine a watch to wear with overalls. He carried it with him in its old red-plush box.

There was a desert town in Nevada, a cluster of bleached buildings, a general store, a dusty street. The old saddle-maker behind the saloon smiled when the lanky boy bought a secondhand saddle, bridle, boots and spurs.

Eddie Rohn hired out to a rancher.

The kid, the cowboys called him. But he rode always, rode his gentle wrangle horses conscious of riding, of rhythm and balance.

Now he was riding the rough string, the horses in the remuda that bucked every time. He rode anything, now. And asked for his time.

"I'll be drifting." He caught a freight from the little town, but he wasn't drifting.

"Butte," the poster read. "Rodeo." And the date, in red letters on the side of an abandoned barn. He had the top down on the old Model-T he had bought for twenty dollars. His saddle and bedroll filled the back seat; he sat quite a time looking at the poster, his hat shoved back, his eyes serious, boyish.

He was ready now. He ate his supper at a little roadside restaurant just outside the city, and when he turned from the counter he could see the lights of the city on the hill. He ate slowly, and there was a strange loneliness in him. There was only a young truck driver eating there, boasting to the waitress. She leaned over the counter so her breasts were prominent. "You a rodeo rider?" Her voice invited him.

He looked up in his odd, frank way. "No." Maybe he would be.

Her voice was a little cross. "Well, you look like a rider. Bet you got long strong legs."

He grinned at her. "They're pretty long."

She smirked. "Bet you do ride." She turned suddenly and glared at the young driver, a hand light on her hip. "I hate a fellow's always talking and bragging." She banged the cash-register drawer, and watched Eddie Rohn go.

The morning sun was hot on the flat; he sat, his long legs stretched before him in the shade of a bronc chute, smoking. He heard the crowd, the harsh voice of the announcer, the thunder of hooves. The first of the professionals was riding. His turn was near. He looked at the smoke curling up from his cigarette, his eyes serious. That morning he had walked with the great, with Steve Earl. He had tramped with them into the pine-board shack to pay his entrance fee. He had only five dollars left.

That didn't matter. He was going to place. Not win, like Steve Earl, and those, but place. And then he'd have a hundred dollars. His name was on the books, his money was paid; he had the receipt in his pocket.

He remembered the manager speaking: "Where you from?"

"Around Idaho Falls."

In the little hot room, a room filled with silk shirts and fancy cowboy boots, a voice had said, "Potatoes." He had flushed, felt defensive about the Broadway Club, about the dances, about his folks, about the little farm he had almost forgotten. But he had grinned in that small room. He knew how well he rode. They'd see.

Now the sun rose higher; the shade of the chute retreated. He moved his legs and pushed back his hat.

He saw a girl. She was coming toward him, a cowgirl, but not dressed so fancy. At first he thought she was plain, but her eyes—well, her eyes were funny. They were blazing with anger.

CHAPTER 4   She was walking into the sun, her eyes blind to him there in the shade of the chute, his long legs stretched before him. He pulled in his legs. "Hey," he said, grinning.

She stopped and stared into the shade. Her eyes were angry again and she began to stride on. Then she stopped, and when she turned there was a kind of smile on her face. She walked slowly back. "I didn't see you."

He got up. "Sit here in the shade." He stood until she sat down, then he slumped beside her. "You're in an awful hurry. Going somewheres?" He grinned again.

"No." She looked at him, then away, her face drawn. "I lost my purse."

"Where?"

"In the crowd. There was a lot of pushing—" She looked at him, helpless. "It was my money to get home on." The words sounded like some cheap story.

He said evenly, "How much do you need to get home on?"

She cleared her throat. "I couldn't take—" She grew rigid, sitting there.

"You could pay me back."

She glanced at him. "Well—"

"Five dollars?"

She nodded, throat dry. "Yes."

He stretched his legs out, reached in his pants pocket and drew out a crumpled bill, handed it to her. She held it casually until he looked away, then stuffed it in the pocket of her short jacket.

He moved closer. "You a contestant?"

She started to speak, then hesitated. "N—no."

He said, "I didn't think so."

She bridled a little. "Why?"

"You look like the real thing, like you really know horses."

"But you said—"

"Lady bronc-riders are like actors. You look real."

She said, "Are you real?"

"That's right." Then his eyes were on her with a curious boyish frankness. "And I'm going to be the best rider in the world."

She couldn't look at him until the sound of his words was gone.

He said, "You don't believe me."

"Well—"

He grinned. "I had to tell somebody. You know anybody here?"

"No."

"We'll go somewheres tonight."

She was suspicious, but canny. "That'd be nice." She smiled, and looked at the string of his Bull-Durham sack hanging from his pocket. "Have you got a cigarette?"

His hand went to his pocket. "Sure. Only this here Durham, though."

"Oh. Oh, I don't like Durham."

"I'll go over to the stand and get tailor-mades." He moved his long legs, stood a moment in the shade, and moved into the sun.

He chuckled suddenly. "If you'll loan me that bill a minute—"

Her eyes were sharp. "You haven't any money? But you—"

"I got my entrance fee paid."

She had to look away. "Why aren't you at the chutes? They're better than half finished."

He sat down slowly. "Only the amateur stuff. Professional don't come till later."

She said, "Where did you ride before?"

"On ranches."

"I mean shows. Cheyenne? Pendleton?"

He looked at her. "I never rode in a show."

She stared at him. Then she looked away and fiddled with the string on her hat. He might have a chance, amateur. Not professional. Not with men like Steve Earl riding.

And when he lost his entrance fee he'd be back for the five dollars.

He said, "I drew the last ride. That's a good time to ride, last."

She nodded, embarrassed.

He said, "They'd remember the last ride."

She nodded.

He said, "You'll watch, won't you? We know each other." His eyes were like a little boy's. She couldn't meet them.

When he was riding she'd be on the streetcar. She felt a little sorry for him, yes. But she'd find out his name from somebody, and send him the money.

"I'll watch you," she said. He moved away looking back at her, and when he climbed over the chute she turned to go.

Yet, she turned back. She stood there.

The sound of his name bawled through the megaphone was lost in the cheering for the rider who finished before him. The crowd was impatient for the last event, for the cowgirls, the lady bronc-riders. Nobody had ever heard of Eddie Rohn.

Through the narrow slats of the chute she saw a whirl of dust, and horse and rider in the middle of it, pitching and tossing. Few around the chutes bothered to watch.

She looked at the idle men, at the little stir along the chute as the cowgirls grew silent and prepared to ride. They didn't care about Eddie Rohn. He was lonely as she . . .

Suddenly she lifted her chin, and walked close to the chute, peering through it.

At first she watched coolly, level-headed. He was riding pretty well. His long body moved easily with the pitching horse, but she noticed a kind of looseness in his riding.

"Sit back a little," she whispered. "Back a little in the saddle."

Then as the bronc turned and sunfished, she lost the coolness. "Sit back. Back in the saddle." She leaned forward.

Then they began to watch, all of them. There was a kind of grace in his riding, a sympathy with the bronc's bucking and sunfishing. Seconds ticked by, the judges were silent in the bunting-draped stand.

But his riding was loose. That he stayed up there in spite of the looseness was the thing. He was almost trick riding. It was almost—

Suddenly he was sprawling, arms outstretched, clutching at air, sprawling in a heap in the dust. On his stomach.

At first there was silence from the grandstand, but he grinned and shook his head when a pick-up man rode near him. Then the crowd laughed.

Lona watched soberly as he began to limp back toward the chute, his long gait awkward, painful. She fastened her eyes on his big black hat, lying just in front of the gate. She whispered, "Leave it there. Don't pick it up."

Every eye in the grandstand was on that hat, his dignity out there in the dust. "Leave it there. Don't pick it up."

She watched him bend his long body, slowly, and pick up the hat. He turned to grin at the crowd and limped on again, the hat in his hands, his nose bleeding, shirt torn.

She stood aside as he climbed down the chute beside her. She spoke quietly. "Are you hurt much?"

He tried to look away. "Hell," he said hoarsely. He glanced at her. "I didn't do very good." He slapped the hat against his knee, dusting it. Then carefully he creased it. That was the end of the ride, a clown's ride, a little comedy, a big grin and a bloody nose.

Great thunderheads loomed on the horizon behind Butte, moving heavily across the sky, casting thick damp shadows. It was still, and the smells from the chutes, horse sweat, leather and dust banked up against the grandstand.

"Ladies and gentlemen . . ."

Now you were going to get your money's worth. Now you were going to see something against nature, something perverted. You were going to watch women feel pain, deep.

The wind billowed out the bunting on the judge's stand and carried the sound of the band along with it, the fifes screaming and the trumpet blasting out the "Stars and Stripes." The last drum roll faded into silence, and distant thunder echoed. The announcer bawled again:

". . . for the Champeenship of the World . . ."

The first cowgirl was riding.

The sick smile she had for the crowd was gone as she sat in the tossing saddle. There was little skill to it. The stirrups the cowgirls used were hobbled, tied beneath the bronc's belly. If she kept her feet in the stirrups, she stayed on top. She paid for the ease with a murderous beating. She felt every lunge, every twist. They were lucky who didn't see her face, thin and white as death, and the strange agony there. And as the gun spoke the end of the ride, sixty seconds, and the pick-up man rode out beside the bronc and picked the girl off, she was limp and raggish before she remembered the smile.

Five build-ups for Bonnie Earl. Bonnie was tinier than them all, her smile was sunnier. Light and bright and gay she rode the sleek black Midnight, her white jacket opening as he bucked, showing the green silk shirt beneath. Her pretty face was serious and set. She rode as light as music, a rhythm that caught the crowd.

The gun roared. The pick-up man rode out and picked her off. She scrambled down from his arms like a child unwilling to be helped; she hurried the long distance smiling, smiling to the bleachers, to the grandstand, the shy little smile.

"Please like me," it said.

The bleachers applauded, the grandstand applauded.

She raised the gauntleted hand and waved.

Now thunderheads had rolled over Butte, the shadows were dark and still. Bonnie Earl had waved one last time at the crowd before disappearing over the side of the chute. Even those who had paid four-fifty for their seats did not complain. Yet—they felt a little cheated. Somewhere among the milling horses in the chutes was a horse called Lady Killer.

A drunk started it. He had been calling to the riders from the grandstand, drinking from a flat flask, waving at the riders, bawling advice.

"Where's Lady Killer? What's wrong with Lady Killer?"

People pretended not to notice it, the announcer in his stand pretended not to notice it, but it was there in the arena, the question.

Another drunk answered from the bleachers:

"They're yellow. They're afraid of the son of a bitch."

The crowd tittered.

The first drunk bawled back, "We want Lady Killer!" And the other answered, "Lady Killer! Lady Killer!"

You could see the announcer then, small in the stand way down there.

"Well, folks," he said. "Seems like we got some cowboys in the crowd today!" The crowd laughed. "Or maybe cowgirls. Sissies." The crowd laughed.

"We want Lady Killer," the drunk bawled again.

"So you want Lady Killer," the announcer shouted. "The big drunk sissy in the grandstand wants Lady Killer. O.K." Pause.

"What's holding you? Why don't you come down and ride him yourself?"

"We want Lady Killer." Several voices now, from all sides, baiting the announcer.

Bonnie Earl hadn't heard, at first. She was smoking again, calm and proud. She'd ridden her horse, she'd made a hit. And more than that, she had fought a battle with herself and won. She wasn't getting old, she wasn't getting scared. She'd drawn fairly. She'd have ridden Lady Killer. . . .

Then she heard.

"We want Lady Killer."

And, "Fifty dollars . . ."

She knew what drama was. She knew what she should do.

The announcer drew himself up. "Fifty dollars," he shouted. "Fifty dollars to anybody'll ride Lady Killer. . . ."

She went weak. She should go out there, and stand in the deserted arena, and say, "All right, friends. I'll ride him." That was the thing to do. And she couldn't do it.

Pride gone. Everything. Steve, too. In a minute she would be sick. If she only could get mad, could save her pride—what was left.

She turned then, holding the side of the chute. And she saw Eddie Rohn.

The moonstruck girl was still with him. He was holding his hat, and the girl was looking up at him. Something in their helplessness angered her, something in the way he held his hat. Bonnie's voice was clear.

"You ought to trade that hat," she called to him. "You ought to trade it for a straw one!" Her laughter then was light and lilting, gay and desperate. There was a little answering laughter from the men around the chute.

Somebody said, "Bet he can ride a potato digger."

"Bet he can sure straddle a row of spuds."

Eddie Rohn looked up and reddened, for Bonnie's eyes were still on him. He held his hat tighter.

"Get your straw hat," Bonnie said, "and ride Lady Killer."

He looked at his hat, and grinned again, and shrugged his shoulders, and was aware of Lona's eyes on his face. He couldn't lose them. And then he felt her hand, hard on his arm.

Lona shifted her eyes to the pretty face of Bonnie Earl, held the round eyes a moment with her green ones, and spoke loud enought. "We'll see," she said. "We'll see who needs straw hats." She spoke softly to Eddie. "I'll be back," she said, and turned and left him there by the chute. She walked swiftly away toward the arena, into the wall of sound where the man was still bawling, "Fifty dollars. Fifty dollars to ride Lady Killer . . ."

Now the squeamish sat on the edge of seats. It shouldn't be allowed—this ride could spoil the day, the memory of Bonnie Earl's small gloved hand and the smile could be lost in tragedy.

They saw a girl sit motionless a moment on the tall bay horse; there was no color about her, no bright shirt, no gleaming silver on belt or boots. She sat straight, and she didn't smile. She had her head tilted forward, her eyes on the neck cf the horse called Lady Killer. Quiet-standing, head down, Lady Killer was a spring ready to snap.

The plain girl made the first move. Raised her arm.

Brought down a quirt.

Lady Killer snapped, rocketed. Five straight leaps ahead, ten, twenty, straight for the wire fence at the side of the arena. A horse wanted to kill. Straight for the fence. In a moment would come the squawk of taut wire.

But Lady Killer whirled. Turned inside out. And the plain girl was still on top. Her hat had slipped from her head and hung at her back; her hair was flying. But there was no pain on her face.

Lady Killer lunged. She loosened in the saddle at the turn, and kept riding, riding like a man. She wouldn't be thrown. She rode too well.

The gun roared, the pick-up man rode out. She didn't notice him. And then they saw the quirt again, saw the girl raise the quirt again and bring it down and down and down, her eyes hard. When she passed the pick-up man Lady Killer was not bucking, but loping straight.

She left Lady Killer there in the corner of the arena, his sides heaving, streaked with dust and quirt marks, sprang down toward his shoulder and nimbly away. She did not look back as she walked away. No smile for the crowd. No wave . . .

The rain began to come, and the old grandstand smelled of it, of rain on rotting wood. The crowd moved away, and the band played, muffled, behind them. Lightning flared behind the gaunt hoists on the hill, and in the mountains around Butte the thunder roared.

Copperville was a suburb of Butte. With miles of emptiness to the right and left, the shabby houses and stores and bars were crowded together along a twisting street that not so long ago was a creek bed.

There lived Italians who worked in the mines and spoke their soft fluid language, who laughed and sang sadly. For they were an uprooted people afraid of space, of the bare rocky hills and the emptiness. They sang their songs, ate their foods fried golden in deep fat, covered with strange red sauces. They could not understand. . . .

Could not understand the young among them, shrewd, sharp young ones, aping Americans, hating Americans, making Americans pay for the golden food, for the fluid language, and a Latin's way with a song.

Copperville was a long street of night clubs, garish with lights that almost hid the dark alleys. The old songs a man loved to hear in his house were sung for money, backgrounds for drunken quarrels and nakedness, for little scenes behind drawn curtains.

"Don't. You shouldn't do that in here. . . ."

LA TRAVIATA. In red lights.

ITALIAN VILLAGE. Lights blinked like jewels.

LA ROSA. The blinking lights formed a rose.

The crowd pressed around the big green-covered crap tables, leaning over, rolling dice along the felt tops, watching dice bounce against the cushion.

"Six the hard way."

They pushed and called, and stood beside the roulette wheels, big silent wheels turning on silent axles; players kept drinks beside them, drank absently and called odd, or even, or seventeen on the black. The little ivory pellet clicked into grooves, and somewhere the orchestra played.

I can't give you anything but love, baby.

A couple had been standing in the entrance, pushed by the moving crowd. The couple moved out of the way, trying to keep their dignity, and the young man in the new white shirt kept fingering his polka-dot tie as if the knot weren't right, as if that was why the big Italian hostess wouldn't notice him. He kept smiling; he felt, now, his lack of a coat. His girl's blond hair was carefully combed, and she wore a new cheap print dress. Her lips were bright with a lipstick called Flame.

When the hostess came near again, she spoke over the young man's head to a late couple, dressed for a night club. When the couple had crossed to an empty booth, the hostess at last met the young man's eyes. "What you want?" she said.

"I wanted a place for us to sit," he said. He felt naked, strange before the big woman's gaze.

Oh, I can't give you anything but love.

"Where's your coat?" the big woman asked. "We don't let anybody in without coats."

He swallowed. "Maybe this booth right here?" He motioned to the booth beside him, a cramped, after-thought of a booth, two benches and a board between, there near the entrance. There was no tablecloth on the board.

The hostess chewed her gum with dignity, and looked shrewd. "All right," she sighed. "Sit there unless somebody wants it."

"Thanks," Eddie said. "Thanks a lot."

He helped Lona into the booth. They were silent a few minutes, sitting there, looking around. Lona said, "You were fine, to get this table. They're pretty full."

He flushed. "Wasn't anything."

"It's right here where we can see everybody coming," she said.

His ears were red. "Wasn't anything." He picked up the cardboard menu, and his eyes moved down the words. "Tell you," he said, "we'll have a cocktail."

"I never had one. Are they good?"

"Not so much," he said. He glanced out into the room where the dancers moved now; whispering feet moved, and the lights were turned low. A single spot caught on jewels and silk and satin. He said, "At the Roseland, down home, they got a great big hall with mirrors, hanging up, and lights on it, and there's colors sprinkled on the floor by it when you dance."

She smiled. "I'd like to see that."

He said, "And I'm going to take you sometime, Lona. I know the fellow owns it. We can get the best table easy." He followed her eyes out to the dancers. He said, "Your dress is a lot nicer than those."

She didn't move her eyes from his. "You like it, Eddie?"

"A lot better than those with no backs or things. None of us Rohns much like things like that." His eyes were soft on her. She was like a girl at home, decent and generous, not like those here. If he'd ever minded knowing she had to pay for the evening, he didn't now. He felt his throat tighten. "You're swell."

Her eyes didn't leave him. "You, too, Eddie."

He looked away. "I'm not so much."

"Eddie . . ."

In a moment his eyes came back. "Yeah?"

"Eddie, you're going to be the best rider in the world."

His lips moved, and he grinned. "Who says?"

"I do."

He shrugged his shoulders. "I guess that's good enough for me."

She had a little mirror, and he watched her fix her lipstick, watched her secretly doing this intimate thing. He said, "You needn't worry about the money you said you'd loan me to get a tire. Or the bill here, either. You're going to get it all back."

She put the mirror away. "I know it."

He said, "We always pay our bills, us Rohns. You can ask anybody around the Falls, they'll say that." He thought of the little farm, and the rich dark soil, and his dad in a clean shirt.

"You'd like my dad," he told her. "You can ask anybody around the Falls about him." He laughed self-consciously, and felt for his watch. "This here's his watch he gave me. Look." He handed the old gold watch and thick chain across the table to her. "Listen to her tick." His eyes were proud and confident. "She's full of jewels." He took back the watch. "My dad likes good things."

"I'll meet him sometime."

"Guess you will, all right. But you needn't be scared. He's just folks. Won't wear neckties. Don't put on no airs." He laughed again. "Likes to take my aunt down a peg or two. She's a schoolteacher. A regular lady."

"She sounds fine."

"She likes all nice things. Went to Chicago with some other teachers and brought back a lot of little rugs from a fair, some special kind, worth a lot. She's got the rugs and a lot of other nice stuff in the Falls, nice chairs and tables." His eyes were modest, his voice thoughtful. "Someday she'll give me all that stuff, I guess. Don't know what to do with it. Give it away, I guess." He said, "Look here. I keep talking. Let's dance."

She was light in his arms, and smiling, and her eyes shone so he pressed her closer. *Tiptoe through the tulips with me.* "You're a good dancer, Eddie."

"I learned to the Roseland. Maybe—you and me—sometime

there." He pressed her close, looking up at the spotlight, smiling, knowing the end of this.

Mrs. Eddie Rohn.

Mrs. Eddie Rohn is sure a fine girl.

Be sure and ask Mrs. Eddie Rohn to the party.

That Eddie Rohn did all right for himself, I'd say.

Eddie Rohn's aunt left all those nice things. She said, "Eddie, I want that fine girl and you . . ."

Lona said, "Eddie, what are you going to do now?"

"Oh," he said, "follow the shows. Cheyenne. Denver. I'll do better next time."

"That was a bad horse you had."

"Wasn't so tough." He looked into her eyes. "I—could ride him now."

"You could?"

"Because of what you said."

Her lips parted. "Because I said what?"

"You know."

"What, Eddie?"

"That I'm going to be the best rider in the world."

The music had ended, the lights were up, the spotlight was gone, but the magic was close. They walked hand in hand to the cramped booth near the door. He walked straight. *Take a look here. This is my girl.*

He said, "Look. One of these days I'll be making two, three thousand dollars a year." It was good to see her eyes come to him.

"That much, Eddie?"

"Oh, anyways that. And look. After a couple of years, a bank would help a fellow get a little place somewheres. You know, just a little place, and a fellow would sort of settle down."

She said, "You'll have to work this winter. After the shows are through."

"Sure. Breaking horses. There's a lot of tricks I don't know yet."

She started to speak, and stopped. She had the empty glass in her hand. Nothing left in it but a twist of orange peel and a half gone lump of sugar. "Eddie. You could work for my grandfather."

Glancing across the room, he put his hand on hers. "Maybe I will." He saw himself helping an old man, felt himself bringing new life to a little ranch somewhere. Nothing more natural than that. And then—and then—

She said, "He's got a lot of horses. A lot need breaking."

"Sure," he said. "I could help him out."

"We're near Sentinel," she said.

"Sentinel," he repeated. His eyes got a faraway look. "There's a place I always heard about when I was a kid, up around Sentinel."

"Yes, Eddie?"

"A big place," he said. "You must of heard. The Bart Ranch."

She looked at her glass. "How did you know about the Bart Ranch?"

He moved his shoulders. "Why, bet I could tell you the name of every big cow outfit in Montana. Why," he said, "I could of touched old man Bart one time. Had a great big car parked in front of the Bonneville Hotel. Somebody called him Mr. Bart."

He remembered the sun on the street, the hot breeze flapping the gaudy banners. The sun was hot on the black leather seats of the big car, and the young fellows watched and caught a glimpse of the cool green potted palms inside the lobby. There was a band down the street. The bellboy had been small and neat beside the big man.

"Yes, Mr. Bart," the bellboy had said. "Yes, sir!"

Eddie said, "I never forgot."

Now the crowd was dancing again, and the spotlight was on. But for him the band was playing in Idaho Falls, and his heart was beating. He leaned across to her. "Maybe I'm no Bart, but I'll bet if I got somebody right for me—somebody to help me—just being around, like." He smiled. "Look. I'll be following the shows, and I won't see you. But none of the girls in the shows'd mean blooey to me. Not even the prettiest." He'd never seen anything like the way her blond hair fell across her cheek. Sort of choked him up. He said, "If I was to know that you was—my girl—" Frowning now, he was, and his eyes were worried. He wet his lips, watching her. "You don't have to say now," he said. "You can think it over."

She dropped her eyes to the table. "Eddie, I don't have to think it over."

He said, "Then—then you—"

"Yes," she said. "I'll be your girl."

He let out a breath, and whistled softly. "Oh, Jesus."

She nodded. Her eyes were moist.

The waiter was beside them, waiting, waiting. She reached into her pocket, and the waiter still stood. She reached under the table and found Eddie's hand, and he flushed a little, grinning at her, and felt her strong fingers before he took the bills.

Funny, to get engaged like that, her giving him money. He didn't have a ring, but he gave her Edward Hiram Rohn.

He said, "I don't even know your name. Just Lona?"

"When you come—ask for Lona Hanson. At the ranch."

He said, "Everybody must know you. You must be pretty popular."

"Sentinel's just a little place. Everybody knows me."

"Just Lona Hanson?"

She nodded. It was going to be hard to explain to him about the Barts. It was going to be hard to hurt him. And he would be hurt.

The orchestra played in the half darkness, and couple after couple moved a moment through the spotlight and were gone. *Somewhere in old Wyoming lives a girl I love.*

The violins were muted and high in the melody, reaching and reaching for something beautiful.

"Just Lona Hanson," she said, and touched his hand.

CHAPTER 5   U. S. Highway 91 runs through Sentinel. South and west, past the Star Garage it goes, through the Cabbage Patch, the rickety little cabins and tarpaper shacks of the poor, of the drunks, of the old men and women too proud to go on the county. It cuts through shabby little truck farms where they get the greens for the Arrow Grocery, the turnips and native lettuce.

And then Sentinel is behind, and ahead on the highway the heat waves rise up, shimmering. Now in the fall the sagebrush is dying, smelling of dust, and the harsh little leaves crumble in your hand, but each clump still catches the blue tinge of the distant mountains. Here a dirt road shoots off from the highway and wanders up toward the soft gray foothills to some long deserted dry-land farm. Only a rusted stove there now, and a woman's shoe, twisted and shrunken.

Here is the Cross-Roads: two saloons, a general store, a post-office, and the stock corrals and pens beside a spur of the railroad. There is a boxcar there, silent, empty. Below it, in the hollow of the rusting willows, is all that's left of a fire a hobo made, thin restless ashes and a blackened lard pail.

Turn off the highway here. Travel west, along the base of the foothills, toward the mountains. You see the stream, now. They call it Lost Horse Creek, and along it the fields are dry and fall-brown. The fields belong to the Barts. Twenty thousand acres.

There is the Bart Ranch. There have been other buildings, other clumps of trees against the low foothills, but these are larger, and there is the great yellow-brick ranch house.

Turn off the road. Go through this gate of peeled poles with the bleached buffalo skull on the crosspiece. Up this twisty, dusty road. This is the way to the Bart Ranch.

There are seven straw-mattressed bunks in the old whitewashed log bunkhouse of the Bart Ranch. In the little light that filters through the dust-filmed, cobwebbed windows you can see that on top of the straw mattresses there are gray sheep blankets, and if a man is fussy, a tarpaulin over the blankets. Some men bring their own bedding, rolled in a bedroll, and the ranchers think these men are steadier. A man with a bed has more pride.

There are usually six or seven men working for the Bart Ranch, and when more come they sleep in the barn. Their names don't matter, for they drift like tumbleweed. Sometimes they write their names on the cover of the Sears Roebuck catalog or on the toilet wall, out back. Or they leave behind a pair of boots or shoes, or a ripped pair of overalls on a nail behind the stove, and that is all that's left of them.

Once a man came to work there and drew a picture in pencil on the wall, a bucking horse and a man being thrown into a cactus plant. The others always pointed it out to new men.

Like as not that fellow got to be a real artist, and they wondered if he ever remembered them.

"He could draw anything, that fellow. He'd draw a picture of a girl with lots of curls on her head and pretty mouth, just as real . . ."

They are the loneliest men in the world.

There is an old victrola in the Bart bunkhouse, from the second-hand store in Sentinel, and a pile of dusty records, and the music makes them forget for a little their loneliness, or reminds them that other men are lonely too, and that is comforting.

Sad, sad songs, songs of broken homes, repentant criminals, blue-eyed children still in death. They order the records from the mail-order houses, and they listen. Maybe that night they write a letter to somebody.

They fix the fences and break the horses, cut out the cows, move them to good grass, to the fields in the fall and the range in the spring; the choreboys split the wood, milk, clean the manure from the floor of the old log barn.

"You going to town Saturday?"

There's got to be a future, and the future is Saturday night. They could be sitting there in a bar, just sitting there, having a drink, and a fellow could come up and say, "You're just the man I want. I got a swell job for you. . . ."

Or they could meet a girl. A man could meet a girl. You know how it's a woman makes a man get ahead.

They don't know women, and they don't have women. There is the girl they dream about, and she is everything their mother was, but dressed in white, with a big hat and cheeks like roses.

They will never possess her, for there is no room on a ranch for a hired man and his wife, not unless she is the cook.

Oh, sure. Sometimes a fellow gets married. He draws his roll from the boss, three, four hundred dollars, and gets the train for Salt Lake. There's this girl, there. They party around, and maybe get a room, and like always he wakes up with a big head and her asleep there, and him in that gray room listening to the lonely sound of the city.

The quart there on the chair.

Jesus, he is lonely. He could make a go of it, if he had a woman. She could get a room in Salt Lake, make a home there, and he could send his money from the ranch.

Sure, sure.

And what did she do? He blew into Salt Lake this time, had a bath and shave, didn't even stop for a drink. Bought a box of candy, them chocolate ones with cherries inside.

He didn't even poke the guy he found there at the room (and the new floor lamp with the fringe) the room he was paying for.

She said, "What do you expect me to do, sit on my tail?"

He got awful drunk.

"So. . . . You're going to town Saturday?"

There are the girls in the Dixie Rooms, Alyse, Alma, Tiny. They get a man drunk and cheat him, and take his money in the little room.

"Alma's some kid."

Alma always remembers his name.

The Bart house was a mansion.

Other ranchers, when their means and their families grew, simply added other rooms to their log cabins, and these became sprawling, ugly, comfortable houses, sometimes whitewashed, with maybe a scraggly vine on the sunny side, if there was a woman about. There was little difference between the family house and the bunkhouse.

The Bart house was a great cube of yellowish brick with a mansard roof, eyed with little ovals that stared across the valley at the acres. Behind it rose a scrubby hill, scarred with outcrop-pings of gray slate and grubby patches of sagebrush. The corrals, the maze of pens, barns, sheds and alleyways were at a respectful distance, down by the creek.

In the hall of the ranch house, facing the heavy front door, hung the gold-framed portrait of Bert Bart. He was sixty when it was painted, the prime of life, and he looked like the Kaiser. There is the same finely chiseled nose, the imperious chin, the upward tilt of the mustache. The eyes were colder than the Kaiser's, greenish. They followed you up the hall, never relaxing the watchfulness that had made the Bart Ranch one of the largest and richest in the state.

You couldn't believe that this man had once been poor, that he had lived in a whitewashed cabin up a gulch that everybody said would yield no gold. You couldn't realize that this man's hands (see the hand in the portrait resting on the stick, see the seal ring) had felt the aching chill of icy water as he panned the pay dirt out of Lost Horse Creek, the winter the others had struck camp and gone, the winter he and his wife and son had lived on sourdough and boiled potatoes.

For now his name stands in a heavy black book, a great Bible-like volume labeled "Prominent Men of Montana," and under his name is that of his son Tom Bart, and his granddaughter Ruth, and his great-granddaughter, Lona.

Now there is the portrait in the hall of the ranch house. See the massive gold chain across the vest, and the fob, the profile of a golden steer with a ruby for an eye. The cold eyes watch still and judge, ruling the house, and the twenty thousand acres.

He has been dead fifteen years, now.

The door opens, and Lona's heels are loud in the bare hall. She wears a blue shirt, full-sleeved and belted tight at her young waist, and she smells of horses and out-of-doors. She tosses her light hair back from her flushed forehead, and pulls impatiently at her leather gauntlets.

And now she stops. Stops suddenly before the great portrait. Here eyes are as cold as her great-grandfather's. Her mouth narrows to a thin line. But she is not looking at him. She is looking below him, at the small brass hook where two keys should hang, the keys to the big Pierce-Arrow.

One of them is gone.

CHAPTER 6   It was not an ordinary car. It was the biggest, most expensive car that had ever been bought in Lost Horse Valley. A long, gray, Pierce-Arrow touring car. Now in 1928 it was six years old. You'd see it sometimes parked in the hot street in Sentinel, before the Implement Company or the Montana Mercantile, and flanking it were the new cars, the Buicks, the Hudsons of the ranchers, the Fords and Chevvies of the townspeople.

It had the new balloon tires. The sun beat and glinted on the seats, and from them rose the hot rich smell of real leather. A heavy, thick walnut wheel had smooth grooves for gripping, and a clock in the dashboard ticked with a precise sharpness that meant jewels.

Listen: turn on the ignition of a Pierce, and there is that click-click-click. You don't have to have an ear for motors. When she took hold there was a surging whisper of power. Look. The head-lights are a part of the front fenders, arrogant, different. Five thousand dollars. The new cars look impertinent and cheap.

"What's that? A Pierce?"

"That's Tom Bart. The Bart Ranch."

Tom Bart had spent that morning in his office, the room crowded with things of his father's day, oak and brass and leather and plush, and engravings and stiff photographs of trotting horses. The gun rack was his own, and the guns. He didn't like hunting—he didn't like to kill. But he liked the guns, the heft of them, the shiny blue barrels and the smooth heavy stocks, the knifelike sights. He liked to spend rainy days polishing the guns. He had a box with gun-bluing and fancy oils, swabs and cloths. He liked to show visitors his guns, to handle them there in the office, to take one and aim it out the window at the mountain called Baldy there in the distance. He liked especially the German Luger, flat, compact, savage. One of the hired men had given it to him after the last war—that's what the men thought of him. It lay with a clipful of shells in a special plush-lined box he had had made in Sentinel. It was good to think of it, lying there clean and blue.

He liked to sit there at the rolltop desk, comfortable in the swivel chair with the sponge-rubber pad, thumbing over things, going over old letters from friends. He had a great many friends. He had signed a good many notes.

And he had these letters from people, thanking him. All his life he had given people sound advice. He felt a helpless amusement that his own affairs were in such a mess. But it was worth it. His father was known in the state as a fine gentleman. His father had earned that. He himself was known as a good fellow. That was worth it, too.

His daughter understood this. Not his granddaughter. She had asked to look at the books. He had put her off, and when she left he had locked the desk. When she wanted to find out something, she found out.

Now the window was open, and the sagebrush smell floated in. The ranch hands had been loading manure on wagons that morning, and that came in, too. It was pleasant enough, at a distance.

In his father's day the room had been dominated by the big desk, the swivel chair, the deep chair of black leather with fringe. Each cubbyhole of the desk was labeled, each neat little drawer:

Taxes.
Insurance.
Land.
Cattle.

Tiny printed cards fitted there inside the brass frames on each cubbyhole and drawer. And fifteen years after his father's death, there were drawers whose contents Tom didn't understand.

Three drawers full of check stubs, disbursals of some four million dollars. Business letters. Rows of ledgers. A hired man's name (where was he now?) and after it, one lb. tobacco @ forty cents. O'alls, 90¢.

Sometimes Tom went through these ledgers that reached deep into the eighties, shuffling the pages as he would a pack of cards, marveling at the system. Tom kept check stubs too, but he didn't like to look at them. It simply reminded him of all the money that was gone, and it made him nervous.

Tom Bart kept ledgers, too, and they had an important place right there beside his father's, but they got confused. He couldn't remember how many pounds of tobacco a man had bought, or how many books of cigarette papers, or how many pairs of socks and overalls. It generally had to be straightened out with the man himself, and together they reached some figure that satisfied them both.

"Well, now, let's see," Tom would say seriously. "You must have had me get you about three pounds during May and June."

"That's about right."

"Did I get you anything else?"

"Some overalls. And you gave me five dollars out of your pocket that time."

"What time?"

"Time I was going to Sentinel."

Tom would look at the ledger. "It doesn't say anything about it here." His finger would move along the items. He would say in his slow drawl, "We'd better not mention that five dollars because it will just ball things up."

He was probably the worst rancher in the state. True, he looked like a rancher. He was tall. There were crow's-feet about his eyes, little wrinkles from staring into the distance. He was staring out of the uncurtained window this morning, hearing the noon sounds about the ranch, the men coming in from irrigating, and the iron-wheeled wagons on the stones by the side gate. The whole house smelled of boiling onions and turnips and stewing beef, yet it seemed very far away. He had been thinking of his father's funeral.

The old man had been laid out in the front room, dressed in black broadcloth, with the great seal ring on his hand. The whole valley had come in and out that morning and afternoon. Ranchers came on horseback or in buggies, and there was a stir when the president of the bank in Sentinel arrived in his Cadillac. Everybody went out to look at it.

It was rather like a housewarming. There was a good deal of food, and a lot of people, certainly more than Bert Bart would have allowed in the house. And through them Tom Bart moved, respected, deferred to. Suddenly, on this day, he came of age.

He was born that day, really. Born, but an old man. His father had lived his youth, lived it until the day he died. His father had been youthful, pushing, had taken chances, gloried in success, spurned failure. Bert Bart had never known how to be old. His son had never known how to be young.

Now suddenly the twenty thousand acres and the cattle were his. The desk with the cubbyholes was his to open. He locked it and unlocked it. Responsibility was his, thirty years too late. How strange they had been, those early years, how purposeless. One scene summed it up. He had even dreamed about it.

He saw himself sitting in the bunkhouse with the men, trying to be friendly, trying to be one of them. And they snubbed him.

Each of them knew with just what amount of insolence he could be treated. They were afraid of his father, and they attacked him through his son. It was safe enough. The son didn't write the checks.

And now, suddenly, he wrote the checks.

Tom smiled. But it wasn't funny. Not funny to be an old man who was weak, and had been afraid.

There was not much time. He had ten or fifteen years to be Mr. Bart, and began to do all the things he wanted to do.

He bought fine horses. No other man at an auction had a chance. He bought cars. He went to stockmen's conventions, handsomer, more picturesque than any of them. He lined them up before the longest bars and bought the tallest drinks. He allowed himself any foolish thing he wanted. He was good to everybody.

All you had to do was sign a check.

What folks don't know won't hurt them. He was glad Lona had been at the rodeo the day the Irwins came.

They were not real ranch people, Danny Irwin and his wife. Danny was forty, with a long gentle face, and a back stooped from tuberculosis. Everybody was stronger and smarter and more pushing than he, and even though he signed his name Daniel, everybody called him Danny. Everybody but his wife.

She called him Dan. It was one thing she did to bolster his self-respect in a world of strong, smart, pushing people.

She had been his nurse. Dark-haired and shy, she had dignity, and she understood pride. She knew that the only thing that might save Danny Irwin was a high, dry climate, but she made him ask her to marry him before he knew it, too.

She would never humiliate him with pity.

She had arranged everything. She saw the advertisement for the land in a Montana paper. It was more reasonable than she had hoped for, and she and Danny had inspected it with the jovial real-estate agent.

"Look, Dan," she said, her face radiant. "Look at the creek running through the land. Our own creek! Fish, and water for the land." A bright, bubbly creek, leaping over the stones.

The agent said, "You have high-water rights, you know." Betty

Irwin smiled. It sounded good. But it meant that only flood water was theirs, that every other inch was measured through a head gate, and belonged to Tom Bart, to water Bart land far below. Gold was weighed no more carefully.

"High-water rights," she said. She and Dan stood together and looked across the valley at the vague blue of the mountains, where the sharp peaks needled the pale sky.

"Some view," the agent said, and looked away.

She had been afraid to come to Tom Bart. He was more than a neighbor. He was king of the mountains, lord of the valley. A week in that country and they knew of the greatness, the magnificent tradition of the Barts.

She sat on the edge of her chair in Tom's office, and let Danny talk.

"My wife and I," Danny said, "thought we'd better come to you for advice." He spoke softly, a smile on his long, gentle face.

"Yes," Betty Irwin said. "We knew so little about—Mr. Fogarty said we had high-water rights. It sounded like a fine thing—"

Tom Bart frowned. "Well," he said, "I don't know. Fogarty should have explained that high-water rights mean exactly nothing. And water's the life of the valley. Your land's dead without it. You can't make a red cent."

Danny said, "Maybe he didn't realize that we wanted to ranch. *Had* to ranch. All we have is tied up in the land."

Tom Bart frowned darkly. "Well." He glanced at Danny Irwin, the cheek bones pushing at the transparent skin. He frowned as his father would have. "You're in a pickle."

Mrs. Dan Irwin lifted her chin. "Then the land's—worthless."

"Afraid so," Tom said. "You signed the papers. You can't sell it—" he shrugged. "Nobody'll buy it." He looked at Danny again, tall, thin Danny, trying to smile, understanding that he was whipped. Tom Bart knew what would happen to that smile.

He looked at Betty Irwin. She had on a tiny black hat, black and unexciting. He could have told her a thing or two about hats!

"You're in a bad fix, you folks," he said darkly. "There's only one way out I can see, take it or leave it." He growled at them. "You're going to have to use my water."

He never forgot the way she looked at him. Something about her eyes, and too proud to cry. What difference did it make if a few hundred Bart acres went dry? A man had to think about making people happy, when he had only a little while to be Mr. Bart.

And there was this other thing. There before him, in a blue cover and red tape, was a deed to land. Not good land. Only the lonesome gulch where Bert Bart had struck gold. Old Bert had let it go to a wild-cat mining company when it was no use to him. Tom Bart had bought it back.

A sagebrush flat, a lonely copse of cottonwoods, gullies cut deep with cloudbursts, hard little eroded rock hills, like biscuits in a pan. And the ghost town. A few rotting cabins and frame buildings staggering along a dry creek bed, windows staring off.

Young Tom Bart had walked the street.

Above the town was the graveyard, a boothill, sunken graves hidden under tangled brush, wooden headstones slanting, rotten.

Tom Bart knew the men who lay there, the women.

It wasn't worth fifteen thousand, but to ride alone among the little hills, to sit and think in a doorway you knew . . . and to talk. Yes, to talk. When you are seventy you have a right to talk to yourself if no one hears.

He listened to the stillness around the ranch, the stillness of saddle horses in the barn, chewing hay at noon, the stillness of the fall wind blowing through the fur of that dog there, of the horses and the men, who had gone shortly before into the bunkhouse.

He leaned forward toward the window, listening. He would hear his granddaughter next, coming in from outside. And then— her boot heels were sharp, staccato on the porch. He slipped the deed into a drawer, and closed the rolltop desk.

How like a boy she was, the boy old Bert Bart had wanted. John, he was to be. He was to inherit the earth.

Well, Lona was stronger than any John would have been. She did a man's work, at eighteen. Riding, bossing. He hadn't done it.

He liked to think that it was an old man's whim that she should boss the ranch, but already she was wiser than he had ever been.

Her eyes were as cold and judging as the portrait in the hall.

She was in the house now. He heard her heels click in the hall, and stop.

He got up suddenly and moved a little stiffly, but quietly, to the door of his office and closed it. She needn't know that he had not been outside all morning. He locked the top of the desk. She need not know about the deed.

When the bell rang he went down the long bare stairs to dinner, looking about for something to talk about at the table. How lucky he looked at the hook under the portrait where the car keys hung. The used and the spare. There was only one key there. He would speak about it. It would be a little talk.

He wore the small business frown he hoped would fool his granddaughter, and he let it smooth into a smile as he sat down at the table.

Lona was already there, seated, her face flushed from the fall air, sitting straight, chin up, as she sat in the saddle, hair blown a little, eyes sharp, mouth firm. But damn it, she wasn't happy. He knew, and was sorry. She thought the Barts were more—had more—than they had.

His daughter Ruth was there too, at her place at the foot of the table, nervous, uncomfortable alone with her daughter. She always slept late in the morning, and her fresh dress was not wrinkled or soiled from any kind of work. Powder, a little rouge, white hands and a beautiful full mouth. Her eyes, always gentle and questioning, lit when Tom sat down, smiling first at her, then at his granddaughter.

"Well. How are my girls today?"

"Fine, Dad," Ruth said.

Lona did not look up, helping herself to mashed potatoes. She said, "There were thirty-five head up there. They should have been turned out last week."

Tom Bart chuckled. "Well, it's not human to get around to everything on time."

Lona said, "I suppose not."

Tom turned to Ruth. "Well, Ruthie, what did you do this morning?"

"Well," she said, "I swept and cleaned the bathroom. . . ."

There it was. How utterly foolish, how frivolous, to clean a bathroom when outside, on twenty thousand acres, important and vital work waited. Old Higgins, the foreman, was gone, and had been gone for a year. He had made the mistake of being friendly with the hands. They took advantage of it, and nothing got done.

Lona had talked Tom into firing him. She was right, of course. He was old and friendly. But at the last moment Tom Bart would have backed out.

Old Higgins had a bottle in his suitcase, and after a few drinks he had come to the front of the house to say good-bye. He had said good-bye to Ruth. There were tears in his eyes, and he kept remembering when she was a little girl.

"You were such a pretty little thing, Miss Ruth."

He remembered all the old days, the great old days when Bert Bart had trusted him so. He had another drink, and went upstairs to the office and solemnly shook hands with Tom.

"I don't blame you, Tom Bart, for firing me. I'm old and useless now." It was perfectly true and Tom knew it, but already he was figuring some way that the old man could draw his wages and just stay on the place.

But Lona had come to the office then, dressed in her riding skirt, armed with the awful vitality that shamed both Higgins and her grandfather, who were having a drink and figuring things.

"Good-bye, Higgins," she said.

Ruth felt rather like old Higgins. She had cleaned the bathroom, had taken a light broom in her hands and pushed it across the floor, stooped to a dustpan, and what was that compared to riding across the fields in the cold air, shouting, driving cattle from the brush, turning them out of a gate and counting them?

Ruth could do none of these things, and hated them.

The silence fell, and her daughter sat there, cheeks flushed, eyes cool. They were strangely beautiful eyes, but not gentle, Ruth thought. They were green, and did not often look at you, and for that reason were more forceful when they did look straight, as those of the portrait did. Her hair was as light as her mother's was dark, and it was bleached at the ends from the sun. Her blue denim shirt was open at the neck, tanned that far down; her hands were rough and strong. Firm mouth and chin. And the eyes.

The vegetables had come to the table in the battered old silver dishes with the B on them, and the tablecloth was white linen, as always. Ruth and Tom used the white linen napkins, but Lona's was set aside, neatly folded and starched.

It was hard to keep one's eyes off the napkin, Ruth thought. Folded and starched. Elegant. As she and her father were folded and starched and elegant. And twenty thousand acres outside, and a girl of eighteen.

From the back dining room came the laughter of men, scraping of chairs, talk. Tom Bart seized his little subject, meant to weld the three of them together.

He cleared his throat and laughed. "I went through the hall," he said, "and I was noticing that the spare car key is gone."

The little subject was wrong. He knew it even before he finished speaking, recognized one of the moments that would end in the pushing back of chairs, the quiet closing of doors. He and his granddaughter would be alone at the table, and he would stare unhappily out the window at Old Baldy, the great snow-capped mountain in the distance where he had tried to lose his thoughts for fifty years.

He hoped suddenly that one of them would say that the key had fallen down, and had been picked up and placed somewhere, or that it had been used because someone had forgotten to replace the other, or . . .

Lona looked straight at her mother. She said, "How in the world could a key get off that little hook? It's all you can do to get the used one off."

"Well," Tom said, "It might have got juggled. Maybe hit by a broom handle, or something."

Lona said, "Then the other one would have fallen off. I think it's funny." She still looked at her mother.

Ruth felt her eyes and looked up smiling, a little blankly, to gain time. "The spare key? Oh, it must be there." She got up and hurried into the hall. They could see her there under the portrait, stooping and feeling along the small turkey red carpet, there where the nap was long. Lona watched her coolly.

Ruth came back. She made a little helpless gesture, palms out. "It's not there."

Lona said, "I think it's funny."

Tom finished chewing a piece of meat. "Well, it will turn up. A little thing can get lost."

Ruth said, "Maybe the cook knows."

Lona said, "I doubt it."

Ruth began to eat, then suddenly she pushed her plate a little forward. "Well, I certainly didn't see it."

Lona rested her elbows on the table and looked at her mother. "Don't lie," she said. "You took it. You've got it hidden somewhere."

CHAPTER 7 At most of the ranches in the valley, they all ate together. Only seniority gave the rancher and his family a place at the head of the long table.

The Bart house had two dining rooms. The front for the family, the back for the men, a long narrow room with a long narrow table, almost prisonlike. Long ago an artistic cook had hung up a calendar with a picture of a lovely fragile girl in a yellow picture hat, driving a yellow roadster. The breeze heightened the roses in her cheeks, and tugged at the thin gauze scarf about her neck. The calendar said June, 1919.

The kitchen was large, with a cement floor, and over it scores of cooks had trudged, complaining of their feet as they strained over giant roasts in the oven or stood, at six o'clock in the morning, frying pancakes for the men, the men who built the fences around the acres, trailed the cattle, broke the horses, thousands of pancakes for nameless men.

In the beginning there had been only Chinese cooks, secretive, yellow men who wore quiet blue slippers. It had been Bert Bart's idea that a Chinaman knew his place, but after the turn of the century Chinese couldn't be had. Then there were white male cooks.

There was complaining in the bunkhouse.

Men were not clean. They did not wash their hands after certain duties. There were feuds with the hired men, and favorites among them. One man would get extra peaches in his dish. Men cooks were sullen, or drunk. There were rages, and no meals on the table. There were practical jokes.

Then there were the women cooks. Nice, clean women, but they distracted the men. The choreboy didn't get his milking done on time. He mooned about. The men quarreled among themselves, and once there were cries of rape.

It got worse. Now women were used to city ways, to moving pictures, to dancing on Saturday nights, to friends and laughter. A new cook would stand in the kitchen in her traveling clothes, and look out for the first time across the sagebrush to the lonely heights of Old Baldy in the distance. Oh, the loneliness of it! The coyotes howled at night, and there were always men outside the cabin where the cook slept, prowling about, they said, and only a little wooden latch on the door!

They left behind them the cheap magazines they had brought, wire coat hangers, a tin of cheap talcum. Jonteel. (Remember the little parrot on the shiny black tin?)

Old women came, old steady women, complaining of their feet, swollen and spread with drudgery. They showed you bulges on their shoes, slit to give a bunion room. They spoke of tragedies, of daughters with worthless husbands, sons with fast wives; but old or young, they couldn't stand the Bart Ranch, and this puzzled them, for they had worked in lonely places.

And then Mrs. Dean came.

She had married at forty-eight and was a widow at fifty, but what a two years, she said. She had never meant to marry; all her life she had worked on ranches and farms around Spokane, Washington, fifty dollars a month and keep. She often thought of Mr. Dean with regret, but someday she meant to have a little restaurant along the road somewhere, maybe a gas pump too. It cheered her up.

Now she stood at the sink, sopping some grease from around the drain. She raised her head suddenly to listen, for the piano was playing in the front of the house. Lovely sad music that reminded her, somehow, of Mr. Dean, and of her mother, who had died a beautiful death. There it was again! What a lovely lady Mrs. Ruth was!

Ruth Bart Hanson was thirty-five years old. She didn't look it. Lona was born when she was seventeen. She was the kind of woman younger men dream about. There was something unhappy about her, and valiant.

She was tall, with long slim legs. Her skin was clear and white. Her black hair was pulled back, parted in the middle, softly rolled at the nape of her neck. Every gesture she made was gentle, every movement graceful. Her eyes always held a shade of fright, but kindness or tenderness would make them soft. There was weakness about her. She never raised her voice.

Now in her bedroom she was hurrying, dressing, packing. There was the leather case, fitted with crystal bottles and straps and compartments, and her big traveling bag, both open on the gumwood bed, her wedding bed, nineteen years before. There were matching pieces, a bureau, a dressing table, awkward in the bare room. The painting she had done to the washstand and woodwork was not successful, nor were the curtains she had made. Two rag rugs covered only the worst part of the splintery floor.

She had washed hurriedly at the washstand. There was a bathroom upstairs, but the water had to be carried up. Much of the Bart Ranch was like that.

A single light bulb hung from the high ceiling by a twisted cord, and the small flowered shade did not help much. It had been futile to do anything to the room, for always outside the window was the ruggedness, the ugliness, the strength of the Bart Ranch. Ruffled curtains, flowers on the washstand, rugs over splinters couldn't change that.

She stood a moment looking out. The brown fields stretched to the mountains. The day was dying, getting cold, and a hired man shoveled manure near the barn. Once he looked out across the fields at the settling clouds.

Snow . . .

She stood there, one arm in the sleeve of the smart jacket of her suit, feeling wonder; she supposed there was always one moment greater than all the rest, a moment of wonder, almost of holiness. Here it was. She was going away.

It wasn't what Lona had said about the key—what did words

matter, what did the key matter? It was the look, the look that said, "You make me ashamed. You drink." One of a hundred, a thousand looks, but this was the one that did it, this was the moment of wonder.

No more to know the room, cold in winter, to wake to ranch sounds, smothered by ranch sounds, overwhelmed by a vague sense of guilt at being a part of nothing, at being—nothing.

She would never come back. The snow clouds settling on the mountains were final, the closing of a book.

She glanced at the traveling bag, full of shoes, expensive pumps. *Charge them to Thomas Bart.*

The alligator purse, the chiffon handkerchiefs, the filmy gowns. *Charge them to Thomas Bart.*

Able to charge things, but never any money. Never any knowing *this is mine.* Always within the power of others to give, even kindness. All her life she had wanted to give—knowledge, kindness. Nobody had ever wanted it.

Would that make you drink?

But the drinking she did—it was not offensive. She wasn't loud. She went to her room. And she could meet people, be kind and gentle. It wasn't true that she looked loose, and stumbled. Simply not true. She was always aware of everything. Everything.

She knew when she had had a drink that the keys to the car would disappear. It was humiliating to go through the hall, to know the emptiness of the little hook. To know the keys were in the pocket of Lona's riding skirt.

Once she had said, "Where are the keys, Lona?"

And Lona had looked at her.

Suppose Lona had said, "I took them. So you couldn't smash the car."

So she had taken the key, the unused key, and hidden it in her room, in a special place that nobody knew. Nobody at all. Nobody could hide it from her. Nobody could cheapen her.

And tonight when the house was quiet, she was going to take the bags down to the garage. She was going to take the car to Sentinel. And take the train.

She had sixty dollars. And there was fifty more in her father's desk. He'd understand.

She need no longer dream.

She had dreamed as a child. A long-legged little girl in starched dress and hair ribbons, curled up in the living room on the couch, reading Scott. Mists and beauty and gallantry. Ranch life was never a part of her. No riding, no walking. The hot winds on the flats, the clouds on the peaks never moved her except to fear. But she would watch the sunset from her room in the cool of the evening, the flames and the gold on the soft-flowing hills; killdeers made their far-off cries.

She had found music. Long-legged little girl with hair ribbons sitting straight at the piano, playing Mozart. The Queen of France had listened to that music—put a small slippered foot forward in the minuet.

The little girl played on rainy afternoons when the mud was deep outside in the corrals and the saddle horses stood with their tails to the wind, played when the men came in the back dining room, their chairs scraping on the cement floor, their laughter loud, in another world.

A boarding school in the East. Long-legged little lonesome girl in uniform moving in clean narrow halls, hearing laughter in small rooms, closed to her.

"Oh, she's a Westerner. Nobody knows *her*. . . ."

Couldn't answer back, little dreamer wanting home. Not Montana. Not mountains and freedom and space. Only the quiet of the ranch house, high ceilings, wanting to play the most beautiful music in the world.

They couldn't send her back to school. She married a ranch hand, a grinning happy-go-lucky breaker of horses, a bronc-stomper with a big mouth and a wide grin. She had lied about her age, fled across the state line, married him.

And came back with him.

They couldn't do anything. Her grandfather's green eyes grew colder. Her father hung his head. There was slamming of doors, and empty chairs at dinner, and a solution. The Barts brought the breaker of horses into the house, made him foreman, tried to make a gentleman of this big genial cowboy who had married a Bart.

Jim Hanson.

She never blamed him. His crudeness offended her, for love to her was gentle and misty. But she didn't blame him.

Jim Hanson ran away with the cook.

They talked of it in the valley, in the kitchens of the ranch houses, in the depot, in the hotel in Sentinel. Ruth stayed in her room. It didn't matter. She was going to have a baby. . . .

She swayed a little, looking down into the bag of shoes. She listened.

The sounds were all the old sounds set against the awful silence of the house, of long halls, six bedrooms, huge rooms with space for silence to wait, and through it cut the sounds from outside.

Branding cattle out there. From the corrals the dust rose and calves bawled as the hot iron seared, and there was the rich sweet smell of blood. Shouting, and the flash of blue denim shirts in the gray fall light. And a flash of red.

Lona was wearing a red shirt that day, red with long full sleeves.

She steadied herself against the bed, fumbling at the sleeve of her suit. She was not drunk. Not really. For a time, even after the words at the table, she had not drunk at all.

How fine it would be to leave the ranch without a drink, to leave knowing that she was strong. But she kept thinking of the full bottle, of the boarding school, of Lona—

There were glasses downstairs.

She had paused at the piano, and played a little, and still thought of the bottle, and of the years in that house.

She had taken the glass down from the shelf carefully, but it clinked against another. She hurried with it to her room, cupped the thin coldness in her palm.

The bottle was at the bottom of the clothes hamper. There was always a tightness that grew into panic as she groped down and down through the clothes. Maybe it was gone . . . maybe Lona . . .

There were other places to hide whiskey. Under the mattress. A pint could be hidden in two shoes. Put the pint in, cover the neck with the other shoe. Leave it there with the other shoes. You'd never see, never suspect . . .

Or empty the bottle into the cologne bottle. Right in sight, and nobody saw. . . .

She put the bottle on the dressing table, there beside the box of face powder, the Coty box, the little orange round box embossed with fluffy powder puffs. Right there. No, the glass . . .

Lock the door.

Five o'clock. Not long to wait now. Mrs. Dean had put the meat on. Smell it. Then six, and the dinner bell, then men's voices in the back dining room, and the pause in the front dining room. No words, just the pause.

Then—seven, eight, nine. Lona would go to her room. Tom Bart would go across to the cellar to the electric light plant, shut it off. The door would slam. Then he would go to his room.

Be careful. Wait. Give them time to sleep . . .

Hurry down, into the car, with the key. The unused key. Used just this once. Flight.

Chicago, that was the place.

Did they wonder what she'd do? She knew. She was going to teach music—a nice little apartment, and the students coming. A grand piano, rented (bought later) near a big window, and a single vase of flowers on a stand. Only that. She—she knew she could teach. You can teach anything you love as much as she loved music. Something in you touches others. You don't know what it is, you just have it. Others feel it.

Ruth Bart Hanson. *Teacher of piano.* White, steel-engraved card behind glass.

"Ruth Bart Hanson? A fine pianist. A great teacher."

"She has some *quality.* Something that *touches* you . . ."

"Oh, yes. Ruth Bart Hanson. Charming."

She reached suddenly for the bottle. Why must she now think of Miss Avery?

Miss Avery lived in a spindly little wooden house in Sentinel, with a tiny porch with gingerbread, and two thin pillars like spools piled up.

The windows (why should you recall the windows?) had an opaque, wavy look, and the heavy glass curtains were always close-drawn. There was a little wooden sign tacked to one of the thin pillars: *Julia Avery, Teacher of the Pianoforte.* Once, once long ago, the letters were of gilt.

Sentinel had been proud of her, for there it was considered fine to have gone to Normal School, and Miss Avery had gone beyond that.

"Miss Julia Avery has returned to Sentinel from Conservatory."

There had been a concert, and Miss Julia Avery smiling and clasping flowers to her breast there on the platform of the high-school auditorium. Her parents, shy, came to bow too. There were not many such evening for the parents of Julia Avery.

A long time ago. The parents of Miss Avery had died as poor as they began, and Miss Julia lived in the small bare house, changing nothing, rarely coming out except to see her friend, a thin, gray woman with a pince-nez, who worked at the Public Library.

Miss Julia Avery had taught Ruth piano. Ruth was about fourteen, then, and Miss Avery about thirty-five. She had not much changed. Even then, she had seemed thin and gray, with a nervous, timid smile. The lesson was at two, and the bare house smelled of closeness, of unaired clothing, and of cabbage.

Always at two Miss Julia would be eating. A bit of crackers and milk, or some canned soup, right from the saucepan. She always dabbed at her mouth as she unlocked the door at two, and then that timid little smile.

"I was just having my luncheon." Dab-dab-dab. "My luncheon."

Anybody else in Sentinel would have said dinner.

There was an upright piano in the small bare sitting room, an old black Weber and a round stool that turned on a great screw; Miss Avery sat beside her pupil in an old wicker chair, and the strands of the wicker were parting. A window, rather high in the wall, shed small light on the end table and a copy of *The Etude.*

Only that.

"Now, that's almost right. No, you didn't make a mistake. Perhaps your—perhaps I'm hurrying you. No, you didn't make a mistake. Your finger just slipped, Miss Bart. Oh, Miss Bart, that's right!"

It was awful, the relief, the gratitude, when Ruth handed her the dollar.

"Oh, *thank* you, Miss Bart. And you played just lovely. Oh, *thank* you. . . ."

Why must she now think of Miss Avery? Why must she now sit here with tears in her eyes?

How she had wanted to do some magnificent thing! To turn suddenly at the end of the lesson and say, "Miss Avery, here is a hundred dollars." It might as well have been a thousand. A hundred was a lot even now, when all you had was a kind of doubtful allowance. . . .

Ruth got up. She walked nervously the length of the room, and back. Feet beautiful in pumps. Every movement relaxed into beauty. Her jacket hung smartly from her shoulders.

"Charge it to Thomas Bart. . . ."

She closed the small bag, snapped the catches. Six o'clock.

It was now less than five years since the Episcopal Guild gave the dance, just before Christmas. They had bought baskets with the money, and canned foods, turkeys, nuts, oranges, and these things were tucked into the baskets. They drew up a list of the poor of Sentinel, and Ruth volunteered the Pierce-Arrow to help deliver these things. She was not a good lady-bountiful; she hated poverty, hated squalor. She ached inside, frightened at want, but Bert Bart had built the Episcopal church.

How strange that the name of Julia Avery should appear on the list. It had never appeared before.

"I can't do it. I know her. She gave me lessons. I would humiliate . . ."

They said, "Not so much as a stranger."

She grew stiff, tight inside. She hoped Miss Julia Avery would not be at home. Then she could leave the basket—go.

But there she was, ringing, as she had rung.

She was so small, Miss Avery, hesitant and puzzled and then that small timid smile. "Oh, Miss Bart. Mrs. *Hanson*. I forget so. Oh, sixteen years . . ."

Ruth had stood there, and then went in, with that awful basket, and sat almost automatically on the old round stool at the piano. She said, "I came—I thought this little present—because of old times, Miss Avery. Just something foolish." And smiled. No one was proof against that smile.

Miss Avery said, "A merry Christmas I will have indeed."

A car went by outside, lights on. Shadows moved across the ceiling. At City Hall decorations were up for the Christmas Eve dance. Businessmen were having Tom and Jerries in the Pheasant. In a few minutes Schumann-Heink would sing over the radio.

Stille Nacht, heilige Nacht. . . .

Miss Avery sat in the old wicker chair.

Ruth smiled again. "I wonder if you'd give me a cup of tea."

"Oh," Miss Avery said. "Oh, can you—will you stay?"

"I should very much like to visit. I was rather lonely." To hell with the dance.

"Oh," Miss Avery said. "And I *have* something—"

She had a box of chocolate cookies. They made tea together in the kitchen. They talked, they laughed. Oh, they had such a time. But then—it was all over.

They had a red candle burning in the window. Miss Avery seemed afraid now, the magic gone. She spoke timidly. "I wonder if—for old times, Miss Bart. If for old times you'd play the little Mozart."

Her eyes—well, what could you say of the eyes of Julia Avery?

Ruth spoke softly. "I had hoped you would ask me. You see," she said, "there are not many in the world who understand Mozart as we do. You and I, Miss Avery."

She sat down on the old round stool and played the poignant little first sonata in the small cold room. Miss Avery sat in the wicker chair. For a long time she didn't say anything. Then, "Oh, Miss Bart. I had forgotten there was so much beauty in the world. You see—you see, I don't play much now. My hands."

They were stiff hands. When Ruth took her hand at the door and pressed it, she felt it stiff and crooked, like a claw.

Old Forbes the coroner said Miss Julia Avery died of malnutrition. Starved to death, in Sentinel, Montana, alone, unable even to wash the few dishes in the sink.

Seven o'clock. Now from the bunkhouse came the loud voices of hired men, the sound of water hitting the ground, thrown from a washbasin. Dusk was deep, but Ruth stared out across the twenty thousand acres, at the dirt road that twisted down to Sentinel. Beyond was Butte. Beyond was—Chicago.

She turned suddenly, and her eyes held terror. Suppose no student ever came to that rented room in Chicago. She saw herself sitting alone and sick at a rented piano, the flowers withering in the vase, a sauce pan on a burner.

But then in a moment she knew it was all right, for she had made no move. She was still Ruth Bart Hanson, daughter of a man with twenty thousand acres. It would be unpleasant, yes, to face her father, who would smile as if he didn't know she was drinking, to face her daughter, who knew.

But she was not going to starve in a rented room.

Suddenly she reached for the box of Coty powder, the little round orange box with the powderpuffs. She lifted the lid carefully, and the big puff inside. And there, just below a skiff of powder, was the key to the car.

In the dusk of her room—the room no one could take from her—she sat at her dressing table and put her head down on her hands.

This had happened so many times.

CHAPTER 8

When Lona was small she was often with her great-grandfather, old Bert Bart. She carried to him up there in his big dark room the freshness of the out-of-doors, and of youth. He always questioned her closely. What was everybody doing? What was his son doing? Carrying out orders, not taking advantage of an old man?

"What are they up to now?" he'd ask her. "Go down behind the barn and see if they're fixing that fence. You love great-grandpa, don't you? That's more than the rest do." In his age he was not afraid to let his old eyes fill with tears.

Or, "What's your mother up to today?" he would ask. "Is she doing some useful work? Playing that piano? She ought to take more care of you. Her little girl." Tears again. "Don't mind," the old man would say. "Great-grandpa will care for you."

They were alone against the world.

As she grew older it was strange to leave the out-of-doors to come in at suppertime to the great, high-ceilinged house, always cool, always shadowy, even on the hottest days. She could mark the end of a thousand days standing there in the dark hall under the portrait, remembering that outside there was life, sun and dust, talk, men sweating. And now, beyond the hall, her mother sat playing the piano.

But not always. Once she had stood in the hall at the end of a day and seen her grandfather, Tom Bart, with his arm about her mother, helping her upstairs.

"But I don't want to go up," her mother kept saying. "Let me alone. I don't want to."

And later, Tom's saying, "Your mother's sick, darling."

There was something weak and unclean about sickness, something of darkened, unaired rooms, of rumpled bedclothes, stale breath and hopelessness. "Sick?"

"Yes. Don't go up, Lona." Softly.

But when her grandfather had gone to the bunkhouse, she had gone upstairs. The reddish sun, low on the horizon, shone through the narrow window at the end of the upper hall and blinded her. She had begun to tiptoe near her mother's room, her eyes on the closed door. The click of the latch on her mother's door made her stand suddenly still, a little girl in boy's overalls, bobbed hair bleached from the sun.

The door of her mother's room creaked, opened a crack. And eyes looked out. Lona stared, and her mother's eyes stared back. Then the eyes smiled. "Darling," her mother said, and the word sickened her. She turned and ran then, and the word and the smile followed her, clung to her. There was no one to tell, for old Bert Bart had been dead now for several years.

Tom Bart was proud of the Freed-Eisemann radio set on the living room table, proud of the cost of it, of the big smooth-turning knobs, of the little knobs and the tubes that glowed inside the polished mahogany box. An uncharacteristic thriftiness in him made him use the headphones rather than plug in the great curved horn: he felt it was easier on the radio; but occasionally the room was filled with dance music from the Brown Palace in Denver.

I can't give you anything but love, baby. . . .

"There now, Lona." He had looked proudly from the big horn to his granddaughter. "How is that? How'd you like to be dancing to that?"

She had gone upstairs; he opened the polished mahogany box and looked in at the glowing tubes and things, wondering what it was he had said this time.

Why didn't Eddie come? There in the bedroom she would think of him, of his sitting with some girl across a table in a room where there were lights and moving shadows and music.

She was ashamed of her secret; twice she had gone to her closet and taken out the things she had worn when she was with him, the same underthings, the cotton dress, the silk stockings, the high-heeled shoes, and put them on. At first she had sat there in the dark on her bed. Then she had walked across the room, conscious of the shoes, afraid to turn on the light, for the light and the mirror of the dressing table would make it real, this longing and loneliness. But of course she did it: locked the door, sat before her mirror under the bright light and put on the lipstick.

Later she wiped it off carefully and put the stained handkerchief far back in a drawer where she wouldn't come across it in the daylight.

She had heard men in the bunkhouse talk of having girls in dreams, of getting satisfaction. They joked coarsely, and she had seen young men have a hangdog look, listening to the joking.

Now she knew what it was to dream like that, for she had felt her arms reaching for Eddie; she woke holding the pillow close, and struggled against consciousness, trying to feel again his touch, to remember the things she was saying, the look in his eyes when she said them.

At last she sat up in bed, reached for the light. She sat again at her mirror and spoke his name; her eyes frightened her, cheapened her, and she let them wander to the reflection of the room, the chair, the curtain, the bed, and finally the door.

Her mother was standing in the doorway. Watching her mother

in the mirror and the frame about it made the two of them intimate a moment, close, two of a kind, one in depravity. She was almost afraid of her mother—as if her mother had seen—had seen what? The longing? The intimate things?

"Lona—are you all right?"

"Yes. Of course I'm all right. I couldn't sleep."

"You called out—spoke."

Lona picked up the hairbrush and began to brush her hair, thinking of the handkerchief in the drawer. When her mother left, she was still trembling.

Now in the fall there was a false Indian summer in the air, hazy, and the smoke from fires in Idaho hung close about the high timber and shrouded the peaks. More than ever the Lost Horse Valley was isolated, a pocket of silence. Still, the strange warmth was disturbed by sharp thunderstorms that began in the evenings and lashed the valley all night: telephone poles were down, bridges out, and all night there was the sound of rushing water.

On one of those dead, golden smoky days Tom Bart rode away from the ranch, straight in the saddle, the sun bronze on the silver mountings of his bridle.

Supper without him was strained and silent; Lona faced her mother at the table. Mrs. Dean answered the tinkle of the service bell.

"What's happened to the old gent?" she said. "There's a wild storm coming."

Ruth spoke quietly. "He won't be back for supper."

"I see he won't. Well, if he don't mind cold boiled beets. Mr. Dean always sort of liked them." She left the silence behind her, and into the room came the muffled laughing and joking of the men in the back dining room.

At nine the house was cold and damp; small drafts scurried up the hall, and the old plush drapes moved. The voices and the harmonica from the bunkhouse had stilled, and over the place was the monotonous putt-putt-putt of the electric light engine, firing and echoing against the barn.

Ruth sat reading a fashion magazine, looking up occasionally, glancing at Lona, who sat watching the sheet lightning through the high window. "You can always hear that echo when it's damp," Ruth said. "Always. You'd think the damp would stop the echo. Absorb—"

And the echo. Ruth said, "Lona, what's wrong?"

Lona turned, stared a moment. "Nothing." Composed, now. "Why do you think there's something wrong?"

"Because you—look like that. And speak like that."

Lona turned away and walked toward the hall. "There's nothing the matter with me," she said deliberately. "I'm going to find Grandpa."

The old-fashioned chandelier blinked and blinked. Ruth said, "He'll be back in a little while."

'There's a storm coming. I can't just sit."

Her mother's eyes were troubled. "I wouldn't bother him, Lona."

"Bother him? What's he doing?"

Ruth said, "He'll be home in a little while."

Lona moved on into the hall, and Ruth called after her. "Lona." She hesitated. Then, "You'll find him in one of the old cabins up there."

Lona stood in the hallway. "Where?"

Ruth's hands moved in a small, defeated gesture. "At the gold camp."

"The gold camp? Why would he go up there?" Her eyes were sharp, suspicious.

"He goes there sometimes."

"Why?" She was pulling on her gauntlets. "We don't even own that land now."

The road up the gulch was little used, worn deep years before by wagons carrying supplies to miners, by swaying stages; it was a phantom road to a phantom town.

Lona felt small at the wheel of the big car, leaning forward, peering through the windshield, trying to see; the road wound through gullies in the low black hills, along grades. Hidden rocks jerked the steering wheel. Ahead, lean gray rabbits darted blind into the blackness.

She had had to get out of the house, to think, to wonder what had happened to her. She seemed to be two people: the girl on horseback, riding, bossing, confident, sure of her place in the house, sure of her right to twenty thousand acres. Now she was somebody else: a girl who dressed up in clothes and sat on a bed in a dark room. Now in the car she felt herself becoming that girl again. She gripped the steering wheel tightly, afraid of changing again, afraid as she had been of the house since supper, afraid she would go to her room and sit there with the light off like— like some crazy person.

What was wrong with them—all of them? Why did her mother drink? Why wasn't she happy? What was it that was so ugly about seeing her mother alone in the living room at the piano, or simply sitting? Why should her grandfather ride off alone and sit alone somewhere in a ghost town? It was more terrible because he didn't look like that kind of man. You couldn't see his face, his kind, genial, somewhat weak face and think those things of him.

And now—she was getting like them. Nobody could help her. Nobody could know the shame of dreaming as she did—and nobody could help but Eddie. Why didn't he come?

The rain came suddenly, slanting, cold and hard, and the wiper began its breathy wheezing; the road led through a deep ravine just wide enough for the car, so steep that now and then the lights left the road and shot away into the dark. She stopped the car when the road leveled, and sat a moment.

She began to strain to hear through the rain—as if there should be some sound—some voice. There was only the rain on the top of the car.

Just below, in the hollow, lay the ghost town.

The lights of the car overshot the town, but she could feel it down there, feel it. She switched off the lights.

In the darkness the darker shapes of the tumbled buildings grew solid, the false-front of the old hotel, and the saloon they had called the Palace; close about it the foothills pressed.

The first lightning came.

It was a dull, broad, bloated and bluish lightning, then bright; it stalked across the country on thin red legs. Beside the car the rain gathered in cuts and gushed down the hill.

Why was she afraid? He wouldn't be doing anything when she

found him. Only sitting in one of the cabins, dreaming away his life. Then why—

She lit a cigarette, and read the familiar label on the package before the flame went out. She rummaged in the glove compartment, her fingers touching familiar things, and finally the cold smooth cylinder of the flashlight. She pressed the button: dead.

She began to pound it, bang it against the seat: dead.

She pulled her coat about her, slammed the door. The silence pressed in, and then the rain. She bagan to walk down the hill, crab-like, her boots slipping in the wet clay.

Flash . . .

The ghost town had only a single street, and the leaning black buildings were close, pressing her; just over there the creek rushed, full, swollen, lapping and sucking at the bank.

She paused on the verandah of the Palace Saloon. High up there on the steps the wind caught her skirt and tugged it, twisted it about her legs. She could see the little cabins crowded against the creek bank like black cubes.

She groped for a match, and then clawed and clawed through her pockets, her hands catching in wet cloth.

The matches were wet. The hollow sound of the creek came to her.

Flash . . .

The thunder faded into the liquid roar of the creek. She stepped back. Now she knew she's seen a horse, and the silver on a bridle. Right there. Panting she stumbled down the steps—and stopped.

He was in that cabin. Right there.

He was talking. Pausing and talking.

He sat at a table, and there was a candle, a candle throwing a feeble nervous light. A small light, and his face was pale and sickly as he spoke directly into the corner of the cabin. His lips moved slowly, but his voice was flat and sank into the rotten logs. He said, "I wish you'd never bought the God-damned ranch."

Her eyes followed his voice across the room to the corner, vague in a thin pool of light. He said, "We're all afraid. Afraid of everything. And afraid to leave."

She moved closer, eyes hungry for someone real in the corner.

But there was no one there, only the thin pool of light.

She started toward him, then stopped. For in his face she saw what her mother saw in hers, what she saw in her mother's: loneliness that sickened and twisted. She turned away, began to walk away, afraid. Afraid of deformity.

The steering wheel was real and solid. The drone of the motor kept the sound of his voice from her mind. Now the headlights reflected crookedly on the high narrow windows of the old house, black in the rain, lonesome under the hill, the rotting core of the Bart Ranch.

"We're afraid. Afraid to leave."

So was she. Lonely and afraid.

And then she saw it—the little Model-T standing in the driveway under one of the scraggly trees. She slowed the car—stared. Stopped the car and slid across the seat, got out, hurried, ran toward the Model-T, and began to smile.

Eddie was sitting behind the wheel in an old yellow slicker, his hat drooped with rain; but he was good, he was kind. He wasn't afraid.

"Eddie," she whispered. "Eddie." Even his name was good. "I kept wondering," she said. "Wondering and wondering." She was smiling and smiling. The dreams were not evil, weren't ugly. She belonged to him. She did belong to him, asleep or awake. And he wanted her. He had come.

She opened the door of the little car, and slid in beside him. She touched his arm. "Come on inside, Eddie."

He shook his head. "I already went in."

"Please," she said. "You're cold. I'll fix coffee."

Don't you see that we'll hold the cups in our hands and be there together?

He shook his head again. "Lona—why didn't you tell me?"

Her voice rose a little. "Tell you—tell you what?"

"About—about—"

About the hall. That the hall in the Bart house is paneled in mahogany. That the staircase is wide and circular, and the eyes of the portrait are a gentleman's eyes.

She knew. She said, "Because it doesn't matter. It doesn't matter."

He said, "It does—to me."

She watched him a moment, saw him lean forward, his hands moving, moving to the spark lever and the gas lever. He turned the key, and his leg touched her, feeling for the starter. He said, "You'd better get out."

The starter ground, the engine chugged. "You'd better get out."

She wasn't looking at him now. She was staring across at the house, and her eyes moved to the side of the dark window, to her room. There is a floor there, and a curtain and a bed and darkness —and nothing.

She spoke slowly. "I'm going with you."

He spoke above the sound of the engine. "What?"

"With you. I'm going with you. I'm afraid." She kept staring at the house, and his eyes followed hers, trying to understand.

He tried to laugh. "What have you got to be afraid of?"

She came to him suddenly, and held him, trembling. His hands moved on her, trying to quiet her. The rain fell from the scraggly tree. "Afraid now?" he said. And then he felt her head move against him. "If you won't be afraid," he kept saying. "I won't go. If you won't be afraid . . ." There was the rain on the top of the car. "Because," he said, "I don't want you to be afraid."

Mrs. Eddie Rohn will have a diamond ring.

Cost a hundred dollars.

He smiled in the dark, and the wind kept circling the old dark house; the rain gathered and fell from the leaves of the scraggly tree.

C H A P T E R 9   The Bart Block, at the corner of Bart and Rice Streets in Sentinel, was a two-story building that had been built in the late nineties in the red brick-and-sandstone era. It had a spired cupola that jutted over the sidewalk, the pointed roof tipped slightly like a rakish hat. The Barts were no longer connected with the building: even in the beginning the money that Bert Bart had put in it was only a fraction of the cost, but the fraction made the building possible, and his surname in square capitals with the date, a mass of Cs, Ds, Vs, Ms, and Xs, was cut deep in the sandstone cornice.

The block was said to be run down; nevertheless, it housed McFadden's Ice Cream Parlor, and Mrs. McFadden was as nice a woman as you could find. Smiling and gentle, she served ice cream to the townspeople on hot summer afternoons, to ranchers' wives in silk dresses and flowered hats, in town with their husbands "on business." They ate sundaes of nuts and syrups chosen from the menu. Schoolboy's Dream (banana, marshmallow, vanilla ice cream, cherries), Fudge Shot, Pung Chow (similar to the Dream except two kinds of ice cream, your choice). It was good to look out the windows at the town, at the hot sidewalks, to relax in the little chairs with legs cleverly made of strands of thick twisted wire.

Next door, the Circle Pool Room was the hangout of high-school boys, seniors in football and basketball sweaters of bright blue with a blocked yellow S. Here the boys came to smoke cigarettes, to leave cigarettes hanging, man-fashion, from lower lips as they made tense shots at the pool table. Here they spoke of girls, of the new babe in the junior class, a hot piece. Nobody had got near her yet. They winked and spoke of a girl named Ruby, the easiness of her, the soft clinging kisses that made you sick when you remembered in the daylight.

They stood at the long counter drinking thick malted milks.

"Hey, Slim. Put a raw egg in mine, will you?"

Slim spoke gravely. "Must a been out late last night."

Sly wink. "No. Tonight."

"You better lay off that cattin', you expect to beat the Crimson eleven."

They sang the high-school song, their arms about each other's necks, pretending to be drunk. "On to Victory, Sentinel, fight for the blue and gold. . . ."

On a high narrow door in the Bart Block there was neat gold lettering. Dr. W. J. Papetti, Dentist.

Dr. Papetti was the most recent of a long succession of dentists. New ones changed very little of what they found in the small dark waiting room upstairs. They brushed the curtains and revarnished the mahogany woodwork. They washed the big bay window in the office so that a patient might look out across the street and fasten his mind on the neat green turf around the railroad station. No dentist ever took down the mammoth carved wooden tooth that hung high over the narrow door of the entrance, a great molar with wickedly curved roots.

Dr. Papetti talked, barberlike, to male patients, of hunting dogs, ball games and fishing tackle. He joked, too.

"Sure you didn't get in the wrong door, Ed?" Dr. Papetti had a toothy grin. "Sure it wasn't just across the hall you wanted to go?" Laughter, embarrassed laughter.

The other plain brown door at the top of the stairs led to the Dixie Rooms.

The usual entrance to the Dixie Rooms was the back one, a rickety zigzag of wooden stairs that rose from the alley behind the Bart Block. At night an electric light on a curved black iron pipe over the door shone weakly and lighted the way up for the cowboys and hired hands.

You pressed the bell. It rang. You heard steps coming, keeping a broken rhythm to the laughter and the harsh music inside. Alma always opened the door. She was tiny, and her fluffy red hair was worn bobbed, long, with bangs.

Smiling. "Hello, there." She limped slightly. On her ankle, faint under her stocking, she wore a tiny gold chain with a nameplate.

"Hello, there, Pete." She never forgot a name. A cowboy in town on his yearly binge knew that. She always remembered something about him. "How's that lame horse you was telling me about? Still got him?"

Inside was a maze of rooms, and when the doorbell rang, rooms were closed off and the new visitor was taken into an empty one. The furniture was the same in each room, a couch, two or three easy chairs, a table for drinks, a mechanical piano, mirror, ashtrays. You sat on the couch and looked down the hall with the closed doors on either side.

"You ain't been up for a long time, Pete."

"I was out to the ranch."

"Don't ever forget me, Pete."

"You workin', Alma?"

She always laughed. "You know better. I'm true to my honey." Her honey's name was on the chain around her ankle.

"How about Alyse?"

"She's busy now."

"When she gets through?"

"Sure, Pete."

There was a ritual, drinks, gin and water in little glasses. Then music, the mechanical piano, and the men walked and stumbled around the floor with the girls. "You dance good, Pete."

"You dance good, too, Alyse."

"You Pete, you!" A little squeeze, dancing.

A girl would sit beside a man in the big chair. There was a horse-play, a fooling.

"Lovey-dovey," they said. "Oh, lovey-dovey." Then there was a seclusion around the chair, and no one spoke or watched the two people there. There was a quietness around the chair that the thumping of the piano didn't reach. *When the red-red-robin comes bob-bob-bobbin' along.*

There was a whisper, and the couple got up, and moved into the hall and down it to one of the small closed doors.

There were the mornings to face, when the rooms were dark and chill in the gray light that filtered through the windows on the alley, when the place was cluttered with empty glasses and dead cigarettes, scuffed rugs, pillows jammed into corners of the couch.

There was this morning to face.

The girls walked listlessly in the small rooms, kimonos belted modestly. They thought of the new girl. The new girl was young, and gay, and fiercely proud of her breasts. They were not like the breasts of the other girls, but rounder, firmer, and pointed.

Now, in the end room down the hall, the new girl was carrying on. The girls walked and tried not to listen, and went into their rooms and came out again.

Alyse said, "Honest to God, Alma, you got to stop her." Alyse stared down the hall.

Alma went down, limping a little, smoking a cigarette, feet soft in slippers. She knocked: you always got to be very careful about knocking.

The new girl didn't say come in. She was only silent a moment.

Alma went in and closed the door. "What's wrong, honey?"

A long mirror was hung beside the bed. The new girl lay there, small, dark, Italian looking. She wore no rouge, no lipstick; she was very young. Her eyes were large and dark, and she stared.

She put her head down in the pillow, lying on her side, and began it. It was not the sound the girls made when they felt sorry for themselves, when they sobbed and cried. A laugh would cure that, or a drink.

This girl was making a soft noise. One hand twisted at the pillow.

"Look, honey," Alma said. It was a bare little room, not yet fixed up with the bows and flounces and pictures of movie stars. The new girl's head was deep in the pillow. The noise grew worse.

Alma spoke suddenly. "Look!" And the girl turned her head. Alma slapped her hard: the sound hung in the small room. The girl gasped, and was silent, staring, lips drawn back from her teeth. Alma said, "I'm sorry, honey. You got to quit." And, "What's the trouble?"

A small gagging sound, then: "Nothing. Just—the weeps." She held the rose crepe kimono over her breasts. Alma saw.

"This ain't just the weeps."

The girl was looking up at her, judging. Her hand wouldn't relax, holding the kimono, hiding her breasts.

Alma glanced away. "He—he hurt you much?"

The girl didn't answer.

Alma said, "Need a doctor?"

"I don't want no doctor."

Alma moved on the bed. "Which one was it?"

The girl looked toward the window. Down there in the alley a truck growled; some man shouted to another. "The—the last one. He had—white eyelashes."

Alma's laugh was quick. "That's a funny thing to notice."

"They was *white*," the girl said. "Fringy and *white*." Then her eyes grew sullen.

Alma said, "I wasn't laughing at you."

The girl brushed a wisp of hair from her forehead. "There was this Rita in Salt Lake. Her folks was Mormons, but Rita believed in stars."

Alma reached in her pocket for a cigarette, put one in her lips and talked around it casually. "Salt Lake's a nice town. Now—feel better?"

The girl kept looking out the window, her eyes away from the cigarette Alma held to her. She said, "This Rita told a girl her baby was going to die, and the baby died. Rita told her. Rita could cure birth marks too." The girl looked a moment at Alma, then back out. "This girl had a little bitty birthmark, and Rita cured it with the stars." It was silent in the gloomy little room. The mirror caught the cold grayness of the alley. The truck below was gone. "Rita said a man with white eyelashes was bad inside. She was looking at me when she said it." And suddenly the girl grabbed Alma's wrist. "Alma! Can a man with white eyelashes make you foul?"

Alma stiffened. "Make you—foul?"

"That's what—Rita said." The girl waited, watching the mirror, and Alma in it. She didn't move.

Alma said, "Do you believe in Jesus Christ?"

The girl moved her lips, whispered. "Oh, yes. I believe honest and truly in Jesus Christ."

Alma glanced at her cigarette. "Then shut up about being—foul."

The girl kept protecting her breasts. "Then—I won't worry none, will I?"

Alma said, "How'd you like something to eat? Club sandwich?"

The girl's eyes were hard a moment. "That Rita never even finished eighth grade."

"Want olives on the sandwich?"

"I had a fellow in Salt Lake. He brought me a whole bottle of olives once, stuffed."

"Double the olives, then."

Then the whisper again. "He won't come back, will he? You wouldn't let him come, even if he wanted? Or—or he could have one of the others." She had Alma's wrist again. "Couldn't he?"

Alma got up slowly from the bed. "You don't need to worry. Those kind just want you once."

CHAPTER 10   In all the little towns the ranch hands stand on street corners outside the saloons and pool-halls waiting to be hired, stubble-bearded, red-eyed men, shaky from whiskey. They are dressed in bib-overalls and shoes cracked from the sour acid that comes from manure around barns. Only the cowboys wear waist-overalls, Levis, and boots with thin, high undershot heels. Only they have a pride in their profession.

When a pick-up truck drives up and a man gets out, strong and steady and tanned, a rancher, they wait only until he has gone inside the saloon, and then they close in after him, and wait idly at the bar, not looking, just listening.

Jesus, they should have shaved.

The rancher speaks to the bartender. "Any men here want work?"

The bartender looks up. "All of 'em do, I guess."

The rancher looks around in the bar gloom, looks at the men. That fellow over there looks all right. "You want to work?"

A man looks up. "Work? Sure, I guess so. What you pay?"

"Forty." The rancher's eyes are around the room again.

"Sure. I'll work."

"Got your stuff ready?"

The man looks at his feet. "Ah—say, Mr.—"

"Yeah?"

"I need a loan, get my stuff." He shuffles his feet. "The bartender's got it."

The rancher takes out a fat wallet. "How much?"

"Ten bucks."

"Well—"

Why couldn't the son-of-a-bitch give you the ten without all them questions? He knows a guy hocks everything.

He follows the rancher out with his bedroll or his suitcase. He's got his watch now too. And his eyes meet the eyes of the others, left behind there.

"Luck, fellows . . ."

They are picked over, chosen, and there are always some left. Too drunk. Weak bodies.

Well, God damn it.

They sit awhile in the high-backed chairs in the saloon, waiting.

When Tom Bart went to Sentinel to hire a man, they always wondered; he would hire a drunk who told funny stories, and once he brought back a pensioner from a circus who spoke of strong women who went on the trapeze and of hippopotamuses who waltzed.

Now he sat in one of the high-backed chairs in the Pheasant Bar reading a ragged, torn, week-old copy of a newspaper. He had been watching the men at the bar, the drifters, listening to their tall tales. He admired those men, their spirit, their hopeless pluck, their wonderful, desperate hopelessness.

He had always wanted to know hunger—to find and make a friend simply because the two of you were lonesome and hungry.

They were talking there at the bar, grave as judges, men with lean, drawn, stubble-bearded faces, a fraternity of wanderers. Tom listened, smiling. They spoke of a bank.

A little bank that looked like a grocery store, in a little town two hundred miles away.

"Seven thousand dollars," one said. Tom could see it all—lazy little town, afternoon sun on the street, a few townspeople gossiping, a few old cars at the curb, and a horse tied there too. Nothing ever happened. Then, suddenly, the bank was robbed.

"Just had a handkerchief tied over his face. By God, he had *guts.*"

"He got clean away." They were with him, this hiding man with seven thousand dollars. He was one of them.

Still smiling, Tom could see the rest of it. A few people running. The horse at the rack raised his head and pulled back. A car started. Somebody yelled. The sheriff stood in the sun, looking up and down the street.

The teller didn't know what happened.

". . . closing time. Walked right in . . ."

Another man at the bar spoke. "Well, them God-damned banks got too much money. Pile it up in them banks and make some bastard richer."

"They're all out to get the workingman."

They were close at the bar, one with the hiding man.

Tom moved up to the bar. He grinned at the men. "What about this bank?" He leaned forward, like them, on his elbows. He was one with the hiding man too, partner in the lonely fraternity.

He set up drinks.

They drank his liquor. Then, as always, they dropped away, one by one, went into the street. His boots, his shirt, his hat, his silver belt-buckle betrayed him. He stood there, feeling his age, embarrassed before the bartender. When he could face it, he walked slowly back to the straight-backed chair.

A man sat there—must have come in from the alley. Had a new suitcase, and when Tom sat down beside him, his eyes moved a moment to it, then went back to his work. The man was braiding horsehair—not simple braiding such as any cowboy does, but that intricate, eye-straining plaiting—delicate, fine, the braiding of men who have endless time and steely patience.

Tom Bart knew braiding. Men on the ranch had given him bosals for hackamores, headstalls for bridles, a lariat of hair, a halter rope. But this was different, this was art.

He leaned over and watched until he knew that the lean young man was watching him, and going right on braiding by touch. Tom grinned, feeling the young man's eyes, and felt a strange chill of embarrassment.

"Didn't want to be nosy, but I couldn't help—I never saw work like that."

The young man held out the foot-long piece of work and looked at it coolly. "Watch chain."

Tom took the piece in his smooth hands. It might have been made by a machine, each link of the same perfect tautness and symmetry. Tom said softly, "I'll give you twenty dollars for this."

"It's not worth twenty."

Tom grinned a little, relieved. Twenty was a crazy price for a watch chain. "Well, I'll give you five, then."

The young man's glance slid from the watch chain to Tom Bart, and again Tom felt the curious twinge. "You said twenty."

Tom flushed, leaned forward in the chair and uncrossed his knees. "Well, I know, but—" He had an odd, trapped feeling: he reached into his pocket for his wallet.

He hired Joe Martin, of course, and it happened he actually needed a man. They drove to the ranch late that night, along the lonely road in the darkness, the big gray Pierce purring, the headlights flashing ahead on the dirt road that suddenly seemed unfamiliar.

It was strange. These nights, driving some young fellow back to the ranch was satisfying to Tom. Maybe he didn't get along with groups of them, but when they knew him—

They took him as a friend, opened up. Told of wives, or daughters somewhere, or a son.

"He's doing real good," they'd say. "Got a garage." Or a store. Or a restaurant. "Got one of them fine big shiny coffee urns. Fine little wife, too. A corker. She's a Baptist."

"You're going to like it fine at the ranch," Tom would say.

And now—it was strange. He couldn't explain his nervousness. He felt pressed, driven—like the feeling you had, he thought, when you lay in bed half asleep and thought you heard your name, a sharp, close, almost wild sound.

He hunched his shoulders. The trouble, he thought, was the dim little light on the dash. It shone on the left side of Joe Martin's face, on the white eyelashes.

Tom let his foot rest heavier on the accelerator. The old Pierce lunged ahead.

Old Art was the first up in the bunkhouse. He milked three cows, carried in wood, cleaned the barn—did any slow, dirty job. The first human sound each morning was the tread of his feet, and then there was the small scurrying under the table, and a scratching of dog toenails on the splintery floor and his little dog crawled out, stretching. She trotted beside him as the sun rose.

"Well, Toots. Nice day." She knew everything he said.

Tom Bart treated Art with dignity. "Well, Art," he would say. "How are the milk cows?"

"Just fine, thank you. The jersey is giving more milk."

"Sure of that, Art?" Tom would be interested.

"I been keeping tract. I never had a cow treat me better."

In the talks Art had with Tootsie, they agreed that Tom Bart was the finest man. "I wish I could do something real nice for him,"

Art would say aloud. "Some big fine thing. Maybe someday."

But one thing didn't change with his coming to the Bart Ranch some years before, and that was the way the other men treated him. He was the butt of jokes: a frog in his bed, cold and wet and moving at night.

Once they composed a letter to the Heart & Hand Club, and signed old Art's name, and the letters came for weeks from strange men and frustrated women.

But the joke they repeated and repeated until it was almost no fun was to tie one of the good silk neckties that Tom Bart had given him around the neck of his dog, and throw her in the creek. When she got out she would run to Art, her hind legs trembling, cowering there, looking up at him. They couldn't help laughing, the wet dog, and old Art's face. Once his dignity had angered a fellow, and the fellow squared off and feinted a blow. Art felt the beat of the hard fist. He didn't move.

The fellow said, "Aren't you going to stand up for your bitch? Aren't you going to stand up for her?"

Art stood with his hands straight at his sides, helpless, trying to understand.

They did not often include him in their conversations after supper, but now they drew him to their side, against the new fellow, Joe Martin.

There was little said when Joe Martin was in the bunkhouse. Somehow, he stopped conversation; they found they couldn't linger in the bunkhouse after breakfast to have a last cigarette. They went right out to work, following Joe Martin.

"He always goes out first, like he's trying to show us up." But they followed him.

They tried to figure him out. They had a few things to work on. He had brought a new suitcase with him, a brand new suitcase, and he kept it locked. He had brought no bedroll. They talked about that after he had gone out, speculated. When he went out the back door of the bunkhouse and walked along the path to the toilet, they kept an eye on him until he went inside the little building, and then they talked softly.

"He keeps that suitcase locked."

Eddie Rohn said, "A man's got a right to do that."

"Sure. But nobody else keeps his suitcase locked. Maybe he thinks somebody here's a thief."

That made them a little angry. "Me, I'd never trust a man with white eyebrows and white eyelashes."

They got around to the main thing, a thing they felt and couldn't say. "He's got a funny look."

"Watch him walk. Like out to the toilet."

There was a rustle beneath the table and Tootsie came out into the room and stretched. Art patted her absently, and ruffed up the fur around her neck. "He looks like he's walking, and he looks like he's dead."

They looked at old Art.

They had never liked a dog in the bunkhouse. Now, suddenly, they began to feed Tootsie there, bringing scraps from the table and spreading down a newspaper on the floor for steak bones or potatoes and gravy, watching her eat while they squatted around. Art was flattered, beaming as they made a fuss over the bitch.

Joe Martin didn't like dogs in the bunkhouse.

"I don't live no place where animals live."

Well, they showed him. They might not be friendly with him, but, by God, if they wanted to feed a little bit of a dog that never hurt nobody—well.

"Eat it up, Toots."

It looked as if they had beaten Joe Martin.

It didn't hurt anybody when Tootsie dragged the ham bone into the room where the bunks were, for the ham bone was clean and no nearer to Joe Martin's things than the others.

And he didn't fall when he tripped; the men lying on their bunks in the darkness heard him stumble. They pretended to be asleep, and breathed evenly.

Joe Martin had spoken very quietly. "Keep that bitch out of here, Art."

The men waited in the silence. Art's bunk squeaked. "I didn't know she left the bone there."

"Keep her out."

Eddie Rohn liked Art. "It was a clean bone," he said.

Joe Martin lit a match and took the bone in his hands; they

could see his face plainly, and tried to listen to the wind outside
rustling the long dry rye-grass.

 CHAPTER 11 Lona was relieved the first night Eddie came
that he made the move to take his bedroll to the
bunkhouse. As they sat there in the kitchen,
drinking coffee, she wondered how to tell him
he must stay in the bunkhouse.

She loved him, yes. Although the moment of oneness with him
there in the rain in the little car was gone (how had she ever said,
"I'm going with you"?) she loved him. But she was a Bart. She
did not make much of mahogany paneling and silver serving dishes
with B on them and linen tablecloths, but they were a part of her.

And the men who worked for you slept in the bunkhouse.

He had said, "Well, I'll take my stuff down now."

She had a plan: by seeing that he got more and more authority
he would gradually be looked up to by the men, by other ranchers,
and at last by her grandfather. It would not seem strange, eventually, if Eddie moved into the room off the kitchen where old
Higgens had slept.

He broke horses that fall; she marveled at his gentleness, his
patience. At times his gentleness irked her; she would have been
firmer. She wouldn't have spent all that time coaxing a horse.

"What are you doing?" she would ask, half jokingly. "Trying to
make a pet of him?" She always wore a little lipstick now.

"I just like horses," he would say.

In the spring he broke horses to harness, and she rode across
the open field with him, hanging onto the seat as the green colt on
the near side reared and plunged. She watched his hands, firm and
gentle. She kept thinking of his hands, of the black hair lying flat
on the backs. Could they be rough or cruel? Alone, now, there was
a wall between them. Had he forgotten the moment in the rain?

And then it was summer, and no more horses to break.

She had felt sorry for the calf too. That's what he didn't understand, that she was sorry too.

Its legs were spindly, thin. It stood leaning against the fence in the lower field, its belly bloated with air, starving. Its mother was lost, or dead. There were always a few such calves, left behind, lost in the willows when you turned the herd out to range.

"There's nothing we can do, Eddie," she'd said. "You can't raise a month-old calf like that. It won't suck a bottle. It would be wasting time."

"Poor little fellow." The calf moved and stumbled, too sick to be timid.

"It might as well die here as in the barn. Even if we raised it, it wouldn't be worth a cent."

It was suddenly important that he forget the calf, that he understand, and forget it. She reined her horse around.

"Maybe," he said. "Maybe if we—"

"No," she said. "Don't think about it. Let it die." It was almost as if the word shocked him. "Or you can shoot it," she said. "If you don't want to think about it dying here, shoot it."

He had looked at her as if the calf were a child.

"I'm not being hard," she said suddenly. "Only sensible."

Riding home, she knew he was thinking about the calf. A part of him was back there in the lower field, knowing the bloated belly, the crooked legs, the old-looking face of a month-old calf.

"There's nothing anybody can do," she said. The sage was blooming on the flat, rich and fresh smelling. It was stupid that a sick calf should come between them that moment, that it should have any importance at all. "Look," she said. The low sun had picked up a piece of broken bottle in the sagebrush across the field. "I wonder what that is."

Now he looked at her. She was sure he had forgotten. "A piece of glass, I guess. The sun's nice on it."

She wanted her remark to be a test: a test that he could take responsibility, that he could be hard when hardness counted, and forget the calf. She felt a helpless anger against the calf now. What was a sick calf on a ranch of twenty thousand acres?

"I'm driving into Sentinel," she told him next morning, "to get some things for haying. Look around the place and see what needs doing." Her grandfather was in his office; he took almost no interest in the place now.

Eddie was standing in the barn door, long-legged and confident in the morning sun, smiling a little. A moment before he had kissed her, taken her suddenly there in the harness room, and kissed her. She had stiffened, then relaxed, but his hands did not move on her. Impatient, she had looked at him in the dusty little room, cluttered with straps and ropes and collars.

"Why did you do that?" There was cheapness in the gloom. He had got through to the girl in the high-heeled shoes and lipstick— and stopped.

"Didn't you want to?" He smiled, self-conscious, confident. Her eyes were on the single high cobwebbed window. For a moment she wanted to hurt him.

". . . into Sentinel," she said. "I'll be back late this afternoon. If you can't find anything else to do, the butcher pen needs cleaning."

There was a deliberateness in his rolling a cigarette. First, the paper, smoothing it, curving it with his finger. Then he opened the tobacco sack with his teeth, poured just enough tobacco, smoothed it. Then rolled the paper, and moistened tongue along the edge. Then the match; the long, long process, the sputtering flame, pale in the sun. The first smoke. "I know butcher pens," he grinned. "I used to be a farmer."

She was pulling on her gloves, fighting for composure. "It's not a nice job," she said. "But there's nobody else. Nobody wants dirty jobs."

It wasn't a nice job—hauling decaying guts out of the little pen on a wheelbarrow. They had to be picked up with a pitchfork, and the rotting fibers parted and fell to the ground between the tines. Heads of beeves, cavities in the brain crawling with small white maggots. She said, "I think the wheelbarrow's behind the barn."

He'd see that there was more to ranching than spurs and riding. And sick calves. He'd find out. There were ugly, necessary, bloody jobs. Branding. Castrating.

There were haying jobs.

The summer sun is hot over the hayfields, and at noon when the rakes and mowing machines stand idle while the men eat, the squat shadows are parched. The horses sweat, fighting flies that bite and leave a drop of blood on a welt.

The sun has soaked through the sweaty hats of the hay hands and dulls thought, but in the yellow heat they remember a cool clump of willows at the turn of a creek where water ran clear and deep, where a fellow used to swim.

They remember wonderful plans that never worked. They remember violence and drunkenness. And now—they've got two dollars a day and greasy meals under a hot tent.

They own nothing; maybe a pocketknife. Maybe a watch. Maybe a cardboard suitcase.

What had happened? Where was the fork in the road?

After noon, their bellies are full, and there is a little life in them, a little zest. Night will come, and the cool stars. A bed of hay feels pretty good. But then the sun soaks through, and the dull thinking begins as the rake wheels turn and turn in the heat. There are fifty days of it, and seven thousand tons of hay on the Bart Ranch.

There is a boss of the haycrew. The boss's son, or a trusted man. He hires and fires. A word from him and you go back to the saloons —to wait. He makes men move. He knows how to fix a cable, repair a derrick, shoe a horse, move a buckrake across a high-banked stream. He walks straight and proud, knowing his judgment might make or break a ranch.

There's nothing fine about haying, or cleaning butcher pens. When you clean butcher pens your stomach twists from the smell. Your hands blister from the pitchfork and wheelbarrow handles, great watery blisters that smart and fester.

She would test Eddie.

Driving back from Sentinel that afternoon she thought of him, bending his back in the hot sun. The sweat would make the back of his blue denim shirt dark. She thought of his blistered hands. (And what if his hands had moved on her that morning?)

"He cleaned the butcher pen," she would tell her grandfather. "He did a good job." It was the ugly jobs that counted—jobs that showed aim and hardness. The men in the bunkhouse would see him there.

The big gray Pierce purred up the dirt road through clouds of feathery dust. Far away across the flat the sun, lurid and red, caught the window of the Double-Arrow Ranch—a big ranch. And the man who owned it had once been a cowboy, started from scratch. She doubted that anyone thought the less of him and his wife for not having monograms on their serving dishes. They ate with their men in one dining room. At bars in Sentinel the owner of the Double-Arrow talked on equal terms with Tom Bart. It was only in the Bart house that this man stood awkward, hat in hand, remembering that long ago his wife had cooked in the Bart kitchen.

Now, Eddie—Eddie's people must be good people. He had pride in his father, and in his aunt the schoolteacher, whose picture was on the shelf in the bunkhouse—a stern, eyeglassed, thin woman. Maybe in Idaho Falls they were well thought of. The big gray Pierce purred. No one would question her marrying him. They had questioned her mother's marriage, but when Jim Hanson moved into the front of the house, tongues stopped wagging.

Eddie must have the pen cleaned by now. Maybe tomorrow she would say, "Look, Eddie. Why don't you go down and get that calf? It's crazy—but if you want to—" She didn't think the calf would be dead by then.

Excitement rose in her as she approached the ranch; she always felt proud of the buildings there under the hill, the maze of corrals and pens (he would have finished by now), the out-buildings, and the great yellow-brick house. The car was powerful under her. Only the Barts had a Pierce. She tilted her chin, sat straight, pressing her back against the seat cushion.

"He did a good job," she'd say.

She looked across the yard to the pens. He was not in the butcher pen. (He would have finished.) He must be in the barn—maybe putting the wheelbarrow away. She parked the car before the house. She always walked proudly when she got home from town, conscious of herself. She walked down to the barn.

It was cool inside the long, low building; the sounds were cool, the whisper of dry hay in a manger, the muffled stamp of a horse. Saddles and harness hung on pegs were dim in the little light that seeped through high-up dusty windows.

She heard muffled voices at the end of the barn in a box-stall, close earnest voices in a small space. Eddie. Eddie and her grandfather.

She walked on down, conscious of the voices, of the barn itself, of the years that hung about the beams overhead, of men long gone who had used those saddles hung on pegs, whose feet had known the feel of those stirrups.

She passed the harness room. In there Eddie had held her, had kissed her in the small dusty room. The morning sun through the window had been cold. (His hands had not moved on her.) That moment was real, alive as his voice down there at the end of the barn.

She walked on down.

Then her grandfather's voice, and a big laugh. "I'll be damned," he said. And then Eddie's low voice.

She looked through the bars of the box-stall, and there they were, the two of them—Tom Bart in his fine California pants and shined boots and big hat shoved back. And Eddie.

Eddie was kneeling down in the hay. His body hid something. She moved, to see around him.

It was the calf—small, weazened face, scrawny neck. Eddie tipped up a beer bottle in one hand. His overalls were splashed with milk. The other hand held the calf's mouth over the end of the bottle.

"By God," Tom Bart said again. "Look at him *drink!*" Tom's eyes were tense. "Why, you little old calf!" Tom said. "Look at you drink. Why, *you!*" He was tense with excitement. The calf struggled, and Tom Bart moved away from the slobbering mouth, glancing at his clean pants and stepping back a bit.

"He's going to be all right," Eddie said. He let one hand move over the small humped back. "You're going to be all right."

Tom's voice was anxious, encouraging. "You're going to be all right. We're going to get that old bloat out of your belly." He glanced up, saw Lona. He didn't seem surprised. "Hello, Lona. You ought to been here. We've got this little old calf drinking. Eddie here—believe me, this kid knows how to make 'em drink."

Eddie looked up. There was a strength and calmness about him, as though the very strength, the quiet, would pull the calf through. He spoke softly. "Hello, Lona."

She spoke quietly. "You two have been having quite a time."

Tom Bart looked at her suspiciously, then grinned. "You bet we have."

"It wasn't easy," Eddie said. She watched him run his hand over the calf, over the scrawny neck and back. "Took us all day, about."

"Yes, *sir!*" Tom said. "And you know," he moved over to the bars of the stall, and spoke to Lona. "You know, I've been thinking." He grinned boyishly, and looked down at his polished boots, dulled a little from barn dust. "I'd like to see Eddie with the hay crew this year. Bossing." He looked at Lona, pleased.

She looked at the two men. They were a good deal alike, as gentle and serious as children playing a game. And she saw the slow-moving machinery, yellow wheat, tired men, sweating horses, and haystacks—seven thousand tons of hay that kept the cattle all winter, the foundation of the ranch, of the house, of the Barts.

Tom stuck his hands in his pockets, waiting. "Well, Lona?"

She spoke slowly. "I don't know." She let them see her confused, flustered.

Now a small afternoon breeze blew down from the moist green willows above the house, stirred the hay in the mangers. The breeze shifted, and caught the stench of the butcher pen. She said, "Maybe he'd better stay up here at the house, instead."

Tom cleared his throat, unsure. Then he said, "Well. If you'd rather he was here—"

She watched them from beneath her hat, saw them glance at each other as if they understood—understood that she wanted Eddie close.

But she thought of the butcher pen too, of the cramped little round corral, still littered with rotting stuff, cluttered with the heads and bones of dead animals.

CHAPTER

12

A man has years that nobody knows, but the tokens are hidden away in a cigar box. A cigar box is nice. The wood is reddish and smooth, and the smell is clean, and cedar, but best of all, a cigar box is small. It doesn't take up much room in a suitcase.

There is a jackknife in the cigar box, maybe. When you were a kid you used to make whistles out of a green willow stick, squatting there in the shade. Notch the stick, girdle the notch, put a lot of spit on the willow and then pound with the knife handle until the bark slipped off easy and left the white wood clean and moist. The sap was bitter.

His dad used to take him fishing. Only this fishhook, now. This old Royal Coachman, this Silver Doctor.

A playing card. That card was from the time he was lucky. Drew it to fill a straight, a jack of diamonds. He's kinda like the Jack of Diamonds, like the song.

> *Her parents don't like me, they say I'm too poor,*
> *They say I'm unworthy to darken her door. . . .*

The few letters are there, on cheap ruled paper.

You see, there was this girl. They got talking, and they had a few drinks, and then another. She cried that night. He was all worked up.

He said, "I'm going to write you a letter."

And, "Oh, I'll write you a letter too. Where'll I write?"

"General Delivery. I'm a rolling stone, darling."

He didn't write, because what good was writing. But she wrote. "I guess I'd liefer die than not see you again. I love you so much with every part of me. . . ."

Jesus, but the years go by.

There are a million cheap suitcases all over the world in all the bunkhouses, and a million cigar boxes, Chancellor, Antony Y Cleopatra. . . .

In the morning they waited in the bunkhouse for her to come. They could see her through the window, striding down, and they always stubbed out their cigarettes and tried to be standing by the time she came in. She would stand just inside the door.

"Art, he wants that ditch cleaned out today." She always gave her orders in her grandfather's name. "Al, he wants you to fix the fence in the east field, there by the creek."

He wants you to do this, to do that. They respected her, even bragged about her in saloons in Sentinel when they were drinking. There was something fine about a woman like that. Only to Eddie were her orders direct now, personal.

"Eddie, saddle up my horse. I want to see how the feed is up Grizzly Mountain."

"Sure." The others were silent.

She had not noticed Joe Martin at first. He was no more than a tall sandy-haired young fellow who sat quietly in the wicker chair by the window when she came in. She had given the men orders from her grandfather that day. And, "Eddie, you can saddle my horse."

She turned then, and noticed Joe Martin. He had made no move to get to his feet, no move to take his gloves there on the table. "And say," she said, "he wants you to go along with Art."

The men were moving about the bunkhouse, reaching for their jackets that hung on nails along the wall behind the stove. Joe Martin reached for a *Western Story* magazine and turned the pages. Looking at the pages he said, "Tell the old man to come down and give his orders. I don't take orders from no woman."

The men stopped, their hands reaching for their jackets. They didn't look at anybody. Joe Martin was looking at the magazine, slumped in the old wicker rocker that had suddenly become his chair.

Lona started to speak, then her eyes were cold. She turned, hesitated in the door to let her glance sweep over the men. Their hands touched their jackets. Then she walked out.

One of the men looked toward Joe Martin and grinned in a friendly way, but Joe Martin did not look up. The men looked out the dirty window and saw Lona walking toward the house, the quirt swinging on her arm.

Joe Martin always left the back dining room first after meals, and he never pushed back his chair to stretch a little and sigh and roll a cigarette, or to listen to the news from the front of the house as given by Mrs. Dean. Again and again, when he left, closing the back door firmly, silently, they listened to his boots on the cement steps, on the footbridge across the ditch, and then they spoke of him.

"He wouldn't take no orders."

"Wouldn't take no orders from no woman, he said."

They talked softly, wisely, and even Mrs. Dean lowered her voice.

"Mr. Dean wouldn't have liked him," she said. "He's uppity. He's got that locked suitcase you said about."

"Well," Eddie Rohn said, "some fellows always lock a suitcase."

Mrs. Dean was not convinced. "Maybe with strangers, but here on the ranch, everybody friendly and neighborly, it's funny. Mr. Dean never locked anything, and was loved by all." She was suddenly silent, her mouth open. The men watched her face. There was somebody in the kitchen, she had heard a creak. She knew the creak a floor made when somebody stood listening by the stove. They sat silent until the footsteps went out into the front of the house again. She knew everybody's steps.

They were Lona's.

There was something strange about Joe Martin. Lona sensed it, knew it. Sensed it because he was suspected by his own kind. Knew it because he had dared to humiliate her.

He had a suitcase, then. A suitcase that was locked. He never left the men alone in the bunkhouse long. There was something she didn't know. It made her uncomfortable, it made her insecure.

These were her acres. The big yellow house was hers, and the bunkhouse too. She had a right to know.

She was going to open the suitcase.

She had a paper clip in the pocket of her riding skirt. She had glanced down at the floor of the living room, and there it was, bent just so. A funny thing to find in the living room—funny to look down and see it, just when you were thinking . . .

But during the next few weeks there was always someone around. Joe Martin was always near. He would appear suddenly.

Twice she had thought the ranch deserted, and then looked down toward the butcher pen and had seen Joe down there with a wheelbarrow.

Her chance came one Sunday.

The men had gone to Sentinel for a last fling before the long grind of haying started. She had watched them from the house as they pumped up the tires of the Model-T. She had heard the tin washbasin fall on the floor, and one grinning man had walked swiftly to the house for a bucket of water. They sang, they joked, their voices were loud and clear in the lazy warmth of early July.

The barn squatted silently in the sun, and down by the corrals the heat waves rose and shimmered. She saw Eddie Rohn stand a moment in the door of the bunkhouse, his white shirt open at the neck to the second button.

And Joe Martin had on a white shirt.

A man got in the Model-T, another got in front of it. They called instructions back and forth, pulled levers, cranked. Then a roar, and the small black car shivered. They climbed over one another getting in, crowding.

She was certain she saw Joe Martin get in just before the car rattled away in the dust. She stood near the window in the big house until the dust was far beyond the board gate by the barn.

She walked slowly downstairs.

Sunday had settled over the Bart ranch house. Ruth sat on the couch, one foot curled under her, reading. She had pulled the shades against the sun, looking cool in a smart cotton dress. Tom Bart was across the road in the root cellar, prodding and poking at the electric light plant. Tomorrow would be washday.

Ruth looked up. "Lona." She put the book down on the couch. "Your grandfather's over there with the light plant."

Lona said, "He's always over there."

"Maybe you could say something. It spits gas, he says. It's dangerous, I'd think."

"He's all right." Lona looked levelly at the pretty cotton dress, at her mother's smooth white hands. What did her mother know about a light plant?

Ruth said, "What's wrong, Lona?"

"Nothing. Just don't keep talking about the light plant."

"I only mentioned it. He shouldn't be alone there." The sound came to them, the putt-putt-putt, and the echo came back sharply from the hill behind the house.

Lona said, "Well, tell him."

Ruth looked curiously at her daughter and picked up her book. The sound of the electric light plant was a Sunday sound like the hissing of the browning roast in the kitchen, like the tinkle of the flat silver in the dining room, like the mournful songs about Jesus that Mrs. Dean sang.

Lona stood in the hall before the coat rack, a great high-backed seat where no one ever sat, with hooks for coats as thick as branching willows. At last she took her hat and quirt and went out.

She walked slowly across the glaring hot expanse of the side yard and down toward the bunkhouse, watching the barn, silent against the hot washed blue of the sky, at the corrals, sagging a little, and the misty blue peaks of the Lost Horse range. She breathed deep the green odor of the standing hay that seeped up from the twenty thousand Bart acres. She couldn't seem to get enough air.

Her heart was pounding now. Maybe, she thought, she might go right on past the bunkhouse, right down to the barn, for a cat down there had kittens. She might look at them. She might go right past the bunkhouse. This cat was white and black and maybe the kittens would be black or white. She might go down and see, and pet the cat, squatting there by the barn where the air smelled of dry hay and sun. This cat—

She turned suddenly toward the bunkhouse.

Inside, she sat on the big table, her feet dangling. She watched the toes of her boots, fresh polished for Sunday; she swung her legs and looked idly about the bunkhouse. They had left in a hurry. There was a crumpled shirt flung across a chair, grayish water in the tin washbasin, and the smell of bay rum hung heavy. A fly buzzed and ticked against the window over by the shelf where they kept their shaving things, an empty whiskey bottle. A round shaving mirror reflected the emptiness, the quietness around the barn. You could see the corrals, too.

Piles of pulp magazines on the big table, *Western Story, Ranch Romances* with a cover showing a cowboy on horseback leaning over to grab a yellow-haired girl up in his arms. She thumbed idly through one, and glanced up unconcernedly into the quiet room where no one was.

But the sudden scurrying under the table left her weak inside, and her hands shook. Her breathing stopped.

The little brown bitch crawled out from under the table.

When she could speak her voice shook. "Get on back there! Art's gone! Everybody's gone. Go on under there!" The little dog went back under the table, toenails scraping the floor. Then silence.

She looked through the door into the sleeping room, around the sagging gray sheep blanket on a string over the doorway that made a kind of privacy. It was gloomy in that room. The little window was dark with dust and fly specks. She stood up, stretched slowly, and walked easily across the room. And through the doorway of the sleeping room.

She stood there. There were the bunks, seven of them. The one against the window was Eddie Rohn's, unmade, the blankets flung back, the old pillow he used rumpled. She felt almost drawn there, for there he lay, night after night, his wiry black hair against that pillow, perhaps thinking of her, perhaps dreaming. Those flung-back blankets pressed around him.

She stood a moment; then she moved her eyes.

For there was the bunk of Joe Martin. Exactly in the corner, the only bunk in the room that was made, smoothly, neatly, a blanket folded at the foot. The suitcase was under the bed. The new nickel lock gleamed dully.

She had one hand thrust in the fringed pocket of her riding skirt, and in her fist she held the bent paper clip. She took her hand from her pocket and looked at the clip. Then, like a sleepwalker, she walked over to Joe Martin's bunk.

She stood quietly there, listening. There was no human sound on the ranch, only the putt-putt-putt of the electric light engine across the road.

She squatted.

She put her hand on the handle of the suitcase and pulled at it. As it slipped out from under the bunk there was a scraping on the splintered floor, loud in the quiet room. Past her a shaft of sun bored like a finger through the dust and made a single bright spot on the floor. She tugged a little at the suitcase. Stopped. Tugged. Now it was out before her. She listened: there was no sound.

She hitched back a little on her heels, awkwardly, to give the suitcase more room. Then, head bent, she inserted the paper clip. She turned it steadily. It began to bend in her fingers. She tried again, impatient with the soft metal. She made a sharp breathing sound—maybe the lock was stuck.

She pressed her thumb against the lock and pushed. The tight little spring snapped free.

She kept still, listening again. Then she began to raise the lid, and bent her head low, to see.

The smell of clothes came up, thick and close. Then the smell of leather, or cedar. There was a suit of new underwear, folded neatly, as stores do it. A new denim shirt was brittle with starch and filler. A new pair of socks were clipped with a U-shaped pin. Cheap leather gloves. And a green metal box. Locked.

Her hand was moist. She burrowed down around, feeling, feeling, and felt the smooth coolness of a whiskey bottle.

She knew hired men seldom kept a bottle. They drank it up. This full bottle, seal unbroken, hinted at a planning, a patience, a waiting for some proper time.

Her hand moved again. A cigar box: that was the cedar smell. She lifted it out carefully, careful not to disturb the square nest of clothes around it. She held it, weighing it. The top was secured by a thin brad that pulled out easily. There was little inside. Some letters. And a .32 automatic.

A .32 automatic is a funny gun to own, flat, blunt-nosed. Not a gun to show: a gun to hide.

But she didn't think it was for the gun that he kept close to the suitcase, that he could appear almost from a shadow when someone was near, that he could walk silent as a cat and simply *be* when anyone was around. She had heard the men talking. . . .

There was something else. She knew it in his eyes, in his walk, in his silence, in his hands. You can read a man's hands. Fingers move and curve just so, and you can read things. *There was something.*

She felt a coldness at her back, kneeling there, a tingling in her spine. She knew why.

Because of course he was standing behind her. She got sick and weak, and fought it like nausea. She swayed, squatting there, legs aching dully.

He was breathing just behind her. She shouldn't have looked. He was stooped a little forward, and his long arms, sleeves rolled up and the light red hair on them, were held out a little. His pale, almost lashless eyes were naked as a snake's.

She stood up, but didn't turn. She looked at the wall.

He spoke softly. "I knew you'd come."

She kept watching the wall, feeling him there.

He said, "I knew."

She turned, then. She reached in her pocket for a cigarette, but she couldn't light it. Not with her hands shaking like that.

"You've got something in there," she said. She thought of his eyes, his hands, and the green box. She said, "I'm not talking about the gun."

He was silent.

The silence told her. And now the feeling came, the sweet flooding of power. She struck a match and held it to her cigarette. The little flame was bright and still.

"I'm not going to say anything," she said, "but it's not because I'm afraid." She looked straight into his eyes. "I'm not afraid of anybody," she said.

CHAPTER  13   In Sentinel the townspeople shunned the hot sidewalks for McFadden's and cool drinks, root beers and lime freezes; certain men lounged in the gloom of the Antler's Club and drank home brew. Householders tugged at garden hoses and thoughtfully watched the little sprinklers scatter mist.

"Hot enough for you?"

"Well, I'll say!"

"Gonna sit on the porch tonight. Breeze out on my porch, and the missus has got cold drinks. . . ."

In the Dixie Rooms the girls rose late and moved about in light kimonos. The rooms were hot and dark, for the sun baked the roof, and heat writhed in the dark alley like a living thing.

"Well, the poolrooms is full of men."

"Out in the country they're starting haying."

"Someways I hate haying time."

"The town is full of men."

The haymen began to come to the Bart Ranch, Model-T's, old cut-down Buicks, Overlands, single men, groups, families with children, women in worn gingham, men in bib-overalls, young fellows of fourteen and fifteen, talking with the twang of southern Idaho, Jack-Mormons hunting a haying job, big money, two dollars a day, three meals and a tent to bunk in.

The families kept together, and at night they sat on the running boards of their cars and listened in the silences to killdeers piping down by the barn where the creek ran and the mist rose and drifted, spiritlike.

Mist is a strange and lonely thing.

They talked those nights before haying began. They boasted of other ranches where they'd worked, spoke with pride of the wealth of their bosses there, and the size of the ranches.

"This place in Wyoming, Jackson's Hole. Had all alfalfa."

"Don't like alfalfa. Hate to mow it, get's stuck in the sickle bar."

"All wads up."

A campfire, there where they had pitched their worn tents, and they sang. All the songs. "Letter Edged in Black." "Little Rosewood Casket." *There's a little rosewood casket, setting on a marble stand, there's a package of love letters, written by my true love's hand. . . .*

Voices rose and fell in the firelight, bewitched with the ancient longing of families with no homes, sons with no families. Always someone played the guitar, chorded in minor key the songs of death, of longing and of sorrow.

They were not good workers. Shiftless, the ranchers called them. They didn't want to work very long, or very hard. A sawbuck is a lot of money, and when you have your sawbuck you grow lazy and thoughtful. . . .

Now, Lona noticed a funny thing. She had seen the hired men and the cowboys, and now the hay men leave the bunkhouse early for work; and she had seen them push back their chairs from meals without lingering over a cigarette.

Joe Martin, sitting with them, made them uncomfortable.

He ate swiftly, and went back to work. He made them nervous. He moved swiftly to each job as if he hated it and could kill it with speed. Late one afternoon Lona had seen him on his back under the axle of a mowing machine, almost blinded by sweat and grease; he talked softly to himself.

She watched him, and beside her stood Eddie Rohn. Eddie Rohn had just finished riding a bronc for the first time. He had ridden well; a girl had watched him ride well; he was proud of himself. Now the breeze tugged at the full sleeves of his black satin shirt, his hat was pushed back, cool looking, and he still wore his heavy silver spurs, proud badge of his profession, and they jingled when he moved. He was proud of his hands.

A rider is proud of his hands. They sense the spirit of a horse through the bridle reins. They know the wild heart of a horse at the end of a lariat. They give slack, and take it up. A rider's hands are a part of brain, not of brawn.

The men working near greeted him, smiling.

"Hello, Rohn."

He always had a grin. "Hi, there."

They were proud to greet him. He was the kind of fellow you liked.

Joe Martin, lying under there on his back, turned his head, blinked back the sweat and crawled out.

The three stood there, Lona close beside Eddie Rohn, the quirt swinging from her wrist. Her eyes were amused and thoughtful. Eddie Rohn and his silver spurs. And Joe Martin, overalls shiny with grease, his old boots run over at the heel, brim of his hat squashed up in back. And his hands . . .

The men working near were silent, working away at the teeth of a derrick.

Lona said, "Joe, how'd you like to boss the hay camp?"

She smiled. She hadn't really meant it. He had hired out as a cowboy, but here he was—his hands were long and thin, black with grease, and his wrist was bandaged where he had cut himself at some ugly job. Sweat traced crooked paths down his cheeks. She glanced at Eddie Rohn, at his shirt and his hands, and felt an odd little sense of power.

Tom Bart took the idea of Joe Martin's bossing the hay crew as his own. He felt wise and shrewd. He had noticed, he said, how

Joe Martin made men work—without even trying. Some men could do that, he said. Why, he said, he'd intended all along . . .

The sun had set red and left a blot of blood on the bare round hill across the valley.

Joe Martin sat alone in the bunkhouse, in the wicker chair, neck bent, reading a *Western Story* magazine. Almost all the men had moved that evening to the hay camp below the house, and old Art and two remaining men played horseshoes out back. When Tom came in he stopped to listen for the silver ring of a shoe on the iron peg.

"Ever play horseshoes, Martin?"

Joe Martin glanced up. "Nope."

"They play a lot down at camp after supper. Say you never played?"

"I don't play."

"Well," Tom said, "haying starts tomorrow." He sat down and listened to the voices out back, curiously distinct in the lowering dusk. "I could use a man to boss the crew."

Joe Martin turned a page of the magazine. "I ain't going down there. I hired out to punch cows. If there ain't that job, you can give me my time."

Getting dark, now. Behind the bunkhouse the game was breaking up, and the men laughed and joked. The little brown dog was excited, and barked.

In the house, Tom Bart said, "I should of given him his time."

Ruth said, "You could do it now." She watched her father. "He doesn't seem—safe."

Lona tossed a magazine to the table beside the couch. "Who?"

"That fellow Joe Martin." Tom turned back to Ruth.

Lona said, "What about him? He's a good worker."

Tom said, "He doesn't take orders."

Lona said, "What about him not going down to boss the hay-crew?"

Tom said, "Says he won't go."

Lona got up. "Of course he'll go."

"Says he won't. Just says it."

Lona said, "Tell him it's orders."

Tom said, "He's funny. And a good man."

"Go on down," Lona said. "Tell him. Don't ask him."

Tom felt the eyes of both women on him. He got up.

Joe Martin was still reading the *Western Story* magazine. He had lit the lamp, and the moths bumped about it and cast wild crazy shadows on the ceiling. Joe Martin was slouched in the old wicker chair, squinting his pale eyes.

He looked up when Tom came in. "Martin," Tom said.

Joe Martin's lips barely moved. "I ain't going down there."

Outside the men had stopped playing horseshoes and their voices floated in from the bench alongside the building, talking softly. They had a smudge going to keep away mosquitos, and the air was rich with the sharp odor of smoldering grass. In the silences they watched falling stars in the black summer sky, craned their necks, watched, open-mouthed, like children.

"Them stars . . . look . . ."

Tom Bart was saying, "You're the man for it." He was sitting on the big table now, dangling his legs.

Joe Martin said, "I didn't hire out for it." Tired, steady eyes.

"Well—"

"You can give me my time." Joe looked back to the magazine.

Then, a little movement at the door. Lona came in quietly. She sat beside her grandfather, swinging her legs, and the quirt swung too. She said, "What's this?"

Joe Martin said, "He was trying to get me down there."

Lona said, "What's wrong with down there?" She fished in her pocket for a cigarette, and lighted it, watching him.

His jaw moved. "Too damn much work. Dirty work."

Lona said, "Yes. But you'd better go down."

He didn't move his eyes. "I already made up my mind."

She took a deep drag of her cigarette. He kept watching her, unblinking, his eyes red around the rims. She blew the smoke toward him. She said, "I'd go down there, if I were you."

She went outside so it would be easier for Joe Martin to back down.

In the evening a haycamp is quiet; the men sit before the tents smelling the mist on the cut hay, talking softly.

They talk about God.

Old man talked about a church, when he was a kid, washed and scrubbed, and his mother there, and the preacher's shouting hellfire and damnation.

"Jesus, he could preach. If I'd a done like he said . . ."

The young men were uneasy. "If you'd a done like you ought to of, and believed in God, you'd a been rich and owned a big ranch." They grinned at the wit of this.

The old man's eyes were grave. "No, but I'd a been closer to God."

The young men laughed. "That would a got you a lot." But in the evening there was a deep hush in the hay camp, a strange peace that forced thought. They fought it, and talked loud and dirty.

Talked about women. About when the thunderheads would tower over the mountains, when rain would streak down and stop haying a day or two. *Say, then!* They'd crank up their cars and go to Sentinel.

"Christ, forty days out here, and no woman."

Boy of seventeen, just shaved last week: "How do you feel, go forty days—without it?"

Eyes meeting eyes. "Why, it makes a man want to bust right out."

They sat in the silence, and one man lit a lantern, and let down the tent flaps. "Wait until it rains. It's bad for a man to go without a woman. Makes a man crazy."

The boy touched his cheek. "Go crazy?" He had heard this before.

"Nature wants you with a woman. When it rains we're going in." They rolled cigarettes, and the cigarette papers whispered.

The boy said, "Take me in?"

The men laughed and slapped their thighs. "Why, you're just a kid. You don't need no woman." But one said softly, "Sure. We'll take you."

I was sixteen, I went. I sat alone on the bare iron bed. I was afraid, but more afraid of not being a man.

They talked loud and dirty, trying to foul the silence outside. The old man smiled because they were afraid.

And they were afraid of Joe Martin.

He was the best haying boss Tom Bart ever had. For now there were no quarrels among the men, small quarrels that started evenings in their tents, playing poker, squatting around a blanket in the light of a smelly kerosene lantern. Little quarrels that grew deep and personal in the long hot hours in the fields, when a man's eyes smarted from glare and heat, nursing hate. Some sore. Some slight, swollen and festering.

Men quit. Machinery was idle in the fields, hay rotted in the windrows.

None of that now. The men were one, hating Joe Martin.

"Move the derrick. Right here. On the double, now."

When he turned they looked at their hands and spoke from the corners of their mouths. Ashamed they didn't quit, ashamed of their fear for their jobs, of nameless things the voice and face of Joe Martin suggested.

They worked hard.

Each evening they had their revenge on Joe Martin.

They refused to talk when he came to their tents. Silent, they sat looking out at falling dusk, and when he had moved away with that stiff walk they began to talk and laugh. They played the harmonica.

Their eyes met.

They watched him alone in the tent he shared with Art, squatting, cleaning his automatic. "Funny kind of a gun for a fellow to have." They listened to old Art down by the creek, throwing sticks in the water. "Bring the stick, Toots. Bring back the stick."

And when Art came up, he boasted. "He's not a bad fellow. I sleep in the tent with him."

They laughed. "Notice your bitch don't."

Art grew red. "Well, she could if I wanted. Sure could."

The sleeping bag was new. Khaki canvas stuffed with kapok, tight against hayseeds and burrs. Joe Martin kept it neat, kept it made, buttons buttoned.

It happened one noon.

There had been no rain, no chance for town, no rest. The sun shriveled. Dinner was over, and the men sat in the hot tents, a little sick from heat and the sluggish creek water they drank.

Some had dysentery, and it was said that Joe Martin had it too, for all morning he kept riding from the haystack to the willows, and his horse stood at the low entrance to the tangled brush.

At noon Lona rode horseback into camp, cool in a fresh shirt, her quirt swinging from her wrist, her horse shying at the tents that heaved and swelled in the heat. Eddie Rohn rode beside her, laughing and talking, the kind of a fellow a man likes.

"Joe," she called, and Joe Martin crawled from his tent and stood there, spraddle-legged. The others poked their heads out of their tents, squinting, and heard the yapping of the little dog down by the creek. Art was at it again.

"Get the stick, Toots." A little echo. ". . . stick, Toots."

Lona swung off and dropped the reins, and came toward the tent of Joe Martin. Eddie Rohn followed and grinned across to the men, raised a hand to them. And, "Howdy, Martin."

Joe Martin said, "We ought to get the derrick moved after dinner." He stood there.

Lona's voice smiled. "It's hot. Going to ask us in?"

Joe Martin stood aside, and held the tent flap up. There was his suitcase, neat in the corner, and his razor out to dry, a brush and comb arranged just so. And there was the new sleeping bag, neat, smooth, each button buttoned.

Eddie Rohn squatted, cowboy fashion. Lona sat on the sleeping bag, and slipped the quirt off her wrist. It lay in the dirt. "You're late moving the derrick, Joe. You should have moved this morning."

Joe Martin squatted. His face was haggard. "They're sick down here. Everybody's slow and sick."

Lona smiled. "Sleeping sickness?"

"It's the water. Makes them sick. We need something better to drink."

Lona smiled. "Maybe lemonade. How about that?"

Eddie Rohn laughed, uncomfortably.

Lona said, "What should I do? Boil water for everybody down here?"

Joe Martin said, "Good idea."

"Get big kettles, and boil it," Lona said. "And for horses, too?"

Eddie Rohn grinned again, and Lona patted the sleeping bag.

There was silence in the fields and in the tents, for the little brown dog had stopped barking. There was the clink of harness where a team was tied to the hitching rack.

Then—the rustle of canvas at the tent flap. Art stood there, big overalls bagging, friendly voice smiling in the silence. "Hello, Miss Lona. Come down to see us?" He came inside, stooping. "Come down to pay us a little visit?" He squatted in his corner. "Nice to have visitors."

"Why, hello, Art. How is everything, Art?"

"Why, just fine, Miss Lona. How is everything to the ranch?"

"Why, just fine, Art. Everything fine here?"

Eddie Rohn held a short twig in his fingers, and dug a hole in the soft earth. Joe Martin stared through the crack in the tent flap.

"Just fine, Miss Lona. Is everything—hello, Eddie! Everything fine to the ranch? You still breaking horses?"

Eddie looked up from the hole he dug. "Sure am, Art."

"Well," Art said. "Must be mighty nice to be breaking a few. Nice for a young man, not dirty work like this." Art's laugh crowded the tent. "Seen you ride in," he said, and grew bold. "Nice for a young fellow to ride with a pretty girl."

Eddie Rohn flushed; he grinned, watching the twig hole.

Art grew bolder. "Seen a movie. There was this pretty girl riding along, and this cowboy, he rode along and began to sing a song. This girl was the daughter of a big rancher." Art kept looking from face to face.

There was a scurrying at the tent flap, a blundering, then the small wet head of Tootsie was in the opening.

Lona spoke quickly. "Hello, Toots." You could see the dog hesitate, and her head moved as if she wagged her tail. Lona said, "Come here," and patted the sleeping bag.

The dog looked from face to face with bright brown eyes. Then wriggled in, slinking along on her belly where long brown hairs dripped creek water. But before she reached Lona, she stopped.

Stopped and shook.

The water flew. Flew in drops dirty with mud. Shook again, and there were ugly brown spots on the sleeping bag.

Joe Martin stood. The others jumped up, looking at each other.

Joe Martin moved. Snatched the quirt from the ground, lunged forward. He had the little brown dog down in the corner of the tent, the muscles beneath his tight shirt played. He crouched . . .

The dog began to yap, high, shrill. Then one long yap like a moan. Joe Martin's arm rose and fell, rose and fell. He crowded closer, and began to kick.

"You bitch," he said. "You dirty bitch."

Eddie Rohn moved. Moved in between Joe Martin and the dog, pushed in, crowded in, hunched down and got in, grabbed Joe Martin's arm, pushed him back. Joe Martin lunged and Eddie lost ground. Eddie grabbed Joe Martin's wrists. They struggled, arms jerked up and down, and the cords bulged in their necks.

Nobody spoke. Only a hoarse breathing. Then a word, single and sharp.

"Joe!"

Lona stood straight. She had the quirt again. "Joe."

In a minute Joe Martin stopped struggling. Eddie Rohn threw him off balance, and he caught himself against the tent.

They went outside. Nobody spoke. The men were coming from their tents, and not looking up, they began to hook up their teams. Art walked to the willows toward his team, eyes straight ahead. The little brown dog limped behind.

CHAPTER 14   The newspaper lay on the couch.

It was not the weekly local paper, the *Sentinel Examiner,* the small sheet that recorded births and deaths and visits in the valley, and told how to remove rust spots from sheets.

It was the big Salt Lake paper.

The postoffice at the Cross-Roads was run by an old couple who quarreled gently while they sorted mail.

"And here's your paper, Mr. Bart," they said, and Tom took the sack of mail into the cold dryness of early November.

All day the paper lay on the couch in the living room. Ruth had sorted out the magazines from the mail-order catalogs and circulars for bull sales, and had gone with them to her room. She had not even taken the tight brown wrapper off the paper.

The paper went next to Mrs. Dean.

Mrs. Dean liked to read. She liked those murder magazines best. They had pictures of real houses and real people and real trunks. When you worked on the Bart Ranch it was sort of hard to remember that exciting things like that really happened.

The paper was nice too.

By two o'clock she was ready to read. The dinner dishes were done, the roast for supper simmered in the oven. She took the paper from the windowsill by the sink, and looked out for a moment at the dead autumn fields, the gray hills, the distant ragged blue peaks. Sweater about her shoulders, she hurried toward her little cabin through the tall dead rye-grass.

As soon as she got her feet up she reached impatiently for the feature section with the big drawings of men lying in their own blood, shot by gangster bullets, and society women with ropes and ropes of pearl beads around their necks.

Mrs. Davidson in happier days before her mate killed himself and left the former Follies beauty destitute.

Follies beauty! One of them actresses, fur pieces, and champagne with bubbles. But behind that grandness there was a lot of misery, Mrs. Dean noticed.

. . . jewels worth fifty thousand dollars. . . .

Mrs. Dean breathed heavily, and read on.

. . . rose from obscurity.

What was obscurity? Mrs. Dean knew. It was being nobody, it meant having poor folks in a clapboard shack, and everybody quarreling, and everything dirty. You rose from it, and had ropes and ropes of pearl beads, or twenty thousand acres.

At four o'clock she sighed, stretched, and sat on the edge of her bed. Well, maybe you could get lowered again to obscurity. Maybe you could get lowered to destitute . . .

Maybe her beads weren't pearl, but she still had them.

Had that insurance money too.

Outside the sun was sinking, a cold light seeped in through the heavy glass curtains sent out from the big house. She folded the paper carefully and took it with her across the yard to the kitchen.

After supper the hired men picked their teeth thoughtfully, and carried their dirty dishes into the kitchen.

Mrs. Dean looked up. "There's the paper. On the window."

It was good to rest in the bunkhouse after supper. The bunkhouse was your home. You had your bunk there, and your suitcase with your things in it. Your dark blue suit for town was hanging away from the dust in the closet with the other fellows' blue suits. All good fellows, and fine to talk to.

It was good to read a little. Them *Western Story* magazines piled on the big table got stale after awhile, but this fellow Shorty in one of the stories, he was in every magazine, a story about him. There was this mean sheriff that was in cahoots with the robbers, and Shorty was the deputy sheriff. There was one of them big ranchers had a daughter with hair like honey in long curls. She sure was sweet on this Shorty, but just when you thought maybe they was going to get hitched the story ended.

Them stories got stale.

The bunkhouse wasn't wired for lights, but there was a good lamp. And the newspaper on the table. The funnies was good.

The men sat silent, resting from the day, from riding after a bunch of steers far from the home ranch. It had been cold and the wind sneaked through their mackinaws, and made their ears ache. All afternoon they had thought of the bunkhouse, the bright light of the lamp, yellow and warm, the talk after supper, and reading a little.

"Maggie and Jiggs is sure good this week."

"I read it. Old Jiggs sure fooled her this week. He put his fancy duds on and then he put his other clothes on and went to Dintv Moore's."

"Last week he got caught. She threw a vase at him."

"A woman will do that, you get caught."

"You get caught fooling with another woman, they'll do it."

"My woman was always a-waiting. By God, they watch enough, they'll see something!"

A dry chuckle. "She throw an old vase at you?"

"I'd a clipped her. She took the kids to Idaho Falls. Guess she's hashing down there. She don't write. Never wanted a fellow to have fun. Liked a little fun herself, before the kids came. That's a funny thing . . ."

They thought about this. "Want to throw the paper in the wood box?"

"Old Art read it? He's down milking. He likes a newspaper."

"Funny old bastard. I wonder does he get anything out of a paper."

Through the dark window of the bunkhouse the men watched the flicker of old Art's lantern down by the barn. It shone on the milk buckets. It cast a weak pool of light on the ground where his dog trotted busily ahead of him. When she looked back, little brown eyes glistened.

"Well, my little dog."

She didn't sleep in the bunkhouse any more.

Art lifted the latch of the barn door and it squeaked in the frosty air.

"Go on in, Toots."

A man needed something. It was nice to have Toots.

Animals were nicer than people. In the newspapers you could read all about things animals done. There was Tom Mix's horse, could count to six with his foot. There was a seal in the paper, name of Sharkey the Talking Seal.

Dogs saved ladies from forest fires and pulled people out of Puget Sound. And in tonight's paper . . .

There was this big fine dog a man in New York had.

This man went to his bedroom with the big dog and a newspaper, and shot himself through the head. They found the dog there, being faithful. And it said one of his paws pointed to the headline that said *Market Crashes.*

They spoke of it in the Sentinel Implement Company, where you bought harness, coils of rope and parts for mowing machines, they spoke of it there at the long counter, waiting for little packages of rivets or bolts or machine oil, ranchers and townspeople talking in the hushed voices used when they gathered for funerals.

They spoke of it in the lobby of the Sentinel Hotel, where the ranchers met, stiff in their store suits, awkward in town.

"Ed Williams," they said. "Charley Wentworth," they said. "The Circle-Bar outfit, the Haynes Livestock." They spoke as they did of the dead. They murmured the great names of the West, Anthony and Myles, the Hood Livestock Company, the Double-H. Legendary names.

"Harry Haynes was a fine man," they said.

"Remember Charley Wentworth. Talked to him at the bull sale in Ogden." (Talked at the Bigelow Hotel, the lights and the music from the dining room, the handsome women in the lobby. Charley Wentworth could have *bought* the hotel. Could have bought *Ogden.* Wore his ten-gallon hat like a badge anywhere. New York. In London he had dinner with Dawes.)

Sons of the West's great families, names that had trailed cattle from Texas in the seventies, proud of their beginnings, a grandfather who started with a pair of oxen and a two-wheeled cart. . . .

The great ranches were crumbling.

There were small, ugly things. Papers to sign. Strange men in automobiles who came to inspect the land and the cattle, arrogant men from banks with briefcases, hard city men who somehow had a right to sit in your house and crucify you.

The big places went first, the lavishness, the openhandedness, the loose kind of feudalism. Too many taxes, too much expense, nothing coming in. An eighty-dollar cow worth twenty.

"Why, Harry Haynes was a fine man. . . ."

Houses boarded up, weeds in ditches, barns sagging. Sheriffs' sales, and strangers bidding. They spoke of it in the Implement Company and in the Sentinel Hotel.

But the Bart Ranch stood.

There was the great old house, with the things in it from England. Dust rose from the sprawling corrals where men branded cows and broke horses. Tom Bart rode on his land, astride a fine horse, and the sun flashed on the silver mountings of his saddle.

The ranch was a fortress, the Bart name a banner. There were much bigger ranches, there had been richer ranchers, but the Bart Ranch stood.

"Is the Bart Ranch . . . ?" People who had never seen the ranch asked it. People who had never seen a Bart.

It was more than the big house. More than the twenty thousand acres. It was hope, and pride.

Oh, old Bert Bart would have been proud. He had not kept those careful books for nothing, made his bargains. He had built well. The foundation was solid.

But the walls were rotten.

The bar at the Cross-Roads was crowded. Here cowboys came when they had finished loading cattle in the chutes across the tracks, and when rumbling freight trains passed the squat log cabin shook. Passenger trains whistled for the flagstop, and in the bar laughter and talk stopped, and drinking men stood a moment staring vacantly. A train shrieking off across the flat did that to a fellow.

Talk and laughter was loud now, a man walked unsteadily to the mechanical piano, the front prettied with mottled panes of orange and green glass. You dropped in a dime and the piano played tinny and strident. The little lever at the side had been moved from "piano" to "banjo." It was gayer.

> *Mary Lou (da-da da da da)*
> *Mary Lou (da-da da da da)*
> *Cross my heart (da-da da da da)*
> *I love you. . . .*

Talking, drinking men. They grew suddenly friendly or thoughtful or remote. They watched the rows of glasses behind the bar and looked into their own eyes in the mirror behind. There was a punch-board, and you could win a little bit of a cedar chest for your girl, with candy inside. There was a big calendar with a picture of a girl in a big light blue hat. She held a bunch of roses against her breast, and underneath it it said "Forever Yours."

> *Mary Lou,*
> *Mary Lou,*
> *Cross my heart. . . .*

The two cattle buyers at the end of the bar talked softly and earnestly. They were dressed in the uniform of their trade, store suits of good quality, expensive high-heeled boots, stitched with rows of colored silk and inlaid with bits of colored leather. Dress boots. They wore their big cowboy hats easily. Ranchers and cowboys liked to see the buyers dressed this way.

One of the cattle buyers set down his drink and turned it in his thumb and fingers, picked it up and set it down again squarely on the moist ring it had made on the bar. He looked up.

"That's a hell of an old tune."

"They got it all the places. It's like the one, *When the red red robin comes bob-bob-bobbin' along*. They play it all the time."

"It was great days, though."

"Now it's Hoover days."

"He said Al Smith would grow grass in the streets."

"Christ. I could mow all the grass Hoover can grow in the streets."

The other looked puzzled, then laughed. "That's pretty good, Ed."

"Well, it's the truth. I was up to the Bart place today. Offered the old man twenty bucks for his cows."

"He gonna take it?"

"Don't know. You know Tom Bart. Laughs and smiles and you never know what he thinks." The buyer's voice got a little tight. "He's *got* to take it."

"First I knew the Barts got to do anything."

"Old Bert was rich, but they can't coast forever."

A car stopped in front of the saloon, and the bartender went out to sell some gas. The men in the bar turned to look out the window at the car and the women inside, two plump, blond women. Some of the men winked at one another.

One buyer spoke again. "I was in the bank at Sentinel," he said.

They glanced at each other. The buyer in the black hat said, "What'd you hear?"

The buyer in the white hat fiddled with his glass. "You know old Barton. Never says much. Way he says it."

"Well?"

White Hat spoke slowly. "He said maybe Tom Bart would sell."

CHAPTER

Tom Bart had put the advertisement in a vacation issue of a big magazine. Keeping dudes sounded sensible to him, businesslike. There was that big house, all those rooms. All the cooking had to be done anyway. Good idea to get some of that money the dudes were spending. They'd pay anything, he understood.

He worked for a long time on the advertisement, writing with a soft lead pencil.

"You'll help, Ruth? You'll help me guide them around?"

"Of course I will, Dad. You just tell me what you want me to do."

"All right, Ruth." He finished the ad. "How is this, Ruth? 'Come to a real ranch.' That sound pretty good?"

"That sounds fine, Dad. Would you like to take some pictures of the corrals and horses?"

"Why, I never thought of that, Ruth."

He did not ask Lona if she would help. She was too busy. But he showed the ad to the men in the bunkhouse when it came out, all slick and shiny, in the magazine. *Come to a real ranch.*

He didn't know whether they would come singly or in droves, but no matter—there was a lot of room, and some of them might like to sleep in tents around the place. He understood dudes did things like that. Seventy dollars a week was a lot of money.

"Well." He looked at the ad. "They'll be here any time." He gave the ad a week to work, and then for the next week he met the train each evening in Sentinel. He wore a new pair of boots, a new silver gray Stetson, a dark blue gabardine shirt with pearl buttons, and a great smile as he waited in the old Pierce beside the depot, waving to acquaintances, nodding and smiling.

And each night the train came and went, the newsstand opened and closed, the bicycles of the grade-school boys went off up the street, and Tom Bart stood alone, watching the red light of the semaphore.

He always tried to sneak into the ranch house when he got back. He was tired of saying that nobody came.

Ruth always waited up for him. "Would you like a cup of coffee, Dad?"

"You shouldn't have stayed up, Ruth. They'll be along one day. Any mail this afternoon?"

"How about a game of cribbage, Dad?"

He would grumble. "You must get sick of playing cribbage."

She always looked so pretty at night, he thought. It was fine to have a pretty daughter, and she played cribbage, too. And when they had finished the game they went into the kitchen for crackers and cheese. "Ruth, I don't know what I'd do without you," he'd say, and brush the cracker crumbs off the blue gabardine shirt.

The dude who came caught him unawares. There was a telephone call from Sentinel, and he hurried to the garage and went to the depot. He didn't remember the gabardine shirt.

He was a blond young man, this dude, tall and bony, quiet, but anxious to please. He always got up early in the morning, and you'd see him before breakfast, walking hatless around the place, looking at the buildings, at the fields that stretched and stretched below the creeks. The dogs liked him, especially Tootsie, and you'd hear him talking to her and laughing when she barked.

He had come to breakfast that first morning with Lona. She had not introduced him, and there was a small awkward silence as Mrs. Dean smiled and put on another plate, a little scraping of chairs as the young man stood there, looking out the window of the back dining room.

He had said, "It's a beautiful morning."

The men went right on eating. After breakfast they hurried to the bunkhouse to have a last cigarette before they went out to saddle up or catch their teams.

Joe Martin said, "Isn't it a beautiful morning?"

They began to laugh. They said it all week. "Roll out of your bunks," they said. "It's a beautiful morning."

Clyde Barrows was thirty years old, his voice was soft, and he never raised it. He had come West because he believed, and his mother believed, that a change let a man get his bearings.

Clyde Barrows was a failure.

Morning after morning he awoke at the Bart Ranch, the smell of sage in his nostrils, watching cracks in the plaster or stains where the rain had come through amorphous, shapeless stains.

He thought about failure. The concrete object of failure was in the closet there, in his otherwise empty suitcase, in a cardboard box. Four or five hundred sheets of yellow paper.

A novel.

Oh, everybody thought novels, and wrote novels; but they were not prepared. Not prepared to give their lives to it, to think of nothing else. Not prepared for the apprenticeship, the million words, and outside of a story or two in small magazines no one ever heard of—to have nothing to show for it but a sheaf of yellow copypaper.

Now it was with a dragging, twisting embarrassment that he remembered his years of work, his dismissal as unimportant the things other men did. Young men he knew, young men with money and family behind them, had already gone up and up in their worlds. They sold things well, performed services; junior members of firms, they rated desks and offices of their own. A brass name-plate is an accomplishment.

Something tangible, worth money. Not a sheaf of yellow paper in a suitcase.

If it were not such a strange book it might have been published. Already there would have been reviews and advertisements, and people wanting to meet Clyde Barrows.

But it was a book of impressions that tried to do for language what Cézanne did for painting: broke up the whole into small parts, each interesting and beautiful in itself. The life of a boy.

There was a curious dreamlike quality about it that fascinated, a shocking nostalgia. There was a scene of a boat crossing San Francisco bay, and someone singing "Smiles."

There was an ambulance, and two white-coated men came to the house.

There was a strange meeting of father and son in the cellar of the house. Near the furnace, and the hot-air pipes reached up through the floor . . .

The book ended when the boy was twenty.

There was the hope, and the feel of the weight of the manuscript in his hands, and stamps, and mailing. And the wait.

Three publishers.

Not for us. Not for us. Not for us.

And a fourth publisher. That letter was clear and shimmering. *This is one of the most remarkable things we have seen.*

This is one of the most . . .

You have got to get a unity. This is going to be hard, because it will have to be a unity that has never been found before. The very nature of your book. . . .

A letter from the editor-in-chief.

He didn't know what to do. Where to begin. Nothing like it had been done before.

What was wrong? Why couldn't he put this final piece in the jigsaw puzzle? He couldn't find the piece. There was the agony of almost having something, of being hungry, with food in sight.

There was the thought of being thirty, and no brass nameplate, and nothing done. There were the mornings watching the crazy cracks in the ceiling of the bedroom, and the shapeless stains that meant nothing.

He talked with his mother, for his father was dead. His mother had remarried, was wealthy now. Helen Winston, her name was, always sane, always right, critical of a man who accomplished nothing. Her point of view was real. He took her money, and came to Montana. Maybe there he could find what he wanted, what he needed.

In the Lost Horse Valley pianos were common enough, in the town of Sentinel and on the ranches, the kind known as the upright. Brides often brought a piano into a husband's unmusical home.

You had to have a piano just as you had to have plants in the house, wandering Jews, snake cactus and geraniums. The piano showed you had a feeling for culture, the plants that you had an interest in nature and enough sense of duty to water them.

But by the middle of the twenties there had already begun the Decline of the Piano. Nobody could play it but older women who used it on Sundays to chord out hymns, flappers and sheiks who vamped out "Kitten on the Keys" and the "Alcoholic Blues," and children who sat together on the bench and worked out chopsticks.

But the pianos remained in the houses. They were great, massive, hulking instruments of some dark wood, often black, often with fluted pillars up the sides, often with intricate scrollwork along the front so the sound could get out, and the scrollwork might be backed with red or green silk. The piano was a piece of furniture that didn't blend well with anything else. It had a character of its own.

The piano was moved in the room with great difficulty, requiring the help of a man.

"I wish you'd help me move the piano over there by the window. I'm sick of it where it is."

"My God, are you going to move it again? No matter where you put it you ain't satisfied."

"Well, it's better under the window. Maybe you could get Ed to help you. Don't scratch the floor."

"Why don't you give this damn thing away?"

"Who you going to give a big heavy piano to? Besides, I'm going to start Myra on piano pretty quick."

It wasn't right under the window, or anywhere else. They tried to transform its useless character with special scarves for the top, scarves of plush and fringe, and plants were set here and there. The top was lined with photographs, easel like.

"Lovingly, Alice."

"To a real friend, Gladys."

"Billy, from Aunt Anne."

The circular stool (with clawed legs) on a screw pivot was seldom used except by an extra guest who sat there restlessly, turning this way and that, or by children who frankly went round and round on it.

The fact that there was a piano in the home caused parents to force children into "taking piano," not for musical or ambitious reasons but because they wanted to see it used, no matter how badly. The piano was too big to go unused. It represented too much money.

There were first the scales and exercises, one a tricky affair called "The Rocking-Horse." C, D, E, F, G (and then the rocking part) C-G-C-G-C-G-C. The mechanical interest in this exercise and the lack of thought it took to play it made it a favorite with any child. "Can't you play something else, Harry?"

"I was supposed to practise it. Old Miss Grantz said."

There was the "Cuckoo Waltz," a thumping bass and small piercing notes in the treble, and this was interesting if played several octaves apart. And at last there was the "Tiger Lily Waltz," bass and treble and black notes. Here lessons ended.

"He just ain't musical. My folks wasn't neither. Ed's father always hated music. Said you couldn't hear yourself talk."

But the piano remained and it made the woman in the house nervous. "I wish you'd help me move the piano over by the door. It looks funny there by the window."

The piano in the Bart ranch house was a beautiful thing, not an upright, but a grand, and there is nothing more beautiful than a good grand piano. The mahogany glistened, and the little gold-plated lyre above the name meant fifteen hundred dollars. It was one of the magnificent presents Tom Bart had bought for Ruth in the days of the war, when steers were selling at fourteen cents a pound. It stood there in the living room, aloof, alien.

There was little for Clyde on the ranch. Hours upon hours to think, and not ready to think about—the book. Afraid to try, afraid he couldn't. He spent a good deal of time in the living room, where it was cool and shadowy, where the air was moist and thoughts grew like strange shapeless plants.

He found Ruth there one late afternoon. The sun spilled red dust in a narrowing path across the carpet. She sat at the piano, and he watched her a moment from the hall, then crossed the room quietly to the couch. He wasn't sure why. He began to watch the movement of her hands and fingers, working through the strict theme of a sonata, a thing bound within restrictions, narrow with limitations.

But the emotion was there, more poignant for order and form.

She went on playing. His mind was on the theme, following it, heard it twisted, tortured, and always the same. Maybe she wasn't playing as well as he thought—couldn't be—but he was leaning forward, tense, listening for something—for some answer. The tenseness was over his body, tight, ready to snap .

Now the music began to flow, logically, moving to a climax as surely as water to the sea. Flowing on a theme—a single idea. One fist tightened. He almost had it, had something.

She stopped abruptly, leaving the thing unfinished, crying for an end, and his heart pumped.

She was smiling.

He couldn't keep the catch out of his voice, his eagerness for completion, fulfilment. He said, "Please don't stop."

She looked very tired. "I've said all I've got to say." Her hands rested on the keys, fingers stretched out for silent chords. A little pressure, and the sound would come. Major. Augment. Minor . . .

The chord she did not play, the ending she had not made tugged at him. What a pianist she might have been! Self-conscious now, she watched her hands. He watched her, hesitating. He said, "Please tell me something."

It was a moment before she turned to him. "Yes?"

"Why did you never leave here? Why did you stay?"

The sun was gone. The narrowing path of red dust was only in the mind. The clock was louder in the dusk. She smiled.

"Does it matter much, now?"

He kept hearing the chord, shimmering, water in sunlight, unheard.

It was only on Sundays that Clyde saw anything of Lona.

Haying was on, and in the fields and at the hay camp work went on as usual. The sun beat down so that the taut blue denim across men's legs and thighs grew hot enough to burn. Heat waves shimmered up from the acres of curing hay, the stale water in the can under the wagon grew warm, and if there were polliwogs in it, they died. Work horses sweated, the collars around their necks rubbed off the hair, sores festered and ran, the flesh grew soft and the collars cut deep.

But around the ranch house the haying season was quiet. The cattle were in the hills, on the range, feeding high in the mountains where silent little springs slipped out beneath the rocks.

The sheds around the ranch were empty of mowing machines and rakes, the barns empty except for Lona's saddle horse, and Eddie Rohn's. A boy of fifteen did the milking while old Art drove the derrick team in the fields, and the boy cleaned out the barn, hauling the sour manure.

Sundays during haying were even quieter. In the bunkhouse Eddie Rohn washed his clothes. He got out the galvanized tub and carried hot water from the house. He shaved off yellow soap into the tub, great thick chips, threw his clothes in, took off his shirt and threw that in. Then he sloshed the clothes up and down with a long stick, bleached and splintered white from many washings. Later he bathed in the same tub, in the room where the bunks were, away from the window.

The choreboy sat on the big table where the magazines were and played cowboy tunes on a mouth-organ, cupping his hands around the instrument so he got a mournful sound, a kind of ooo-waa-ooo-waa, sad and longing. Beside him was a *True Story* magazine, and later he was going to read it. There was a picture of a big fellow carrying a pretty girl into a bedroom. You could tell because there was the end of the bed showing.

On Sundays, Lona stayed in the house. Clyde Barrows always thought of her sitting on the footstool pulled up near the ornate round stove that had no fire in it. She would sit there staring at the nickel trimmings on the stove, her longish sun-bleached hair in her eyes, her hands clasped around her knees, leaning forward. She would look at her fingernails, close her fist and study them closely, absorbed. He had seen her fumble for a cigarette, and then for a match. He knew she didn't have any. He leaned down over the stool and offered a lighted match.

She looked up, blankly. "Oh, thanks." With a little shaking of her head so the hair was out of her face. "Oh, thanks." She began to study the cigarette. It annoyed him a little.

What did she think about? She never went to town. Never saw a movie, heard a phonograph record. She left the room when her mother played the piano. Yet he felt she talked and laughed outside the house.

She didn't read, didn't read the *Saturday Evening Post*, as old Tom did, or *Vogue*, as her mother did. He expected sometime to find her reading the cheap magazines they had in the bunkhouse. She didn't. In spite of little education, blue denim skirts and sun-bleached hair, in spite of that she gave an impression of breeding.

He always noticed her on a horse, and there he had never seen anyone so secure. There was a haughtiness about her whole being, a kind of insolence.

"Let 'em eat cake," he had muttered once as she rode off. He was ashamed of himself.

Because she had an awful responsibility, carried a tremendous load, fought a hard battle. And she was losing. She must know that.

What did she fight for?

The house typified it. A great ugly old house of brick. The house was piped for water, there was a great coffinlike bathtub upstairs, and a toilet, but there was no water except that carried by hand. There was electricity, but some rooms had no fixtures, only the naked taped twisted wires sticking through plaster. There were radiators throughout the house, but no furnace in the damp cellar.

Magnificent plans, gone wrong.

She fought the sagging of barns, the breaks in fences and dams, low water, low prices for cattle. And she was losing. She was ignorant of facts, of failing banks and tottering industry. Of starving men and women huddled in freezing rooms.

She was up at six and in bed by nine at night. Her boot heels beat staccato in the long halls. She drove herself and the men, trying to save a doomed structure, a dead feudalism.

And failing.

Was it just recently she had begun to bite her nails? She was smoking a lot. Too much.

"Here, Lona. Here's a match."

"Oh, thanks." The quick movement of her head, and the hair out of her eyes. He would watch her. He began to feel sorry for her, no dances, no pretty clothes, no music, no powders and perfumes or a hat with flowers or feathers. . . .

And he fell in love with her.

She knew it. It sometimes gave her a strange pleasure when she knew he watched her ride away with Eddie Rohn. She supposed he was jealous, supposed he imagined what Eddie Rohn said to her, and she to him. He would imagine Eddie's touching her, whispering things . . .

Eddie Rohn hadn't done much, yet. But he was going to. She wanted him to.

She had turned in her saddle once when they rode away from the ranch after dinner. She had never seen anyone so lonely looking as Clyde Barrows.

"He ought to eat more," she told Eddie. "He's too thin."

"He looks like a fellow that's been sick a lot."

She said, "I like to listen to him talk. That Sunday he rode with me he kept talking about artists, people who paint pictures."

Eddie Rohn said, "Oh."

Clyde Barrows had asked to ride with her. It was embarrassing to ride with him because he looked funny. He wore a ten-gallon hat of her grandfather's and it didn't suit him. He wore those baggy overalls that didn't fit anywhere, and he didn't sit right in the saddle.

While Joe Martin reported to her, Clyde wandered around the stack asking questions. She wished he wouldn't. When he turned his back she knew they winked and said something about the Goddamn dude.

But they said nothing before her because they were afraid of her. They were lucky to have jobs that year. Every poolhall was full of men.

They rode up from the long flat yellow fields toward the foothills, and from the gradual rise they could look back and see the haystacks going up, little by little.

She pulled in her horse. "Let's get off here."

They stood and looked.

There was yellow in everything. The long flat field was greenish-yellow. The clumps of willows that marched along the creek were yellow-green. Even the blue of the sky was washed with yellow, washed sea-green, and when the loads of dry hay plumped down on the stack from the derrick there was a swishing, rustling sound, and the dust billowed up into the sun like powdered gold.

Suddenly she dropped her bridle reins and reached out her arms, stretching for what she saw, the warmth and the brilliance of yellow.

He was watching, too. "It looks like a Van Gogh."

She said, "What?"

He spoke softly. "Van Gogh was a painter. There was sun in the things he did, the yellow of the sun."

She was curiously angry. She had always thought that no one but she ever noticed the yellow in the fields, subtle but always present. It was a secret, and now this dude had it. It wasn't all hers.

And yet she supposed it was because he had the secret that she let him kiss her. She had never been cooler, and the kiss meant nothing, but she wondered what would happen if she had put something into the kiss.

One day Eddie Rohn was going to kiss her, and she would put something into the kiss.

Something yellow.

High in the upper end of the valley, past the small ranch of Danny Irwin, near a mountain spring and a clump of pines, was a log cabin, squat and low. It had been built as a shelter for the cowboy who kept the cattle from drifting across the state line into Idaho. There was a little log barn below it for two saddle horses. The rider was always gone all day.

In the little barn were the two horses of Lona and Eddie Rohn. She had wanted to check up on the rider's supplies.

In the cabin there was a small cook stove and a homemade table piled high with old magazines, and saddle and boot catalogs. The ceiling was low and there were only two little windows. It smelled of a single man: cooking, oiled leather, fresh-split kindling wood and the smoke from stale Bull Durham. A whiskey bottle was filled with saddle oil and filmed with dust.

There was a battered portable phonograph, open and dusty, and a high leaning pile of records. "My Pretty Quadroon." That was a sad one. "When the Work's All Done This Fall." That was a sad one.

Two handmade chairs were pulled up near the table. And in the corner was the bunk, made of boards, and the bedding was spread with a heavy gray tarpaulin.

It was cold in the mountains, for the wind blew over snow-drifts hidden deep in the close timber. The sunlight was thin and whitish.

Eddie Rohn made a pot of coffee and Lona watched him from

the bunk. There was something nice about a fire going in a stove, a loneliness and closeness. They smoked awhile. She kept watching the end of her cigarette and then she looked at him. He was right there beside her and when he laughed she had a little weakness inside.

She kept wondering how it got started, that it wasn't right to do what you wanted, when you both wanted. When you were hungry you ate, when you were thirsty you drank, when you were sleepy you slept.

"This is good strong coffee," she said. "It makes me feel funny."

"Too strong?" He leaned a little toward her.

"Uhh-unh. Here's a cigarette."

He said, "You're all shaky. You nervous?"

She said, "Sort of."

"What you nervous about?"

"Well," she said, "if the rider came in it'd look kind of funny, us sitting here like this."

"Yeah," he said, "it would." He was still leaning close. He had a good smell, and the muscles of his arms showed through his shirt. "But you said he never came."

She looked away. "You must have known a lot of girls. A lot of kinds of girls."

"Mn-hm." That sound was sort of in his throat. His hair was thick and black and wiry. "I never knew a girl like you."

She said, "What kind did you know?"

"Just girls." He looked a little remote.

She began to insist. "Was there any girl you treated—nice? Like you do me?" She was lying back a little, talking in a friendly tone.

The road twisted down through the sage, and there was no one coming, no speck far down the mountains. He stared out of the window a minute, twisting his neck.

He said, "There was this one girl."

She had a beautiful name. La Verne. She lived with her grandmother and grandfather in a little white house, in the Falls.

Lona said, "What was she like?"

He said, "Just a girl, I guess."

It was Saturday night, and all the lights were on in Idaho Falls. Neon lights, and the lights from store windows flooded the street,

*where the people from the farms were all dressed up. He had on
his blue serge suit, and a haircut, and La Verne was standing on
the corner with a girl friend. He had a drink of corn under his
belt, and felt good.*

She said, "What was her name, Eddie?"

"La Verne."

She laughed. "That's a funny name. The kind of a name from a
movie magazine."

He looked at her, a little hurt. "It was her name, though."

"Say," he had said, "would you like to take in a movie?"

She stiffened and looked a bit haughty. "I'm with my girl friend."

Lona said, "Did you like her a lot?"

Eddie said, "I just knew her."

*"Come on, La Verne," the girl friend said, "or I'll tell your grand-
mother."*

*"Tattle-tale," La Verne said in her beautiful voice, and laughed.
He was laughing, too.*

"She's an old tattle-tale," he said.

Lona said, "La Verne is an awfully funny name, Eddie."

*The clock in the court house struck midnight when they were
on the porch, and the porch light was on, and all the little bugs flying there. Inside was a big plush couch. She was so beautiful, like
a doll, he was afraid she would break. She had on a cotton dress,
tight across her breasts, and they strained at the cloth so you could
just see the tips.*

Lona said, "Did you kiss—La Verne?"

He made a little grin at her.

She said, "You did, didn't you?"

*He kept saying her name all the week they put the hay up. They
went to the Roseland in a pal's car. The pal played steel guitar in
the orchestra and wouldn't be out during the dance, and he knew
he'd sit in the back seat with La Verne and hold her gently, and
ache, not even touching or kissing her hard because she was so
lovely.*

*The doors of the car were closed, but he heard the orchestra
and the whining of the steel guitar. When it's moonlight on the
Colorado, how I wish that I could be with you. La Verne hummed.
And suddenly he touched the breasts and kissed her hard and the*

*ache came up in him, and he got rough. He got rough and rough
and she lay very still, whispering to him, and it almost drove him
crazy—her lying there and whispering and whispering. . . .*

Lona watched his face. She closed her eyes as he looked at her
and whispered, whispered, "*Darling . . . darling . . .*"

He relaxed his elbows to be heavy on the breasts under her shirt.
There was the whiteness you could see and the hardness you could
feel. He wanted to be heavy.

"Oh God," he said. "Oh God, darling."

And it was a funny thing. He had hated La Verne, after. La
Verne had cried. And when he got her over that she was sharp with
him, and he hated her touching him. But with Lona it was all
turned around. He loved her, and was afraid of her. He rode a little
behind her on the way back. Clyde was standing there by the
corrals, looking at them.

Eddie unsaddled her horse, and she left him and began to walk
toward the big house. In a few moments Clyde followed her. She
knew he was behind her, and she kept walking. She wondered
why she wanted to hurt him, couldn't understand it, and couldn't
stop wanting to.

They were both in love with her.

CHAPTER 16   Beside the bunkhouse, just outside the window,
there was a small patch of brown weeds, stiff,
thin little weeds, with thinner little branches
like feelers. Now in September they were dry
and brittle. And sensitive. They picked up little
currents of air, tiny vibrations, and they twitched nervously in the
dusk, moved by forces that even the rusty willows by the creek
did not feel.

Supper was over. Joe Martin sat in the bunkhouse by the window cleaning his automatic, and when he glanced up it was not at
the men, nor to listen to their talk, but to watch the nervous little
weeds thoughtfully. He was not like other men. He didn't brag
about his gun, tell how straight it could shoot, how much he paid
for it, who owned it before. He just sat there handling it, feeling it,
rubbing it with a little cloth. He kept it in the suitcase.

Two men were playing checkers on a board so old that the yellow pasteboard showed through the black and red in diagonal paths. They played heavily, slowly, and Art hovered over them watching. They had spoken to him before about the suggestions he had been giving.

"Shut up for Christ's sake." They hunched their shoulders.

Art was always hurt when they spoke like that to him, and he always moved away. After awhile he pumped up the kerosene lamp and brought it over near them.

"Here's the lamp when you need it," he said eagerly. "When you need it, it's right here." He hovered over them, his lips moving, making little jerks of his neck and wrists when they moved wrong.

The Kid, fifteen almost sixteen, almost a man now, sat in the wicker chair straining his eyes, reading the *True Story* magazine with the picture of the man carrying the woman. He bit his lower lip, his eyes eager. He had his leg thrown over the side of the chair.

"*My God, darling,*" Robert said. "*I want you in the very blood of me. I've got to have you, darling, I must. . . .*"

She pressed against him and suddenly all was . . .

The Kid moved his leg.

Eddie Rohn was kneeling on the bunkhouse floor beside his saddle. He had a tomato can filled with neat's-foot oil and he dipped a torn piece of overall cloth in it and rubbed the saddle. He almost hated to work with his saddle now. He kept thinking of how he had been going to be the best rider in the world, and here he was, twenty-three, working on a ranch. He couldn't leave, either.

He had said, "We gotta get married, Lona."

"Oh, we've got to wait. I've got to wait."

She always seemed to be waiting for something. But he couldn't leave. He frowned and dabbed at the saddle. There was something about the feel of her . . .

Clyde Barrows sat in his room at the big house. His pigskin bag was on a chair by his bed, and it was packed. Every good broadcloth shirt folded neatly, every pair of socks folded once over, a morocco belt coiled.

"Your folks must be rich," Lona had said.

"I guess you'd say my folks are rich," he had said, and she had looked at him strangely because the word folks sounded strange, affected, in his mouth.

He had written a letter. "She is as strong as granite. And as hard, I suppose, but she knows what she wants. I wish I knew what she wanted . . ."

He had written the letter over and over, for his mother was a snob, a possessive snob.

He looked at the suitcase. It had been packed for over a month.

Lona was worried. She sat on the footstool and smoked and worried. She had let them turn a thousand head of cattle into a field to hold them until the haystacks were fenced in the larger field below. They all worked so slowly. The feed was short where the cattle were, and it worried her.

She'd speak to Joe Martin, really speak to him. He had been getting insolent, but never quite insolent enough. It was hard to tell when a man like him had got too insolent.

He was insolent to Eddie Rohn too, but there again, you couldn't tell. Eddie just looked at him in that way of his. Lord, a good Mormon was good, all kinds of love and charity and fairness!

But she got weak thinking of him. His goodness melted right into her.

She should have hired another man. Those cattle . . .

Tom Bart was happy. He was in the root cellar across the road working with the electric light plant. He was the only one who understood it. It was fine to hold the spark plug in your hands, to touch up a gasket, and to know that nobody else could do it. When it stopped, they had to come to him. It was deep dusk now, and cold in the moist dusk of the cellar. He'd better hurry and get it fixed or they'd all be without lights.

Only he knew about the light plant.

Ruth moved about her room, to the window and back, to the window and back, smoking. Dusk was deep in the room and in a little while she could turn on the light. When you turned on the light tiny roses showed through the shade, invisible before. Oh, clever as hell.

"I'm going through hell," she kept thinking.

Before the deep dusk fell she had stood looking out the window at the patch of weeds down near the bunkhouse. The weeds were trembling and it was going to storm. One of the bad September storms. She had always noticed it. Clever of her to notice it. Clever as hell. But they did tremble.

Then the deep dusk fell and she kept walking about the room. There was some brandy in the clothes hamper and it had been there for a month and she wasn't going to touch it. Wasn't going to.

She turned suddenly to the window, stood there motionless in the center of the dusky room, rubbing her hands as if they were cold. She couldn't see the weeds now. But they were there. Trembling.

Tom Bart had got the light plant fixed, and he kept thinking about it as he shaved the next morning. He poured hot water into the basin from a big blue pitcher and rubbed the steam off the mirror with the flat of his hand. He leaned forward to look at himself, bending at the waist, posed there. He liked to have finished some useful task just before he left the ranch because then he didn't feel so guilty about leaving. He could pass the portrait in the hall with his chin up. Pass his granddaughter too. When you were afraid of the young he supposed you were really old.

He felt old. He had worked hard over there, overheated himself, and by the time he had finished beads of sweat stood out on his forehead. The short walk to the house in the open air had chilled him.

That morning early he coughed.

He had tried to hold the cough back. His room was next to Ruth's. She had heard it though. He hurried to light a cigarette before she came in, a robe over her nightgown. She had stood there in the doorway, the room gray with dawn, and he puffed at the cigarette.

"Did you cough, Dad?"

"Oh. Hello, Ruth. Cough? I breathed smoke up the wrong alley and it sort of backfired."

"You didn't get chilled last night?"

"No. Oh, no, I didn't get chilled."

She was always looking for coughs. She gave them an important name. Chest coughs. And when he got one she made him wear that long scratchy underwear he hated. She could come up to him, grasp his wrist and turn up his shirt cuff to see if he had it on, a doubtful smile on her face. She had to be sure.

He understood. She had to feel needed. But damn it, he hated that underwear. He cut the sleeves off a pair and wore them when she insisted. Then when she turned up the cuff . . .

But that morning before he shaved he put on the long underwear. The cough was deep and it scared him a little. He explained it away when she questioned him again in the bathroom.

"It's good for driving," he told her. "Driving in an open car, long underwear is all right."

He supposed when you got old, things like chest colds scared you.

She left the bathroom and he hummed a bit because he was sure he had fooled her. She wouldn't have let him go.

Great bluish-gray clouds were hanging over the mountains and it seemed as if the whole ranch were shut away in a little pocket. At breakfast Lona had a tightlipped look, and the men had rushed through their breakfast to catch teams and leave for the big field and the unfinished haystacks.

Something was going to happen. Tom Bart lathered his face and leaned forward again. It always seemed that everybody rushed around when he was getting ready to go somewhere, as if they did it on purpose to show that he shouldn't go. Well, he was needed in Ogden, too. They were having a stock show down there and he wanted to buy some bulls. He had reserved a room at the Bigelow Hotel and everybody he knew would be there. He was a big man there. Mr. Bart. They liked his liquor and they liked his stories.

Damn, the house was silent now, the gray outside, the clouds, and all he could hear was the razor scraping over his whiskers.

Smelling strong of shaving lotion he went into the garage. He guessed he'd better put the side curtains on, great bulky flaps of canvas and celluloid with little oval eyes for fastening. In a moment he was working fast, his hands all thumbs, as if someone were watching, ready to stop him. It was the damndest thing.

He had just finished when he saw Lona striding up from the barn, walking swiftly, her quirt swinging as she walked. He pretended not to see her.

She found him there and he had to turn. He was trembling. It was the damndest thing.

"Grandpa, I'm glad you didn't get away."

"Oh, Lona. What's up?"

"I sent everybody but Eddie down with the wagons to fence the stacks. It's going to storm."

Tom said, "Well?"

She said in a determined voice, "I hate to spoil your fun, but it would help if you'd put off the show for a day and help us move those cattle. If it storms the cattle will crowd the fence and break in below to the hay."

He stood very still. He looked pretty nice. He had on a new suit, and his best boots, his best hat. His bags were all ready in the back of the car, and he'd got those side curtains on.

There were all those friends down there, and the room at the Bigelow. Lord, he wanted to get away from the ranch.

And then he laughed a little. "All right, Lona. I guess you're right. We'll move them."

Now he was changing clothes again, putting on the old boots, the old hat.

Ruth came into his room. She sat on the bed and began to fold his good pants. "I don't think you ought to help, Dad. It's going to storm. It's raining already. It will turn to sleet."

"Oh, maybe not." He went on dressing, and she sat there on the bed and rubbed her hands. A cold draft sneaked up the hall.

She said suddenly, "Dad, don't go. You'll get all cold and wet. Please."

He chuckled. "I'll be all right. Those cattle really ought to be moved. Lona knows her business."

"I know she does."

She sat on the bed in his room and heard his boots clump downstairs, down the hall, past the portrait. He took a mackinaw from the closet and went out the door. She watched him walk alone to the barn, leaning forward into the rain. Mr. Bart going down to see about his cattle.

She saw Lona lead two saddle horses out of the big barn door, saw them both swing up, the old man slowly. Saw them ride away into the mist, the old man sitting proud. Mr. Bart running his ranch.

The house was cold and damp. That place in the ceiling of her room would leak again. The mud would be deep in the corrals and on the roads. The water in the well would taste of earth.

She had seen those weeds trembling.

She sat on the bed and pretty soon she'd go down and ask Mrs. Dean for a cup of stale coffee from the back of the stove.

She fastened her mind on the ticking of the clock, the tall mahogany grandfather's clock that stood in the living room, a room dark now as evening, choked with the roar of the storm outside. She sat very still on the couch, chain smoking, watching the brass pendulum swing.

It was a part of the tradition, that clock. Wound once a week, a Saturday night ritual. She remembered Bert Bart, straight and tall like the clock, moving toward it with the dignity that twenty thousand acres give a man, walking to it, unlocking the narrow glass door, putting his strong elegant hands on the fluid brass chains, and pulling so the polished brass weights came up, and up, and up.

She could see the dull light catch a moment on the brass of the pendulum in its passage. See the shape of the dull light, the hourglass shape.

And Tom Bart always walked to the clock, self-consciously, remembering his father and the square shoulders of his father, the look of his broadclothed back as he stood there.

They both wound it. They kept it at its incessant ticking, measuring their time.

She lit a cigarette and crushed a smoldering butt. Those rattling windows, those drafts under the door, those long moldy drafts. Now the keals would begin, now the stains would begin, the groping, shapeless stains on her bedroom ceiling.

It startled her when they came in. She heard them in the hall, heard the storm, raw and unmuffled behind them, the click of the door. And she heard her father coughing.

She found him up in his room stooping before the cold little woodstove, blowing up the draft, trying to start it.

She watched him with a curious feeling of finality.

"Let me, Dad." She got him into bed first, and covered him. Then she turned to the stove, her hands heavy, fumbling.

He said, "I'm tired, Ruthie." His eyes were closed.

"Wait a minute, Dad." She went to her room and burrowed in the clothes hamper. The bottle was almost full. And there was another.

"Good." He smiled a little. "You have one, too."

"All right, Dad." But she looked around quickly when she heard boot heels on the stairs.

Tom Bart said softly, "Close the door. Lock it. This is our party, Ruthie." Outside the sound of heels stopped. He called loudly, "Go away, Lona. Your mother and I are talking." The heels hesitated and retreated.

The bottle was gone by midnight, even before Clyde got back with the doctor. The telephone was dead, the house completely silent except for the rain beating on the high old windows.

She knew he was dying. When he dozed she slipped out of the room and moved downstairs.

She knew the phone was dead. It had gone early in the storm yet she stood there before it. If she could reach the doctor, see if Clyde had got through to him. She turned the crank for central. Only a dull, grinding sound. She tried again.

Lona stood beside her. "You can't ring it. It's dead."

Lona looked half scornful, half frightened. She hadn't changed her clothes, her boots were muddy, her hair lank, uncurled.

Ruth tried again. Still the dull grind.

Lona said, "Don't do that. You've been up there drinking and you've got him drunk too."

Ruth turned, very slowly, and looked at her with a curious gravity. "He needed it. I didn't drive him out of the house into the storm."

Lona said, "What are you talking about?"

"I'm talking about him. You drove him out and he's upstairs dying."

Lona sprang, slapping her mother hard, and there was the sound of it in the hall.

Ruth held the curious look of gravity. On her face was the look of the Barts. She simply looked at her daughter, steadying herself at the telephone.

CHAPTER

 17

Old Foss who published the *Sentinel Examiner* picked out the large type that spelled GRIM REAPER, and the smaller type that spelled PROMINENT RANCHER CALLED.

"Tom Bart is dead."

Well then, you've got to look in the bureau and see if there's a clean shirt, if there isn't Ma'll iron one soon's she gets done sponging her navy wool.

You got the chains on? Christ, it's rained a week, it'll be nasty driving and nasty at the grave.

The neighbors arrived all morning, up the valley, down the valley, old touring cars with side curtains, old Dodges, Studebakers, chains flapping through the deep black ruts, slapping against the road fenders. Ka-bang, ka-bang, ka-bang. Ranchers and their wives sitting straight in the high-wheeled old touring cars. Ka-bang, ka-bang, ka-bang. A long line of cars parked near the Episcopal church, a line stretching from the Star Garage to the Courthouse.

Inside the church the organ sobbed, a sickly light oozed through the stained-glass window over the altar. Clyde Barrows sat between Ruth and Lona. They had the front pew, near the organ. Ruth's face was hidden beneath a black veil. Black suit, black furs.

"The days of our age are three-score. . . ."

There were not many cars in the funeral procession. The grade up the hill to the cemetery was steep and slick with mud. They watched from the town below. Once it looked as though the hearse wouldn't make it. Not many cars . . .

People that the gentle, dreamy old man had helped, lied for, signed for, loaned to. Not many cars though, for it was raining, and he was dead.

But the Irwins were there. She had Danny bundled into sweaters and coats from the wind and rain. "Oh, Dan," she said, "he was a good man." When they lowered the coffin she buried her head on her husband's arm. Then back down the hill the procession moved. Ka-bang, ka-bang went the chains.

Now when they talked about the funeral late that afternoon they spoke, as they always did, of the casket.

"Say it cost fifteen hundred dollars."

"Just like the Barts."

"Waterproof, all sealed."

Well, the bottom of the grave was all water. They had their supper, those ranchers, in the Sugar Bowl Café, and they ate carefully and properly, as you eat in town. The women dabbed at their lips, very elegant. And they thought about Ruth Bart Hanson, in all that black, her white face when she lifted the veil, her weakness, and her pride. The king's daughter, left a shabby, tottering kingdom.

They were home from the funeral. Clyde had gone to bed, and Ruth was in her room. The whole house that night was filled with the sound of rain. The lightning was gone. The thunder was still. There was only the constant low roar of the rain, and the rushing of the creek down near the bunkhouse. Lona had opened the front door, stood a moment in the cold dampness and heard it, and watched the shimmering white light in the bunkhouse window, the Coleman lantern. She had gone back to the living room and sat on the stool beside the cold stove.

It had never occurred to her that her grandfather would die before her mother had—well, something. The pattern was that her grandfather would die and she would hold authority.

If her mother had begun to drink steadily it would be the same as if she weren't there at all. A responsibility, but one she knew how to handle. But sober, her mother was strong and dangerous.

Lona thought things she was ashamed to think. But why pussy-foot? Face the fact that it would be years before she got the ranch. Years and years.

How beautiful her mother had been at the funeral. How soft her voice as neighbors spoke to her, how clinging her expensive scent, how soft her furs.

"Please don't stay up too long, Lona."

That sentence had not been halting, as before. It was almost a command.

Everybody knew that drunk people couldn't handle affairs. Drunk people were like people not there at all. You could go to court and get guardian papers. And there were institutions. They treated people well there and tried to cure them.

Lona sat on the stool and looked at the nickel on the stove. The rain roared louder—or was she listening hard now, just this minute?

If her mother began to drink again . . . she watched the nickel on the stove and studied her strong hands.

She was already in bed, in bed in the cold, bare little room, when she heard the knock at the front door, if it had been a knock. It didn't come again. She supposed that was because all the lights were out. If it was a knock.

The rain had gone on so long that the corrals were bogs of deep stinking mud. The men had idled in the bunkhouse the day of the funeral, but Eddie Rohn had ridden twice into the big field to see that the cattle were not crowding the haystacks. His woolen mackinaw was drenched through. The cinch of his saddle was caked with mud, each strand stuck to the next as the mud splashed up against his mount's belly. The cattle had stood quietly against the willows and watched him riding by.

In the bunkhouse they were still playing poker when he rode in before supper. They had a gray sheep blanket spread out on the big table and they sat along the side and two of them sat on the table and dangled their legs. They peered at their cards, for the bunkhouse was deep in gloom, and nobody moved to light the Coleman lantern because that would be a break in the chain, and the game would stop until after supper. One hand more . . . one hand more.

Joe Martin won steadily. They were certain he was cheating. His long bony fingers were quick on the cards. Only the thin skin across the pads of his fingers kept him from feeling the spots, feeling the red of the hearts or the black of the spades.

They had heard of a fellow who could feel red and black.

They hoped they would not catch him cheating. They hoped he would not drop a card or do anything funny with the cut because they would pretend not to notice. They were short with one another.

When a man had a good hand he would put it carelessly down on the table, face down, and roll a cigarette, watching the paper and the tobacco closely, smoothing it delicately, wetting the paper delicately with the tongue before he bet. Steady as that damn Joe Martin.

They scowled at Eddie Rohn when he came in because he broke the chain of play, him and his wet-smelling mackinaw, the freshness about him.

"Might as well pump up the lamp."

Eddie Rohn seldom played. He was the kind of a fellow that would give ten percent to the Mormon Church. But a hell of a lot nicer than Joe Martin.

They were nervous after supper because they wanted to play and win back some money, but they were stubborn and waited for Joe Martin to suggest it. He sat near the only lamp reading a *Western Romance.* That made them angry and they were short with each other. They played a good loud scratchy record on the phonograph.

Judge said stand up, boy, and dry up your tears,
You're going to prison for twenty-one years. . . .

The damn rain kept coming and they could hardly see the big house, all dark except for the kitchen windows.

They watched Eddie Rohn greasing his saddle. They read an old Maggie and Jiggs and a Katzenjammer Kids. The Captain stepped on a pie that the Kids put beside his bed and Mrs. Captain hit the Captain over the head. She didn't know the Kids done it.

"Well, good night. I'm going to roll in."

"God damn this rain."

"Going to be wet in the old man's grave."

"The coffin's one of them sealed ones, like a can of sardines."

By ten o'clock the bunkhouse was quiet except for the hiss of the Coleman lantern. Eddie Rohn was staring at a great shadow of himself on the wall and thinking.

They were asleep in the bunkhouse, even Joe Martin who had smoked his last cigarette in bed for the night. The wall beside his bed was scarred with little brown trails of scratched matches.

Eddie Rohn got up, stretched, turned to the lamp and closed the valve, and the lamp grew dimmer and dimmer. In the last blue puff of the lamp he moved toward the door of the bunkroom, and reached to lift the sheep-blanket drape that kept the room dark.

The knock came then, a little knock that rattled the latch of the bunkhouse door, and then another. Eddie jumped for the lamp and turned the valve while it still glowed, nervous faint blue puffs of fingers reaching into the mantels.

CHAPTER 18   Mrs. Irwin looked like a scarecrow. She wore a long overcoat of her husband's and the damp weight of it strained at her shoulders, the mud clung to the bottom like a wide heavy hem. Her little hat was jammed down on her head and the feathers drooped. She had no gloves; her fists were clenched and blue.

Eddie Rohn opened the door suddenly and she was staring into the white hot mantels of the lamp.

He stood aside and she walked unsteadily into the bunkhouse and leaned a moment against the table where the chips and cards were heaped in the middle.

"What's the trouble?"

She started to speak, and tried again. "We're stuck." She took a breath. "Beside the road, back there."

He saw then that she trembled. "You'd better sit and warm up."

He dragged a chair out beside the stove.

"No. Please help us out. Dan's back there."

"You better warm up."

"No. I've got to get back to him. It's cold. He can't—" she looked helplessly at Eddie.

He reached for his mackinaw on a nail behind the stove. "Stuck bad?"

She nodded, and the little feather moved across her face. "Way down in the mud on the side."

"Then I couldn't get you out with my tin-lizzy." He hesitated. "I'd have to get the big car."

She spoke quickly. "Then get the big car."

He said, "They're asleep in the house. I'd have to ask."

She still trembled. "I'll wake them. Don't you see—my husband's back there in the cold." She started for the door.

He said, "I'll go. Wait here."

He knew where the key was. When he took it off the hook he felt as if someone were watching him.

He gave her a drink of whiskey to warm her up, and she gagged on it, but took it. He helped her in, gave her a coat of his and tucked blankets around her.

"Would you bring a little whiskey for Dan?" she asked.

Now in the front seat of the Pierce he watched her face in the dashlight as she stared through the rain on the windshield. She leaned forward to brush off the steam. She looked very young and tired. The chains flap-flapped slowly, hitting up under the fenders; the heavy old car ground through mud and ruts, lurching and splashing; rain fell in sheets and he stopped the car twice to get his bearings and wipe mud off the headlights. When he opened the door to get out, the loneliness of the sodden foothills crept in, the silence rolled down from the dank sagebrush.

"It's farther than this," she kept saying, and grew tense when the car skidded. The blackness kept coming toward them, light splashed, and black pole after black pole, the fence crept by. He kept noticing her perfume, like flowers, and the heater warmed the odor. She was all wrapped up in blankets from his bed.

In high school boys had liked her and girls had liked her, and they told her things. She always knew the words to songs, and would write them out in her round hand.

"Say, thanks," they would say. But the boys never asked her to the moving pictures.

She was thorough, and she helped the football boys with their algebra. They would sit beside her and pat her shoulder. "You're a swell kid," they'd say. But they never asked her to a dance.

The girls told her things about boys, because they could trust her.

What was wrong with her? She used to look in the mirror in the little room she had with the people she lived with and worked for. Well, she wasn't bad looking. Too serious, maybe.

But what she didn't know was that there was something decent about her that frightened people.

She read everything she could lay her hands on. Good, cheap entertainment. She might as well get used to good, cheap things, she'd never have anything else. She was going to be a nurse.

And the internes never asked her anywhere.

But someday. It might happen any time. Someday she might be walking down the hall and . . .

He was lying in a bed in the hospital. There wasn't much hope for him. He was dying, they said. His cheekbones poked through his skin, but he had a wonderful, quiet smile. Daniel Irwin, his card said. Pretty soon she found she was his special nurse.

And do you know what he said one day?

She had come to his room with the thermometer. She had stuck it under his tongue, and put her hand a moment on his forehead. He tried to say it when he had the thermometer in his mouth. She took out the thermometer so he could say it better.

She had cried all night about it, and wanted to tell somebody, but it was really too wonderful to tell.

"You know," he had said, "you're beautiful."

Now it was night and she was driving in a car with Eddie Rohn, and he had wrapped her in blankets from his bed. The wind and the rain closed them into a small still world. She had watched silently when Eddie got out and sloshed through the mud to wipe the headlights, watched him scrape his feet on the running board. How many times she had done that!

Now she was sitting here, watching a man do it. For a hot moment she resented Eddie, the broad thick shoulders and chest, the strong hands. It wasn't so much to be well, strong. It was something to be brave, too, and patient, and kind.

She was unreasonable, and knew it. Eddie's smile when he

opened the door of the car was reassuring. "We'll make it," he told her.

She smiled shyly. "I know you can."

Her hand flew to the door of the car when the headlights of the Pierce fumbled and splashed on the old Dodge touring car. She hurried through the mud to her husband.

"You're all right, Dan? You kept warm?"

"Yes. I'm fine." He spoke through chattering teeth. He was tall and stooped, he was embarrassed because he couldn't walk six miles through mud and water. She listened closely for a small word from Eddie Rohn that might hurt him.

Eddie Rohn said, "Say, you're in deep. Look, if you'll hold this chain while I hook the bumper—"

Dan straightened. "Yes. Yes, I will."

"Dan," she said, "let me."

Eddie Rohn said, "You stand back. Or get in the car."

She sat there, shivering in the cold car, watching Eddie sloshing around in the deep mud that clogged and held the high wheels. She thought, "He's nice. Awfully nice . . ."

Eddie had said, "I'm going to follow along. Just in case."

"Oh," she said. "You don't have to do that. It's just here the road is slick. Up above, the gravel—"

"I'll follow along," he said. The two cars crawled up the slick black road, the big Pierce followed the old Dodge, and the rain washed down beside them.

There was no electricity on the Irwin place, but the kerosene lamp in the kitchen was bright and comfortable, the yellow light on the linoleum and the range. In the firebox the wet wood sizzled and popped.

Danny said, "Maybe you'd fix him a cup of coffee, darling?"

"Yes, I will, Dan. Of course." She took her husband's arm and led him off into the bedroom. When she came back in the fresh dress and dry shoes she felt strangely shy. The rain beat on the roof dully, and it was warm in there. The draft of the range sucked.

Eddie Rohn said, "You'd better sit down. Let me fix the coffee."

"Oh, no," she laughed. "I'm not used—" and suddenly it was a betrayal to say that. "All right," she told him.

She sat watching as he opened the cupboard doors, found the coffee and the shining pot. It didn't look as funny as she thought, seeing a man make coffee. It looked—nice.

"Do you want sugar?" he asked.

"I don't know—"

"Better have some," he said. It was strange. She felt soft, small, cherished. That was it. Protected.

He was talking, talking of horses, of riding. She didn't understand much. She didn't listen. She just watched, the straight strong shoulders, the kind face. "Stand back there, or get in the car," he'd said.

All her life she had done things for herself, for others. No one had ever helped her, sheltered her. Not ever. No one had ever ordered her about, either. Or waited on her, and grinned, as Eddie Rohn did now over the cigarette he was rolling.

"I wish I could do that," she said, and looked into her coffee cup.

He had to touch her hand to show her. The thin rice paper wrinkled to nothing in her fingers, and tobacco scattered in gold flakes to the floor.

"Oh, I can't do it. You see? Helpless . . ."

And then it came, in the silence of the kitchen, the sound from the bedroom. He didn't notice, but she did. It was a cough. You couldn't have heard it, unless you knew that it came from the useless struggle of muscle and flesh to rid itself of death, a soft little cough that others didn't understand.

She understood. And understood that the rule wasn't that man did things for woman, but that the strong did things for the weak.

She said softly, "It's late, Eddie. You'll be worn out tomorrow." She stood up. "Thanks for the help. Dan and I appreciate it."

She stood in the door watching him drive off, watching the ruby-red tail light. She stood there, tired. But proud. She went into the bedroom then, and in a little while she lay beside her husband, and tried to give him the warmth of her body.

Eddie Rohn put the Pierce in the garage and walked around to the front of the big house. In the distance the lightning had begun again, and it reflected in the faces of the ranch buildings, and in the big narrow windows of the house.

It was only two steps to the hook under the portrait, and he felt the sharp end of it in his fingers. The sudden light in the hall and on the stairs blinded him; he glanced quickly up the stairs. Lona came down slowly, in a man's bathrobe that made her look small and young.

"What did you do?" she asked shortly. "Get the key?"

He said, "I just came in. I didn't mean to wake anybody."

She said, "You woke me."

"I'm sorry, I didn't mean—"

She stood on the stairs, so that he had to look up. "How did you know the key was there?" she asked.

"Well, I saw it one time. I saw your grandfather—"

"I heard that girl's voice," she said.

"Yes. Mrs. Irwin."

"What did she want? Why don't you say what she wanted?"

"They were stuck. I had to pull them out."

She said, "So you came in and got the key to the big car."

"Yes. Their car was deep down."

She was beside him now, looking up at him, very close to him. "Her husband stayed back in the car, and *she* came for the help?"

"Yes."

"She's brave, isn't she?"

"Don't talk like that. If you could of seen her and him—"

She smiled then. "I'll talk any way I please. Waked up in the middle of the night, sneaking in, telling me how to talk—"

He turned then. He was going.

"Eddie—" She was before him, and then in his arms. She was going to cry. "I'm all upset—about my grandfather."

Then they were sitting on the couch in the living room, with only the light from the hall. She cried then, and lay quietly in his arms. He kissed her, and felt tired and shabby.

He kept looking out at the crooked lightning.

"Oh, Christ," he thought, "I'm lonely." The gutters were full and the rain came down the side of the house in a sheet and slid, crooked, down the windows.

CHAPTER Ruth could not remember having waked so early before. Dawn was just creeping into the room, and through the open window came the early morning moistness, the dew that lay on the fall-brown stubble in the fields, the moisture that made a thin coat on metal objects, the wheels of mowing machines stored in the sheds, a dew that brought along the clean bitter smell of the willows along the creek.

She was wide awake. There were no sounds outside yet, and no sounds in the kitchen below. It had been years since she had seen the emptiness of the kitchen, the big bare zinc-topped table, the big black stove.

Curiously satisfying to be the first one up.

She started a fire of fresh-split kindling. The coffee she made boiled up quickly, and she took a big cup of it to her room and sat drinking it near the window. In an hour or so Mrs. Dean would come hurrying through the rustling dry weeds, carrying the alarm clock.

She took half an hour drinking the coffee. The peaks in the distance had begun to glow red from the rising sun. Then the roof of the barn took on the red tinge, then the roof of the bunkhouse, and finally the new sunlight began to sweep the valley, a swelling scarlet tide engulfing twenty thousand acres.

She had a strange feeling of birth. She hadn't changed. But now she was a person. She had a purpose. She was mistress of the Bart Ranch. In three hours she and Lona would drive to Sentinel and there Barton, the banker, would read the will and make everything legal. She felt rather humble. . . .

Then a tremendous energy. She would walk an hour before breakfast, feel the sun in her face. She stubbed out her cigarette and rummaged through the closet for a pair of flat-heeled shoes. Those high heels were impractical. What she needed was good sensible walking shoes.

Well, these oxfords would have to do. And a stout pair of cotton stockings—well, these silk ones would do now. She found an old felt hat; she stood a moment in the middle of the room. Some gesture was required this morning . . . well, she knew what it was. She stooped beside the clothes hamper, rummaged there and brought out an unopened quart of brandy. She wrapped it in her suede jacket and carried it quietly but swiftly down the stairs, past the portrait, out the front door and around the house. She breathed deep, took long swinging strides, mistress of twenty thousand acres.

She knew she could never learn all there was to know about ranching. Too late for that. Lona would see that the ranch work was done. But she could handle the money. It was simply a matter of spending as little as possible. Not even clothes.

Not on anything! She had the blood of old Bert in her too!

She felt the weight of the brandy in the jacket.

Below the bunkhouse and behind the willows, out of sight, was the dump. There in a ravine the refuse of the ranch was piled up, wheels of discarded haying implements, frames of rakes. The battered and peeling back seat of an automobile, springs poking out and tufts of horsehair showing through. Mounds of tin cans. Those furthest away had lost the labels, reduced to rusty shells. Old broken chairs, braked with twisted rusted wire. A bird cage. (Now, where had that come from?) Greenish bottles. Rotten cloth and steel—a corset. Piles of rubbish . . .

She stood looking at it. The first rays of the sun touched the rubbish heap, and it blurred before her eyes, but she was smiling. She unwrapped the bottle of brandy, looked at it. Then she threw it.

It didn't break. It rested right under an old kitchen chair, right beside a cold-cream jar that must have been Mrs. Dean's.

She was serious a moment, watching the bottle, thinking a sentimental thing.

"There's my unhappiness . . ." Her whole past.

She turned away. At that moment it seemed the whole ranch came to life. A dog barked. She saw the glint of sun on rattling milk buckets. Eddie Rohn had run in the horses and they milled in the corral. A gate squeaked. A door slammed. There was talk in the bunkhouse, laughter. A thin blue column of smoke came up through the straight black pipe. The sun was everywhere.

While she dressed, she thought of the car, knew that this day she was going to drive it, that her daughter would sit beside her.

For at least two years, from the time that Lona began to drive, Lona had always driven the car and she had sat there, pretending not to mind, pretending that the accident on the bridge into Sentinel had been forgotten, pretending that her father wasn't referring to that when he said, "You'd better let Lona drive, Ruthie." A gentle, small punishment.

She had attempted escape by seldom riding in the car with Lona, never going to town when Lona went, then she needn't be humiliated.

She was going to drive today. It seemed as if the whole day hinged on that. In the fifteen minutes it took her to wash and put on make-up, the symbol had grown and bloated.

She could hear Lona in her room, could hear her steps, the tap-tap of her boot heels, then the pad of stockinged feet, then the firmness of oxfords.

Ruth stood still, listening. She glanced down at the garage doors. Then the panic took hold. She must get in the car, behind the wheel.

She hurried down the stairs and almost ran to the garage, pulling one sliding door open enough to squeeze in sideways.

She sat panting behind the wheel, chilled because the garage was cold. She took a startled glance into the rear-view mirror. Her eyes were wide and frightened, her lipstick smeared a little, her face dead white, and after a few moments she realized she was gripping the big polished wood wheel until her hands hurt. There was no sound in the place but the sharp ticking of the Elgin clock.

Set in the doors of the garage were small windows, opaque with grime, that turned the brittle December sun a sickly gray. One corner of the garage was piled high with old tires, tires from the Pierce, and cars before, the two Franklins and the Stearns-Knight. A tangled, rusting mass of tire chains, license plates, old jacks, a gallon jug of oil. She fiercely thought of each object, going over each one, putting off facing the fact that Lona would come into that garage, open the doors wide and stand beside the car.

She would say, "Mother, I'm driving."

As if Lona had spoken, she gripped the wheel harder.

Nerves. She watched herself in the rear-view mirror.

Then she smiled. The generous thing, the kind thing, would be to ask Lona to drive. To show that rivalry was done. It was enough to know that you *could* drive, that you had the right, the power.

She was composed when Lona finally opened the sliding doors wide. Ruth slid over from the wheel.

"All ready, darling?" she said. "I wish you'd drive." Hers was the power—to be generous. "I feel much safer when you drive."

If only Lona had smiled.

BARTON, 1894.

Such, in the exact center of a granite block, was the inscription high on the cornice of the Sentinel Trust Co. You never noticed the old red-brick façade, the narrow, high windows with wavy glass. Your eyes rose immediately to Barton, 1894.

The bank was a climax of years of land, mine, and cattle dealings, sharp bargains that mellowing years had made legendary and honorable.

"Oh, I tell you, Peter Barton has a head on him!"

Peter Barton was a businessman and gentleman, courteous, dignified, and shrewd. When he spoke he held you with steely eyes. He used the words "sound," "free enterprise," "stability." "Harum-scarum" dismissed many people.

Tom Bart was "harum-scarum."

Peter Barton sat in his private office. He had pulled two straight chairs up before his desk, one slightly to the rear of the other.

The will of the late Thomas Bart, which he had himself witnessed, lay smooth on his desk, legal in blue cover and tape. He had read it through several times that morning, moving his lips behind his full beard.

He couldn't for the life of him understand how Tom Bart had come to make so sensible a will.

He had given his secretary orders not to keep the Hansons waiting. The Seth-Thomas clock ticked away. Peter Barton tapped his long fingers on his desk and made a little tent of them, waiting.

He heard first the soft voice of Ruth speaking to his secretary, then his secretary's crisp tones.

"Mr. Barton is in."

Mr. Barton rose and bowed from the waist. He came forward to seat the two women, but they had already sat down, Ruth in the forward chair. She wore black, and the silver fox scarf softened her eyes. She was smiling a little, her knees crossed, head tilted confidently.

Peter Barton looked away from her.

At Lona. She was uncomfortable in her rough tweed suit, and he had the impression that the sleeves of the coat were too short for her, the skirt too long. She had greeted him shortly. She had her hands thrust in the pockets of her suit.

He said, "I have here your grandfather's will." And added, "And your father's." He bowed a little toward Ruth. "Let me offer my sincere sympathy again."

Peter Barton began to arrange things on his desk. A pencil was moved. The pen in its swiveled onyx base was moved. A desk calendar. The clock ticked and the cold fall sun filtered in through the single window. "I suppose you had a good trip to town?"

"Yes," Ruth said. "My daughter drove. She is a good driver."

Peter Barton made a little bowing motion. "I can imagine she is capable."

Ruth smiled. "Dad was very fond of her."

Peter Barton said, "Our whole system is founded on family unity and the control of the most capable member."

Lona looked up sharply, sat up and removed her hands from her pockets. She crossed her legs and began to look at her nails.

Ruth said, "Naturally, Lona will look after the land and the cattle. She knows the work." She smiled. "She's done a fine job. We all realize what the times are. Dad didn't seem to care much, toward the end."

"Good," Peter Barton said.

Ruth looked puzzled. "Good?"

Peter Barton said, "I am glad you understand the—situation."

Ruth said, "Naturally I understand the situation. Dad and I—" She frowned slightly.

"My impression," Peter Barton said, "was that you expected to inherit it. I was afraid the will might come as a shock." Now he had the will in his hands, leafing through it, holding back the sky-blue cover and the red tape. "Of course, you will receive fifty dollars a month. The land and the cattle, of course, go to your daughter. But since you know . . ."

Ruth had fixed her eyes on the wall behind Peter Barton, on the Seth-Thomas clock.

They couldn't see her eyes beneath the small black veil.

She stood up. She stood as tall as she could, and drew on her long black gloves. She turned, smiling at Peter Barton.

"Of course I knew. Dad and I—were always very—close."

CHAPTER "You can join your mother shortly," Peter Barton said. "It's better she's gone out to wait."

"She doesn't understand business."

Peter Barton rearranged the pencil. "Your grandfather didn't understand business."

Lona put a cigarette between her lips, and Peter Barton leaned forward to light it. She said, "Then, the estate is in a mess."

"Probably worse than you think."

"I doubt it." She inhaled deeply.

He was making a little tent of his fingers, and watching her closely. Her answer pleased him. He said, "I was your great-grandfather's friend. Bert's. He trusted me."

"And my grandfather?"

"He gave me small chance to be trusted. He got—responsibility too late. You don't misunderstand me?"

"I don't."

He said, "I hope you will trust me as your great-grandfather trusted me."

She looked at him, thoughtful. "I have no reason not to trust you."

He liked her reservations. He said, "Good." He looked at the calendar, flipped a page.

"What are you about to say?"

He looked up at her, levelly. "I advise you to sell the ranch."

She spoke promptly. "No. I'm not going to do that." Her eyes were cool.

He said, "Please hear me. I can get a buyer. You can clear the estate, and a sum will remain, sufficient—"

"I'm sorry. I wouldn't consider it."

Peter Barton made a little tent of his fingers. "You realize that you sell cattle for less than it costs to raise them. Since the crash, you go behind each year."

Impatiently. "Yes, of course I realize that. I've done everything but write the checks for two years. But I will live—in poverty—before I give up the ranch." She kept looking at him. "My mother and I."

Peter Barton made a laugh. "I suppose that is a fine attitude. But it isn't feasible."

"Why isn't it? This slump won't last forever."

He picked up the pen from the desk set. "Because this bank holds a note. An outstanding note. The times require that it be paid. When due."

She looked at him, but her eyes were in the Bart house, darting over the furniture, how much this would bring, how much that would bring. The car . . . there was some Wedgwood, some silver. Horses—there were her grandfather's fancy horses. "How much is the note?"

"The note is for fifteen thousand dollars. We hold a chattel mortgage."

For a moment she couldn't look at him. She leaned forward and stubbed out her cigarette, kept her hands busy on the opened pack. She said, "I suppose he needed the fifteen thousand for expenses."

Peter Barton said, "I hesitate to tell you why he wanted it. Understand that a bank is not interested in ethics." Outside the traffic moved on Bart Street, there were heels on the pavement, a car backfired. The sun had moved away from the little window. "The mortage we hold is good security," he said. "It isn't the note we hold that makes me urge you to sell, it's—the times."

Her eyes were level and cool on him. "Please don't hedge. Why did he want fifteen thousand dollars?"

"He wanted it to buy a piece of property."

She was puzzled. "Property? I can't recall—any additions to the ranch. He never said—"

Peter Barton laughed. "He wouldn't have. He bought up a piece of wasteland from a wild-cat mining company. Where the gold camp was." Watching her, his eyes shifted a little.

Her eyes were hard. "It's worthless. You know that. Assayers have been all over that land."

He tried to stare her down. "I'm not interested in motives. I was not close to him. Please remember that."

She spoke coldly. "The deal was a fraud. They tricked him."

"Perhaps."

She got up, thrust her hands in the jacket of her suit and walked slowly over to the window and looked out into the street, cold in the pale sunshine.

Fur-coated young women, shopping. She'd known them in high school. They were pretty. The young women down there moved their lips, smiling and talking, walking on Bart Street toward the grocery where naked Christmas trees in wooden stands made a little forest. The young women would gather for parties, they would dance. They would speak a tongue she didn't know.

But those women down there were walking on Bart Street. She was a Bart. That must never be forgotten.

At last she spoke, there by the window, almost musing. "Before my grandfather died—did you ever have the impression that he was—queer?" She kept looking out the window at Bart Street. The pretty young women buying a Christmas tree. On Bart Street.

"Not queer. Only very foolish."

She said, "He used to disappear from the ranch for days. No one knew where he went. He never said."

"Yes?"

"He used to go to conventions, dressed like a dude at a rodeo. When he died the bills started coming in. Stores I'd never heard of."

"He spent a great deal."

"I have heard men laugh at him, men he'd bought drinks for. He heard them too. And he'd laugh, and say it didn't matter. Only a man who was—queer—wouldn't have minded."

"He had a great many friends."

"I wonder," she said. Then, in the musing voice, "I used to go to the root cellar, there in the hill where we keep the light plant.

He had leaned forward across his desk, watching her closely. "Why do you want to think he was insane?"

"Did anyone else ever hear him?"

"I don't know. I can swear it's true."

"Perhaps his age—"

"He wasn't so old." She turned suddenly from the window, her lips tight, as if she'd got hold of something. She sat down and leaned forward, seeing it all. "I found him one night in one of the old cabins, on this land he bought. I wondered why he was there. I see it now. He was sitting in a chair. He looked like he'd been crying." She hesitated. "He was talking to himself."

She watched him, her eyes urging him to see it as she had, the lightning that night, the smell of rotting wood, the smell of death.

Peter Barton was silent a moment while the Seth-Thomas clock ticked. From outside the faint sound of typewriting came. He said, "What are you getting at?"

She cleared her throat. "I think—he was insane."

He had leaned forward across his desk, watching closely. "Why do you want to think he was insane?"

"Because I think there is a law. If the mining company made that deal with a crazy man, I think—"

Peter Barton looked at her. "You'd go to any lengths."

She was gripping the arms of her chair. "Yes. To any lengths."

He said, "I don't know about the law. I'm not a lawyer."

She fished for a cigarette, still watching him. "I can get one. A good one. And witnesses."

A tent of his fingers. "You're forgetting one thing. One most important thing."

The afternoon light was fading, and now the corners of the office were almost hidden, and it seemed as if as the light faded the ticking of the clock grew louder, that it pushed at the light . . .

She said, "What am I forgetting?"

He said, "You're forgetting his will." He patted the folded blue cover, flat against the desk. "If he were judged insane his will would be invalid."

"Oh," she said. And, "Yes. I see."

"And then," he said, "then his land would go to his daughter. Not to you."

She stared at him. Before she could speak he said, "I wouldn't start anything, Miss Hanson."

Then he smiled, and began to look through some papers. A

strange little smile on his thin lips. "You know," he said, "half an hour ago I wouldn't have extended your note. But somehow— now—"

She found her mother in the Sugar Bowl Café behind one of the monk's cloth curtains. Her mother was drinking coffee, and the ashtray was piled with cigarette butts.

Her mother's smile irritated her, but she kept it inside her. "Everything's settled."

She'd have time to think. The note was extended. . . .

She must begin to think. She thought on the way home, driving the powerful old car, gripping the big polished wood wheel. It was cold that night, and the windshield frosted over. There was only silence in the car; far off there to the left were the lonely little lights of ranch houses.

She stopped the car once, and began to scratch the frost off the windshield with her fingernails. A coyote was howling off in the dark of the field.

It was going to snow. She could feel it. The air was heavy.

She would marry Clyde Barrows. He was rich. It had been in the back of her mind all along.

CHAPTER 21   Mrs. Dean was having what she called one of her blue mornings. When she got up in the pitch black of morning, her back ached around her kidneys. Cold as sin outside—the dry weeds sticking up through the snow, rattling as she moved along the path to the kitchen. Winter was a sad time. She had all that insurance money, but this morning it just seemed a responsibility. She was just a poor woman. Nobody knew about her back. Nobody cared.

December was bleak; cold weather had come, but little snow, a crippled, sick season. In the corrals cold choking dust was stirred up by running horses, hooves drumming frozen earth. The valley was gray, the stubble in the fields weak as sawdust in the bellies of the cattle.

Never, Lona thought, was the house so large, so empty; and it was always cold. It had been Tom Bart who built the fires, who made big jobs of little jobs, whistling and shaving kindling just so, stooping to blow until the flame caught. Now icy drafts had the run of the house, whisking along the dark halls, whipping up the frayed edges of rugs in rooms, chilling legs. The house seemed false, incomplete; she was aware of the half-finished attic, of naked two-by-fours, of lathes without plaster. And the stale cold was everywhere.

She was nervous. She had little time to be with Clyde. She was outside most of the time, and exhausted at night. She wondered how to be most attractive to him—disturbed, not by her deception, but by her need of him. She had noticed that he watched her when she gave way to fatigue and simply sat thinking.

"You're tired, Lona. Is there something—?"

She had thought, "Yes. There's something. Ask me to marry you." She had said, "No—I'm not really tired." And then her smile.

On the other hand, there was Eddie. If Clyde asked her—

She must keep Eddie too.

It would be a matter of morals with Eddie. Somehow, she was going to have to overcome his whole background—his poor, stiff-necked proud father, his schoolteacher aunt, his belief—deep as the black soil of the little farm—that good was good and bad was bad.

Her weapon was bribery.

He wanted a pair of spurs. She remembered his eyes—childlike —on the spurs in the catalog.

You can buy a pair of spurs for three dollars, machine-made, the shanks soldered on, the cheap brittle steel blued. They rust. They don't make you proud.

You can buy a pair of spurs for a hundred and fifty dollars.

She remembered his eyes. It was a small catalog of bridles, bits, spurs. Even the saddles were mounted with gold or silver. Dream saddles, dream spurs—things no cowboy expected to have. Tom Mix had these things. Hoot Gibson. Sour grapes: cowboys would sneer at a pair of spurs inlaid with a hundred small pieces of pure silver, set in a rose-and-leaf design.

"Who the hell'd want any such damn stuff?"

In a thousand bunkhouses men sat beside stoves at night (close to a hot stove your overalls smell funny), eyes on the spurs.

Spurs were important. You not only saw the spurs, saw the sun on the silver, but you heard them; the rowel in the shank jingled. You were the man with the Garcia spurs.

She remembered Eddie's eyes. He could quote the paragraph beneath the sketch. *Inlaid with 100 pieces of pure silver. The finest spur available* . . . He was a little near-sighted. He had his neck bent, head forward, eyes squinting. She had wanted to run her fingers through his rough black hair. They sat together on the big table in the bunkhouse, legs dangling. The afternoon light was cold and gray through the window, but the heat from the old black stove was almost stultifying. A washbasin simmered on the stove; the dampness touched and released the odors of men—bay rum in the bottle under the window, boots and shoes behind the stove, wet leather and sweat. Whiskey. Tobacco in an open can.

"Say," Eddie said. "A fellow had these spurs, he'd be all set." She knew he looked at them every evening.

"They're fine spurs. You'd have them all your life, like your gold watch."

"Sure." A shutting out word, a forgetting word. She always wondered if he shut out the picture of the bed at the cow camp.

She sent for them that week. It was before Christmas, but she did them up with Christmas paper. It was the first Christmas package she had ever wrapped up. The red tissue paper whispered, the silver ribbon was smooth in her fingers.

She had been afraid, handing them to him. He had looked so stern—innocent, maybe. She thought of his father, and the school-teacher aunt (there was the cheap photograph on the window, a thin, pinched, proper woman).

"Say," he said. "What's this?" His hands were clumsy on the ribbon and paper. And there were the spurs. "Why, say," he said.

"Do you like them, Eddie?" She smiled, and hurried on. "I know," she said. "I know—maybe you don't want to take them." He was getting a stubborn look. "But, look. You can get me something nice. Something for Christmas."

"Say," he said, "I couldn't take—"

Oh, she knew. Couldn't take a gift from a woman. Old man always had pride. Us Rohns. Ask anybody in Idaho Falls. "You can give me something real nice," she repeated.

He wouldn't talk about them, didn't really look at them. He put the box—and the spurs in it—up on the shelf. "Eddie," she said, and watched him take down his mackinaw from behind the stove, his back to her. "Eddie, wait here. I've got to go up to the house."

She'd leave him alone with them. Give him time to think, to put his mackinaw back on the nail, to walk over to the box, to wait, to put his hands on the box and look inside. *Inlaid with 100 pieces of pure silver. The finest spur available.* There was a funny weight about a good spur, a feel, and the rowels made a sound.

She would always remember the fence post, a corner post in one of the flat fields five miles below the house. It had rotted and sagged; in the sagging the taut wire fence sagged and cattle were getting out, wandering down the road toward the Cross-Roads.

She had meant to send Eddie to fix it. She changed her mind.

"Eddie," she said, "catch your horse this morning and ride down after those cattle." Joe Martin had already left the breakfast table.

Eddie said, "Don't you want me to fix that post?"

"No. Anybody can fix that. But those cattle are going to drive hard."

He was proud of being a cowboy.

Now she watched the bunkhouse door from the window in the dining room. First, Joe Martin went out. A little later, the other two men. Then old Art; he whistled. His little dog slunk around the corner of the bunkhouse.

She lighted a cigarette, and waited. It was not often you rode after cattle in the winter, but when you did you wore boots—even if it was cold. Or Eddie would. With boots you wore spurs.

She stubbed out the cigarette, and lighted another. It didn't used to be like this, she thought, little crises, always pricking, little schemes she had, the terrible importance of somebody's words.

What did it matter if he wore the spurs? Why was it *now* that counted?

It was now that counted, because this was the moment. If it happened now, everything would be all right.

She glanced suddenly at the bunkhouse door, a weathered door, once painted white. The paint was dry, thin, chalky, rubbed off on you. But it was white. And the white moved, flashed a moment in the gray day. The door opened.

Eddie hesitated in the door. Then walked out. He swaggered a little; he had on the spurs. That took vanity—cold tight boots on a cold morning. But his vanity had a quality, it was virile, male. She despised him a little.

She would set the post herself.

She caught up a team in the corral, lonely there, running to corner first one horse, then another, choking in the cold brown dust.

His feet would be cold, now. She hoped they would.

And then she remembered his gentleness, his closeness, and the hundred times she wanted to run her fingers through his hair, the hundred times she had touched him without his knowing, her fingers on the cloth of his overalls.

She harnessed the team, hooked them up, and drove team and wagon down beside the barn. High in the seat there she was lonely again, the lines stiff and cold in her gloved hands. The very length of the thin lines stretching across the team's backs was lonely, and the long frosty shadow of the barn.

There was a new post down there, half in shade, half in the pale sun, the shady half hoary with frost, the sunny half bright with cold frost-sweat. A big post.

She began to struggle with it. She could barely move it.

There must be some leverage she could get. She stood straight, looking for a smaller post—something for leverage, something anyway to loosen the post from the frost under it. She looked away from the coldness, across the land. That always made her feel better. But the stretch of it like the stretch of the lines and the barn shadow was lonely. There was something lonely about the paleness of the sun, the weakness of it.

She looked at the post again. Clyde was coming toward her in overalls and one of her grandfather's bright checked blazers.

His voice and laughter were warm. Now at least there were

two of them in the cold. He kept laughing. "What are you trying to do?"

She looked at the post and frowned. "Trying to get that in the wagon. I'll tell you," she said evenly. "I hate the damn post." She looked up, half ashamed.

He laughed again. "There are things even you can't do."

"Well, I can try," she said. "No damn post—" She stood back, stepped quickly out of his way to watch him load the post.

It didn't take him long to set the post, and when he'd finished he took off his gloves and looked at his hands. "Say," he said wonderingly. "I've got blisters."

She said, "You're proud of them, aren't you?"

He laughed. "Yes."

"You did a good job," she said. "I couldn't have done it. I guess I knew that when I started." She stooped to pick up the crowbar, to help him. "Are you warm enough?" she asked. "Are your feet cold? I've been afraid your feet would get cold." He shook his head.

She let him drive the team back, and when the narrow little wagon trail crept over the curve that hovered above the ranch she said, "Look, Clyde."

He glanced at her, followed her eyes. She said, "Look at the land." She was silent a moment. Then, "You know—you mentioned that artist one time. I've always thought of it. The yellow sun. I look down there—"

"Yes?" He was close to her. The horses waited; the tug chains clanked, light and cold. Below them the big field stretched, remote and lifeless, and along the far fence the ground was marshy under the weak yellow stubble. There rose up a strong fleshy smell of rotting roots and cattails.

"I wish I knew more," she said. "About things. About artists, and color. I've never known anything. I'd never heard of Van Gogh. I never knew about sun and shade." She kept her eyes on the field. "I wish I knew about yellow."

He was watching her. "With all you have," he said, "you don't need to worry about anything."

She was silent a moment. "I don't know. I always wanted to be enough for myself. Now—I think I don't have much."

That was it. He kissed her. She closed her eyes, and kept her mind on the field stretching below her. He was speaking again.

Then she was saying, "Yes. Oh, yes, I will." She felt tired, felt wicked, felt hurt at the voice inside her. *Is this how it is? Is this how it is when a man wants to marry you?* But she still felt the field down there, cold and bright as silver, and secure now. The strong fleshy smell of the swamp was solid.

C H A P T E R At the Cross-Roads bar the beer company's calendar was turned to December, and the pretty girl in the picture had nothing on but a red bathing suit trimmed in white fur. She was under the mistletoe. There was a Christmas tree behind the bar, and a simmering kettle of hot water for Tom and Jerries.

There was a Christmas tree in the Dixie Rooms, and Alma had presents for the girls, a picture of Richard Barthelmess in a white celluloid frame that looked like ivory for Tiny because the boy Tiny used to go with in Salt Lake looked like Richard Barthelmess, lots of perfumes, pink-colored ones and lavender-colored ones in little glass bottles, and fancy soaps for the others.

There was a Christmas tree in the window of Rodney's department store, and the bright white floodlights shone way out into the snowy street and children gathered there, longing for the Flexible Flyer and the Lionel Electric train that ran around and around forever.

When it was bedtime, when the lights were turned off in the houses in Sentinel, there were reflections in the upstairs halls, light shining on the tinseled trees, little sparks of light. The tree was there. In a few days there would be things under it.

The old magic of Christmas came again to the Lost Horse Valley.

It was part of the magic that people should come.

"Ed wrote and said him and Millie would get in on the twenty-third."

"I was coming over to your house to tell you Bob's folks are coming."

"Now, I'm glad to hear that. Old folks like Christmas."

"Old folks and kids."

"I always say Christmas is for the kids."

They had always said it, and it was a lie, because the magic got them too. It was a time when everybody must be together. It was a time to remember that once things had been good, and only good.

"We was all together, then." It was before Dad started drinking, or got sick. It was before Al went bad. It was when Alice was so good in the school play. It was before somebody lost his money, or his wife.

Now, look in the spice box.

"You got to go to Sentinel and get some sage. Can't make dressing."

"How about the whiskey for Dad?"

"Well, yes. But don't tell Grandma."

"Hell, she knows he takes a little at Christmas."

"Well, yes, but she likes to be fooled."

And that's what you remember at Christmas, that once everything was good. And for a moment that time was here, and now, and real as a pine bough and a bright red ribbon.

After supper the tin-lizzy that belonged to one of the hired men rolled away from the Bart Ranch and left behind it neat little tire-patterns, diamonds and grooves. Joe Martin left boot tracks at the gate leading to the main road when he got out to open it. They had all gone in those few nights before Christmas, all but Eddie Rohn.

It was comfortable and stuffy in the bunkhouse, a little steamy, and the washbasin still held dirty water that the Kid had forgotten to throw out. Too excited. They had promised him something.

After supper they had kept saying to the Kid, "I'll bet you're going to back out. Again."

"Oh," the Kid kept saying, "you go to hell."

He kept grinning at the older men, shy, but a little proud. He had dressed up fit to kill, and even shaved.

"You ought to put some cream on your face and let the cat lick it off," they told him.

"Oh," the Kid said grinning, "you go to hell."

Then they said, soberly, "You're all right, Kid. You're all right." You see, they were like the Kid once, scared and slicked up, face red and shining, and they knew how you felt in your stomach.

They even gave the Kid a little shot of whiskey before supper, and he stood there as tall as they, skinnier, but as tall, and it didn't do much for him but make his face redder.

Mrs. Dean saw they'd had a drink when they came in for supper.

"You ought to be ashamed," she said to them, "giving a young fellow like that a drink."

"He's a man now," they said.

And even Mrs. Dean understood a little of what was going on. There were certain things men had to do, so you might just as well close your eyes. She gave the Kid the biggest piece of pie, and remembered not to pat his head.

Eddie Rohn watched them from the little frost-cleared place at the window, watched them until all he could see was the little red tail light bouncing along. He felt sorry for them. They had nothing.

He had Lona.

They had decided to go right after supper. They had filed awkwardly through the kitchen, through the big front dining room, keeping their eyes on the rug. They had stood beside the desk where Lona sat, writing their checks. They thanked her when she handed the checks to them, but when Eddie's turn came she said, "You going, Eddie?"

He thought he would, Christmas coming, and everything.

She moved her eyes away from him. "I'd like to talk to you tonight." The other men were filing out, tiptoeing. She put the pen up.

"Why, sure," he said.

She said, "I'll be out after awhile." She looked at him.

They kidded him a little, but Joe Martin didn't. Joe Martin kept still.

Eddie watched the tail light of the tin-lizzy. In a moment he knew he was going to be happy, happier than he had ever been in his life, but he kept putting off that feeling, playing with it. She was coming out to see him.

And Jesus, this was Christmas. She'd given him a present. Well, he had one for her too, and he was going to wrap it before she came out, and give it to her. It was a brush and comb set, but there were lots of other things besides a brush and comb. There was even a little round box with a hole in it that you shoved hair in to save. And it was silver, too. Real silver.

That's what the woman said. God, that had been terrible, standing in there at Rodney's with all the women, buying the present. He knew it was a good one when he saw it. Big, fancy box, and little places for each piece of stuff, and the little places padded with white silk. He was going to ask the woman about it, but— oh, he didn't know. There were things a woman did in her bedroom you didn't talk about. He remembered even with his own mother it was sort of funny in the bedroom, like there was something there that was only for his dad.

It was wanting that along with the rest made a fellow want to get married.

He let the happiness come now. There were shirts thrown over the chairs, and boots in a pile under the washbasin. Grinning, he emptied the basin, threw the water out into the snow and slammed the door against the cold. The latch clicked like a sleigh bell. He began to hurry picking things up, straightening up.

He wouldn't make a half-bad husband. And there was a lot of things he could tell kids too. He could tell kids about the way you could make a pen for a pet rabbit, and how you could make little strong harnesses for gophers, and the way you could step on tin cans sideways and make them clamp on your feet and walk on them.

He wondered if her mother liked him. Her mother was a real lady, as fine a lady as his aunt who was the schoolteacher in Soda Springs, who talked nice that way with no wrong words.

His kids were going to talk with no wrong words.

He got out the broom and swept the floor clean of cigarette butts and the corks of bottles they had had. Jesus, he felt sorry for them.

You know what he'd done? Well, he'd got some of them red

stickers, them red Christmas flowers with pointed leaves, and some Santa Claus stickers. He'd got white tissue paper, a whole roll.

He bet she didn't think he could wrap a present. Well, he could.

It wasn't much of a package, really. Not much. Not as big as he thought, and the paper kept tearing and where he got too much spit on the stickers the paper sort of messed up and had to be fixed with more stickers, but he bit his lip and squinted and got it fixed.

He had felt each piece before he wrapped the box, washed his hands first though because of that white silk stuff. And he had looked in the mirror, held it right up there by its shiny handle.

He had grinned at himself. He wasn't a half-bad-looking fellow. Look at that chin! He stuck the chin out and made a big frown. Mean and tough. Then he grinned.

"Hell," he said, disgusted with himself. Now, there it was. There was the package on the table. He put two old newspapers over it.

He sat down, watching out the window, watching for her shadow to fall against it.

When he used to go to church down to Idaho Falls they used to tell a story at Christmas time, and they kind of had a play about it. There was this Mary, this wonderful Mother of God, and there she was in this old barn with this little Baby, and everybody came to see Them.

You knew all the time that Mary was a girl name of Eva Mayfield, her old man had the place on Swede Creek, but you forgot. And you knew the Baby was a big doll belonged to one of the kids. You even forgot it was Idaho Falls.

It was just Mary and that Baby and all them sheepherders coming, and it was funny afterward to go outside where all the sleighs were, and everybody talking and laughing in the dark and lighting up their lanterns, and a few having drinks to keep out the cold.

It was warm in the bunkhouse. Maybe he dozed, because when he looked up she was there, Lona was there, and he had the funniest feeling about her being there, and just grinned at her and said, "Hello, Lona," softly. "I been waiting."

"Hello, Eddie." She sat down on the edge of the table pretty near the box under the newspapers. When she moved he smelled the perfume she had on, a little trail of it. Her cheeks were red from the cold. She was a pretty girl, a fine-looking strong girl.

She seemed nervous. She would be, coming out like that, him alone there. Well, there was nothing wrong about it when they were alone because he loved her.

She said, "I want to tell you something." There was a magazine beside her and she looked at the picture on the cover, and traced it with her finger. She said, "I was talking to Clyde."

"I been waiting," he said. "I guess they must all be in bed, in the big house."

She said, "I don't want you to say anything. I don't want you to say anything when I tell you something." She looked at him, searching his face, and then back to the magazine.

He watched her, puzzled. You couldn't tell about girls. They said things you didn't get. "All right," he said.

She said, "There are lots of things we've got to do, and don't want to."

That was a woman for you. He said, "I don't get you."

Her eyes challenged him. "You've got to promise not to get mad."

"Why, no," he said. "I won't get mad. Honest."

She said, "You've got to remember I love you. You've got to keep remembering that."

He was beside her now, his arms around her, feeling her warmth, the soft-hardness of her, but she wouldn't relax. She said, "I was talking with Clyde tonight. I—I'm going to marry him."

He kept holding her, and then it seemed his arms were paralyzed. He couldn't feel. He said, "I thought—we was—that we was—" Now his eyes were fixed on the magazine and the picture. He saw himself alone on some cold station platform, with his saddle wrapped in a gunnysack, and the whistle of the train blowing mournfully. Then for a minute he didn't think at all.

Her voice was small and tight. "Don't say anything. I don't want you to leave here."

His chin was a little stubborn. "If you don't love me, I gotta go."

"I do love you!" Her voice was sharp. "I'll come—here. When you're alone. I'll do—whatever you want me." She was looking at the old blanket sagging between the rooms.

His voice was flat. "I couldn't. Maybe rich fellows who don't care except about—maybe fellows like that." Not him, not with his good family.

A race of panic in her voice. "I love you."

"Then you don't love—him."

She hurried. "No. I don't love him." She said, "I love you."

He spoke slowly. "Why do you want to marry him?"

"Because. Because he's got money."

His eyes grew a little hard, and you saw the chin. "I didn't think —you'd—" he said, "that's not—right."

She choked up, and looked directly at him so that he saw the tears in her eyes, shiny and teary and hurt and afraid. "Don't you see—I've got to—take care of my mother."

"Oh," he said softly. "Oh," softly. "Jesus, I'm sorry." He put his arms around her, and could feel the softness of her. They sat there while the clock kept ticking in the bunkroom, while the draft of the stove sucked and sucked, and a draft moved the sagging curtain between the rooms.

She had buried her face on his shoulder, and he could feel the wet of her tears, and the smell of her perfume, and her hair. Her breathing was hot against his neck. He moved a little so he could see her face, but she moved at the same time. "I—want to go in there with you."

Now he spoke huskily. His stomach was doing things. "In the room, there?"

She nodded and went ahead, slowly, as if he were pushing her, but of course he wasn't guiding her; her hair hid her eyes. It was cold in there, so cold that they got under the blankets and warmed up, lying there, because hands are cold against flesh.

They took a long time, and once in awhile she'd push at him. "You can't go now. You can't—go."

He said, "You poor kid." The heavy brown quilt was dusty and musty smelling.

She whispered, "You can't go because of what you're doing."

"You poor kid," he said. "Oh, you poor kid."

After it was over she cried softly in his arms and kept her face against his neck, and he could feel the wetness and the warmth all mixed up with the brown quilt.

In a few hours he'd love her just as much as he had an hour before, for she could do that to him every time. Everything that happened under the quilt was beautiful, and he saw himself alone, and wanting her, alone with his saddle, after all that beauty.

He felt childlike, hurt, and he saw himself on a hot flat on the rodeo grounds, red flats and brass instruments. He was alone and sad, and that's what drove him on and on to be the greatest rider in the world.

He pulled a little away from her. "I got to go," he said.

C H A P T E R

 23

Clyde had got a Christmas tree. It wasn't much, but he had got it himself in the patch of timber a few miles above the ranch. He was proud of it. Proud as he had been of the blisters. He didn't have blisters now. He had callouses.

When he got back with it just after noon the snow clouds were coming down like dark gauze curtains. Lona had already ridden away into the fields to see when the cattle should begin to be fed for the winter.

Ruth had promised to help him decorate the tree. Lord, he thought, I'll never grow up. He sat alone for awhile in the chilly living room looking at the farm journal, at pictures of silos and bunches of cattle. The stove was hot enough, but there was still little heat.

That tree was going to surprise Lona.

Why didn't Ruth come down?

There was no one around the ranch, and only the thin smoke from the crooked little chimney in Mrs. Dean's shack showed any life, smoke drifting to the ground about the brown stalks of rustling rye-grass that poked up through the snow.

The big clock struck three, and he listened until the last faint shimmer of sound drifted off, like smoke.

But Ruth must have heard it. There wasn't much time before Lona would come.

"Cows," the farm journal said, "fed on this silage will fat-ten. . . ." A cold draft scurried through the house and poked into corners.

He felt there had never been any gaiety in that room, no one had ever laughed or been foolish. There had been piano music, but always serious, longing. The room might be shaken by anger, but there had never been gentleness there, or generosity. The old man in the portrait probably had seen to that.

Now again the brass gears of the clock began meshing, moving, preparing to sound the half hour, and it was a long time before the dull gong shivered out its tone.

No sound upstairs. Only the smoke from Mrs. Dean's chimney.

He went into the hall, glanced at the portrait, and moved up the wide stairs. The carpet was badly worn by all the feet that had moved up, step by step, to a colder level, the long hall, the rooms (and almost always closed doors) opening off like cells.

Tom Bart's room, his big bags empty now, in the closets; Bert Bart's room, larger than the rest, stuffed with black walnut furniture, marble-topped tables and plush. The room of Tom Bart's wife, long dead, the eastern aristocrat who had married the Bart money and died having Ruth. Drawn shades, green gloom. Lona's room, a bed, a chair, a half-open door.

He hesitated before Ruth's door. He dreaded knocking: the knock would echo in the hall, intruding on dead Barts. It was a foolish thing he and Ruth were going to do. And a foolish little tree.

He knocked. . . .

That afternoon the snow fell softly on the Bart Ranch, shut in, isolated small spaces within the range of Lona's vision. She rode alone there in the fields. The cattle pressed close to the fuzzy, indistinct willows, out of the wind, and watched. Willows and cattle and space.

She was dressed in heavy wool pants and mackinaw, and a scotch-cap pulled down over her ears. Once she had seen a haystack across from her, and two men working around it, propping up a fence that kept the cattle out, but she did not ride near enough to speak.

Eddie Rohn was gone.

He had spent the morning in the bunkhouse, and from the big house she had heard him. She had seen him walk to the shed where he kept his little black car, and he had driven it out in front of the bunkhouse. He had come to the house with the water pail, and she had heard him speak to Mrs. Dean, and go out again. The back dining room door clicked shut.

The morning was a long time for him to get his things together, his suitcase, his can of tobacco, his blue serge suit that hung in the dark closet in the sleeping room. He would roll his blankets, tie them, his face serious.

When she came to the bunkhouse, he was shaving. No shirt on. Towel over his shoulder. There by the door she stood, proudly. Handed him his check.

"Here's your check."

"Thanks." He took it.

And last night—in that other room, through that sheep blanket that sagged, a curtain over the other door, there on the bed he had said, "Darling, darling." Only a sheep blanket made those words secret, theirs.

There was another barrier, but it was between them now. She said, "What are you going to do?"

He shrugged and grinned. She knew what he was going to do. In a few months the rodeo started up in the south, traveling north. But in the meantime there was the waiting in the poolhalls, the nights in small towns, in shabby rooms. He had to live on something.

His rickety little Ford was out in front, and the tracks in the snow led back to the shed. A small black Ford naked and cold looking there in front.

He said, "Take care of yourself."

She loved his hands, his wide hands and the hard nails and the hair on his arms. On the backs of his hands were the little patches of hair, little islands, smooth lying, black. She loved his smile that seeped right inside her, and the strength of his long legs, how they had pressed against hers, and moved.

She stood straighter. She remembered that he had failed once, that he had failed and come to her, and it gave her a kind of hold on him, you always had a hold if you knew a weakness. She had made it clear that she remembered his weakness, smiling when he mentioned the rodeos.

She had heard his big, boyish, bragging words. "I'm going to be the greatest rider in the world. . . ."

She said, "I'll be watching the papers for you."

He had only shrugged and grinned, standing there with a towel in his hands. She couldn't tell what he thought of her, how he felt about—last night. They had been in that room and she had been afraid that someone would come in, and then she hadn't cared.

They said that men hated women afterward. That men didn't get over the hate until the next time they got her on the bed, and even then they hated her really, but pretended so they could get her there.

But you see, maybe men hated because other women cried and tried to cling, tried to be close to a man in the morning when he was sick of it.

She stood close to him now, but still straight and proud. He held her check in his hand. It was larger than what he had coming —much larger, and she couldn't afford it. He wouldn't notice.

Eddie. Eddie, you don't have to go.

But he couldn't take what he wanted. He wasn't strong.

Already the afternoon light was fading, and Ruth, alone in her room, watched out the window as old Art walked away from the bunkhouse toward the barn to finish one of his endless chores. His dog followed.

If only she could get over feeling sorry for everyone.

Her eyes rested on the washstand that she had painted in cream and decorated with a circle of blue flowers, dots and green triangles to resemble leaves, and she was conscious again of painting it, the weight of the can of paint in her hands, the feel of the brush in her fingers, how it rubbed and blistered a finger. And then the smaller brush, for the blue flowers, and the tiny can of blue paint.

The can was somewhere.

Down from the ceiling hung the long twisty green cord of the electric light that ended in the fluted linen shade. When it was lighted you saw blue flowers and green leaves; the design matched the design on the washstand, a striving for order, a repeated pattern.

Old Art disappeared into the barn. It was almost Christmas for him too. Did he remember other Christmases? Did he long for something that Christmas would bring—or bring back?

Look at the dog now, following.

There was a little pine tree downstairs, not a very good one, thin of branch, not shaped right. Clyde had brought it back proudly but it wasn't much of a tree. But—the first in the house for many years. You would have thought her father would have made a lot of Christmas, but he hadn't. One of his strange blind spots.

She was going to decorate it. Going to get out the box of things, strings of tinsel, of colored glass, things she hadn't seen in years, and she was going to recapture something.

A small tree, lost in the big room, under a high ceiling. The tree was going to take her back twenty years.

Oh, she knew she couldn't go back. Nobody can go back. You can't go back because you aren't you any more.

And yet, and yet . . .

She felt suddenly close to Lona, closer perhaps than she had ever been, for they were faced with a common danger.

The danger was a woman.

Clyde had said, so casually, that his mother was coming. There was a rudeness in her coming. There was only one reason why she would come.

To find out.

There were things that Lona didn't know, that people were often judged by different standards than she knew, by charm, by modulation of voice, by manners or travel or education or long background of family.

Lona had none of these. The woman was coming to find out.

A strong woman, because Clyde was weak. Perhaps too weak now to stand by a decision. The woman was going to hurt Lona.

Curious, that it would take another woman to bring them together. Lona must feel the danger too. Lona was proud. Her pride was the greatest thing about her, and the woman would leave her with nothing

There is always a little spot of time, a point in time you can measure. A time when two minds meet, two paths cross, two people become a family.

Solidarity.

That would save them. The woman might notice the old house getting shabby, the worn carpet on the stairs, the plumbing, the heating, the outbuildings needing paint, the age of the car. She might be shrewd enough to know that twenty thousand acres can suck you dry. She might sense the breath of decay.

But the woman would see too that even here in the West breeding counted, and she would see that the Barts had breeding.

She lifted her chin. Ruth Bart Hanson would show the woman. Lona would be proud.

She turned to the second knock on the door. She would go down now.

 CHAPTER 24   The sun gave a bold sharpness to outlines, a cutting edge to objects against the snow around the house, the barn, the bunkhouse, the corrals. The smoke rose straight from the chimney of the Bart mansion, thinned and disappeared. In the fields the cattle stood on the east side of the banks of snow-heavy willows, their hides gleaming red like copper in the sun, motionless, and their breath condensed to vapor. When they moved there were new tracks in the snow, deep and black in the slanting sun rays, and tracks of timid, scurrying animals along the endless winding snake-like sagging depression where the creek ran, where the water gurgled far below the ice. The mountains, thirty miles distant, white to their bases and girdled with the black-blue of timber, had a painted look, a hugeness in one dimension.

The valley was still.

So still that the creaking of a twig, the slamming of a door, the clink of a latch hung like a tangible thing.

Hours, now, since the blackness of early morning when Lona, dressed for town in the tweed suit, had come shivering down the stairs to open the draft of the stove in the living room, and stood near the warmness, feeling the familiar objects around her, but conscious of strangeness. She was uneasy.

She was to marry Clyde that week; she was afraid that something would happen.

She let a chunk of wood tumble into the stove just as Mrs. Dean slammed the back dining-room door, and the sound made her start.

It was hard to start the old Pierce. Old Art trudged behind her from the kitchen with pails of boiling water for the radiator. He hovered about her as she squatted and stooped to turn the pet-cock under the radiator with a pair of pliers. He poured the water into the car and the steam rose and vanished but the smell of oil and dust from deep inside remained.

"It's going to be a fine day," he said. "Good day to go to Sentinel for Mr. Clyde's mother. You'll see all the nice things in town, the Christmas things." He spoke carefully, anxiously.

"Yes." The morning star was still bright.

He went on. "Tootsie didn't get up this morning. Wanted to stay under the table where it was warm. She don't like to get her paws cold."

"You'd better get another bucket of water, Art."

"Yes, I will, Miss Lona."

She was ashamed of the car. The leather seats were shabby and cracking. The battery was feeble, and the starter ground and almost stopped. When the big motor started she raced it until it roared, until it was docile, idling, and the exhause went pa-pa-pa-pa. She took off her gloves and worked at the side curtains, fumbling with the tiny oval eyes and slippery catches until her fingers were numb. She shook out the robe and hung it carefully on the cord across the back seat. She drove out and parked before the house, and the dim headlights spread a sheet of yellow across the snow.

There was coffee in the kitchen. Standing, she drank a cup beside the kitchen stove, and heard the men in the back dining room, scraping their chairs, ticking their plates with knives. There was one less place set there, and there was Joe Martin. He made a half smile, more intimate than old Art's talk, more knowing, contemptuous.

She carried a cup of coffee into the front room and handed it to Clyde, hating herself for the deceit in her smile. He was better looking in his suit than he was in the overalls he had begun to wear. He was too thin for them. They sagged. He needed padded shoulders.

"Good morning, darling."

"Good morning, Clyde. Here's coffee."

"Thanks."

"The car almost wouldn't start."

"You might have let me."

"Nobody understands it but a Bart." She laughed a little.

He kissed her, and she felt the roughness of his coat and the softness of his hand. She said, "I don't suppose your mother ever rode in such a car. I hope she doesn't freeze."

He laughed. "New England winters are no better than Montana winters."

They lit cigarettes. In the half light of dawn they stood there and watched the cold gray horizon. She shivered. In less than a week they would get up like this, and he would have slept with her, and the softness of his hands and his thinness would be intimate.

"Are you cold, Lona?"

"No." The cigarette lit up her face.

"You shivered."

"It was cold outside. Have you heard Mother upstairs?"

"Not yet."

"I'll go up."

"Why not let her sleep? There's no reason for her to go with us."

"It would look funny to your mother."

"No, it wouldn't."

"I'd rather have her come along."

She stood before the door of Ruth's room, and hesitated before she knocked. She always felt like this. Awkward, and strange. Ruth's low voice answered at once.

She was not up, she was in bed. But her dark hair was brushed and smooth, the pillows were piled high behind her back. She had a white cloth across her lap, and little bottles and sticks were on it.

"Good morning, dear," she said.

Lona looked at the file, the orange sticks, at her mother's hands, soft and smooth as the cloth.

"Why aren't you up? We're almost ready to start."

"You go ahead, darling. That's all right."

Lona said, "But you're going with us."

Ruth had the buffer in her hand. Under it her nails grew pink and smooth.

"I think I'd better stay here." Her voice was confident. "There are things to do, Lona. You should come back to a lighted house, and things warm and nice."

"But she'll expect you with us."

Ruth smiled and shook her head. "No, she won't, dear. You'll see I'm right."

Lona had a cigarette in her hand. The match snapped and flamed. She would say it reasonably, she would not sound impatient, or angry.

"But I *want* you to come."

Ruth looked at her daughter, and the buffer stopped, and moved again. "I'm going to stay here," she said, and smiling, pleading, "Lona. Trust me for once."

Now the sun rose, and the smoke rose straight from the Bart ranch house. The outline of the shabby old Pierce was sharp against the snow.

Clyde drove. She had only to suggest it. Now his mother would see him taking a man's place, and that was probably what his mother wanted to see.

He was not a good driver. As many times as he had been over the road, he couldn't tell where the ruts were and the big car skidded and careened. His face was tense.

She sat on the edge of the seat, wanting to show him how to drive.

He was upset, she thought. Anybody could see that. There were long silences as they drove, abruptly broken.

"Will you light me a cigarette, Lona?" And the smile that went with it.

It seemed that he smoked incessantly. She tried to keep from thinking about him, about his mother, about marrying him. About her own mother.

Watch the country. Watch the endless miles of snow and sage-brush on either side, the glittering sharp brightness of sun.

Cold in the car. The heater—hot air from the manifold—scarcely worked at all, and through it seeped the sickening smell of exploded gasoline. If he wouldn't smoke so much—

She had heard that if smoke made you sick, the thing was to smoke yourself. She should have eaten some breakfast, not just that coffee.

But the insolent look of Joe Martin in the back dining room—that knowing, impudent look . . .

Her tongue was raw and dry, and the cigarettes tasted bad.

Suppose he ran off the road. They'd have to wait until someone came along with a chain. You couldn't even see the road now, for snow.

His mother, then, would have to wait at the station, wondering. Maybe she would go to the Sentinel Hotel, and sit in the big leather chairs, wondering, then call the ranch.

Well, in that case, when they finally did meet her, there would be a point to start a conversation.

"We got stuck. We couldn't get back on the road until . . ."

They could keep talking about that, and there would be no intimacy. Nobody would ask questions, say anything about marriage, or futures.

But eventually there would be questions, glances.

Nearer town small roads from the foothills converged on the main highway, and there were other cars going in. One had a Christmas tree on the running board, and there at last was the town ahead.

There were children with sleighs in the streets, and a gaiety everywhere, cars at the curb, the brightness of Rodney's store, and the smell of it in the street. Customers behind the frosted show windows of the Arrow Grocery. Turkeys, cranberries, and the scales that hung from the ceiling.

The sound of people and laughter and movement came suddenly, and she knew that the town saw the car and spoke of her

and of Clyde and of everything that had gone on for fifty years.
". . . the Barts. And that's the fellow . . ."

She sat straighter. She pulled at her stockings, twisted them so
the seams were straight, brushed at the coat of her suit.

And there were the things they said about her mother . . .

They would drive right to the station, avoiding old friends of
the family, old men who remembered her father, her grandfather,
her great-grandfather, old women who remembered that once
there were other Bart women, old Bert's wife, Tom's wife, beautiful, proud, grasping.

She wanted to wait in the car in front of the station. Already the
townspeople had gathered there, meeting, talking, catching the
excitement of the noon train's coming in, carrying the excitement
home to their houses.

The express wagon lumbered out. A lot of mail today. Talking
and laughing, and going into the station where there was steam
heat, where the magazine covers were bright on the newsstand,
where you could meet a friend.

Far out into the white distance the railroad track reached out of
town, and the semaphore was still set against the train's coming
in, a great arm on a post. It always fell before the train came, and
you could hear it slam.

Her eyes were on it.

Far up the track the rails curved around a low round hill and
vanished, curved around a low trestle there, and underneath a
warm spring seeped up melting the snow in the winter and the
bright green of cress and moss was there.

The semaphore arm slammed down.

Bang.

The train flew around the hill, leaning against the hill, a moving
black quarter-circle, and there were plumes of steam. She moved
her fingers, stiff with cold, and wished she had gloves, not because her hands were cold, but because they were rough. Clyde
slipped his arm around her shoulder, and she grew a little stiff.

The roar of the train was deafening, crashing against her mind,
and the door of the station opened and the people crowded out to
watch, standing respectfully back from the train.

They got out then and began to walk.

"She'll be down at the end," Clyde said.

There was only one bit of movement down there. A porter stepped down and began to put luggage out, quickly and carefully. He was grinning and talking.

"Yes, ma'am! Yes, ma'am!"

There was a great pile of luggage.

The porter in his white coat was shivering with cold, but he still laughed and said, "Yes, ma'am," straining under the luggage he carried. The woman followed him, talking and laughing with him. She seemed to ignore Clyde and Lona, talking to him.

"Now, you take care of that wife of yours, George!" she said.

"Yes, ma'am!"

"Don't you let her run around with those other fellows! You tell her she's lucky to have a thoughtful fellow!"

"I sure will, ma'am!"

"Why, I don't know what I'd have done without you, George."

The porter staggered under the luggage, grinning. Their voices were clear.

"Right there, George. Put the bags down."

He put them down.

"Now then!" The woman opened her purse and took out some bills. "There," she said, "there's a present for you to buy that wife of yours something. You show her you can buy presents too."

"Thank you, ma'am." Great grins, and white teeth, and bowing and happy mumbling, leaving. The train pulled out, the porter stood on the platform and waved, and the woman waved back. She had not so much as noticed Clyde and Lona. Then she turned, and suddenly the full force of her personality was on them.

"Darling!" And a kiss on Lona's cheek. The woman was not beautiful, but she was beautifully groomed. Her speech was that nice balance of affectation and naturalness, the soft broad "a," the care with the vowels, the crispness. Her clothes were subdued and expensive. Not much more than fifty, her hair was gray and shingled, smart. Everything was smart, her hat, her luggage, her shoes, and she had a terrible self-confidence. More than that, family-confidence, blood-confidence, money-confidence.

She had a world, and belonged there. Expensive cars, and clubs, and busy late mornings planning charities in sunny rooms and lunch and fittings and music, and others like her, successful men and God in well-built churches. Family crests in the bedroom, pride in cold, frugal Puritan ancestors. A white house with green blinds and white pillars and decor.

"Darling!" You can always tell expensive perfume, and expensive furs have their own warmth.

Lona stood there in the good rough tweed suit, but it was shabby. She had no gloves. She wore no hat.

She could think of nothing to say. Embarrassed, she felt cold, stiff, inadequate, even frightened.

The woman said, "Clyde."

He kissed his mother, and she kissed him, and they stood a moment, locked there, he, tall and thin, a part of her world, fitting in it. "Mother."

Lona stood, watching. She dreaded the moment when they would start toward the car, wondering who would go first, who should go first. If only she could think of something to say, but even her voice was inadequate.

She kept telling herself, "I'm a Bart. This is my town. My family . . ."

But for a moment what she was and what she had was nothing. Outside there was something bigger, more important, more ordered, more stable. She stood there.

There was the old Pierce.

And Clyde's mother was laughing softly, walking along. "Look. The car! The glory that was Greece—"

"That's my car," Lona said. "We're going home in it."

C H A P T E R

25

In the bunkhouse they got to talking.

The fire was lit and beginning to glow on one side so that the wall smelled. The gasoline lamp hissed and their shadows, as they sat there, were black and stooping against the wall. In the big house the cook passed back and forth across the shaft of light that poured out the kitchen window, and they watched it. The sudden heat inside made them a little drowsy and philosophic, the knowledge that outside it was fifteen below zero. They were a little under the spell of the evening. Dusk had fallen at four-thirty, and shortly after that a flight of wild geese flew over the gray fields, honking, making their unworldly sound like the crying of lost souls.

From the swamp in the distance rose a damp stench of rotting roots and stalks, and the wet fur of little water animals.

Old Art was playing a game with his dog. He would put out his hand to her, stooping there beside the table, and she would put her paw in his palm. He would draw his hand away, then she'd try to reach it again, wriggling toward him. Now and again he glanced at Joe Martin, wondering if Joe noticed that Tootsie was back in the bunkhouse these weeks since it had got so cold.

But Joe Martin was reading his *Western Story* magazine.

It was at this time of evening that they chose their subjects for the evening's arguments, talks about women or family, politics or religion, and sometimes a curious mixture of all these things, for they all made a fellow what he was. You couldn't get away from that.

One of them said, "Old Hoover's the one caused it." He looked levelly around the room. "He had it all fixed with them financeers. They got money in them big banks with bars in front."

Another said, "More than that. The Pope of Rome's mixed up in it. The Pope of Rome's trying to get this country in his clutches."

Art said, "Why's he doing that?"

They looked at him as if he were a child, and he looked back at Tootsie, embarrassed, trying to forget his foolish question.

"Why," one said, "there's places in this country where everybody's Roman Catholics. They're always saying them prayers that the Pope of Rome will get this country in his clutches."

The idea was dangerous, there was silence in the bunkhouse.

"There's them nuns, too. They got them specially for them Roman Catholic preachers. You don't think no man's going to do without women, do you? Oh, no. And them preachers can't go places like other fellows."

"I knew a fellow knew a Baptist preacher used to cheat on his wife."

"Well. A lot of them Baptists are regular, same as you and me. I had a cousin was a Baptist."

"There's them Jews, too. Fellow told me they was trying to get the country in their clutches."

A little silence. "I thought you said the Pope of Rome was trying."

"He *is* trying. All them damn people are trying. Matter of fact, the Pope of Rome and them Jew preachers are working together."

The thing was, there was danger in the country. In this bunkhouse it was warm. There was a bright light, and friendship, and in a few minutes supper was going to be ready. But there was danger. They could be fired, and they had been talking in town. There weren't any jobs. There were people starving, and they could be next. Their future depended on the will of one person. She could fire them. She could lower their wages. They worked around to her in an oblique fashion, because Joe Martin was sitting there, saying nothing, and he hated talk.

But he had hated Eddie Rohn, and he must hate her too, because of Eddie Rohn.

"Them Mormons don't need no nuns," one said.

"They just find a pretty girl, and bang."

"They got to marry her though."

"That's what I meant by bang. There's all this talk about not letting them do that, but they do it. There's never a night that a Mormon can't get what he wants."

They pondered this wonderful thing, a whole houseful of women to make a man feel big.

And then, "Eddie Rohn, he was a Mormon."

This was the way to cultivate Joe Martin, and it angered them that they wanted to cultivate him. They hated him, but he never worried about things. He didn't give a damn whether he had a job or not.

One said, "Old Eddie Rohn's probably got a lot of girls. Good-looking fellow, and lots of women like them clean kind of fellows."

Joe Martin didn't even look up.

Another said, "Them clean kind like it just as well as the next."

Joe Martin turned a page.

One said, "He coulda had any woman he wanted. He coulda had her if he'd a wanted. Jesus, you remember how she used to keep watching him?"

Joe Martin looked up.

Another said, "She was sweet on him, all right. She's just like the rest of them women."

Joe Martin spoke softly. "Keep your God-damned mouths shut. You're like a bunch of women. Keep your mouths shut about her."

"Well, now, Jesus, Joe."

He looked at them.

Old Art was glad he hadn't said anything. He got up and walked quietly across the room, and was glad that Tootsie didn't scuff her toenails. The supper bell rang and they went out, the snow crunching under their feet. Supper was late because the cook was fixing a special supper for the front dining room.

Before they left for the ranch, Lona and Clyde and his mother had sandwiches at the Sugar Bowl Café. It was there that Lona realized she was afraid to go home.

She had gotten on with Clyde's mother by simply listening. When Clyde took her hand she made a little wooden smile and went on trying to listen.

Helen Winston said, "You're distracting her, Clyde. I'm trying to tell her about my trip." She smiled at Clyde tolerantly. She knew her gift. She talked well. Her chair was pushed back from the table now, and she had her knees crossed, dangling one foot, studying the toe of her expensive shoe. She had thrown back her coat, and she fingered the long string of amber beads around her neck. She talked in slow, amused tones of things she had noticed on her trip, she painted little miniatures of personalities, faces, the timbre of voices. What might have been rude and prying in another woman was in her an engaging, childish interest, but under it was a streak of cruelty.

"I've always been interested in people." Watching the toe of her shoe, comfortable.

She mimicked cleverly, and could tear apart a personality, slit open a past and leave it bleeding. She spoke of people she had seen for a second, during the change of a train, the drinking of a cup of coffee: a small Italian arguing bitterly with his wife over a lost pocketbook, calling on God and St. Anthony.

"He might better have invoked the Traveler's Aid."

There was a girl of not more than fifteen sitting on a new-varnished bench in a railroad station, pregnant, her eyes swollen, a shabby bag beside her.

"She should have played longer with dolls."

Clyde said, "You're hard on them, Mother."

She smiled. "I don't see why you say that. I simply see what I see."

"There's not much point in talking about the seamy side."

"No. But it *is* interesting, isn't it?" And she was off again, fingering the beads. The waitress, a great, heavy-footed woman with hennad hair, paused and smiled.

"We sure got some swell pie today if you folks want some."

Clyde's mother said, "Well, we sure are hungry. Bring us some of that there pie."

"I sure will," the waitress said. The eyes of Clyde's mother sparkled with amusement.

It was then that Lona was afraid to go home. She had last seen her mother in the cold gloom of the bedroom, and somehow it was sordid, her mother lying awake there, watching her as she stood at the foot of the bed.

Her mother had refused to come to Sentinel. "I'll just stay here."

But it might be all right. It had been all right for a long time. There was no reason to think that—that now—

"Really, darling," Clyde's mother said to her. "Really, you are the slowest eater!" Lona smiled, and hurried.

But her mother was all right. Her mother had been all right in the bedroom. She saw it all again, the dark room, the gray bed against a grayer dawn, the stillness, the rustle of a pillow. It was only that there was something there, something lying there in the room waiting, something unclean.

She couldn't shake off the feeling, the odd smell of a room slept in, the disturbed privacy; for they had grown too far apart to see each other sleeping or naked. They knocked at each other's doors . . .

"Have you finished that there pie?"

The old car was parked in front, and the little town of Sentinel was busy and white and brilliant in the cold sun. There were groceries to pick up, and some tobacco for the men. That took a little time.

Why should she care what anyone thought?

Well, there is the icy feeling, the chill you get when anyone close to you is drunk, when they are cheap and common before strangers.

No, that's not it at all. The woman can influence Clyde. It is a matter of fifteen thousand dollars. If you are beginning to doubt your position in the world when you've got twenty thousand acres, what are you going to think when even the acres are not secure?

She stood at the tobacco counter. "I want a case of Prince Albert, and charge it." The clerk hurried to her, whipped out his pad.

"Yes, sure, Miss Hanson. Anything else?"

It made her feel better. And no one knew the name of the woman in the car. No one had ever heard of her. But they knew the Barts. They rushed over with their little pads.

She got in the back seat with his mother. She sat stiff and straight. Past the Star Garage. Past the little shacks in the Cabbage Patch. Ahead of them the Lost Horse Valley was cold and endless. She was afraid to go home.

Clyde was driving, and she got out of the car to open the old pole gate that led up to the ranch house. Dusk, already, for the trip had been slow, the highway icy, and the county road drifted with fine dry snow. She struggled up to the gate and fumbled with the chain and horseshoe that secured it. It was then that the wild geese passed over, and it made her shudder, the airy loneliness of the sound.

From the garage she glanced at the bunkhouse, squat there in the dusk, and still dark. When the window lighted up it would not be his hand that turned the little black knob on the lamp.

"Well, here we are," she said.

Light in the living room, soft light, and order, but it was empty. When she stood with Clyde and his mother in the big hall under the portrait and looked into the light, she sensed that her mother had just been in that room. Sitting there at the piano probably, sitting there . . .

How is that? How do you know when someone has been there? It is as though the furniture was alive a moment ago, and is frozen now, stiff and silent. The piano was closed. Had it been open? Why hadn't she noticed?

The fire crackled in the big stove.

Helen Winston said, "Take the bags up, Clyde. I brought along some whiskey. A drink will warm us up."

"I'll get some glasses," Lona said.

"I'll be right back," Clyde said. "I'll get them."

"No." Lona spoke sharply. "I will."

Keep busy. Keep your hands busy. You won't have to answer questions, explain. *This was crazy.* This was only another evening. Everything was going to be all right. Her mother would be right down.

But Ruth didn't come, not just then. The electric light plant across the road began to chug and the light in the many-glassed chandelier blinked and flickered.

Lona said, "The lights are bad. Sometimes I wish we were on a power line."

Clyde's mother said, "I rather like the isolation. I've spent all my life with people." She had a comfortable smile.

Lona said, "My mother hasn't been very well. My grandfather's death." She let her eyes fall.

"I'm sorry. Is there anything I can do?"

"Oh, no. She's probably lying down."

She started when she heard the stairs creak, but it was Clyde.

He was carrying the bottle, whistling softly. He said, "Do you think you ought to call your mother? She ought to try this." He held the bottle up. "I haven't seen anything like it since I left home."

Lona said, "We'll let her rest. She wasn't feeling well this morning."

Clyde said, "You didn't tell me."

"I didn't think to tell you." Lona looked up at the lights. "The lights are flickering. I was telling your mother I wished we were on a power line."

Clyde said, "Well, if you think you'd better not call her."

Lona turned to his mother. "Would you like water with it?"

"You don't have a little soda?"

"I'm afraid not. We hardly ever drink here. Just when men come in. They usually take it straight."

Clyde said, "I'll get some water from the kitchen." He left them there. The light from the chandelier made the amber beads blood-color.

"My grandfather was the only one could work it right." Lona held her hands in her lap.

Helen Winston laughed. "I guess I follow you, but it's hard. I didn't know my son could be so exciting."

Lona smiled and looked at her nails.

Clyde came back with the water. "Here it is. I'll mix them."

She should have been talking, saying something, playing the hostess. She had no idea how to do it. There on the table were the new magazines. The *Cosmopolitan,* the *Literary Digest.* She said, "The magazines came yesterday. There's a light over your bed. Tonight you can read."

Clyde's mother said, "That's nice. What magazines do you have?"

"Well, there's the *Literary Digest* and the *Cosmopolitan.* You've probably seen them. They're good."

"Yes, they're good."

"My grandfather always liked magazines, and we never stopped them." Lona picked one up and handed it to her. "Here."

Clyde said, "The drinks are ready."

Lona said, "We'll probably have time for just one."

It was the next two hours that counted. Get the drink down, have supper, keep busy. Maybe they could walk, get out of the house. She might drive them somewhere. Then if her mother came down and found the room empty, she'd go back upstairs.

Maybe her mother was really sick. They had pretended that, once.

"Your mother's sick, dear." Her grandfather had said it, and her mother had been in bed. But she had smelled the whiskey, and her mother was dressed, lying there.

"Your mother's sick." Strange, how gradually you come to understand things. She could pretend now. She could even give her whiskey, and keep her there in bed until Clyde and she . . .

Keep her mother there, force her, push her back into the room, onto the bed . . . beside her they were talking, and she was talking. The lights flickered, and they were talking about the trip again, painting their little pictures. Chicago, Boston, people Lona had never heard of, a tight little world of their own.

And now Clyde was standing and smiling, but not at her. He looked past her, to the hall, and she heard it, the creak on the stairs.

It wasn't what Ruth wore, and yet it was the right dress. It was black, slender at the waist, and the skirt flared and swirled. She wore no ribbons, no beads, but there was color—the red, red rose on the skirt.

She stood in the big doorway. She was proud and poised. She came toward them, walking with the easy grace, walking in beauty, and Bert Bart had never dreamed of dignity greater than this, this woman without jewels, with only that way of holding her chin, of wearing a red, red rose.

She said, "I am Lona's mother."

It was only a second before Clyde's mother rose and came forward. "And I am Clyde's." Smiling, she turned to her son. "Will you fix another drink?"

He was strangely clumsy, fixing the drink, and Lona, torn and confused, shabby in the good tweed suit, watched him fumble with the glasses. She watched her mother's easy gestures, listened to her mother's voice, gentle and beautiful, her easy conversation. Lona's voice had been tight and fighting, but she had felt strong because she was handling a situation.

There hadn't been any situation. Now they began to talk around her. Her mother took her hand and led the conversation back to her, but it veered away. Clyde's mother was watching Ruth, and there crept into her eyes that alert, that interested look. Lona kept hearing her say, "And then this woman, this gorgeous creature came in . . . that bleak old house . . . those lonely miles . . ."

And then, "This woman . . . you should have seen my son . . . you see, she's quite a young woman . . . fumbling with his drink, watching her . . ."

They were having another drink now. Lona watched her mother

raise the glass and felt a hot satisfaction. They wouldn't think so much of Ruth if they knew—if they saw—

She looked down at her hands, motionless in her lap, and made the little clutching gesture. If they knew of the bottles in clothes hampers, the eyes. She kept looking down at her hands, rough hands that you couldn't hide. They didn't know the fear, the watching and the fear.

Wasn't her mother's voice different now? A little high, faltering?

Clyde's mother said, "You two run along. Your mother and I have so much to say." Two gentlewomen with secrets. But wasn't her mother's voice . . ?

There was quite a bit left in the bottle there on the table, and the women had begun to talk intimately, had begun to lean toward one another, laughing and talking.

She went upstairs with Clyde, and to his room with him. "This is better," he said. "Alone." He spoke softly, intimately, and she was not afraid of him, only disgusted with his soft voice. He said then, "They're getting on well. They'll talk about us."

She tried to make that room a refuge, a soundless refuge where she couldn't hear the voices. "Yes, this is better," she said. They were on his bed and he kissed her, his face a little flushed, and she kissed him back.

When I am kissing him I don't think so much about them.

He slipped his arm around her. "They're getting on fine," he said. "I knew she'd love you."

She moved a little nearer him. "You shouldn't do that, Clyde."

His lips were on her throat. "Why not? Why not, darling?" His lips vibrated against her throat. In a moment he would sort of pull her back.

"I love you," he said.

She whispered, "Oh, I'm glad . . ." And stiffened, trying to hear, thinking of Clyde's mother's eyes, of her questions.

She sat up and glanced at him, smiling a little. He had taken her mind off them for a little. She said, as if teasing him, "I think we'd better go down now, Clyde." Nothing was real.

She stood up, afraid now. Now she had to get downstairs, and she stood impatiently beside the bed while he straightened his tie.

They were still talking. There was a new bottle. Whose? Had she looked everywhere, was there more?

Helen Winston was smiling, and her face was a little flushed. Rich people didn't look like poor people when they drank. As she moved toward the table she noticed her mother's eyes. They were still and troubled.

Ruth looked up. "Oh, darling." Clyde stood behind Lona and put his hands on her shoulders. Ruth watched them for a moment, the gentle hands on the girl's straight shoulders. Then her eyes softened, and she smiled.

Helen Winston said, "Let's all have another drink," and she leaned forward and began to mix them. The glasses clinked and the clock ticked. The room was bare and cheap in the yellow flickering light. Everything seemed shabby and cheap and unreal.

Ruth reached for her glass.

Lona stepped beside her and stood there. She said, "Mother— don't you think you've had enough?" She couldn't keep the coldness out of her voice. She was cold inside and tired, disgusted by the man beside her. "Don't you think you've had enough?"

Helen Winston looked up, suddenly alert, eyes a little hard, questioning.

Lona stood straight, watching her mother.

Clyde said, "Now, let's not—" Then he laughed. He said, "We're all tired. I'll tell you—" He turned to Ruth. "Play a little." He turned to his mother. "Mother, she plays beautifully."

His mother's voice was soft. "Please do, Ruth."

Ruth stood up, hesitated, the full glass still in her hand. She put it down carefully, very carefully. "You know," she said, "we are tired. And I have a headache. I think I'll go upstairs."

In the silence they watched her move from the room, and heard her go quietly up the stairs.

Lona sat alone in her room, at the dressing table.

Do you know the quiet of this house, the quiet as long and dark as the halls? And it creeps, hunting small frightened night sounds, creaks and taps.

She put her cigarette down on the edge of the table. It glowed there, and made a tiny hissing, spitting sound.

She had shown Helen Winston about the bathroom, how to empty water into the toilet tank to make it work, and she had apologized for the inconvenience. She had stood in the bathroom with towels in her hand, feeling the rough weight of the cloth, knowing the game was up, that she had lost, that she hadn't measured up to some standard she didn't know. She was alone with the woman, and in a moment the woman would speak.

"These towels," Lona said. "I'll get soap." All she had felt was tiredness, defeat. Well, it was something to recognize it.

She picked up the cigarette on the dressing table, took a puff, and inhaled deeply. There was nothing on the dressing table but a brush and comb. What is the brush made of? Pig bristles. Some of them gone, worn out. Look at the handle. Celluloid? Celluloid burns. She picked up the cigarette and carefully, intently, brought the glowing end nearer and nearer to the end of the brush handle.

A funny, dead smell.

"These towels," she had said, there in the bathroom. "I'll get some soap." There was the washbowl, there was the coffinlike tub, and the electric light hanging from a naked cord.

She had turned to the door.

But the woman had stopped her. Stood before her. Taken her by the shoulders, and smiled into her eyes. "Lona," she had said, "you're strong. I'm glad you're going to marry my son."

She took another puff of the cigarette. She was trembling. She held up her hand and watched it. Steady enough. It was her stomach that really trembled. Then she let the full surge of her triumph sweep over her, and watched what it did to her eyes.

She turned her head and looked at the bed in the corner, the plain brass bed. Each night she had looked at it. She thought of Clyde's gentleness, his thinness. And she would have to know them in that bed.

Well, now, how much do you think she ought to give him, how much of herself?

Not much. Even the wedding night could be arranged.

She got up and walked to the window. The night was strangely blue, the stars on the snow. Her eyes found what she wanted.

The bunkhouse. They were all sleeping in there, the windows were black. There was a bed in there.

Now she could feel him touch her.

Now, in a little while, she could have him. Her fingers closed over her palm, and time stopped as she thought of him.

She must remember all this. The way the night looks. The way her cigarette glowed there on the dressing table. The way her eyes looked in the mirror. She must remember the squat bunkhouse out there in the snow, remember . . .

She froze when she heard the tap at the door.

The breath had suddenly gone out of her. She could only whisper at first. "Come in."

The tap again.

"Yes. Yes. Come in." She sat so stiff that her neck ached, and the ache began to creep down her back. "Come in."

The door opened. She forced herself to look.

It was Ruth.

She was still in the black dress. She stood there in the doorway as she had downstairs, trying to be proud. She started to move and steadied herself in the doorway, a fumbling hand out against the door.

"Lona—"

Lona whispered, "What are you doing here?"

Ruth took a step forward, uncertainly. "Lona, do you love Clyde? Do you love him?"

Lona looked at her mother. Maybe it was her mouth, the way it drooped, and the painful effort she made to keep it straight and proud.

"Get out," she said.

"Lona, I want to tell you. Something his mother said."

Lona rose. She stood there, her nails pressing into her palms, watching the woman whose eyes and mouth could ruin every plan, every hope. Lona's words were cold against the silence.

She said, "Get out. Get out of my room. Don't come here." She took a step forward. "Don't come here, ever."

 CHAPTER **26** There was a brick church in Sentinel, beside a vacant lot. There was a crack running down the front of it, zigzagging down from under the eaves to the little door where they dumped coal, when there was money for coal. The steeple was truncated and pigeons nested in the louvers and croaked there and were dirty, not frightened by the gray-faced Wednesday night worshipers, nor disturbed by the thin tinkly music from the old upright piano, the threadbare hymns to a weeping Christ.

On Wednesday night the church was lighted with only two naked bulbs, and no one could see what you wore nor who you were. A girl from the Dixie Rooms could sit in the back pew. Miss Julia Avery had played the piano there, before her death. It is at night that loneliness comes like sickness.

At last they said goodnight to the minister, standing beside the rickety door, a little cluster of forlorn middle-aged men, young men with thin wrists and bad complexions, pinched-looking women, homely, eager girls. They were all smiling now because they had sung together.

He walks with me and He talks with me. . . .

The minister went back inside the church that was not quite so cold as the winter outside, not quite so bare as the quaking aspen out in front, and the people went down the street past the other church, silent, knowing that if things had been a little different they would have belonged to this other church that had neat lawns in summer, and a stained glass window of ruby red and royal blue. If things had been different . . .

A wedding was going on inside.

Behind the carved altar the brass vases held flowers, and the gold pipes of the organ were vague in the diffused colored light of the big-arched window. But it was silent.

No one at the wedding but the rector, the bride and the bridegroom, and the two mothers.

She knew no one, there was really no one to ask, but she was proud. She said she didn't want a big wedding.

The service was going on. The few paragraphs were musical.

She hadn't wanted a bouquet. They had stood alone in the florist's shop. It had been cold outside, but in the shop it was warm, tropical, the dampness rich with carnation spice, rose odor, the delicate green smell of fern fronds, the moistness of moss. There was vase after vase of flowers in a small glass room, the walls misted with scent, bursts of color flaming from white vases.

The woman there looked at her, at the new shoes, the new winter wool dress, hanging a little stiffly, the new hat and gloves. She had turned away because the woman had smiled intimately.

Clyde said, "I wish you'd let me buy them all for you." He was tall, tanned from working outside in the snow glare. It had done him good.

"No, Clyde. Not even a bouquet. They'd just freeze."

Tucked away in the corner of the small glass room there was a white flower, only one, white and waxy, but the edges were turning dark. It was not meant to be there.

He grinned at her. "What are you looking at?"

She said, "That little white one. What is that one?"

"Gardenia."

"I'd like that one, Clyde."

The woman slid a glass panel, and the scent from inside was overpowering. "Would you like to pin it on the young lady?"

There was a straight pin, the head an imitation pearl, and he stood above her, fumbling a bit, and pinned on the flower. "It looks very pretty," the woman said, and smiled that secret smile.

The rector had almost finished now.

Well, she had protected the gardenia from the cold, holding the collar of her coat away from it, keeping her cheek close to it, giving it warmth until they got to the Sentinel Hotel and picked up the two mothers. She felt tenderness, compassion for the flower. Sorry for it . . .

The rector had finished now. She could heard her mother crying; she felt the small new pressure of the ring, and turned to her husband.

Her *husband* . . .

He was smiling. Beyond him the church was empty. Is this the way it is, she thought, is this the way it is when a man marries you?

He took her in his arms, pressed her to him and kissed her, but she turned slightly sideways so that the flower was not crushed.

Clyde stretched his arm and looked at the luminous figures of his watch, and then brought it near to his ear, to listen. Lona lay asleep beside him. He was silent, listening to her regular breathing. He felt a flood of tenderness toward her and put his arm across her, let it rest there for a moment.

Three o'clock is a strange hour.

From it you move forward or back: into dawn, or back to night. Dead center.

Three o'clock is a matter of two hands pointing to figures, an angle of ninety degrees, arrived at by weights, or springs, or magnets.

Once three o'clock was falling sand in a glass, water in a bowl, a burning candle, or the shadow on a rock. But dead center. Always dead center.

In cities it is black strokes of shadows bold against the face of a building. A hungry rat in a narrow alley twisting through narrower places. It is a telephone ringing in an empty room.

Clyde got up, and his fingers found a cigarette on the dressing table. He lighted it, and the stub of a candle there. There were candles or lamps all over the house in case the electric light plant failed. A feeble little light, playing across the planes of Lona's face, light—soft and caressing, fluid.

He felt very wise and old, knowing the responsibility of a man for a woman.

Still smoking, he stood by the window and looked down at the ranch buildings there. The bunkhouse, nearest. In the moonlight the squat shadow was thick, a part of substance. The narrow path through the new snow to the door was black out of light, a narrow pit that might have been bottomless. He thought for a moment of the loneliness of men without women, dreaming at three o'clock of a girl in a picture hat.

He turned his head, his face serious, to Lona there in the bed.

He had been gentle. Understanding. He supposed that from the first his watching her, his sensitivity to her moods was a preparation for the night just past, the life just beginning. However strong she was, in the matters of men and women she was innocent.

But he would make her happy if it took the rest of his life. It only took time, and understanding, and gentleness. In all fairness, he had those things.

He stood smoking, watching her.

And there was so much more in the world than sex. The girl in a lonely man's dream is not nude.

A world filled with music he could uncover for Lona. The magnificence of Beethoven that made you do greater things than you could. The poignancy of Mozart that made you feel more than you could understand.

He thought of books he would choose for her. Saw them in a case, saw the titles and the covers of the jackets.

A girl with her quick mind—her depth—would one day understand the Italian masters, the grand simple symbolism of Giotto, the impressions of the French. Degas. Cezanne. Chausson, Franck, in music.

It seemed a great deal to graft upon the mind of the girl lying there. See now, how her hair is scattered across the pillow. See her face . . .

He felt very old, very wise.

And then the tenderness flooded over him, and he stubbed out the cigarette; he lay down beside her and put his hand out to touch her.

She pulled a little away from him, and he smiled, remembering the awful responsibility of men.

Helen Winston was leaving. Her bags were packed and the green gloom had descended again on the room that had been Lona's grandmother's; winter sun made dots on the old carpet through worn places in the drawn shades. Although she hadn't gone yet, it seemed there was nothing left of Helen Winston but the scent of her perfume, the echo of her soft scent. Once the wedding was over she didn't exist.

But the house was unsettled. Clyde had ridden away to help

Joe Martin with some cattle, ridden away proudly, waving from the barn. He would return at noon to drive his mother to Sentinel. Mrs. Dean was singing in the kitchen because of the fifteen dollar tip. There had been a kind of high breakfast in the dining room, and Ruth and Helen Winston lingered there until almost ten o'clock, smoking and drinking coffee.

Lona was restless in her room, thinking up little tasks there, straightening out things on her bureau. She looked into her closet, fussed with the spread of her bed. She didn't want to see Helen Winston again except once—once when she left. When she heard the woman's footsteps in the hall she got busy at another task, trying to get the stopper out of a perfume bottle. She frowned, and worked away with her fingers. But she looked up and smiled. "Here. Take this chair. I'll sit on the bed."

"Thank you, Lona. We haven't been alone since I came."

There was a good deal of sunlight in the room, and the reflected glare of the land outside stretching in all directions gave a kind of spaciousness to the room, like mirrors. The land looked even bigger in winter. Something about the white of it.

It had turned warmer, and the snow had begun to melt off the low sloping roof of the barn, and brown patches showed. Art had left the bunkhouse door open and he stood in the doorway shaking a blanket, the dust silver in the air. There was the laziness of false spring in the air.

Helen Winston said, "I came to talk about Clyde."

"Yes."

Helen Winston wore the same French woolen suit, the amber beads, but now she didn't impress Lona. "You'll never know how much I appreciate what you've done for Clyde. He seems a bigger person. I know. I've been father, mother, and friend to him."

"I haven't done much." She felt almost sorry for the woman.

"You have. But I wanted to see that you had. You'll understand when you have children." She looked at her rings.

Lona said, "Do you want a cigarette?" Rather tensely they leaned forward and fumbled and smiled and inhaled, and the smoke was a cloud around them.

Helen Winston said, "You see, Lona, I wondered about Clyde's marrying a western girl."

Lona looked up and spoke quietly. "What do you mean by a western girl?"

Hesitation. "I don't mean to say that the girls he knew were more desirable. Only different. At home there is a kind of pattern—"

Lona said, "And the girl that Clyde would marry would be in the pattern. Good family, probably a rich family."

"Yes. I suppose so. But that makes us look rather like snobs."

"No, I don't think so. You've told me whom you expected Clyde to marry. That's frank. I can be just as frank and tell you that we are the oldest family here, but more than that. We have acres. Here it is acres that count."

"About the acres," Helen Winston said.

"Yes?"

"Well, I'm not a business woman, but I've been around business. I'm not a rancher, but ranching is a business."

"Of course it is."

"Well," Helen Winston said. She looked at her rings, at her capable hands. "I've noticed this and that. You're a brave girl, Lona."

Lona got up from the bed. Outside it was thawing, but her hands were cold. She curled her fingers inside her palms to warm them. Would it be this easy? Would it be right now?

"My grandfather—" she said slowly. "I've had a lot to straighten out."

"I know." The older woman's eyes were kind. "And Clyde is so impractical. It wouldn't occur to him to tell you. But after I spoke to your mother I felt better about it. She seemed so sure you loved him."

"My mother?"

Helen Winston stubbed out her cigarette. "Please don't mind," she said, "my thinking it would make a difference—that Clyde has nothing. My dear, I understand. When his father died I was left without a penny. I never had anything until I married my present husband. So you see, I do understand."

She got up then and came to Lona and put her strong hand on the girl's arm. "You're a fine girl, Lona."

Lona smiled. Somehow, she smiled. "Thank you," she said, "but there hasn't been any question of his money."

She rose and walked to the window, and there outside were the acres, white and shiny with snow, and slipping away from her. Anybody could see. And Clyde. She thought of his thinness, of the close smell of a bed that two have slept in. He had cheated her. He had cheated her from the beginning.

She said, "The Barts have never thought much about money."

She turned then, her hand tight on the windowsill, and looked at his mother, the expensive woolen suit, the soft leather bag and gloves. The perfumed smell of money. She hated her.

"It doesn't matter at all," she said. "I can afford him."

C H A P T E R 27 The calendars from the Sentinel Bottling Works showed a scene of cherry trees flushed with blossoms, and a pretty girl with an armful of pussywillows. It was April.

On the south slopes the water ran down under the snow, eating it, then long brown fingers appeared on hillsides, creeping up and up, then whole brown hands. In the valley the corrals were deep with mud and manure, small ponds low in back pastures reflected animals walking slow in the sun.

You can't come in here with your feet like that.

Well, what's a fellow going to do?

That broom there, and sack—want some coffee?

Roads were deep with ruts, and holes bottomless, and chains of cars loose on the tires. Ka-*bang*. Ka-*bang*. Ka-*bang*.

Mrs. and Mr. Daniel Irwin were in Sentinel Monday, transacting business.

Several people from the upper valley were in Sentinel to attend the party at the high school. A good time. . . .

Mrs. Lona Barrows was in town from her ranch, transacting business.

Clyde had minded. Lona's husband. Lona Bart Barrows. Yet he knew it would be like that. The valley wouldn't put him in a Bart's place. Not right away. Not yet.

He thought about it at night in the bedroom, in that still awk-

ward moment when he got in bed with her. She slept on the outside, manlike. That told him that he could accept favors, and
demand nothing.

The café adjoining the Sentinel Hotel was so successful that
now the formal dining room off the lobby was seldom used except
for gatherings of the Rotarians every Wednesday at twelve-fifteen,
and meetings of the Ranchers' Association. During the week the
darkened windows made almost invisible the two long tables and
the stiffly placed chairs. The walls were of dark red calcimine,
and the bracket lamps here and there on the wall were entwined
with artificial grape vines, the leaves dusty and stiff and edged
with gilt.

On one wall was the head of a thin elk, the glass eyes glazed
and frightened, left from a day when the Elks had met at the
Sentinel. The manager was rather proud of the head. The prongs
on each antler were tipped with tiny red bulbs which lighted
when a cord was plugged in.

Here the ranchers came once a month to talk about range and
prices and land banks, stiff, earnest, good men, confused and afraid
to show their fear. Their land was slipping away. Their cattle
were worth nothing. And they knew only the land.

The laughed at the meetings, and drank too much. The years
behind and ahead were one long winter. The cattle were poor, the
snow still deep, and the wind blew cold across the Lost Horse
Valley.

Lona was not surprised when they asked her to join the Association. Her grandfather had been president. Her great-grandfather had founded it. She knew it was her name they wanted.
Her name on a petition to the governor was worth all their names
together. The name Bart still had a little magic in Montana.

And yet—she was flattered.

She worked hard. She kept the minutes of meetings. She wrote
letters. The old Pierce-Arrow took her from ranch to ranch to talk
over range problems and bills of the legislature. Once the Association sent her to the capital.

She compiled figures. Each night she went through the newspapers comparing cattle prices at Minneapolis and St. Louis,

watched for trends and made her plans, there in the office upstairs.

Cold in that room, and damp, but the ledgers were there, the tax figures, the bills. And there was something about working there in a room surrounded by things of the Barts, maps of the ranch, pictures of important men the Barts had known.

Cold up there. She couldn't remember when the small wood stove had been lighted. Almost hopeless, the plans in that cold room.

But—

She knew her feeling for the ranch. She knew she would be nothing without it. She got deep pleasure in going to the meetings at the hotel.

They were always so glad to see her. Why, they thought, if a woman could weather the times . . .

And she knew it was not for herself that she felt pride in going there, a part of the almost hopeless plans, but pride in the Barts. And each night, through her closed door she could hear Clyde across the hall in the bedroom, the dull tapping of his typewriter.

He wasn't sure when he decided to begin writing again. He wasn't sure where he got the idea that would bring unity to his book. He told himself it couldn't be that easy, the simple following of a theme that occurred and reoccurred. He was suspicious, but it seemed to work.

There was doubt, and he worked haltingly, found he had to twist the theme, torture it, but it seemed to work.

He wrote in the evenings after supper, and the tapping of his portable was faint in the long hall upstairs, through the heavy door. The small light dangling from the twisted green cord in the bedroom was hard on his eyes. The shadow of his head fell against the yellow paper, but he said nothing about a table lamp. There would have been curiosity, questions. He wasn't yet sure.

Now the rewriting of the novel was a rite. Better let Lona think he was writing letters until he could hand her the revised manuscript complete, finished, and *good*. She might not understand it, it might puzzle her, but she was smart: she'd know it was good. A wife would know.

Writing there, he sometimes smiled at his male need to impress her. The ruffled plumage of male birds, the bellow of male animals. A boy frantic on the trapeze. A man with his work . . .

The roots of it? In a woman.

And he was learning self-criticism.

"Why does old Art cut kindling better than I?"

He spent hours helping old Art at the woodpile, talking to him, and Art happily told his kindling secrets.

"That Mrs. Dean," said Art, "does sure like to see good kindling."

He watched Joe Martin mount a horse, tried again and again to match the strange catlike grace. And couldn't—quite.

But it was the book that counted. He tapped a power to criticize it, a power that grew in the fallow silence of the old house, the long quiet hours after six. The floor around the table was littered each night with sheets of yellow paper, bad lines, dead phrases, whole scenes in confusion, stripped bare, and a theme added, the story of a boy fighting to grow up. And out of each evening's work came a page or two of solid work.

Some nights when he finished he sat listening to the electric light engine, putt-putt-putt, hoping Lona would come see him there before the typewriter, see the coffee cup, the cigarette butts on the tray, see him working at a craft where he was master.

And he smiled, a small boy frantic on the trapeze.

His shadow fell against the yellow paper, his lips would move. "I think it's right. Right . . ."

The lamp appeared suddenly.

There it was, an old goosenecked lamp he had once seen in Tom Bart's office, a lamp that had lighted the paper for Tom Bart's letters to friends, and before that the deeds to twenty thousand acres, the strong hand and seal ring of old Tom Bart.

If the novel had talked before, it sang now.

Barrows was a name too. She'd see. Look at this book. And she knew Barrows was a name; knew what he was doing up there in that room, making a possession, the name of Barrows. She hadn't come to him because she was afraid to disturb him. Afraid, but proud.

He tried to catch her eye, to accept her gesture, but got no sign, no movement of eye or lip. Too intimate a thing, that lamp. She was not confident with intimacy. But now in the bedroom he felt a new strength, a new consciousness of his body.

She was just across the hall.

He had heard her come up and go into the office and shut the door. He had hoped for a minute that she would come in and find him there, working on the last page. She hadn't.

Afraid of disturbing him.

Ruth had gone for a walk. He had heard the closet door open in the hall, heard coat hangers whisper, the big door click shut. Mrs. Dean had finished the supper dishes. No sound from the kitchen but the growling of the hot water tank behind the stove.

He sat a moment at his table upstairs looking out the window at the peaks sharp in the new moonlight, still white above timberline. He felt the weight in his hands. His book.

He savored a moment the table where he wrote, memorized the planes and surfaces of the battered little typewriter, fixed his eyes on the coffee cup.

The manuscript was heavy in his hands. A strange introspective work to have finished in this house where even the furniture seemed frozen by taboos. So far, here, from people who understood the agony and indecision and triumph of a book.

But *she* would understand. Lona knew accomplishment.

He turned off the gooseneck lamp, feeling the heat of the bulb in his hand, the warmth of understanding. He wondered if she knew just how much it had meant. Curious thing, light.

Now the room was in darkness.

He stood at the top of the stairs before going down the hall, looked down at the heavy plush draperies on the windows, at the worn plush carpet on the stairs, at the portrait down there, at the cold green eyes.

His book was heavy, solid under his arm. Heavy with the weight of his blood.

He moved along the upstairs hall.

Now he stood before the door of the office. So many closed doors in the house. Everyone so conscious of doors. You always knocked. You were always afraid of something you might see.

He knocked.

Her voice said, "Come in."

He stood smiling in the door. Heavy, the book.

The room was cold. The stove was cold. She was sitting at the desk, a coat thrown around her shoulders, capelike. The room was cold, and the small black woodstove in the corner. Nobody ever remembered stoves in the Bart house.

And then he thought of his book.

She looked up. "Oh. I didn't expect to see you." Then, "Clyde, I'm sort of cold."

He said, "I'll fix the stove right up. Look," he said. "I'm finished."

"Finished? Oh," she said. Her eyes moved back to the newspaper.

He said, "I've got it here, and wanted to show you."

He held the heavy cardboard box a moment, almost hating to give it up.

She looked up again, frowning a little. "Wanted to—show me?"

He grinned. "My book."

He was beside her, and held it before him with both hands. "I want you to read it. I want you to tell me what you think. I've got a lot of faith—"

She pulled the coat about her shoulders. She said, "Is that what you've been doing in there?"

He nodded. "Yes."

She glanced at the stove, and back. She spoke suddenly. "Clyde, can I talk to you?"

He still held the book, awkward now, because he had held it out and it wasn't taken.

Her voice was quiet, earnest. "I don't know," she said. "Maybe your—book, you call it—is pretty good." She kept watching him, hesitating.

He said, "I know—"

She said, "Look, darling, don't you think—trying to write—is a pretty poor excuse for—" She was smiling, trying to make him understand. "Look. Here I am, sitting here, trying to keep this place going, figuring." Smiling to make him understand.

He remembered her hands, strong and quiet on the desk. A pen there for checks. A calendar for decisions. A coat about her shoulders, and the cold stove. Then the strain was gone from her voice, and she spoke lightly, chidingly.

"By the way," she said, "I notice you've taken my lamp. I don't mind working here," she said, "by the overhead light. But Clyde, it was my grandfather's. I sort of like to keep those things together in here—" She was smiling again to help him see. "If you don't mind."

CHAPTER 28 The bedroom of old Bert Bart had a certain magnificence. Each piece of furniture was of black walnut, stained almost ebony, heavily waxed and polished. There was never any question of moving anything: it took two men to carry even the smallest piece, the commode, the top a thick slab of marble. Two chests of drawers were as high as a man's shoulders. The bed was seven feet long, and there seemed to be no way of taking it apart. The headpiece was carved with a hunting scene. Draperies and glass curtains were drawn, carpets were so thick that even bold footsteps were apologetic.

That spring, Lona slept in there alone.

She had caught a cold. She said she couldn't sleep with anyone when she had a cold. Besides, she was tired, terribly tired, working like a man all spring. Only Joe Martin worked harder.

Clyde had smiled a little when she spent the first night there, conscious of the bigness of the room, of the theatrics of moving in there where the first and greatest Bart had slept. The hour before bedtime was now awkward and strained, sixty minutes pregnant with possible sarcasm. And Clyde's smile.

She said, "You know how you feel when you get a cold."

He said, "I know how you feel."

She had started to speak, angry, but—there was nothing to say.

She had begun sleeping there when she got the first plain envelope from a Wyoming town. It contained only a newspaper clipping.

"The winner in the finals . . . an Idaho man, Rohn, who looks as if he has a chance. . . ."

Then a second envelope came, a picture this time, from another town farther north. Not a good picture, a newspaper photograph, but it had caught his smile and the set of his shoulders.

"Sure," he would have said. "Go ahead and take the picture.' He was proud and self-conscious and boyish.

She kept the clippings between the pages of a magazine there by the bed; they were dog-eared now, for she read them by the light of the candle on the little black stand. She read and touched the clippings (his tongue had run along the envelope flap, tasted the glue) shutting out every other thought. She carried the dream of him close during the days, speaking seldom.

Maybe she was queer. She had a new consciousness of her body when she bathed, a new fastidiousness. The idea of any man but Eddie sleeping with her . . .

She could almost see the hurt look in Eddie's eyes.

Well . . .

If only there were a woman to talk to, to reassure her—to say her feelings were not twisted and queer.

One night she took a careful bath. Clyde was downstairs, and Ruth, and occasionally the piano sounded—those same scales her mother had been playing these last weeks, and simple little pieces. She could hear them talking when the piano stopped, voices hovering over the echo of strings and sounding board.

She put on a fresh nightgown and went quietly to her own room where the bottle of perfume was and dabbed a bit behind her ears. She stood before her mirror, her long bobbed hair brushed, the nightgown white. Then she took the candle to her great-grandfather's room, and got into bed.

She reached out for the magazine, opened it to where the clippings bulged. She touched them, held them in her moist hands, and lay back quietly a few moments. Then she blew out the candle and waited, holding the clippings.

It was almost like touching him. He was there with her, the strength of him, the warmth of him, his long legs pressing, his thighs, his weight on her pressing out her breath.

She heard Clyde coming them. She called softly, "Clyde."

She heard him hesitate and then walk down the hall toward her. She held the clippings until his figure was in the doorway, and then she slipped them inside the magazine. "Clyde."

"Yes, Lona."

"Clyde, I heard you talking."

"Yes."

"Clyde, darling. Come here."

"All right. What is it?"

"Clyde." She groped for something to say. "Why don't we—go somewhere tomorrow? To the Irwins'. We haven't called on them."

"I didn't know you liked them."

"You make me out pretty bad." She watched him. He had the shape of a man.

"All right," he said. He half turned toward the door.

"Clyde." She reached out her hand. "Please stay here tonight."

He said, "How about your cold?"

"Darling," she said. "Don't talk about that. Just—just come here."

Charley Evans, Danny Irwin's hired man, wheeled a barrow of manure out the back door of the barn. He let the handles drop and stood smelling the palms of his hands. Damned if you couldn't smell spring in manure.

Charley Evans had always hated everybody. His gray mustache made him look tired and sad, but his eyes were bright and sharp, watching for the meanness in people. It always showed up. He had watched the Irwins, too.

And now—

Well, damn it, he was soft. He spit in his hands and took the handles of the barrow. He was doing twice the work they paid him for—and they couldn't pay much. He told them they paid him plenty. But he owed the doctor for that bladder trouble and his little insurance policy didn't come free. His friends laughed at him in bars. And his obligation to his niece.

Maybe he disliked his sister and her husband as much as anyone. They were always butting into his business, writing him at Christmas and his birthday (they always got it wrong) advising him in this and that. They had been surprised to hear from him.

"I never liked you much," the letter told them, "especially

Henry. But I am sending thirty dollars that I will try to send every month until you say stop for my niece to be a nurse."

You see, Mrs. Irwin was a nurse.

They were playing a game at the Irwins', all three of them, pretending Danny wasn't sick, that he did much of the work, and Charley told at the supper table how Danny helped move the cattle, how Danny helped haul poles to fence a stack yard, how Danny ran the haycrew.

But Betty Irwin knew. She knew the debt she owed Charley Evans was as great as the debt she owed the Barts.

They pretended it wasn't strange to eat breakfast late some mornings, not strange that Danny and his wife slept on the porch all winter. The extra meal at midafternoon was called tea, and it was made jolly and comfortable.

They pretended there were never times when the light burned all night, when there were spasms of coughing.

The small house was neat and polished, and the furniture painted in bright colors. There were plants in bright pots, geraniums, nasturtiums, ivy, all carefully planned to screen away fear, the fear that never left Betty Irwin.

She felt she had always known death. In the white order of the hospital where she had worked, when the visitors whispered and tiptoed and doors closed softly, a thought kept flashing.

In some room, someone is dying.

When someone was dying they put a clean white screen around the bed so others couldn't see—the last little privacy of someone who had built a house, tasted coffee, turned on a light, expected someone on a train, someone who had loved. When they put the screen around—their rubber soles silent—she would go to the lavatory and stand there, washing her hands over and over.

There always seemed to be a screen around Danny. She painted furniture, planned colors, changed the flowers, and made things match.

"Dan's getting so brown!" But when he rode away from the ranch on his gentle horse with Charley, then she remembered his eyes and his cheeks and his stoop.

She liked to tint the photographs that Danny took, and at night they discussed them; some they were going to send away to a magazine.

They had an old victrola in the corner of the living room, and that corner she called the music room: "Mighty Lak a Rose," and a funny record called "Cohen at the Telephone."

There were magazines, and they belonged to a book club (it took their last cent). There was usually a new book on the small low table, for she was proud of what she called "keeping up with Dan."

The table was cream with red trim that week, and she had put a book on it the day Clyde and Lona called. Not a new book, Dan said. It was called a dividend by the club, an extra, a great heavy book in a special box, and it had upset her. But Dan said it was an important book, so she felt she ought to keep it out.

The book was called *An American Tragedy*.

They found her on her knees busy with a tiny plot of garden. She had empty seed packages skewered into the brown earth on sharp little sticks. She wore overalls and canvas gloves.

She said, "I'm glad you came today. Dan's out with Charley doing something, and I wished somebody would come." Her smile was quick and lively.

Clyde grinned. "I'd forgotten that people visit."

"We thought we'd come over," Lona said. Her hands felt big. "You've a nice little place here."

Betty Irwin said, "That's what your grandfather used to say. He used to come often. I miss him."

Lona said, "We can't stay long. Spring is busy." She felt stiff and tall.

"It won't take a minute to fix coffee," Betty Irwin said.

She talked from the bright kitchen, calling from the sink with the ivy on the sill, waxy-green in the sun. The shelves under the sink were green too. They heard drops of water hiss on the stove. "How do you like that color I've got the table now? That cream and red."

Clyde called in, "Fine. I was thinking, if you got curtains with stripes like that candy we used to get."

Her laughter came so easy. "Do you remember that candy? Yes, curtains like that." She appeared in the doorway. "I'll get out the Sears Roebuck." And then, "What do you think about it, Mrs. Barrows?"

Lona said, "I'm afraid I don't know much about curtains." Her hands felt so rough and big.

Betty Irwin came in with a tray. "Of course you don't. You don't have time for nonsense. I haven't had time to learn about ranching. Not that I ever will. But Dan—Dan's learning." Her eyes lit up. "He's a regular rancher now. We're getting along so fine, the ranch clear and Dan just fine, getting so brown. My, he's like a regular Indian, riding and getting so brown." Just a shadow across her eyes. "Sugar and cream?"

They talked. They leaned forward.

Betty Irwin said, "The friendliness here is what I like. In the city nobody knows you. But here—" She looked into her coffee. "We came so close to making a blunder when we came. I guess we did make the blunder, but friendliness—wonderful friendliness —saved us."

Lona had one hand on the arm of her chair. She was watching it. She looked up. Clyde said, "A blunder?"

Betty Irwin hesitated, afraid for a moment to show this stupidity. "We didn't know, you see. We didn't know. He must have told you."

Clyde said, "Dan? Dan must have told us?"

"No. Your grandfather, Mrs. Barrows. About the water."

Lona moved her fingers. "The water?"

"Yes. And your grandfather—I remember how big he seemed, sitting there in his office, and how afraid I was because everybody knows about the Barts."

Lona moved her shoulders. "What did he do? My grandfather?"

"Well, I never got it straight. But—we had no water for the land here. He—you know how he was. He let us use his." She grew serious. "You see why I like to give his granddaughter a cup of coffee."

The sun through the clean windows made a long tongue of light across the carpet toward the cream and red table. Clyde spoke suddenly.

"Who's reading that?"

"Oh," Mrs. Irwin. "That book. Would you like to look at it?"

"I've read it," Clyde said. "But Lona—" he turned to her. "Have you read it?"

Lona said, "You know I never read anything."

Betty Irwin said, "Why don't you take it with you?"

Lona took the book and weighed it in her hands, and looked at the title. She hesitated. Clyde said, "Go head, Lona. There's a lot more to living than working." He smiled. "When you get as old as I am you'll know."

Lona shrugged. "All right." She put the book beside her.

Betty Irwin spoke cautiously. "Did you like—the book, Mr. Barrows?"

"Yes. I suffered. The man was my namesake, wasn't he?"

"Yes," Betty Irwin said. "Clyde. But not like you, not at all." She made a little face. "Like your wife, I never read at all before I—but I hate this book."

"Maybe you hated it," Clyde said, "but it's a good study of what blood and background can do."

Clyde talked, and in that bright desperately cheerful room the book came alive, the shabbiness, the hunger, the twisted thinking, the despondent shrug of shoulders, loveliness rotted by perversion. There in that room rose the dark of tenement halls, the stench of dirty clothes and urine. Jesus Christ and shabby people huddled in public toilets.

Betty Irwin said, "But what made him—to the girl?"

"Made him kill her? It was what he thought he had to do."

And there it was, a man sick with weakness, and lust, and ego. There was the rowboat in the water, and the depths of the water.

"He was crazy," Mrs. Irwin said. "Wasn't he?"

"Crazy? No. Afraid."

The wife of Danny Irwin looked out the clean window at the clean land, at the spring in the valley. "I don't think people do that. People can get things without—that."

"It's not that simple. People are what they are. You can't know what a child saw and remembered—the sound of the past he keeps hearing."

The silence was heavy. Lona spoke suddenly. "I'll read it."

Betty Irwin said, "We haven't spoiled it for you, I hope."

"No."

Clyde grinnned at Mrs. Irwin, and tension was gone. "She won't read it. I haven't seen her with anything but one magazine for weeks."

"No. I'll really read it."

"You'll work with your ledgers."

"Well, I have to do that."

There was a moment before Mrs. Irwin turned to them, a moment when her eyes were intent on the land outside—frightening, tentative land, only real because of a man. The afternoon sun spilled into the room and glinted on the coffee pot and cups. New, cheap cups, and cream colored, with little red flowers.

CHAPTER The branding corrals were ten miles from the house, near the foothills where the drainage was good, a gaunt, lonely enclosure most of the year. But now in May the corrals were alive with bawling cows and the noise rose with the dust and moved out over the valley, smokelike. In smaller corrals calves milled around the fence, and in the center of one was the fire, blazing and crackling, and the heads of the irons in it, B for Bart.

A man rode among the calves, roped one by the hind legs and dragged it struggling and bellowing to the fire. Another man threw the calf on its side, a third helped to hold it down.

Then the iron, the burning of hair (see how yellow, how solid the smoke is where the iron hits), the searing of flesh, slick and raw beneath the red iron. Then the castration, the scrotum held with the thumb and first two fingers, the knife, and then the blood oozing down the leg. Joe Martin castrated, and he threw the testicles into the fire where they roasted and burst, white and puffy.

Lona watched from the top pole of the fence, her red shirt the only brightness in the gray, dusty corral, and a hot little breeze tugged at her full sleeves. There was something good about seeing all the cows and calves in the corrals there below you, to look up and see your land around you, as near as you could get to having it in the palm of your hand.

She made the little clutching gesture, watching.

Clyde was throwing calves, and when he put his weight against them the cords of his neck stood out. His face was dirty, streaked with sweat, his lips cracked. She watched, and a smile crossed her face.

She climbed down quickly from the fence and walked over to the fire. She said, "I'll get my horse. I'll rope awhile."

She caught Joe Martin's eye, glanced at Clyde, then back again to Joe, and smiled a secret smile. Joe Martin winked and felt the blade of his knife with his thumb.

She began to rope, threw the rope easily with a free wrist motion. She hardly ever missed the big calves. They were branding faster now. She kept watching Clyde, the cords in his neck, the little uncontrolled motion after the weight of each calf, the way his arms dropped for a second after each one, paralyzed, useless for a moment. She brought calves in faster. Clyde was breathing through his mouth, licking his cracked lips and spitting, but there was no spit.

Now the other men caught on. She was joshing her husband. Even the Kid was grinning, carrying the branding irons faster and faster. It was a funny thing to see a man over thirty begin to stagger a little after each calf.

She tired of it suddenly. "I'm through roping now."

She led her horse out of the corral and climbed up on the top pole, looking out. The sage was blooming now in late May, and the gray-green grew fainter and softer toward the mountains, and the lines of the hills were fuzzy and fluid. Then the mountains, and she could almost feel the cool wind in the pines, the sudden coolness of a little park there where the snow still lay deep, where springs ran out from under clear and cold, up there where the Bart cattle would range in a few days.

It was like having everything in the palm of your hand.

She needed thoughts like that, reassurances of her strength, for there was the note held in the bank in Sentinel.

Sometimes it seemed hopeless. She sent down five hundred head of cows the fall before at twenty dollars each. It cost her more than that to raise them. Fences were sagging, no money for poles and wire. She skimped and saved on everything and was so coldly reasonable when Ruth asked her once for the fifty dollars of the will that Ruth never asked her again, but waited until those times when Lona gave her three dollars or five dollars.

"Here's a little something we can do without, I guess."

Ruth had begun to appear around the house in clothes meant for town or traveling.

But Lona had symbols that gave her courage. One was the portrait. She always glanced at it when she went upstairs. Another was the house, heavy and grand, and durable as the hills. Another was Bart Street in Sentinel.

And there was the humidor.

It had belonged to Tom Bart, a heavy metal tin, like a tobacco can, but the top was bronzed, and the sides were covered with pigskin. He used to keep cigars there, Coronas. In the top was a blotter behind a piece of screen, and he used to put a little rum on it, or sherry, to keep the cigars properly moist. The humidor was almost hidden behind a stack of books on the top of the bookcase, *Grasses of the Western United States, The Winning of Barbara Worth*, some cattle and boot catalogs, Blucher's, Hamley's.

It had always been a secret place, a place to think about because you were forbidden to go there, but even as a little girl she had gone there, and slipped the red and gold bands from the cigars and hidden them, and counted them, used them for chains, used them for rings, too big for even her thumb.

There were still one or two cigars there, but now she hid money there, and when she put the money in a little excitement rose in her. She waited always until the room was empty. No one had ever seen. Small sums, a little change she had extra when she came back from town, a few quarters, halves, dollar bills, silver dollars, even a five dollar bill. Once she had bought a part for the car with the money, once a part for a mowing machine. The sum never amounted to more than fifty dollars, but it was a symbol. Of strength, of courage.

And of secrecy.

No one dusted there. No one knew. She could look up from her place beside the stove and see it, without seeming to, and it satisfied her. There were a lot of things people didn't know about. There were a lot of things they didn't know she thought and planned.

She had no interest in the movie that was playing in Sentinel although it was one of the new ones, a talkie, and they had just gotten the equipment at the Hartwig Theatre a year before.

"I thought you didn't like movies," she told Clyde. "You always said you didn't."

"Well, I like them now. And we could have dinner at the Sugar Bowl." He spoke a little sarcastically, she thought. "We can have a regular blowout."

"You always said you didn't like movies, only plays."

"There are no plays here. Not even *Uncle Tom*. It's all relative. Here I like movies."

"But the movie's two weeks away."

He was a little crestfallen. "I thought we might make our plans and get some fun out of it."

"I'd rather not go, Clyde. They hurt my eyes."

"Well," he said, "maybe your mother will go."

Lona laughed a little. "I don't think a movie and the Sugar Bowl is her idea of fun."

"I wonder," Clyde said. "I wonder."

She thought no more about it. She began to get the machinery ready for another haying, and rode out after the horses in the hills. Joe Martin was going to break some to the wagon, and it excited her to think that in a few days she would be up there in a wagon racing along like the wind behind an untamed colt that dragged the wagon and the gentle wheel-horse as well.

She had let another man go—there were only five left—and made up for it by learning about the machinery, about the gears of a mowing machine, the transmission of the tractor.

She didn't notice particularly when a box came from a dress shop in Sentinel, addressed to Ruth, a shop at which she had closed the Bart account.

Clyde and Ruth left the ranch for Sentinel and the movie one evening after supper. The sun had just gone down and the sky over the peaks was flame-colored, and on the tops of the foothills, on the flat planes, there were jagged gold patches like fields, and higher up the shadows of the sunset were purple, soft, like mantles. The killdeers had begun to sing, and their song had a moist quality, like the mist from the creek.

Clyde had put the top down on the car and the old Pierce purred along. Ruth sat beside him in a suit of light green wool, and her dark eyes shown with pleasure.

"You don't know how much I've been thinking about this, Clyde. It's the kind of an evening when there's excitement in the air. As if something would happen." She breathed deeply.

He said, "I've felt that way too. I've been reading the advertisements for the movie. Bebe Daniels and John Boles at the peak of their careers. According to the *Sentinel Examiner.*"

"Yes," Ruth said. "And the technicolor is superb, the very peak of the cameraman's art. Magnificent scenes, tastefully arranged . . ."

They laughed and lit cigarettes, and the sky was flame and the motor purred. "We'll make the second show," Clyde said. "And then," he paused significantly. "Late supper at the Sugar Bowl."

Ruth said, impressed, "I can't believe it."

"But you must. A tempting array of dishes to choose from, subtly seasoned."

"Yes," said Ruth, "and handsomely served up. Oh, Clyde, it's not for the likes of us."

"We can hope, Ruth." They laughed until Ruth's dark eyes were moist.

They sat in elegance in a loge, two wicker chairs with fairly comfortable seats, twenty-five cents extra. They exclaimed over the organ pipes, gilded, high on either side of the screen, and the puffy-cheeked cherubs with trumpets on the ceiling.

"Of course," Ruth said, "you realize that this magnificence is an old story to me. I have been often to this theater."

And then it was the last scene, the entire cast on the screen, and singing.

Life's completer, Rita, when you are near. . . .
All I ask from above
Is one day your lips will say I love you. . . .

They lingered for a moment in the loges, then walked out, the last ones, alone. The little ticket booth out front was deserted, dark. They stood under the marquee, dark now, and a man with a ladder was changing the lettering. By the light of a distant swinging street lamp they watched him reach in a box for the big black letters.

SUNNY SIDE UP

Somewhere the motor of a car fired, gears ground in the distance. The man folded his ladder and vanished, a phantom.

The silence of twelve o'clock in a little town began. The theater was on a narrow alley and they looked up it. There was a rickety zigzag of stairs leading to a door on the back of an old brick build- ing, and at the top of the door a weak electric light glimmered. The door opened.

Now a man stood on the steps, and a woman in the door. "So long," she said clearly.

And the man, only a dark shape, stood there. "So long, Alma." In a moment he turned and walked down, his steps sounding wooden on the stairs. The door closed above him. He stood a mo- ment looking up, and then walked down the alley. In a few moments Clyde and Ruth began to walk too.

There was night life in Sentinel, and those who were part of it gathered at the Sugar Bowl Café; brakemen on freight cars, the night telegrapher, the girls from the Dixie Rooms, truck drivers, people on a party.

They had a camaraderie. They knew the strangeness of the night, the look of a car parked in an alley, a cat's prowling, branches mov- ing over the face of a street lamp. They knew the shadows and told time by the moon.

They were gay, and rapped on their coffee cups with spoons, and many of them had been drinking. Women were easy to talk to, for early in the morning women are lonely and insecure. They ate steaks and apple pie. They were sentimental, and almost every night they sang, sentimental songs a few years old, a dream they had almost realized, happiness never forgotten. Outside the streets were dark and silent, and the windows of the stores and houses were blind with night.

There was a row of booths along the wall, little cubicles with heavy monk's cloth curtains, almost all pulled, and inside men leaned across the tables on their elbows, their shirts unbuttoned, and women crossed their legs and showed the inside of their thighs; there was tenderness and intimacy. Over the tops of the booths cigarette smoke floated up to the grease-smoked ceiling that was geometrically flowered in metal bas-relief. Sharp women's laughter, scraping of chairs, and a voice low, telling a story, or a lie.

The waitress was big and tall and blond, and her face was blurred with powder. It stuck in the down on her cheeks and altered the shape of her mouth and crusted a little around her lipstick.

She pointed to one of the booths. "There's a party in there from Salt Lake, traveling man, a regular card." She smiled archly, and rested the point of her pencil against her pad. "What you folks having?"

Clyde and Ruth sat at the counter. Clyde said, "What's good?"

The waitress said, "Steaks."

"Steaks," Clyde said. "Rare."

"Nobody has them rare," the waitress said, and waited.

Ruth said, "Let's have them the way they're having them."

"Okie-doke," the waitress said. "And—?"

Clyde said, "French fries."

"No," the waitress said. "I wouldn't tonight. He gets mad. He don't like to fix French fries tonight."

"He?"

"The cook. They kept ordering French fries last night and he said damned if he'd fix any more. A traveling party from Idaho Falls said by God he'd fix them himself and went in the kitchen, he'd been hitting the bottle, and him and the cook bawling around the kitchen, and finally the traveling party left. I wouldn't order French fries."

Clyde said, "What are *they* having?"

"Hash-brown. He likes to fix hash-brown."

There was a phonograph in the back, and a good-looking girl

came out from the curtains of a booth and put a record on. She danced tight against the man who followed her out. They went back in. Somebody began to sing in the back booth. The other booths took it up. The woman sang a kind of alto, and there were whiskey tenors.

> *Remember the night, the night you said*
> *I love you—remember?*

Clyde and Ruth hummed, and as the singing died away, Ruth stubbed out her cigarette and watched it.

The waitress came near. "Always liked that song. Takes a body back." She moved down the counter and stood looking a moment at the wall.

Clyde said, "I wonder what it takes her back to?"

Ruth kept watching the stubbed cigarette. "To a car beside a dance hall, and the lights coming out, and there was this man. And this night."

Clyde said, "You're the first woman I could ever talk to."

She was lovely. Her eyes were grave. "Thank you."

The waitress kept standing there. Ruth said, "What do you suppose happened to the man?"

Clyde said, "He was ambitious. He got another job. New circle of friends."

"And the old circle?"

"He was her circle," Clyde said.

"But she saw him once after that."

Clyde's eyes were serious. "How did you know? Yes, she saw him that one time. She could tell the set of his shoulders. She remembered that."

Ruth said, "Do you suppose he remembers?"

"I don't know. He's gone a long way. New faces—new things. You know."

Ruth said, "I wonder if she still hopes—someday—"

He started to speak, and kept looking at her.

The motors of cars sound good at night in the cool moist air. Ruth said, "There is something I want to ask you." There was only the light from the dashboard. "I've always been afraid to ask. Afraid of the truth, I suppose. I'm not afraid, now."

Clyde looked straight ahead at the road where a jack rabbit bounced blindly before the car. He slowed up. The rabbit bounced into the ditch. "Ask me."

"Well. You've heard me play."

"Yes."

She said, "I'm not young. I'm past thirty-six."

He spoke slowly. "I'm older at thirty-one."

"No. But—do you think there's a chance for me to go away—and teach?" She fumbled for words now. "Just—children. Nothing grand. I don't have grand ideas now. But—could I?"

He was silent. She waited, her face turned toward him, the dashlight soft on her cheek. Then he said, "Yes, you could. But it's more than your playing. There's something in you that youth can understand. I used to think that was a disadvantage. But it isn't, Ruth. By God, it isn't."

She had turned a little, watching him. "You really mean that, don't you?"

"I've thought about you a long time. Once I asked you—why you stayed. Remember? And then I didn't even know—"

"You didn't know then—?"

"What kind of woman you were." His hands were tight on the thick wheel of the old Pierce-Arrow. He stared ahead. The low black hills moved beside them.

He said, "The kind of woman who sees a man working, and brings a lamp to him."

She kept looking at the glove in her hand, pulling at the fingers. She said, "It wasn't generosity." She turned back in the seat, watching the road. "I'd read your book. Took a chapter, when you didn't know." He could hardly hear. "I didn't mean to pry. It's only—" He strained to hear. "It's only that I never knew anyone who had your talent. Your courage. I suppose I wanted your courage."

Now the ranch buildings were ahead of them, black planes and angles and bulk, up the twisty little road, and the few scraggly trees whispered against the false dawn. A dog barked. And silence. Then the headlights flowed up against the side of the house, flooded the garage.

They stood by the garage doors a moment, stood with their hands beside them, and there was a moment apart from time. He moved.

She spoke suddenly. "Don't say anything. Please. I'm very happy."

Gravel crunching in the darkness under their feet.

They groped for the light in the hall. Dark shapes of heavy old furniture bulked, and the clock ticked. Through the dining room, through the hall, they saw the blade of light under the kitchen door, sharp and yellow. They moved toward it.

"Somebody forgot . . ."

They were tiptoeing, whispering, their hands before them. Ruth put her hand on the dull glow of the brass doorknob and turned it. The light in the kitchen almost blinded them.

On the table was a cup and saucer. The coffee pot simmered on the stove. And beside the cup and saucer was an ashtray almost filled with stubs. The kitchen was hot, and filled with smoke.

Lona stood, smoking, watching them, and the light from the naked globe on the ceiling glinted on her hair. She was very tall standing there, watching them as they blinked in the light.

"Well," she said.

"Mmmm," Ruth said. "Coffee."

"Smells good," Clyde said.

Lona didn't look at him. "Well, mother. Have a nice time?"

Ruth was puzzled. "Why, yes. Lona, you sound so—funny."

"You had a nice time at the show, and dinner at the Café?"

"Why, yes."

"It must have made a big hit—that green dress."

Ruth was looking down at the dress. Then at Lona. Then away.

Lona went on. "I remember, now, when the box came. From the store. I was too busy to think about it then. Too busy trying to keep this place together. This ranch."

Ruth's hand had moved and found the handle of the coffee pot. Her fingers twisted and moved. "Lona—I have a right—"

Lona seemed to smile. "Just when did you steal the money?"

Ruth kept watching the coffee pot. "Lona, you've never given me—or let me—"

"Tell me. Tell me when you stole it. Did you plan it a long time? And then sneak downstairs, like you used to sneak—"

Clyde spoke suddenly. "Lona. Listen, Lona."

Lona went on. "Some mothers help. My mother—"

Clyde moved. And then turned suddenly and went. He remembered it: Lona tall under the naked light, and Ruth, her shoulders narrow in the green suit, her fingers twisting around the agate handle of the coffee pot.

CHAPTER 30   There was a pleasant nervousness in all the ranch houses in the valley. Ranchers got out their suits from closets, wives got out flat-irons and sponge and pressed, their eyes harried, trying to do many things.

"You always look nice in a store suit, Jim. Don't see why you don't wear a suit more."

"Well, I always hate to leave the place here. Something might come up."

"Oh, now, Jim, you got to get to the bull sale. We need bulls."

"Yes. Yes, I got to do that."

Ranchers always felt guilty about leaving the ranches, guilty about the potted palms in the Butte Hotel, and the big comfortable chairs in the lobby, about the Spanish-looking girl at the cigar counter with her deep, softy voice and her hair all coiled and shiny, the crystal chandeliers in the dining room, the little dark bars where a man can drink.

"Jim, I can't get this spot out. It's paint."

Betty Irwin was sure that Danny's lung was healing. He was standing straighter, for one thing. He was putting on weight. Why, those overalls were almost—almost tight! He didn't cough so much at night, and for some time she had been able to look calmly at the handkerchiefs he hid under his pillow. There were no pink stains.

"Dan," she told him sternly, "I'm tired of washing so many handkerchiefs for a man who doesn't need them. Sick and tired of it!"

"Well," he said, grinning. "Bossy, aren't you!"

She sang and hummed a great deal; when she did the housework she got little flashes of pleasure that left her standing motionless with the mop or broom in her hand, shocked with happiness.

But she had timed the visit to the doctor in Butte carefully, to coincide with the bull sale and the rodeo. Then, you see, if they left the doctor's office silently (and the little meal somewhere when they both tried to smile) then there would be the rodeo to take his mind off the shadows on a square of black glass, the shadows that said you've still got to hope.

That had happened so many times.

In spite of her happiness, she was thin and nervous. Driving their old Dodge, even to Sentinel, exhausted her. On the last trip for the mail an oncoming car had frightened her; she had almost run off the road. She had brought the car to a stop, and sat there trembling. "Oh, I'm sorry, Danny. Sorry." And had begun to cry, there beside the road.

And now: "You'd better let me drive the car to Butte," he told her seriously. "I'm not afraid for me, but for you."

"I'll not let you," she said indignantly. "Maybe you can drive *back* if—if the doctor says." And then she brightened. "And if we need help, Eddie Rohn will be there. It would be nice to ask him to drive us back. He might like to spend a few days with us."

She remembered Eddie—that night in the mud and rain. He helped people. He understood. Why, she wouldn't be afraid to ask him anything. "We could get Eddie, if we needed."

Then there were the clothes that had to be got. She found a small blue hat with a veil and some shoes with three-inch heels in Sentinel. Danny bought a new pair of dress boots and a new Stetson like ranchers wore in town.

She was proud beside him.

You could order suits from Sears Roebuck. On the yellow order-blank it told you how to measure: chest, leg and crotch. Natty blue pin-stripe double-breasted suits. When the suit came you could get the cook to press out the wrinkles from the box.

Mr. Joe Martin, C/O Bart Ranch, Sentinel, Montana.

Lona had gone back to sleeping in her own room. There were no more of those nights she hated, lying there, pretending sleep, pretending she didn't feel Clyde's touch. The issue was never brought bare and squirming to the surface now, as it had been when she had said, "Oh, Clyde—*please*." And had sighed.

He had not spoken, there in the darkness, but lay still for a long time, as if even the further withdrawal of his hand—the whisper it made against the sheet—would be ugly.

It had worried her because she did owe him something. He was a good worker, doing more around the ranch than she had ever believed he would.

But something had happened to him now. He was different. Strangely confident.

Nobody suspected anything when Lona said she was going to the bull sale. She had prepared for the trip: she had sales literature about the house in conspicuous places, pamphlets with pictures of fat bulls standing in straw, and the pedigrees.

Beau Domino 16th, out of Belle Domino and. . . .

The rodeo and Eddie Rohn was not mentioned.

But Clyde wanted to go. Every excuse she could think of for his not going fell through, and she worried at night, wondering how she was going to see Eddie alone. She must, for this was his chance at the championship.

Closer and closer he had edged up to that championship—she knew every show he had ridden in, every prize he had won—not much money, but—fame. She must be with him that night. He would remember that she was with him when he started, when he was just a kid with big hopes—he would remember. She had a *place* in his great hour.

She would think of some way to be with him. If there were no decent way to do it, she would simply tell Clyde.

She shuddered at the bald thing she would have to say.

The morning they were going to Butte the early sun poured in her window, and she stood facing it, stretching her arms to the warmth. *She had a place in somebody's success.* She was going to see him. She had begun to form little sentences and greetings.

"Hello, Eddie. Darling, I haven't seen you . . ."

"Eddie, I waited. I never wanted anyone but you . . ."

"Eddie—you've got to take me."

He must take her. Don't you see when you want to give yourself he's got to take you? They would make some plan together, sitting at a table.

Before she dressed for town she went into the garage to run out the old Pierce. She hadn't opened both garage doors, and there was little light coming through the dusty panes of glass. The place was damp and smelled of dead exhaust smoke, oil, rust. She thought about chains for the Pierce, and remembered another set somewhere in the pile of rubbish and old tires in one corner. She began to pick through the pile of stuff there, coughing in the dust. She found the chains, and turned.

There was a shadow on the wall; she had seen it rise to meet her, looming. She started, and made a little protective motion toward her face.

"Joe!"

His almost lashless eyes watched her, compelled her. His thin lips smiled. "What's wrong?"

She spoke with a trace of hysteria. "Don't do that again!"

"Do what?"

She stammered, flushed. "Sneaking. You sneaked. You don't make any noise."

"Sorry," he said. "I wanted to ask you something."

"Well, don't sneak. What do you want?"

"I want to ride in with you." He made a thin smile, and did something with his eyesbrows. "To the bull sale."

Her mind jumped to the ledgers in the office. He had almost no money coming. He'd bought a saddle, a bridle, and something else. "You haven't enough to go to the Cross-Roads," she said.

"I'll make it," he said.

Her eyes were suspicious. He seemed to know something. Then, "No. I can't let you go now." She felt the walls of the garage around her, and a tension. She found herself waiting for him to speak. And waiting.

He put his hands in his pockets and looked at his boots. "If your husband wasn't to go," he said. "If your husband wasn't to go, he'd be here to look after things."

She glanced at him again, then back to the wall. "You'd have to ask him," she said softly. "It's up—up to him." She stood still, watching the wall. Joe Martin walked toward the house.

Clyde came down in a few minutes. He was shaved, and smelled of the clear green lotion he used. He wore a clean shirt, still open at the throat, ready for a tie. "Lona—would you mind if I didn't go?"

She made a disappointed face. "What's wrong?" Crossly.

"It's Joe. He wants to go. He says he hasn't had a vacation since he came here."

She stooped to pick up the tangled chains. "Yes, not even to Sentinel. That's not my fault. Besides, he didn't come here for a vacation."

"I think you ought to let him go."

She couldn't meet Clyde's eyes. "Well, if you think so. But you're foolish to be so good."

"You don't mind, though?"

"Mind?"

"He wants to ride in with you. You wouldn't—afraid or something?"

She made an impatient gesture.

Now Joe Martin sat stiffly beside her in the front seat of the Pierce. He didn't smoke unless she suggested it and handed him one of her Camels. He was careful about brushing off the ashes from the new double-breasted blue suit.

Happy, she remembered the sun in Sentinel when she stopped there at the bank to cash a check. The sun glinted against the show window of the bookstore next door, and she remembered the color there—the red and blue fountain pens spread out fan-wise, and the jewellike green and blue bottles of ink.

She stepped to the curb. "I'll get you some cash," she said. "A loan. Fifty enough?"

He had made no move to get out of the car. He said, "I can get by. But I need this cashed." His old wallet was limp and tattered.

"Yes," she said, "I'll change it." She took the bill he handed her and started across the walk before she glanced at it. She stopped there in the sun. She glanced back at Joe sitting there in the car, smoking one of her Camels. She came back to him.

She said, "This bill is a hundred. This is the first hundred I've seen since my grandfather died." Her eyes questioned him.

He said, "I didn't get it from your grandfather."

She was about to speak sharply to him for some insolence she sensed, but the sun was bright on the window of the bookstore, and she was going to Butte. She turned and walked inside the bank.

She knew the teller behind the brass gate, a mild, soft-voiced old man with nimble fingers. His eyes were honest and shrewd; she could not account for her nervousness.

"This check," she said. "And I'd like some tens for this." She passed the hundred under the grate.

The old teller took it. She smiled at him. He said, "You don't often see hundreds these days."

She couldn't explain her nervousness. There was no reason to lie, no reason to impress the old teller in the gray coat, but she resented his mild interest.

She spoke stiffly. "My grandfather," she said, "always liked hundreds. He always had them around."

And then the old teller was busy again with his soft nimble fingers. "Hundreds are nice solid bills," he said.

She waved to Joe Martin when she left him in Butte, for he looked lonely standing on the corner there under the big sign of the Rialto, the place where they gambled. She had laughed once before she let him out, as if she were about to speak of the bill, but some perversity, some small twisted secrecy kept her silent.

"Have a good time, Joe," she called to him.

There were others there, hired men in town, shined boots and shoes, stiff blue suits, satin-striped ties, and their big hats. They stood there talking, lonesome for the bunkhouse already. They would blow a summer's check, and then it would be gone. But if they still had a ten-spot they didn't have to sleep alone.

It was a smart shop. Surprising, but there it was, sandwiched between a saloon and a hardware store; an entrance of black shiny tile and chromium, and nothing behind the thick plate glass show window but a single hat, a pair of long gloves, and a flower.

The black-suited saleswoman wore a pince-nez that dangled from a ribbon at her molded breast. There was a heavy carpet, and flowers everywhere.

"Is there something?"

"Yes. A dress. I'd like to buy a dress." *What would he like? Oh, what color would he like?*

The woman raised her brows a little. "What did you have in mind?"

"Oh, I don't know."

The woman looked at the shabby suit, the shabby bag. "Something—reasonable?"

Lona lit a cigarette. "Just let me look." She looked about for an ashtray, her hands shaking a little.

"I'm sorry," the woman said. "But that's rather an expensive suit." Lime green that almost matched her eyes, and a flowing cape.

"How much is it?"

"One hundred and fifty dollars."

"I'll try it on. And shoes. Do you have shoes?"

The woman smiled. "One moment. I'll get Mr. Mann. Mr. Mann is shoes."

There was a little room with drawn curtains, and a long mirror. When Lona came out the woman took a breath and hesitated. "You—you do wear that well. When you came in—"

Lona said, "I know."

The woman was anxious. "You look so lovely," she said. "May I—may I suggest something?"

Lona watched herself in the mirror. "Yes."

The woman made a gesture. "Your hair. If you could have your hair fixed. The bangs—perhaps as they are, but more—even. A little curl at the ends perhaps. Just a bit." There was an eagerness about the woman. "And a beret. This one. You don't mind?"

"Of course not."

"You could model," the woman said. "You look so confident and happy. Perhaps," she said, "perhaps the young man will buy you a flower. Some small white flower."

Lona walked into the hotel, head high, chin up, alive with happiness. She stopped for a moment at the cigar counter, bought cigarettes and a few magazines. That first time—she and Eddie had had cocktails. A champagne cocktail. She tipped the bellboy. "Whiskey," she said. "A quart. And a quart of champagne."

The boy left her. She sat a moment in the overstuffed chair, she picked up a magazine, let her fingers run over the slick cover, and opened it. The story, a boy and girl. The illustration was large and bright colored. It was a good sign, she thought, that the girl looked rather like her—the same hair. An omen. She put the magazine aside and let happiness flood over her. He would be with her in this room. She closed her eyes a moment.

Betty Irwin never remembered coming down the stairs of the doctor's office in Butte.

It was a sprawling old brick building, tenanted by doctors and lawyers, and a mining assay company.

Assayers, she remembered. Assayers, the glass window in the door, pebbled so you couldn't see through, and the gilt lettering. Brown wood paneling in the hall, fresh-varnished brown, and those thin corrugated rubber rugs that ran endlessly through the long halls, the disinfectant and the so distant peck of typewriters.

And she remembered a wicker chair, and Danny beside her, an old ashtray on a thin stand between them, the tray filled with butts. They were supposed to go down into the tray when you pressed something, and she had tried and tried. Wouldn't work. And there were the gray faces in the reception room, the blank faces. Old copies of *Field and Stream. National Geographic.*

Danny had grinned at her. "These sure are old magazines," he said. She had smiled. Her confidence was gone now. This was the fourth time in that office, waiting for a word that would never be said. The same magazines, the same faces. But not the same hope.

"Look at this cartoon," Danny said, leaning close. "See?" He had laughed softly.

She smiled. *How cold your hands get. . . .*

Do you know how much I love you? If I told you, you would be afraid. You would know I couldn't live . . .

"And look at this one," Danny said. He leaned close, pointed to the cartoon. How white his hands were, through the roughness. He'd worked too hard. He'd tried too hard.

A window in the waiting room faced the blankness of a brick wall, and a window there, a lace curtain, a flower pot. There were people behind that window, planning and laughing and having dinner.

You'll never know how much I love you.

Danny had reached over and put his hand on her wrist. "Hello, Betty," he said. And that smile. "Look," said Danny, "here's a newspaper, about the rodeo. What do you say we take it in? How'd you like to do that?"

"Oh, fine," she said.

"Eddie Rohn's going to ride," Danny said. "I'll bet he wins. I'll bet he wins, and do you know why? Because we know him. That's the reason."

"Yes," she said. "I guess he'll win." Everybody was going to win but the Danny Irwins.

"We could have dinner with him," Danny said. "How would that be? We can get hold of him—"

"All right," she said. So after it was over they could sit across from Eddie Rohn who was young and strong, and then she could look at Danny.

She could hate Eddie for his youth and strength.

"Mr. Irwin," the nurse said, "Doctor will see you now."

"I'll wait here, Dan," Betty said.

She waited there in the reception room and looked at the jokes Danny had showed her, remembering the smile he asked her to share. She watched faces; they meant nothing now. For now they would have his shirt off. Now they would have him stand before the machine. The machine that told.

Then the purple-blue, quivery light.

It must have been an hour; the faces had changed. She moved her eyes to the window. The sun had moved away. She looked back.

And there—was Danny, following the nurse. Her eyes flew to him, searching. She knew every line of his face, suspected his smile.

But the nurse was smiling too. And the doctor. The doctor said, "He mustn't strain himself at all. Not at *all*. For at least six months."

Danny came to her like a sleepwalker. "Betty," he said, "I'm going to get well."

She went to pieces. "Oh, my God," she said. "My dear God." She kept sobbing and clinging to him. She pushed him away, looked fiercely into his face. "You wouldn't lie," she said. "You'd tell me if you lied," she said, and began to sob again, clinging to him.

The doctor watched. Watched her. "And I insist," he said, "that someone else drive your car tonight."

The only seat Lona could get that afternoon was in the bleachers. There was a drunk beside her with a child's balloon who kept snatching off the hat of the woman before him.

Across the flat the smelters belched smoke into the thick fall air, it hung heavily over the bare black hills, and through it the sun was orange and hazy.

A rider had just finished, and there was silence down in the arena. Down near the chutes a few men moved, and in the judges' stand men in big showy Stetsons moved their heads and jaws like puppets.

There had been good rides. A horse had bucked into the wire mesh around the grandstand, broken its neck, and the rider was carried off in a stretcher. Women had screamed.

Now, the silence.

Lona's hands were clenched, her nails digging into her palms. In a minute her man was coming out. He had sent the clippings. In a moment he would ride—for her. High there in the bleachers she had a moment of aloneness, and her throat tightened.

He was riding to show her, to hurt her. But it was a good hurt.

He was only a figure now in a cloud of dust, riding a ton of horseflesh, and she was standing with the rest of them, crying out to him.

"Ride him, oh darling, ride him."

And in that sixty seconds Eddie Rohn left the sleepy little farm world in southern Idaho behind him. The day's champion, today. First money. Next year, New York. Boston. London.

This was seeing your man win. This. She sat back, spent. She waited until the crowd had gone, and felt again the sharp aloneness and the thin fall sun on her face. She stepped carefully down the steep stairs of the bleachers, a lonely, happy figure in new shoes.

She hurried through the fine gray dust beside the empty grandstand. Below were the chutes, the alleyways and pens and corrals, and there a few horses milled about; dust rose like copper plumes. A few riders still lounged there against the fence. There was a gold glint on a whiskey bottle. She felt the nostalgia, and walked faster, singling out the men, watching for a shoulder, a gesture, listening for a laugh, his laugh.

"Hello," she said. "I'm looking for Eddie Rohn."

They looked at her suit, her shoes, and they took off their hats. "Why, ma'am," one said softly, "why, he was here a spell back. With some folks."

"Might be down around campgrounds."

She said, "Thank you."

A tent was pitched on the camp grounds, near a cut-down old Maxwell, ashes from a fire stirred before it. Inside the tent a baby whimpered, and the thin voice of a woman was singing. *Go tell Aunt Rhody, the old gray goose is dead.* . . .

The woman wore a gingham dress. She was rouged, and thin and tired. She stood now in the door of the tent, holding the baby.

"No, ma'am. I ain't seen hair nor hide of him. But I know him."

This woman knew him. How is he? she wanted to ask. Is he happy? Does he laugh?

She spoke shyly. "That's a nice baby."

The young woman looked soberly at the baby. "Spitting image of Charley. Him and me always used to stay at the Commercial. I got with the baby and Charley got all fidgetty and nervous. It's hard on some men. But he'd rather have this kid than do good this year, I tell him."

"Do you think Eddie Rohn's at the Commercial?"

"Oh, I know he is." Lona turned. Suddenly the woman flushed. "You wouldn't have a cig, would you? Charley took ourn."

Lona gave her the Camels from the new suede bag. "Keep them."

There is the cat in the window of the fruit store, curled against the window so the fur is flat, and the oranges are piled and dotted with deep patches of shadow. There is the sidewalk. Do you remember when you first touched the knob of the door that leads upstairs?

You were afraid. You are afraid now.

She clicked the latch and went up past the first landing, past the night bell. *Ring for Landlady.*

One sick brown fern still languished in the small bay, and there was the table with the ledger and the pencil dangling from the string. The elegant old woman hadn't changed: her felt slippers whispered down the hall. She put her hands on her hips and cocked her head.

"Yes. He's staying here." Her eyes said nothing. There was music down the hall, and when a door was opened for a moment voices leaped out. A splash of light lay across the dingy hall, and a splash of sound.

"If you'd tell me what room?"

The old woman grew haughty and pursed her lips. "Well, room 6." Then her eyes lit up in triumph. "But—he's out."

"Out?" Lona was conscious of herself, of an awkwardness. To cover it, she opened her bag and looked inside and rummaged there a second. "You say he's—out?"

"Yes. A lady and a gentleman called. I—seen them." Then, slyly. "Were you wanting him, dearie?" The old woman raised her eyebrows. "He probably went to Copperville."

Here are the brash, cheap, shoebox-shaped buildings with fancy fronts, stuccoed like Spanish, black-glass tile like *moderne.* La Golondrina. The Top-Hat. Cars were jammed on both sides of the narrow snakelike street; points of light caught on shiny fenders. Here on the curb a woman pulled at a man's sleeve.

"Come on. *Come* on. I want to dance."

And out beyond, behind the buildings, the flat stretched from the backdoors up to the hills of Butte; out there in the darkness the weeds were sick with arsenic fumes from smelters.

"Get drunk on me, will you?"

The doors of La Tràviata opened and closed, and the Rocky Mountain Café and the Golden Arrow were crowded. The Italian hostesses were pretty and fat, proud of their satin gowns—so smooth over their stomachs and breasts. Some had little mustaches, and their sweat was scented with flowers.

"No tables left. We're full here." Too damn many spongers come in. Look around. Don't buy. "No—no tables."

Booths lined the walls and curtains were pulled, and on the floor they danced: rodeo riders in silk shirts, miners in cheap blue suits, black shoes, pointed toes, fancy ties.

I can't give you anything but love, baby.
If you're sick, there's the john.

She had to park the Pierce in an alley. A cat jumped out from a garbage can and ran, stretching its body in the light of the headlamps, sprawled around a corner. She slammed the door of the car and caught her cape.

"Oh, damn," she sobbed. He would leave just as she got there. . . .

That always happened.

The Traviata was nearest. No room to sit. She stood by the door, and stared back at the Italian hostess. Each time the door opened, her eyes lit up. He wasn't at the bar. In the lady's room she washed her face and put on fresh make-up and wiped off her shoes with a paper towel. *If you found him now, you couldn't talk. You'd cry.*

She watched the booths when the curtains parted. She walked slowly beside them, trying to hear inside. Not his voice.

She stared back at the fat Italian hostess. Her shoes began to pinch.

Two hours in the Golden Arrow.

Two hours in the Rocky Mountain. In all the small back rooms roulette wheels turned, smooth on axles, clockwise, and the man threw the ivory pellets into the steel frame, counterclockwise, up under the lip. And the wheels slowed and the pellets fell into slots.

She kept watching the door. She glanced at the wheel, and craned to see the number.

"If red comes up this time, I'll find him."

She watched. All the hands and fingers pushed money out. The wheel turned, the pellet slowed.

Click.

"Eighteen. Even. Red."

It could have come up black. But it came up red. Red. Do you see? She felt the trembling in her stomach. There was only one place left: La Rosa, at the end of the street. There the quivering neon lights outlined a rose, pale pink petals, pale trembling green leaf. She was tired, and a little sick.

"I'm sorry," the Italian woman said. "It's too late. We're just closing now."

She held her hand on the doorknob. "Please." *Can't you see I'm smiling? Can't you see I've got to come in?* "Please, I'm looking for someone."

The Italian woman was large, her arms white and fat, trying to close the crack in the door. Lona pressed close.

"The door's got to be closed. No more comes in," the woman said. "Watch out for your nose."

"Please," Lona said. She began to push the door, her neck felt tight and strained. She braced the new shoes on the sidewalk, pushing.

"No," the woman said. "No, no. We close." She leaned her weight against the door. But Lona was stronger.

"I must get in. I'm looking." The door was wider.

The deep Italian voice became whining, feminine. "You're hurting me, lady. You got my hand pressed—" she looked about wide-eyed for help.

"I want to come in. I'm looking. Please."

The woman's voice was high. "Oh, Tony!"

People were looking. Lona pushed. The woman's big breasts were heaving, eyes womanly, frightened. "Oh, Tony!"

A fat dark man, chest-hair growing up under his open collar, pushed forward. "What's a trouble here?"

"Tony, help. This woman. She hurts my hand."

"Please," Lona said, and spoke around the woman. "I want Eddie Rohn. Tell him Lona."

"Eddie Rohn?" the big man said. "Rohn? Oh, let her in," he said.

The woman stepped suddenly from the door, lips pursed, curved in a smooth smile, and Lona stumbled against the freed door.

She stood in the middle of the dance floor; the people were looking. She pushed at her hair, tried to fix her beret.

And saw him. He was sitting in a booth. He was just the same. The mouth, the chin, the shoulders. She could imagine his voice.

Her eyes were stinging, hot, and she smiled. She would have to break down that dignity of the Rohns, the pride the Rohns felt when a woman came back.

You see, she'd found him. Everything was going to be all right. Everything was going to be different with her than it had ever been before. There was a strange hope in this night, a beginning.

She started toward him, still smiling, fighting back the tears, smiling. How could she tell him what the night meant?

Suddenly she stopped still. He—

He was with somebody. Then she moved again. It was still all right. If it had been strangers—but it was only the Irwins.

The Irwins. Danny was sitting there, quiet and smiling and talking across the table to Eddie. And Danny's wife. She looked again at Danny's wife.

But she kept smiling and moved toward the table. Just being with him, that's all she asked. Just this night, for the beginning. Her eyes stung again. But they'd go. The Irwins would go.

Now she stood beside him. "Eddie," she said, and her eyes searched his face when he turned. He had more confidence. He knew people looked at him now. But all the old feeling for her was in that look. Yes, it was. The trust and the anxiety and the love. And then she saw the look—like a shadow—rest there, the dignity of the Rohns of Idaho Falls.

She felt it, too. "I'm glad I found you," she said, and slid into the booth beside Eddie. She couldn't keep the shake out of her voice. "I looked everywhere," she said, and took off her gloves. A night like this didn't happen often.

"This is a wonderful night," Betty Irwin said.

"A lucky night," said Danny.

Eddie didn't say much, but she knew. He loved her; it made him silent.

She said, "I—" and flushed. Somehow she would show him, tell him when they danced, that this night was a beginning. Just give her a chance to show him that nothing mattered but him.

Close beside them the musicians moved, the dull redness of light on a violin, the sound of A. Light on brass and white coats, and the white, smooth keys of the piano. The musicians talked softly, and there was the whisper of a page of music.

The music was close. There was a small awkwardness in the booth. Danny's wife put her hand on Eddie's wrist. "You go ahead, Eddie. Dance with Lona. There isn't much time."

He flushed and hesitated.

Danny's wife smiled. "Go ahead." She turned to Lona. "He had asked me."

Eddie was still dignified, a little stiff against her. She felt old, loving him, understanding his pride. It would break in a minute. She spoke into his ear. "Eddie. I've waited so long. So long, darling." A whisper.

He didn't dance well. He sounded very young. "I've been pretty lonesome too, Lona."

She pressed close. "Oh, darling, were you? Honest, were you?" Her cheek brushed his shoulder. Nothing would ever spoil this. Couldn't he see how little it took to make her—different? She said, "Some way, we've always got to be together, Eddie."

His breath was warm on her cheek, her palm pressed flat against his back and the very life of him was firm and warm under her fingers.

There in the corner where the light didn't reach she whispered again, there where other couples were slow-moving shadows, intimate, mingling. "They'll go," she said. "Pretty soon the Irwins will go." She moved her head so she could look in his face in the little light. "I'm so—happy." He must feel this magic.

"They called me," he said, "at the Commercial."

"That's all right," she said. "They'll go." And whispered, "We've got to get rid of them."

And he said, "We can't."

She glanced at him. "Oh. Oh, yes, we can. They'd understand." Her palm was tighter on his back. "If we told them it had been so long."

They were in the shadowy corner when he spoke, and the figures moved in darkness. He said, "I've got to drive them home."

Then the figures pressed in and in on her, hot, sweating bodies, close, close. If she could get out, get away from those dancing shadows there . . .

She managed to speak, managed to argue, managed to keep her voice quiet. "But Eddie. But darling. I've—I've got a *room*."

I've got a room and there I meant to show you that I can't do without you. That you mean more than anything. That I'll do anything, be any way . . .

He wouldn't understand the bigness of this night. He said, "She isn't up to driving home."

Her eyes went to the woman there in the booth. That woman wasn't sick. She was a woman with a secret, that woman, a woman in love. A sly, pretending woman.

"Eddie," Lona said, "do you believe that? Do you really believe she can't drive tonight?" Her fixed smile was ready to crack with laughter. Her eyes darted to Danny Irwin, sitting there too. Quiet, he was, trusting, smiling. Couldn't he *see?* Couldn't he see what was in his wife's eyes? Didn't he know that he was sick, old . . .

How did he know what happened that night when Eddie drove with his wife in the rain? Hadn't he seen his wife put her hand on Eddie's wrist? Didn't he know what happened when flesh touched flesh?

"Eddie," she said—and the smile could break into a laugh—"do you honestly believe that?"

"Yes," he said. "I believe her."

What had happened, then, to the feeling of his flesh against her palm?

They had said goodbye—as if nothing had happened. She could feel that old, strained smile. They had left her alone in the booth, in the new suit, her eyes on the door they had opened. And closed.

CHAPTER 31   The hotel room was small.

There was a sepia print of Beethoven playing before Mozart, and a print of a bunch of flowers in a vase, the blues faded, the reds turned brown. There was barely room to walk between the bed and the dresser. Not much nap to the carpet.

There was a plush easy chair by the radiator under the window. She sat there. The metal bed lamp threw a little path of light across the bed; the new cape tossed there, the new beret. There was light on the dresser too.

It caught the two glasses turned upside down on a metal tray, the clear glass pitcher, and highlighted the thermos jug of silvered glass, the stopper chained to the neck by a thin string of bright metal beads. A Gideon Bible in mock black leather stamped in gilt, and a telephone. The whiskey was in the empty drawer below, and the champagne.

She sat very still. She reached carefully over to the windowsill and picked up her new purse, unsnapped it, hunted there and found the nail file, a long sharp one. The deep little grooves crisscross, this way, that way. She looked at it, and began to file her nails. She put the nail file back in the purse and sat quiet again.

The radiator banged, cooling, and when the sound died away she picked up the purse again and took out a cigarette.

It might have been the picture of the piano up there that made her think of her mother, maybe the whiskey in the drawer. Now the whiskey, the picture, and her mother were bound together. Now after an hour of smoking, and the radiator banging, of looking out the dark window at a silent street (the dark little alleys run back up the hill), at a garage that said OPEN ALL NIGHT, blinking, blinking, now the churning longing had quieted.

The whiskey is in the drawer. Why do you suppose your mother drinks? Can it kill longing?

See the little ashtray of green glazed glass, the box of matches, upright. Green hat. Green tips on the matches.

You should have put the new green cape in the closet, put the purse out of sight, the new purse with nothing in it but a compact, a few dollars, cigarettes, a nail file. What are you going to do now? Go to bed? Take the pillow in your arms?

The bottle is in the drawer. You can get it without looking at the champagne bottle. Just reach in. Don't look.

She got up, her blouse open at the neck, her skirt twisted from moving this way and that way in the chair, crossing and uncrossing her legs, feeling her forehead.

She poured two fingers into one of the tumblers, and took it into the little bathroom. She set it on the glass shelf over the bowl, and let the cold water run.

Look at the little cake of soap still in its green crepe-paper wrapper, the little shiny black paper band around it. Palmolive.

"Look," her grandfather used to say. "Here's a little bar of soap . . ."

Nothing had turned out. Sometime back there when Tom Bart brought a little bar of soap, something had gone wrong. And this was the end of it, waiting for the water to get cold so she could drink two fingers of whiskey.

She swallowed the whiskey and swallowed water before she breathed. In a moment she shuddered. She sat down on the edge of the tub. Look up through the glass shelf and see the soap there. She watched it, her eyes oddly gentle.

She had eaten nothing.

The second drink was easier. She watched herself in the mirror. She was pretty. She raised her eyebrows, and raised them again, critical. Yes, pretty.

A pretty girl could hurt a man. If he came to the door this minute, she would simply look at him. She would look at him as she looked at herself, raised eyebrows, coolly.

"You could model," the woman said. She stood straight, her breasts pointed out. In the bedroom she walked slowly across the floor, glanced over her shoulder into the mirror at the pretty girl walking there.

She didn't give a damn. She really didn't give a damn. She leaned against the window, looking down into the dark street. She watched the street coldly.

She could hurt a man.

Do you know what? She is going to have another drink. Do you know that men hate women to drink? They are afraid of a woman when she drinks. She sees through them, then.

Lona, you've got to stop drinking. It hurts me when you drink. You should have thought of that before.

Cold eyes, staring down into the street.

She took the bottle into the bathroom, put it on the little glass shelf.

She stood still. Maybe that was the telephone next door. Hundreds of rooms in the hotel . . .

She listened. She swallowed the drink, and set the bottle down carefully. The ring again, and again.

It surged over her, the longing, the churning, the weakness. She remembered everything, his smile, his warmth, his mouth. She fixed her hair, buttoned her blouse, straightened her skirt, smiling before she answered.

A clerk's voice said, "Mrs. Barrows?"

"Yes," she said. "Yes."

"There's a man down her to see you—"

"Yes," she said. "Yes. Send him up."

Hesitation. Then the clerk: "Are you sure—?"

"Oh yes," she said. "I was expecting him. Send him right up."

He would have know that she'd be there, waiting. He would wait until she was settled in her room, then he would come. She would wait forever. That was one of the things he must know she'd do. Wait forever, wait and wait.

Not a loud knock.

She forgot to walk proudly, slowly. She ran to the door. "I'm coming," she called. "I'm coming." She opened the door and stood leaning against it, smiling into the hall. There was a lamp on a bracket out there, a rose-colored fluted shade. The man beneath it didn't move until she spoke.

"Oh," she said. "Joe."

His cheap blue suit was rumpled, his shoes were dusty. He had his hat in his hands. She could see his hands, long and narrow, chapped and cracked, strange beneath his white cuffs that were still creased from the box.

Her voice was strange, quiet. "I suppose you want more cash. Come on in."

He looked at her. "All right."

He followed her in.

"Don't stand there, Joe. Sit down. Don't come in here and stand there."

"All right." He sat, awkward, in the overstuffed chair, on the edge of the seat, waiting, his hat in his hands.

"Don't hold your hat like that, Joe."

He let the hat drop to the floor beside him.

She smiled. "That's better." She went into the bathroom. He waited. "How would you like a glass of champagne, Joe?"

"I never had champagne."

She said, "I didn't ask you if you ever had it. I asked you if you wanted it."

"All right."

She laughed suddenly. "I only had champagne once. It's funny, you never had it, and I only had it once."

He looked at her. "You've been drinking."

She said, "What of it?"

"Nothing of it."

"Men always get mad when a girl takes a drink." He watched her. She said, "Well, get the champagne. It's in the drawer there. Go on."

He got up and walked across the room, not awkard now. He had a funny walk, catlike, never any sound. "What's wrong?" she asked. "Can't you see it?"

He smiled. "What's this here wire on top?"

She stood beside him. "Here. Let me show you." His hands touched hers, and she looked up at him. "Joe—"

He looked into her face. "What?"

He must have had a shave. There was that sharp sweet alcohol smell about him. Lilacs and Roses. He had a funny jaw. It would be hard for the barber to get around it. What would he do if she touched his face and said you've got a funny face? His face was blank looking, those white eyebrows and white eyelashes sort of faded. She could handle him. She could hurt him.

"Be careful," she said. "I don't want to get it all over my new suit. It pops when you pull it out."

He looked into her eyes. "Does it?"

She looked away. She said, "Well, go ahead."

"All right."

There was a big mirror over the dresser, and she kept seeing herself and Joe there, strangers moving about and talking like a movie, and she was pretty.

She laughed when the cork came out, and some of the champagne boiled over. She said, "Why didn't you cool it? You do everything wrong."

He grinned. "Not everything."

"I only had it once," she said.

He pulled her down so she sat on the bed. He was a little rough. "Here's how," he said.

She laughed. "Here's how." You only had to be who you were to handle a man. They were always trying to get you to stop drinking, doing things you wanted to. "Joe, why did you want that money?"

He had drunk the first glass in a gulp. He didn't know how to do anything. "To have a time," he said.

She looked at him steadily. "You're having a good time, aren't you?"

He kept looking at her. "We could have a better time."

She was about through with him. She even felt a little sorry for him. He was cheap in his suit. You could always tell a cheap suit, sort of fancy, tight in the wrong places, tried to make a man look big-chested, narrow-hipped. You didn't care about a man's hips or chest unless he was the right one. Men were always hoping somebody wanted them, trying to make a girl want them because of the narrow hips and big chest.

She was about through.

"Joe," she said, "did you ever have a girl?"

"Sure," he said, "I had a girl."

Some little cheap girl who thought he was wonderful. His hands were narrow and ugly, his wrists bony, long arms. Some cheap little girl thought he was wonderful.

She laughed a little. "You're wonderful, Joe. You must get pretty lonesome out at the ranch."

His laugh was an echo of hers. "Sure I do."

She spilled a little of the champagne as she poured. "Were you ever alone much with this girl?"

He was close to her on the bed. He moved his hand. "Hello, Lona."

She moved away. "Don't call me Lona."

She was through now. It was tiresome, what she saw in the mirror—the two of them sitting on the bed. A rotten movie, same thing over and over. This is where she came in. "You're not supposed to call me Lona."

Joe said, "And all the champagne to finish."

She spoke a little haughtily. "I'll get your money. You can have twenty dollars."

"Is that all?" he asked. "Look," he said, "I don't want your money. I've got more than you've got."

She laughed. "That's pretty good, Joe." She kept laughing quietly, and put her spread-out hand behind her on the bed and tried to get up. Her legs felt funny. She kept sitting there, thinking about it.

She watched him go into the bathroom. He ran water in there. Well, he'd slick back that whitish hair now and go. She kept sitting there, looking at the dresser mirror. She'd hurt him. Now he could go.

She had a self-satisfied smile on her face when he came out of the bathroom. He moved swiftly, softly, smiling at her, coming toward her steadily. She couldn't look close at him. The picture was blurred in the mirror. She couldn't see all of him.

"Honey," he said. "Listen, honey."

She opened her lips, and then he had his hand over them. He said, "Don't, honey. Don't do that."

She was lying on the bed, kicking. He stopped that with his leg. She strained, breathing hard through her nose. She was strong; she couldn't move.

Carefully he took his hand away from her mouth, and she made a hard smile at him, still breathing hard. "I'm going to scream, Joe. They'll take you away."

"No," he said. "You won't do that. They said you expected me."

She stared.

He took the pillow and pressed it over her face. Black under there, and he kept pressing it. She waited.

He took the pillow away, smiled, and held it above her. She turned her eyes toward the window. If she could get that nail file . . .

"Let me up a minute," she said.

He shook his head and brought the pillow down. Under it her breath choked her, hot and wet. She stopped fighting.

And then he was whispering. "Honey, lay still. Just lay still a minute, honey." And whispering again. "I don't want to use the pillow on you. I want to see your face . . ."

He was hurting her now. Down in the dark Butte street the sign kept flashing.

C H A P T E R 32 Lona was afraid.

She wondered about Joe Martin. He didn't try to see her alone in the barn, the garage, but when he was near she was conscious of her breasts and legs; his aloofness troubled her. And there was the matter of the cattle in the lower field.

She always went down to the bunkhouse shortly after breakfast to give orders, striding down the path, the small quirt swinging from her arm. The men were silent, respectful, quiet as she smoked the best part of a cigarette, sitting on the big table. Her eyes moved about the room and rested on their private things, their razors and lotions on the windowsill, their magazines, their tobacco. As she smoked she would let her cigarette hang from her lips, and draw on her gloves, smooth them on her hands, pull them over her fingers, squinting through the smoke.

This moment with the men in the bunkhouse was the core of life. Her will dug ditches, branded cattle, broke horses, built fences, moved men to sweat in summer heat and winter cold. Dust rose anywhere on twenty thousand acres when she spoke. This moment began when she reached over her head in the morning to pull the chain on the light. She didn't need an alarm clock. Something in her blood woke her.

And then this silence of respectful men.

"Tell you what," she'd say, "this morning we'll move those cattle. Two of you fix that fence on the east side. . . ." Then they were moving quietly to the wall for their jackets. They were lucky men to have jobs, and they knew it.

A week after the rodeo in Butte she overslept.

She woke in a panic—the whole pattern wrong. Not because Clyde was gone. He was in Sentinel, waiting for a shipment of lumber.

The room was cold, the weak November sun floundered just below the hills behind the barn; through the crack in the door came the stale smell of grease, and the sounds of seven o'clock, the scraping of dishes, the iron kettle pulled across the stove for the dinner's pot roast. And the silence.

She glanced out the window. No one moved near the bunkhouse, a cold little log shack pressed under gray dawn light, and the smoke wisped out of the chimney faint and blue.

Mrs. Dean had pancakes in the warming oven. The coffee was cool and bitter.

"Well," Mrs. Dean said, "you sure slept in. I guess your husband's gone and all. Used to sleep in myself when Mr. Dean went to Spokane. Woman can't sleep with a man flouncing and acting up. Egg?"

Lona ate carefully, slowly. She would treat this calmly.

She put on her hat and jacket, picked up her quirt and gloves, and lighted a cigarette. She walked slowly to the bunkhouse, and hesitated once in the middle of the yard to examine a funny looking rock. If they were watching, they'd see she was deliberate. As if she'd planned . . .

You couldn't see through the window into the bunkhouse. Too much dust (how the dust settles inside when the windows are moist from men's breath and the steam from the washbasin), too many fly specks, and the cheesecloth a neat man had hung for a curtain.

The latch on the door was cold. You had to give a little push to get the door open. She had fixed her face, her eyes directed toward the old wicker chair by the window. Joe Martin's chair.

She was standing in the middle of the bunkhouse floor. There was the table with the magazines, the top of it carved deep with the initials of men long gone away. There were the stacks of *Western Story* magazines, gaudy covers of women swept into the arms of men on horseback. A dusty guitar hung on the wall, a string still humming from her last footfall.

Everyone was gone.

The chairs were empty, quiet on their rockers; an alarm clock inside the bunkroom pecked away at the silence as she stood listening, stunned. She walked slowly over to the big table and sat on the edge, dangling her legs, pulling on her gloves, squinting through the cigarette smoke. She sat there a little while, looking into the empty room.

She took off her gloves and looked at her nails. She looked up at the sudden scratching at the door, a little bark, then quiet, waiting.

The serious voice of Art. "Now, Tootsie," he said, "I'll let you in. I always let you in."

At first he didn't see her. He was leaning over, patting the dog as he entered, stooped over her, and as the dog moved he moved along beside her, petting her and talking.

He smiled his anxious, friendly smile at Lona. "Good morning, Miss Lona. Slept late, didn't you. Me and Tootsie are talking about things. We been all over the yard looking for a shovel."

Lona lighted another cigarette, watching the match. She said, "Where are they?"

"Oh, they've gone out to work. It's way past seven." He smiled gently.

"I said, where are they?"

"Oh, they went to the lower field to bring those cattle up to good feed. There ain't no good feed down there, he says."

She watched him, squinting through the smoke. "Who says?"

"Oh, Joe Martin. He sees everything."

Lona spoke quietly. "What are you doing, Art?"

He spoke gently, respectfully. "Like I said. Me and Tootsie been looking for a shovel. Joe Martin said to fix the dam by the aspens."

She said, "Get a horse. Tell Joe Martin to come here."

He looked at his feet, hesitating. "Well, Miss Lona, Joe Martin—" He tried again. "That dam by the aspens—"

"You won't go then, Art?" She fixed a smile on him.

He said, "Miss Lona—" How could he tell her how Joe Martin had stood there, and the other men already gone out, quiet, and Joe Martin talking through thin lips. He had been afraid, alone with Joe Martin and the dog at his feet. "Miss Lona—"

She stood up and snapped her cigarette at the stove. "You don't have to go, Art. I'll write you a check."

The lines in his face softened, and his eyes smiled. "Miss Lona, you don't have to do that." He looked at his hands. "I know you can't afford to pay us any more."

She turned slowly. "What's that, Art?"

"Joe Martin. He said if things don't straighten out here there won't be any money." He began to flush. "Miss Lona, I want to say something."

She had the smile on him. "Yes, Art."

It was hard to say this big thing he had to say.

He had thought about it at night, so he couldn't sleep, when the wind rustled the rye-grass outside the window. He would lie looking up at the stain on the ceiling, smoking at night, thinking, wondering if the other fellows guessed the big thing inside him.

He could see himself saying it, standing proud, and saying it, coming forward when the others had deserted her, the grand-daughter of Tom Bart. Like a story . . .

He could hear the silence that would follow his words, only the silence and the sound of the rye-grass outside the window.

Before he spoke he looked out the dirty window at the barn he knew, and the cows inside it that knew him. He looked at the twisty path that led up from the barn to the house.

What he was going to say was so big that everything ugly that had ever happened was gone, the men who laughed at him or teased him. They didn't know how big he was inside.

The waiting at the back doors of restaurants in Sentinel, asking for a little food, and knowing it wasn't his smile that got food, but pity. They didn't know the big thing inside him.

He wasn't always big, but every man has one big moment, and this was his, now, in the bunkhouse.

"Miss Lona," he said. Something was happening to his voice, but he straightened his shoulders and smiled. "I'll stay here for nothing and work." He was big now, and the little dog knew it too. "I'll stay and be faithful."

She looked at him a moment, and then began to draw on her gloves. She half smiled, and said only two words. She said, "You lunatic."

In a few minutes she would go down to the bunkhouse. Joe was back. She'd seen him ride in. She'd go down and say, "Joe,

I want to see you." She would speak to him alone in the barn.

Or she would say it at noon, in the kitchen. She'd be cooking. She had fired Art—crazy old man—and the cook had, strangely, quit over it. It didn't matter. The years knew scores of cooks and old men gone at last.

She'd have it out with Joe at noon.

She should have cried out in the hotel room. Eddie—Eddie would have killed him.

But she hadn't cried out.

Right after she spoke to Art, she should have saddled up and gone to find Joe, called him down before the others. If he'd opened his mouth, fired him. He wouldn't dare tell about the hotel room. If he opened his mouth—what if he did? Who would take his word against a Bart's? Not in that country.

She sat in her room, looking down at the bunkhouse, fixing her hair. She turned when her mother stood in the door, glanced sharply.

"What's wrong, Lona?"

"Nothing. Nothing's wrong. Why do you say that?"

"You're nervous. You—"

"I'm not nervous, so don't say it." She began to comb her hair again. "And Mother—fix dinner, will you?"

She'd see Joe later. Just now she'd sit on the bed. Did you ever dream you were holding the door against some clawing thing, straining and pushing to hold it off, smelling its breath—and feeling the knob turn in your hand?

Clyde came at suppertime. She watched him through the meal. Well, suppose he knew about Butte. Suppose her mother knew: it didn't really matter. The thing that mattered was to fire Joe Martin.

Well, sit in your room, here in the darkness after supper. You've made up your mind. Fire him.

Joe would go. What else could he do? Get rid of him. (And that awareness of her legs and breasts.) She shuddered, remembering his cheap striped suit, his sitting there in that hotel room; she had felt his patience as she had felt his breath later.

Why had she let him in the room at all? He was ugly.

Oh, what people did when they drank wasn't their fault.

Down below, there were lights in the bunkhouse. *If you turn on the lights here in this dark room, you can't see the lights in the bunkhouse.*

She pulled the light cord and blinked in the glare. Why does darkness twist your thoughts?

Look. Now in the light she can see herself in the mirror. She hasn't changed. Nothing has. She is getting her boots on. It will be dusty in the barn. She glances in the mirror. She is tall, her green eyes snap.

"Well," she said. The word cut like a quirt.

She leaves the room, and moves down the stairs. Wide, gently descending stairs. She is always conscious of descending these stairs slowly, with dignity. She has never hurried down. At the bottom is the portrait. Bert Bart.

His eyes were hers. He would have dealt with Joe Martin. Wouldn't have stooped to go himself. Would have sent word . . .

She stood in the hall. "Clyde, will you go down and tell Joe Martin to come up here?"

Clyde looked up from his book. "Yes, of course."

Ruth said, "Is anything wrong, darling?"

"No, nothing's wrong. I want to talk with Joe Martin, that's all."

Clyde went out.

"Mother, play something."

Ruth got up, puzzled. She began a Chopin waltz. "You haven't asked me to play for years."

"I'm tired, Mother. That's all."

Oh, you'd forgotten there were times you had to hear familiar things, sounds, words, music. . . .

She started when the back door opened. The cold draft rushed into the house. She got up, stood with a cigarette in her lips, ready. But the footsteps in the hall were Clyde's. And he was alone. Puzzled.

"Lona, have you—had trouble with Joe Martin?"

She looked straight at him. "No. Why?"

"He won't come up. He's playing—checkers."

"What did you do?" she asked softly. "Tell him to finish his little game? How long would this place last if the help ran it?"

"You asked me to ask him."

"I won't be told what they'll do. You won't carry out anything. I won't ask you again."

Why did Clyde stay with her? What did he want from her? She strode into the hall, put on her hat, picked up her gloves, her coat. She picked up the quirt.

Ruth stood near the piano. "Lona, where are you going?"

She didn't bother to answer.

There was an eerie crystal blueness to the night. The wind whined high in the air and swept ragged gauze clouds over the cold face of the moon; the first snow was silver on the peaks.

The buildings in the yard crouched and had no depth, but there was depth in the blackness that began at the barn door and yawned inside, down to the last stalls where the milk cows were.

Art had milked that night for the last time. She had seen him with the buckets, and his dog trotting behind him.

If she could stop time. If she could go back.

"Art," she would say, "I'm sorry. I don't want you to go."

Mrs. Dean would stay.

If she could go back, Joe Martin would never have come into her hotel room. She would have left him standing with his money in his hands—under the rose-shaded lamp in his cheap clothes.

The hairy Italian woman would never have blocked her at that door.

Eddie Rohn would have been alone.

You see.

And now there was something she couldn't stop. She moved on down the path to the bunkhouse. She snapped the quirt on her wrist. Not much of a sound. She snapped it again, and tried her old charm, walking straight, proud, conscious of her height, of her blood. And her power. She snapped the quirt again.

There was still a light in the bunkhouse.

She walked obliquely toward the window. At first it was only a crack of light, and as she came nearer it grew wider and wider, but still the chair where Joe Martin always sat was hidden. She saw the others, one of them naked to the waist, studying a Sears

Roebuck catalog; the Kid was reading a magazine, his leg thrown over the arm of his chair, hair in his eyes, biting his nails.

Now she saw the edge of Joe Martin's chair, just the wicker back. And then Joe Martin.

Still playing checkers.

She saw only his back. There was something about his back, taut, springlike. The man across the board was nervous. There must have been words: about not touching men.

The game would be over shortly. The man across the board hesitated, afraid to move too slowly, afraid of a foolish move.

It didn't matter. Joe Martin had a king, a king that leaped this way, that way, playing a small mean game with two lone black pieces.

She pressed so close to the window that her will must pass through the glass, must help the small black pieces that staggered toward the king row. She wanted to break the glass, to reach out and sweep away the leaping king. She was trembling.

The other men were watching now. She could see their faces, interested, watching silently. Only the Kid still chewed his nails over the pages of his magazine.

And black—then black made a sudden, foolish move, and paused. She couldn't see Joe Martin's face, only his taut back and his arm, moving forward.

The king leaped.

The men relaxed, grinning, talking to each other.

She wondered how they would look if Joe Martin told them about the hotel room. The Kid would look up for that. She pictured their excitement, their sly, grinning interest. When she came down in the morning to the bunkhouse would they look at her, or would they grin and look away?

If she fired Joe, he would tell them. Any man would tell.

As if he were there, she could see Eddie standing in the bunkhouse, his slow, puzzled smile.

Say, what's the joke?

Oh, Eddie, let me tell you. Let me tell you how it was . . .

Or perhaps it would be in Sentinel that he heard it, or at the Cross-Roads. Bar talk, and her name. And she would never have a chance to tell him how it was.

She turned suddenly, in the cold blue night. With her quirt in her hand she walked back to the house through the rustling weeds.

C H A P T E R 33 There is something religious about a bank, in the silence of oiled hinges, in the ritual of cashing checks, in the words that open guarded chambers, in the hushed voices of the tellers, the remoteness of the director.

Banks are made of stone and brick. Steel is for grilles, steel is for doors; the windows are narrow; and there are concrete places underground, and devices to blind and kill.

Do you believe in banks?

She had the letter from the bank in her pocket.

"Will you come in," Peter Barton had written, "at your earliest possible convenience?"

The note wasn't due.

Clyde had brought the mail from the Cross-Roads the night before. She recalled how the car looked in the winter dusk, moving through the gate, lurching through the snowy ruts to the house.

"Will you come in at your earliest possible convenience?"

She waited two days.

Since Mrs. Dean had gone, Ruth had been doing the cooking. She was not good at it, not quick. Wasteful. She opened cans.

"You've got to cook something else," Lona told her. "I can't afford canned goods. You know that."

Ruth struggled with roasts, braised ribs. Her bread was flat and soggy; she didn't understand yeast. Cookbooks were not clear. Breakfast was tense, everybody conscious of burned bacon, pancakes soggy in the center and scorched outside. Joe Martin had set a dish of oatmeal aside.

And Ruth stood over the stove nervously, smiling, apologetic, trying, bungling. Her thumb was cut deep with a butcher knife, her palm was raw with burns.

"What are you doing?" Lona asked. "Why don't you bind that cut up? What are you trying to do?"

"I'm trying, Lona. But the bandage slips in the water."

"Fix it right and it won't." She hated to see her mother's hands red and cracked and swollen. Lotion did nothing. She hated to see her mother's feet in the shoes she said were most comfortable, a middle-aged woman's shoes, twisted of heel. Her mother bungled, and the apologetic smile.

Clyde tried to help, making the fire mornings, cutting rind off the bacon, carrying vegetables from the root cellar, doing cook's chores. The same apologetic smile.

"Will you come in at your earliest possible convenience?"

She had dressed carefully that morning; her suit seemed shabby. The house was shabby in the dawn, the living room dead with winter and stale smoke. Ruth and Clyde had talked late the night before, and Ruth had played the piano, runs and scales; the monotony made it hard for Lona to sleep: she had called down.

Awake again at two, huddled in her room with a blanket around her shoulders, smoking, waiting in the dark—hoping for nothing. She watched the spark of her cigarette making arcs in the mirror, she thought hard of how a spark will show an ashtray in the dark. The thought of the dream haunted her, the Thing on the other side of the door, and the knob turning.

When would she dream it again . . .

At dawn she came down the old stairs and sensed something wrong. There was no smell of coffee, and she had reached the back of the house before she smelled the smoke from pine kindling.

Clyde was laying the fire, a little puff of smoke reaching up around his hands. He looked up. The smile . . .

"Where's my mother?" she asked.

"I'm getting breakfast this morning," he said.

"It's late. Breakfast is half an hour late. Where's Mother?"

"She's not feeling well. I looked in her room, and she's not feeling well."

"She felt well enough last night. It was two when you came up."

He said, "She's not used to this, Lona. She's never done anything like this before."

If her mother would only pull herself together, and do something about her hands and feet, and stop that smile.

Now the fire crackled. He put coffee on, and he began to cut the bacon in thick, uneven slices, hacking away at the rind. She watched him a moment, and walked into the back dining room.

He had forgotten the spoons. She put them on herself, yanked open the silver drawer so that everything rattled and flew back in the drawer. She could see Joe Martin's eyes if he found no spoon for his coffee.

She opened the back door a crack. The bitter cold outside had pierced the brass doorknob, and it stuck to her moist hand. She pulled her hand gently away. You can tear your skin. They catch weasels with cold brass plates. Put a little blood on the plate, and the weasel . . .

She looked out at the bunkhouse, watched the clear blue smoke rise straight from the smokestack and vanish in the thin winter air. Now the sun rose red and gold on the snow, the rays sweeping the valley. In the bunkhouse a figure moved against the window. The men should be out now, should be harnessing teams, long shadows on the snow, chains jingling. But everything was silent.

There was only the simmering of the coffee, about to boil, the sputtering of bacon.

She could almost see the men in the bunkhouse, sitting, watching the alarm clock. And Joe Martin. . . .

The bunkhouse door opened suddenly and the latch clanked loud. Joe Martin stood there, looking toward the house. She stood rigid behind her crack, afraid to close the door, afraid to move. Afraid of eyes . . .

What would she have done if he had suddenly strode through the snow toward the house? Suppose he came suddenly into the kitchen, past her hiding there, seeing her.

"Breakfast's late. What's the trouble here?"

She closed the door softly. It was as if he had spoken.

She spoke to Clyde. "That's no way to fry bacon." It was burning. "That's no way."

He had that same apologetic smile.

He put on a hotcake, and the batter spread thin across the griddle. She watched the frying cake. When he turned it, it was scorched. "You can't expect anyone to eat that," she said. "You can't expect anyone—"

The smile again. "I guess I forgot something."

"I guess you did."

"I'll make another batch. I'll read better this time."

Her fingers curled. "There's not time," she said, tense. Her voice was rising. "There's not time."

She walked swiftly out into the living room. At the foot of the stairs she hesitated. Suddenly she moved swiftly up toward her mother's room.

The familiar smell of a room slept in, and the night air hung motionless, choking out light, a still, dead air. The bed was badly mussed up, covers pulled, sheets twisted, and her mother's black hair swirled across the pillow. Her mother had always been so neat—now there were clothes flung across the foot of the bed, the bureau drawers spilled clothes.

"Mother."

There was a stir. There had been other mornings like this, strange mornings when her mother lay in bed.

"Yes, Lona."

Her voice was hard. "Mother, Clyde's getting breakfast."

"I know. I have a splitting headache."

Lona hesitated, and looked about the room at the disorder, the slackness. "Mother, things have got to change."

"To change—?"

"You've got to get breakfast on the table at six-thirty. You've got to do something about this—" she gestured—"this mess."

Ruth sat up slowly. "Lona, sit down here."

"No. There's nothing to say."

"Lona, I hoped you'd come."

"There's nothing to say. And there's no room here for headaches and laziness." Something welled up within her. She fought it. She couldn't stop it. Then the words were out. "If you can't have breakfast on the table on time you'd better get out of here."

She turned, moved slowly down the stairs, and sat on the couch in the living room. The weak winter sun slanted through the narrow windows, the pale yellow light exposed the worn places on the carpet, the shabbiness of draperies, the cobwebs on the spider-like chandelier.

Do you remember that once the chandelier was handsome?

The monotonous motion of the pendulum in the big clock caught her eye. She watched it, fascinated.

It ticked twice a second, made a sweep of eight inches, from right to right in a second. She counted. A long time ago she knew you could gauge a second by saying "one steam engine." Took a second to say that. *You were only a child . . .*

"Two steam engine . . ."

If you didn't wind the clock it stopped. If you didn't stand before it once a week and feel the chains and the weights in your hands it ran down; the movement stopped, the pendulum was still.

She got up suddenly and strode to the clock and stood there and wound it; the chains rasped angrily across the gears.

She refused to think of what she had done. It was as if someone else had done it, someone who looked like her, spoke like her, but wasn't she. As if someone else had threatened her mother.

. . . at your earliest convenience . . .

Forty-two miles from the Bart Ranch to Sentinel. In the summer it took Lona an hour, and that meant driving sixty and seventy miles an hour on the highway for the last twenty miles, for the first twenty-two are on the country road, dirt and gravel and ruts, and you know county commissioners never do anything, and if you believe the neighbors there is all sorts of graft going on among the commissioners and squandering of money, and it is hopeless because no matter who the commissioners are, there is still the grafting and the squandering.

She drove fast, for no special reason at first. The chains spanked the back fenders. The loose crosspiece kept breaking.

The Lost Horse Valley was wide and lonely and white, and out from the road wandered little lonely country roads to occasional ranches, little specks of brown out there, a house, a barn, a shed. And in the sagebrush, almost covered with snow, recent silent tracks, neat narrow tracks of coyotes, the small embroidery of mice and weasels. The glare was blinding, the steel-blue of the sky was vague and distant. The low sun could not reach the coulees and ravines high in the hills, and there the shadows moved and faded, quiescent and alive.

She smoked, and tried to recall the security she always felt at the wheel of the big car. The front seat of the car had always been a secret room.

She breathed a small sigh of relief when she saw the small activity at the Cross-Roads, a man at a gasoline pump, a new blue sedan, women with pretty hats, a man with no overshoes and a light coat, California bound. Someone was crossing the highway with a bundle of groceries from the store, glancing up and down the highway and scuttling. Down by the stockyards a brakeman moved alongside a few stockcars, and up ahead a locomotive waited, silent plumes of white steam hovering. A horse tied at the saloon, and a woman was calling for a child.

She smiled a little at a Model-T, a pile of Christmas trees lashed to it, to running board and top and engine.

The sight of them . . .

You see it was at Christmas time last year.

He had given her a present. Was there something in the year, the mind, that repeated itself? Would he remember?

She turned into the highway. She began to drive fast, and faster, urged on by something . . . the big car purred, the wind whipped the side curtains and bulged them out and a dampness came in the car from the steaming river below, snaking along between icy banks, slipping under the ice. She had lost a lot of time on the county road. If the commissioners . . .

Then ahead was the tall black grain elevator, the top like a triangular hat, then the red brick hospital, the big windows and the drive for the ambulance, then the streets of Sentinel, the neat bare trees, and people with bundles. A child dragged a sleigh, struggling to move it across a bare place on the sidewalk.

Already the Christmas trees were lashed to the lampposts.

She hadn't read the *Examiner* that week, but there must be something going on. There were a great many cars in town, a great many from the country, old sedans and touring cars with snow piled on the running boards. Parked all along the streets. There was something funny about it though. No one was dressed up. Everybody seemed to have come suddenly.

As if someone had telephoned, as if someone had called suddenly, and just as they were—at the barn, at the blacksmith shop—they had jumped in their cars and come.

The movement in town all seemed to go in one direction, down Bart Street.

It might be the celebration at the public school, the pageant, the cookies the parents brought, and the high-school band playing "Silent Night"—but the school was deserted, the bare yard, the snow tramped to ice by children's feet. The swings on the big cast-iron frames moved slightly in the breeze, and the pendants of the Giant-Strides touched together, rang clear like bells.

The movement in the town was all in one direction.

The day was brighter, and frost began to fall in the sun, sharp little phantom flakes. It wasn't cold enough to frost the windows of the City Drugstore. Presents there, arranged on snow of cotton and mica, a toy house with a red chimney, bottles of perfume, fountain pens. She could see in the window quite well, because the old touring car in front of her had stopped a moment and held her up. There was a jam ahead, someone was honking a horn. When the sound stopped she could hear voices. She had never heard voices sound like that.

It was just after two, the shimmering sound from the steeple of the Gothic courthouse still hung in the air. She went ahead now. There was a sad little band of men and women from the brick church, each with some brass horn or drum. A dog sat beside them; there was a black kettle hanging from a wire on a tripod, covered with chicken wire that had meshes wide enough for dollars, not wide enough for hands.

But there was no music. The eyes of the little band were on something down the street.

Have you seen the things in the window of the Men's Store? The shoe skates? The dummy in the skiing costume, holding a ski pole? A muffler makes a nice gift.

This is Bart Street. The bank is on Bart Street.

The cornice is of granite. MDCCCLXXXVIII.

There are all those people in front of the bank. You see heads moving, a sea of heads.

She stopped the car. There was a space beside her at the curb.

She jammed the car in it, got out and began to run, pushing and elbowing her way. They were solid in front of her and she had to push, push, and then she began to fight to get through.

She stood at the bottom of the steps that led up to the high narrow doors. A woman pushed by her, ran out of the crowd and pushed by her and up the steps, and clutched the steel bars on the doors, hanging there and clutching.

But the green shades were drawn.

The bank was closed.

CHAPTER 34   She didn't want sympathy or understanding: she told Clyde and her mother what had happened as shortly as she could, but each precise, cold word carried an echo.

The people at the bank had let her in. Not because she was a Bart, but because of the note. And there in Peter Barton's office a strange man in a serge suit had sat and smoked, asking over and over, "Can you raise it? Can you raise it in six months?"

She didn't have to tell Ruth. All that morning the telephone had been ringing, neighbors calling to tell of the run on the bank.

Lona had never been neighborly. She thought coldly that the kindness of calling the Bart Ranch was meant, not for her, but for the memory of Tom Bart. She had never felt comfortable in other ranchers' houses, always felt alone in the rooms, different.

She was fighting alone now.

As she went upstairs, she could hear her mother begin to cry. She heard Clyde say something about loyalty.

She wondered if she were going crazy. When you get a little —queer—do you do the sort of thing she was doing now? She walked on past her own room—tiptoed—to her great-grandfather's room. They mustn't know downstairs. Secrecy was a part of this thing she was going to do. If they heard her, and saw her, she could pretend she was in her great-grandfather's room to get a book or a candlestick.

She hesitated outside the door.

What she hoped to get in there was strength: a weapon to fight what closed in everywhere. She pushed the door open. The stale air, holding the past, lifted her spirits. She did not turn on the electric light, but walked in darkness to the marble-topped commode where the lamp was, the old kerosene lamp, a brass angel holding a frosted glass globe.

It was a good sign that there was still kerosene in the lamp.

How fast did kerosene evaporate?

Well, it had been more than fifteen years since someone else had filled the lamp and lighted it. (She could see and feel the movement of a hand and fingers with a match toward the wick.) It would have been her great-grandfather, just before he died, when he was old, failing, troubled, lighting the kerosene lamp, trying to get that room as it had been.

Maybe when he lighted it he thought of days and nights up Lost Horse Gulch when he and his wife were starving, when he had nothing in his stomach but faith in himself. She could almost see him there in the yellow light (and the shadow on the wall) tall, strong, his proud thin face like the Kaiser's.

But he had never been humiliated—had never sat in a room in the bank and been grilled, forced to answer, beaten down, cornered in that straight chair.

"Yes, I'll get the money. In six months." The window above her was barred. They had her alone there in her cheap clothes; her voice was harsh. She had kept trying to hide her hands, thinking of cheap little girls behind counters, waitresses, halls and dingy rooms. She had her eyes fixed on the heel of her shoe—crooked and run over. It gave her foot a deformed look.

"We must have the money in six months."

Now, look at the yellow light on the wall of the bedroom. The old man had made a map of the ranch. It hung there, a checkerboard of squares outlined in red, each township, each Bart section.

Why was he respected? Because of the little squares drawn in red—the ranch. Her world. She was nothing in the other world— that world of girls behind counters, where it mattered if the heel of your shoe made your foot deformed.

They were still talking downstairs, Clyde and her mother. Seemed to whisper. Suddenly she was exhausted. She moved across the thick old carpet, and stood a moment in the shadows by the bed. And then—her eyes on the map—she lay down. She didn't blow out the lamp: the room was as it was in the old days when the Barts were proud. (The heel had made her foot deformed.) And lying there on the black walnut bed, she got the strength she needed—in that wood, in the fibre and the grain there was something that reached her.

She slept, still a Bart, but she tossed restlessly, as if something in her still rebelled at what she was going to do.

She rode out on horseback early next morning, angry. For the second time her mother had not come down to get breakfast: angry with Clyde for taking her mother's place beside the stove. But the winter air was fresh and clean outside.

Some of the men were sawing wood, struggling with logs a foot thick, piled like cordwood, hauled down by sleigh from Lost Horse canyon. There was the flash of cold sun on the whirling saw, the metal-scream as it bit the logs deep, and the sharp odor of fresh sawdust that meant birth, planning and building.

She rode through the willows behind the house, crouching low to clear the red-brown willows that sagged under new snow. She paused for a cigarette at the wire gate behind the willows, and then turned across the dazzling white flat toward the foothills. She rode up and up; ahead the timber was black, spilling down like lava.

She had a secret place.

It was an isolated patch of timber. There were secret depths where dark shadows moved like thick green smoke; a spring gurgled under a sandstone boulder and trickled off under the snow; there were quick pine squirrels and even a marten. Near the edge a coyote had her den.

An enchanted wood.

The snow was deep. Before she reached the timber her horse began to lunge and flounder, and she felt the trembling, the heart beat, in her knees. She got off where the wind had blown a clearing, and there made a little fire. There is nothing like the smell of burning pine needles.

She lit a cigarette, and turned. She had brought her grandfather's field glasses; she took them from their case and raised them. There below her along the creeks as far as she could see, dotted here and there with cattle, stretched twenty thousand acres. (The heel had made her foot deformed. She had tried to hide her rough hands.)

And now, there below, it seemed as if the white fields turned to green . . .

She knew those bends in the creek, where the lazy water slid around the turn and nudged the willow snags below the surface. The sun through the willows traced lacy patterns on the water: green moisture rose through grass roots.

Where is the muskrat that skuttled, little brown ball of fur, down to the bank into the water, a ripple behind a stone?

Do you remember the fall?

The forest fires in Idaho sent smoke over Montana, and in the evening the sun was red over gold fields. The cook shack for the haycrew is deserted for another year, the canvas roof rolled and stored in the blacksmith shop; the tents are folded. But if you rode there now in the winter you'd see piles of hay nudged through the snow where men had slept. You'd see a green Tuxedo tin, a long willow, brown now, and the shell of a grasshopper on a rusty hook.

These men had been lusty as young wolves, their eyes restless, singing bawdy songs, or Jesus songs.

> *Angel came from the bottom of the pit,*
> *Gathered the sun up in her fist. . . .*

Which one had used the fishing pole?

But the winter is more beautiful.

Frost tinsel gilds the willows: the water glides under the ice around the same bend. A plume of smoke rises thin near a haystack, there where a man is warming his hands. Little animal tracks follow secret trails and disappear inside tiny icy caverns.

She stood straight, there by the enchanted wood. Her's, down there. Not an acre mortgaged. The cattle, yes. But when they had spoken of the land—it had been dark in the back room of the bank, and they had the lights on. How could it be, the tawdry little room, and the bright shining acres?

There must be some law, she had kept saying. (Her voice had been harsh and she had wondered about a glass of water.) Where was there fairness in losing everything you had in the bank because you *owed* the bank?

Well, that's just the way it was.

They had her pretty well talked down. "What are you going to do?" they kept asking. "At least five thousand."

And then they had mentioned the land.

Her body had stiffened in the straight chair. "No," she had said. "You won't take that."

But they would, of course. They could, you see.

"I've got to think," she had said. "I can't think here."

She owned twenty thousand acres. But without money behind it, the land was sterile and dead, dead as land without water.

Now she turned, and her cool green eyes rested there on another spot below, on a clump of trees, a little house (see the smoke from the chimney) and a small barn. Down there they had tried to set out shade trees, cottonwoods, carefully dug up roots and all, brought from the canyon behind the barn. Did they think those saplings would take root there?

You can't transplant things in the Lost Horse Valley. They didn't understand things like that, Danny Irwin and his wife.

And his wife . . .

She hesitated there. She smoked another cigarette, took it carefully from the package, studied the tiny print that named the cigarette. CAMEL. She kicked at the frozen earth, frowned and threw the cigarette into the smoldering pine fire that hissed in the snow.

And Danny's wife. She thought of her now as the Irwin Woman. She brought up the Irwin Woman's face, the smile the woman had used when she had looked at Eddie Rohn in that night club, there before her sick husband, remembered how she had looked in Eddie Rohn's arms, there on the dance floor. *There* she had lost Eddie. *There* began her fear of Joe Martin.

She fought to keep the woman's face there, hating it.

But she hoped the woman wouldn't be at home. There was something—something frightening in the woman's smallness, the woman's dependence, something sly that covered strength.

It was quiet around the Irwin place, snow-deadened winter quiet. The little bunkhouse had a deserted, cold look. The trail toward the timber was dead: that meant Charley Evans was out feeding cattle.

There was a small chicken house of packing boxes and two-by-fours, and panes of glass to let in the sun. A rooster and a few hens stepped high in the snow, picking at things, the sun bright on red wings; they made a sudden squawking noise and flapped in through a little door to shelter. Crazy, flighty things. They flapped wings and ticked their feet over the roost. Then—the silence again.

She hated to see the woman.

They hadn't finished their garage. They still ran their old Dodge under the shed. The garage was still a frame of raw pine lumber, a pile of new boards and hammer and saw. They were slow at things. Danny Irwin puttered so.

She moved around the shed. Nothing is so silent as an empty shed. There was no car in it. The tracks led out, to the house— then away.

Only the woman drove the car.

Now she moved swiftly, listening.

There was that smoke from the chimney, not an old smoke, but hot and new. She moved quietly across the snow, watching the white ruffled curtains. She must keep this silence—as if noise would send help.

There was a knocker on the front door—the woman's foolishness —an enameled cast-iron figure of a Dutch girl.

She knocked with her fist.

She wished he hadn't looked like that—that friendly, neighborly smile. She wished it hadn't been so warm inside, a warmth that rushed to greet her. There shouldn't have been that smell of coffee.

His smile was embarrassed, the smile of a man who is not working at that hour in the morning—it was past ten—who was just having breakfast, wearing a dressing gown of plaid wool.

He had been sitting by the fireplace; there was a book open flat, and a coffee cup on the red and cream table.

He looked better than he used to—not so flushed and thin. "I'll get more coffee. I just had my breakfast." He made a friendly wink, as if they had a joke between them. "What do you think of that?"

"I'm only staying a minute," she said. She felt a funny stiffness in her back.

"I'm sorry Betty isn't here," he said. "If you'd come a little sooner—or could stay—"

He stood until she sat down. He stood, offering her cream and sugar. "Just black," she said. She hadn't asked for coffee. She hadn't asked for sugar and cream, warmth or hospitality. She made no move to drink the coffee, but the smooth brown steaming surface was a point to hold her eyes. "I guess," she said, "your wife has gone after the mail."

"No," he said. "She went up the hill to close a gate." She was aware (he had shoved his hands in the pockets of his robe) of his humiliation. "She won't let me out when it's cold."

She hardly heard him. She listened for the sound of the old four-cylinder Dodge motor. Then the strain began, the words spoken that jerked and jarred, ugly, unnatural as lice in a clean bed. She said, "The ranch belongs to you, doesn't it?"

Brain gone, now, his brain and hers. Only the will was left.

"Why, yes. It belongs to us."

She said, "I mean, to *you*."

"Oh," he said. "Yes. It does belong to me. I'm not surprised you ask." His smile was fixed.

She was straining to hear outside again. "I came over," she said, "on business. I want to be sure I'm talking to the right person."

He got up and threw another stick on the fire. She wanted to rise and help him—to lift the stick and toss it in herself so that the new warmth, the new light and heat wouldn't compromise her. "If there's anything I can do . . ."

Formal, meaningless words, like a phonograph record. The fire in the grate was unreal, a fire in a store window, a prop of plaster bricks, a flame of tissue paper. She felt her jaw move as she spoke, still listening outside. "Yes," she said. "I want you to give me five thousand dollars."

His smile remained a moment, then his eyes changed. He shook his head once, as if he hadn't heard right. "What did you say?"

She put the coffee cup aside on the cream and red table. She hadn't touched it, hadn't used his sugar, hadn't felt his heat. Hadn't asked for hospitality. "I said I wanted five thousand dollars."

His hands took the sash of his green plaid robe; his fingers moved and tied a new knot. She felt the cold distance between his eyes and hers. "You're joking, aren't you?" he said. "It's a joke of some kind."

She said, "For three years you've been using my water. Three years and six months. I want five thousand dollars."

He sat looking into the fire. And suddenly he changed, grew cold. "The water isn't worth five thousand dollars. Over a long period, maybe, but—" He kept looking at the fire. "I couldn't do it, anyway. We haven't got anything."

She kept her eyes on him. "You have this land." That sound outside is the water under the ice. It runs along in the open and then slides under the ice and makes that sound. She said, "You can mortgage your place."

He looked up. "You mean that, don't you?"

She didn't answer.

He said, "I've never asked for sympathy. We made arrangements with your grandfather. He let me use his water; for that, I've been keeping up some of his fence. You've never said before—"

She said, "Keeping up that fence isn't worth fifty dollars. The water's worth five thousand."

He said, "But your grandfather and I had this arrangement—"

She said, "Have you got that in writing?"

He brought out a pack of cigarettes from his robe, held it out to her. She didn't look at it. He took a cigarette. He said, "Please think what this means."

"I've thought of it. I need the money in six months. You can get it in six months."

He had a kind of strength now. He said, "You know I'll have to get rid of Charley Evans."

She didn't say anything.

He said, "Suppose something happens to me—before six months?"

Her eyes were steady on him. His color was better, the bones didn't push so against his cheeks. She said, "Nothing will happen to you."

He said, "Would you mind waiting until Betty gets home?"

She was buttoning her coat.

"All right," he said. "All right." And then, "I didn't expect a Bart to—blackmail."

How had she gotten out?

How do people get out of rooms? Well, a shell comes, thick and hard. You hold yourself so, and so. And speak. That's how you get out of rooms.

She was on her horse, riding home.

Blackmail. She kept hearing it, over and over. The shell wasn't thick enough. Blackmail. There was rhythm to the step of her horse in the snow. Something stirred in her mind. Something old, once close, half forgotten.

Sticks and stones. Sticks and stones. Will break my bones. A pushed-out thought. Sticks and stones will break my bones.

But names will never hurt me.

Ruth was alone in the kitchen.

She had sat on her bed a long time that morning, and she saw the gate shut, and watched Lona's horse disappear into the first small patch of timber above the Irwin place.

She had gone at last to her dressing table, sat there, feeling things with her hands, her comb, her brush, and she arranged small bottles and instruments there in designs.

She must hurry now. She didn't dress. She stood in the closet and felt the cloth of dresses and suits, and took out the old satin quilted kimono. Little tufts of pink and blue wool, small designs of pink and blue flowers. Binding frayed. Didn't matter. She sat on the bed again, crossed her legs to put on a shoe, and kept feeling her foot with one hand, pressing fingers against the arch, looking across the Bart Ranch.

The field was flat and white, a line of willows snaked off down the valley, and there in the middle of the whiteness was the gaunt frame of a derrick. She tried but couldn't think of activity around it, of summer, of far-off warmth, and the blue shirts of men and shouting. Only a frame, a gallows, in the snow.

It was still in the house: she listened, leaned forward and listened, pressing her fingers against the arch of her foot, feeling pressure on nerves. Three vessels under her skin—veins, arteries.

Which was which? One gushed, one flowed. One emptied the heart.

She should have been up two hours before, should have got breakfast. Lona had spoken once before.

There is no room here for headaches and laziness.

Lona would speak again. Today when Lona got back from riding over those white, white hills she would speak. There was something in Lona's eyes. She'd seen it before, in a mirror.

Clyde, of course, had got breakfast again that morning. She wondered where he was, how he had answered when Lona had said, "Where is my mother?"

Why had she been unable to get up, to go into that kitchen, to fry pancakes, to feel the weak light of winter morning? She had gained an hour or two away from Lona. She had locked her door so Lona couldn't come in. Couldn't *get* in. Couldn't open the door and stand in the half darkness and accuse her . . .

She couldn't stand it. Couldn't stand it.

But Lona would be faced, and humility, and shame.

She kept pressing the arch of her foot, the veins and the arteries.

And this time Lona would put her out. Yes, she would. Give her a little money, and put her out.

She felt the gorge of fright in her throat, and kept watching the white hills of the Bart Ranch.

How would Lona say it this time?

Ruth's mind kept feeling around, nudging at something. Nudging and feeling, and scurrying back to the safety of the white, white hills out there and the Bart Ranch.

The thing the mind sought was familiar, almost nameable. Not quite nameable.

A drink?

Maybe a drink.

There was whiskey in Clyde's room. He had bought it for Thanksgiving. Perhaps a drink.

But that wasn't it. A drink only put things off. And Clyde—she didn't want Clyde to see her drinking.

Her mind went out to the familiar thing again. Whatever it was, it was there all the time, more and more real. But still untouchable. A mouse, nibbling . . .

Startled away.

She wondered where Clyde was.

She went downstairs then, in the old quilted kimono, haunted by a sense that she had walked like this before, felt like this before; she must get those dishes done.

Clyde would have done them, but she knew how Lona felt about his doing her work when he had work outside. He would have washed the knife. She believed it was called a French knife, a long triangle-shaped knife, kept sharp on the grindstone in the blacksmith shop, finished off with the steel that hung there from the rack on the table.

Did you ever stand near the tracks of a train when the engine roared past? Something seems to call you from under the wheels, a shy, beautiful voice.

Did you?

She ladled water out of the reservoir in the stove, dropped the knife in the pan, and the dishes on top.

Oh, many nights during the months she had sat with Lona and Clyde in the living room, dreading the moment. The pattern was always the same, and she knew it by heart, knew the look of their faces and the sound of their voices. She might have been a ghost.

It always began when Clyde smiled, stretched his hands over his head and yawned.

"Well," he always said, "guess I'll go up."

Then he always sparred for time, waiting for Lona to follow, to be close to him. He would go to her chair, stand behind it, read a few paragraphs of what she was reading, stand there pretending to read. She never moved or turned to him. He could not see the tenseness in her face as he stood there.

Then he would start out of the room. But he always paused at the bookshelf near the hall door, stopped and looked at the books there, and then stood with one of them in his hand. "Mmm," he'd say, and maybe come back to Lona with the book. "Did you ever read this, Lona?"

"I believe I have," she'd say. "Go on up, Clyde. I'll be up."

"Well," he'd say, "I guess I'll go up, then." He always looked back at her from the bookcase.

The water in the dishpan was almost too hot for Ruth's hands. She took them out a minute, holding them just above the water. She had wanted to say, when Clyde looked back from the book-case, "I'll go with you. I'll go up with you."

She had always wanted to turn to Lona and say, "Can't you see what you're doing to him? Don't you know he has a chance to be big?"

And never did, for Lona would have looked at her with disgust, at the woman who wanted her daughter's husband. A kind of incest.

Where was Clyde now? The window above the kitchen sink looked out on the back pasture where the saddle horses were. There was a long trail worn in the snow from the barn to the waterhole, winding down, and beyond that a fence.

The scream of the woodsaw from behind the woodshed . . . then the silence of the snow beyond the waterhole.

She tipped the water out of the dishpan and listened to it gurgle down the sink, watched it whirl about the drain.

There was the knife. There in the pan. Dangerous thing to have put in the pan, under the dishes. She filled the pan again with warm water, moved her fingers in it.

She could see Clyde now. Across the waterhole, near the fence, leaning over, using an axe or hammer on a pole. She couldn't hear it, for the scream of the woodsaw out there. Strange that he should have ended there with an axe and a hammer and a pole, and the greatness of him hidden upstairs somewhere in a box or a suitcase.

Those pages of his. Would he believe that she had sense enough to tell him what they were?

Her arm jerked. She felt something.

Afraid to look. But she must look. The water in the pan was quite bloody. See the blood moving from the cut, little streamers of blood, feeling out into the clear warm water. Flowing easily. Artery or vein? One gushed. This flowed, out and out, spiral twisting feelers.

She wasn't thinking at all. She raised her eyes and looked across the white, white snow. She could see his arm rise and fall; the woodsaw was silent a moment, and she could hear the thump, faint, delayed echo of the blow on the pole.

And glanced back at the pan, and the water, red-brown now, streamers gone. Jerked her hand out.

Stared at it. Frightened. Her eyes on him again. Wanted to run to him. She was going to be sick. There was a clean towel on the rack and she grabbed it down, tore off a strip, bent her neck and wrapped the neat long cut on her finger.

She had to tell him.

And she was going to tell him.

Oh, but this wasn't the way to do it. She ought to fix her hair, and put on a dress. Lipstick. Feminine things . . .

But she wasn't going to bother. She would go now, like this, in this old quilted kimono.

She would go to him out there just like this, and say, "Clyde, I love you."

Lona rode slowly down from the Irwin ranch. She didn't want to see anyone. She wanted it to be after one o'clock when she reached home, wanted the men away at their work again, sawing more wood. She didn't want to speak.

It was going to take time to get over this feeling she had. Time alone.

She wanted her mother to be out of the kitchen. She couldn't stand the sight of her mother's hands, red and rough, those old shoes she wore, turning so at the heels, her apologies for doing everything wrong. She wanted her mother upstairs.

She didn't want to hear Clyde's quiet voice, the gentleness of it. She didn't want to think of the new strangeness that had come over him. Not her fault.

No one understood anything she did. No one understood the fear of twenty thousand acres. The bank.

No one would understand this last move. Well, they'd never know about it. They'd wonder where the money came from, but no one would ask. Taking, taking.

There is a funny quiet in ranch houses after noon. The fire is dying in a thousand kitchen stoves, embers blinking red eyes in gray ash, a half-burned stick goes *klunk*, and silence.

She let herself in the back dining room door carefully, knowing the little sound it made. The table was still cluttered with bowls and serving dishes, grease in the gravy bowl was white and hard. The roast was cold in a little pool of jelling, pinkish gravy. Salt shaker tipped over.

I will never be any tireder than this.

The egg beater had been used. It lay in a round pool of egg yolk. Roasting pan on the oven, liquid dry and flaky. The big zinc-topped table in the kitchen was littered with spoons and bowls and plates, stacked up as the men had brought them in. Over the sink the alarm clock ticked away, ticked as loudly and busily as if someone stood there, hands in water, as if the bread were rising in the big pan on the stove, as if the floor were wet and sleek with scrub water.

And the dishes weren't even done. Not even started. She stood there looking at them a moment, piled there. Then at the soap box.

Blue and white box with a picture of a tub, and bubbles floating out of it. Keeps clothes white as snow, no scrubbing, rubbing or tubbing. After using, look at your hands.

It isn't blackmail.

Funny how the ticking of an alarm clock soon becomes silence.

There was no sound from the front of the house.

Of course there was the wind outside, but that was silent, and the swaying silver willows outside must make some sound. And the rattle of a window somewhere.

She moved into the front dining room. The table was not set. If her mother and Clyde had eaten, it was in the kitchen. The expanse of mahogany table was dusty, and the light from the window made the hand prints, finger prints, stand out on the shiny surface. Chairs in their proper places along the walls. The English print of a racing stable in a mahogany frame needed wiping.

In the picture the groom is brushing down a stud's hind leg, two jockeys are quieting a rearing horse. The jockeys have faces like mice, and the horse has a head like a rabbit.

Oh, there are lots of things you can think of.

Strange how often you have looked at the pendulum of the big clock. Because it is the only moving thing in the room. Nothing in the room ever moves, not even the people who sit there, for they sit still as statues, looking at something outside, watching.

For a moment she hated the room, the clock, the house. She wanted to stride through the room, change it, drag this chair out, take out that rug, stop the clock, put a new face on things. . . .

The pendulum dragged back and forth.

Sticks and stones.

There was a creak upstairs. She could tell where it was. She looked out into the hall. Moved out there, stood under the portrait. *He* would understand.

She began to mount the stairs slowly, because she was so tired. She took the turn at the landing, stopped a moment, and went on up.

The door to her mother's room was open.

For the first time in her life, she was shy about going in there Not her mother's room. Ruth's room.

Oh, she would go in, speak of the dishes not done, the way everything was not done. She had to. No one understood, but she had to.

She kept looking in the doorway. Something different about the room: maybe not. There was the window, there was the fluted shade hanging from the green cord, the painted washstand, the little woodstove.

She would go in, but this was the last time. You couldn't change people.

Then she knew what was different . . .

There beside the bed.

Her mother's bags. The pigskin traveling case, and the big bag: R. B. H. Then she saw her mother.

She had always known that her mother was beautiful. She wanted to turn away, and couldn't. The sun that stared through the window made the room shabbier than ever. But Ruth . . .

Ruth was smiling, her hands on Clyde's shoulders, looking at him. Those two in that shabby room. And when they left . . .

The shabby silence.

They stood there close.

Clyde said, "Lona."

She tried to avoid his eyes, took off her hat and ran her fingers through her hair. Sudden fear of that room, empty.

He was watching her gently, as if he knew her tiredness, knew *her*, and didn't want her. He said, "We were waiting."

She was grateful for the sun that slanted through the window, blurring their shapes. "You don't have to talk." He was very tall, standing there. Ruth's eyes were the same she had seen in the mirror that night—pitying. Lona spoke first.

"You can take the car," she said. "Leave it in town." She took off her gloves.

Clyde said gently, "You can get the divorce."

She turned. Hesitated when she heard her mother take a step toward her, heard Clyde's quick movement. She went on down to the kitchen.

The blue box of soap was there beside the sink, the pale blue box.

She got hot water from the stove, and dumped soap into the pan, swishing the water, drowning the sound upstairs, the footsteps.

I could have stopped them, but I didn't.
I gave them the car.
Sticks and stones.
I'm not wicked. I'm not.

CHAPTER 35   *The old postoffices are dusty, with varnished dark wood everywhere. Breast high desks, with scratchy pens and thick black ink. Tattered posters: Join the Navy and See the World. A sailor grins beneath a big long gun and* Old Glory.

Reward: $5,000 for information leading to the . . .
See the depraved jaw, shifty eyes, the twisted mouth.
Gilded words over brass barred windows. Stamps. Packages. General Delivery.
Listen, lady. Look again. Watch her look again. Why, she could miss your name in all those letters, easy. Listen, lady.

Lona wrote letters. *Eddie Rohn, General Delivery.* Cheyenne, Pendleton, Soda Springs, Calgary—the rodeo towns. He would come now, for she was free. She could almost see him at some general delivery window, his hat in his hand. Then he would have her letter.

She was cooking now. She closed off all the house except the kitchen, the back dining room, and her bedroom. She never went into the living room at all except on Saturday night.

There were only three men on the ranch now, counting Joe Martin. She couldn't afford more, but somehow Joe got four men's work from them. On Saturday night they went to town—but not Joe Martin. She wondered about it.

Those nights there was safety in the living room, in the furniture, in the weight of the draperies and the chandelier. She could see the portrait in the hall. The front door was always locked, the front porch piled high with snow. If Joe Martin—if anybody came in the back way on Saturday night she could be upstairs in a moment, upstairs in the office where the gun rack was.

But Joe Martin made no trouble.

He relayed her orders each morning. He seldom spoke to her. There had been no rift, except over a dish of prunes. She had not cooked the prunes enough, and as the four of them sat in the dining room she had watched, fascinated, a twisting inside her as if a hand clutched, hurting. Joe Martin had set the prunes aside.

She didn't say anything. She didn't want a showdown.

Yet the showdown came.

She supposed it began with the man she hired in Sentinel. He was young, with a smile. He reminded her of Eddie.

She came to look forward to meals because he smiled, because he was polite, and called her Miss Lona. One night she made an apple pie.

Joe Martin fired him.

She saw him standing with Joe beside the bunkhouse. It was beginning to snow, the early smoke from the bunkhouse chimney floated to the ground. She could see Joe's lips move, and his lips answer. She saw him go back inside the bunkhouse, saw him come out in a few minutes dressed in his suit. He had gloves, but no coat. She couldn't believe her eyes: he walked away from the bunkhouse, out into the snow, through the gate and toward the road. There was something terrible and lonely about it, and the room she sat in took on the loneliness

She stood up, angry. Sending a young fellow off like that into the snow and cold. Why, she'd go downstairs—why, she'd go out— why, she'd—

She would take the key off the hook under the portrait and take the car and drive the young fellow to Sentinel. She'd go down right now. Take that key and slam out of the door. Standing there in her room (and the mountains out there and the fields, twenty thousand acres) she could almost feel the power of the old Pierce. She'd go right down.

The room was cold.

In a moment, she sat back down in the chair. She wasn't afraid of Joe Martin. It wasn't that at all. It was only that she didn't know about the young fellow's work. Maybe he was slack. Joe—Joe probably had good reason to fire him.

December meant thin cattle, thin haystacks. That morning she had scratched a match to look at the thermometer: ten below.

Joe Martin lingered in the back dining room. Lona stood at the sink, wiping a skillet. Outside the dark window snow flew in thick sharp flakes, swirled angrily beyond the electric light.

She hated winter.

She wondered how she stood her thoughts, that moved and crowded, revolved in the hotel room. The letters she wrote were escape; she knew it each time she got out the little cedar chest with the heart-shaped padlock and tiny key. Eddie had won it on a punchboard. Inside was a flat pad of mock linen paper and her fountain pen.

She gave the skillet another wipe. Joe Martin said, "We've got to start feeding." He poured himself some coffee. She pretended not to notice the "we."

"Yes," she said. "In a week, maybe."

The snow darted at the glass, flakes shining in the weak light. He said, "We got to start today."

She set the skillet on the stove. "No. Not today. There's not enough hay to last the winter." She felt his eyes.

He made a cigarette, his fingers steady, sure, smoothing tobacco and paper. His tongue touched the paper delicately. Then, "We're starting today."

She strode to the table, pulled out a chair and sat opposite him.

She reached in her pocket for cigarettes, took one out, tapped the end sharply.

He reached for a match, fumbled, brought out a stub. No head on it. She waited.

Now he brought out a good match. He scratched it with his thumbnail. He lighted his cigarette and placed the match carefully in his saucer, balancing the end on the edge.

She spoke suddenly. "Let's get this straight, right now. You won't begin feeding today. Or tomorrow either. Or the next day. You don't tell *me*. I tell *you*." She took out a match, lighted her cigarette. "Understand?"

She stood up, eyes on him.

He looked at her. His eyes had been like that in the hotel room. And her eyes shifted. Then she heard his quick step in the back dining room, and the door slammed.

Stay away from the window in your bedroom.

The thing was, Joe Martin was right. He knew cattle. She had had an offer for a hundred head of cows, and a lot depended on how fat they were.

But stay away from the window. You can see what he's doing from there.

She washed dishes slowly. She threw some grease into the stove; it burned, flared, exploded a little, huffed and puffed. It left silence.

It was getting light now. The dishes rattled in the pan. She looked out the window over the sink, straining to see Old Baldy in the distance. Up there the snow would be flying like live steam. She wished she had something to read.

You gave Joe Martin orders. He wouldn't dare start feeding.

But don't go upstairs and sit in that chair watching.

She wondered what she would do if she saw Joe Martin getting the hayracks ready, if she heard sled runners squeak across the snow toward the fields: every harness has loose links of chain on the end of the tugs. They jingle like bells.

She left the kitchen suddenly. She stood a moment in the cold living room near the closed Steinway piano; the music rack was bare of albums, nothing left but a fold of popular sheet music, a picture of a lonely figure in an armchair, a telephone silent on a stand.

She went upstairs, into her bedroom.

Stay away from the window.

She stood in the middle of the room. Suddenly she was rigid, listening. If there was anything to hear near the barn, she would hear. If there was anything to see—

She turned toward the window, heard the rattle of chains. She forced herself to watch. She looked levelly at the old sod-roofed barn, at the three teams before the door. And the three hayracks. One moved. (Hear the creak of the runners on snow.) Then another. The third—

Joe Martin wore a mackinaw and scotch-cap, his overalls were tucked inside his overshoes. He moved swiftly, surely. Animallike. He leaped up to the platform of the rack, took the lines in mittened hands, turned the team in a sharp circle and drove away.

She moved her eyes to the little varnished cedar chest on the table beside the plain brass bed.

C H A P T E R 36 — Mrs. Dean had not left much behind in her shack: two wire coat hangers, a cold-cream jar (open, and the dust was heavy over the rancid cream), an empty hand-lotion bottle.

Lona made a fire in the small black stove with the wood still piled neatly there. The draft roared; in a few minutes the tiny bare room smelled of hot scorched dust.

It would be a good room for Eddie. When he finally got one of those letters. She snapped up the shade. The hot dust danced in the cold sunlight.

She had to keep busy.

There was the letter from the bank. She had made it quite clear, she remembered, that she would pay the note in the spring, not now in winter. Why should they write of a possible buyer for the lower field? She had made it quite clear (she remembered that, too) that she would not sell land.

Why should they write, then? There was something strange about it.

She had burned the letter. It was like those chain letters a cook got once. You had to burn those chain letters or something bad would happen. She had watched the hot coals in the kitchen stove, she dropped the letter in, watched the white sheet brown, then flame, then char. She took the poker and stirred the ashes, and stirred them.

She had gone upstairs and written to the bank. The note would be paid in the spring. She was not interested in a buyer. (And nothing was going to happen because she had burned the letter.) She wrote a second letter to Danny Irwin. She wanted the money by the last of April.

Sincerely, Lona Bart Hanson.

In the office the cold winter afternoon light was harsh on the prints of trotting horses, and glinted on the blued guns in the rack. It all had something to do with loneliness.

That loneliness had driven her here to the shack.

It helped to fix this room for Eddie. There was a lopsided broom in the corner. She swept. She turned out the drawers of the bureau. His clothes would be folded there. She would do his laundry when he came. Because he would come. He would come soon.

(She had burned the letter.)

If I open the bottom drawer of the bureau, if I do that, and there is something in the bottom drawer (something of Mrs. Dean's) then he will come very soon.

She didn't open it right then. She went over and sat on the bed and looked at it. You could open it with the two little brass rings set in lions' mouths. What did they call that wood? Cherry? Walnut?

It would be rotten—to have fought and been hurt—and then not find anything in that drawer. (Something of Mrs. Dean's, to make it harder. She didn't ask anything easy.)

When he comes I'll have somebody.

She got up, looking at the drawer, and then walked quickly over to it and stooped, squatted before it. She took the two brass rings in her fingers and pulled. Jerked and pulled (everything swells up) and jerked.

The drawer gave, opened. She closed her eyes. She didn't have to open them. She hadn't seen. If there was nothing there and she didn't know there was nothing there, that wouldn't count against her. Would it? You've got to be fair.

All right.

There was a neat pile of magazines in the bottom drawer. *True Story. True Detective.* Ten of them. She counted them.

Magazines do count. And they had been Mrs. Dean's. You remember she was always talking about her magazines, about the stories, you do remember.

So Eddie is going to come.

Nothing like it had ever happened to her before.

She did not believe in coincidence. Everything that happened to you was something you made happen. You did this, you got that.

But nothing like this had ever happened.

She had gone along the snowy path to the meat house. A few cats followed her, mewing at her feet, hissing and slashing at one another, yellow eyes fixed on the platter and knife.

Frozen flesh has a strange odor, raw and sweet—she lifted down a part of a quarter of frozen beef. She took up the saw and sawed, took the cleaver and hacked away at frozen flesh and bone. Outside the heavy door the cats yowled softly.

It was ten o'clock in the morning. Ten o'clock meant chunks of raw beef in black iron pots. She held the platter piled high with meat. The cats yowled and jumped up on her. She closed the door of the meat house and shoved it with her hip to secure it. And stopped still.

You can hear the motor of a little Ford a long way off. You can see it first, a black speck against the snow, then larger, and the sun flashes on the windshield. It crawls through snowy ruts, then turns off the highway up the twisty road.

She didn't move, watching. The cats kept yowling.

She couldn't move when the little black car putted into the yard and stopped. The door opened. He got out. He saw her there and came toward her.

She looked at the meat platter, raised her eyes to speak, and couldn't.

He said, "Lona, I got a letter."

Her tongue was thick, her throat dry. "Eddie." The cats kept yowling and slashing. She let the platter drop.

He took a step. She touched him first with her fingers before she went to him. She held him so tight that it must hurt him. It must hurt him so he'd remember. She began to sob. "Eddie . . ."

He said, "Don't, darling. It's all right, Lona. It's all right."

She held him tighter. It was so simple. Eddie Rohn was all she'd ever wanted.

CHAPTER 37   Repeal came suddenly: the moonshine, rot-gut, and Monogram whiskey from Canada disappeared. Now came the legal, the peppery Old Anchorage, Walnut Hill. There was a new spirit in the world, people were working, eating, hoping, and sometimes at the bar their eyes went to the big lithograph of President Roosevelt. They talked.

"Hear the Half-Diamond sold some cows for three and a half cents."

"Say! That's all right. Say, things are picking up . . ."

Cars down from the valley stopped outside the Cross-Roads saloon, splashed with mud and water, and a man didn't know how to dress—warm days and frosty nights, and dampness was driven from the earth.

It was good to drink with Tennessee, the bartender, to hear what news he had.

News of old Carter, down country, and his cook and Mrs. Carter. Of a Tuesday night when Jerry King got gowed up at the Pheasant and sold half his ranch to a Texas slicker. Carrie King had hit him with a flat iron. (They turned when cars whizzed by on the highway, thoughtful, and talked again.)

They talked of Danny Irwin, how he did his own work now, how his wife helped him. "Jesus. You ought to see that little woman work."

"Well, somebody's got to. Irwin's man Evans is gone."

They wondered how it was at the Bart Ranch.

"I don't think we ought to do this," she told Eddie. She wanted him those nights, worrying about the letter. Burning it hadn't been enough.

They had the room dark, so the men in the bunkhouse couldn't see a light. And besides, he didn't want the light. He had turned it off. That had hurt her, that he didn't want the light on. Not that she wanted it on—because of the men in the bunkhouse—but his not wanting it on.

She snuggled close to him. "We shouldn't."

"Oh, darling, it's all right. You'll get your divorce pretty quick." She couldn't live without his arms. Only when he held her could she forget the letter. But he hadn't said, "You aren't doing wrong."

Burning the letter hadn't been enough. The neat, clean typing (it had closed "very truly yours," not "respectfully"), the stiff paper had shaken everything. There was a man ready to buy the lower field. That was the beginning of the end of ranches. She'd seen it happen.

Twenty thousand acres made you walk straight in town, chin up. You could be *you*. No matter what you did, you weren't ashamed.

"I don't think we ought to do this," she would say.

"It's all right, darling. It's all right."

What did he mean by all right? That it was all right because she was getting a divorce? All right because there was nothing wrong—and there wasn't—in sleeping with the man you loved? Or were his words a kind of loose comfort?

Suppose he left her. Men hated you to cling. The old vision came up: loneliness, the wind and the drifting snow. She was using little feminine devices, hand-cream, fresh housedresses every day, spending a lot of time on her hair.

"Eddie. Come up to the house tonight, darling."

And that night, "You got perfume on, Lona."

"Do you like it, Eddie?"

And later, "I got to go, Lona."

The panic. "Please, Eddie."

"It's getting daylight." Tenseness in his body. She hated this. "Please."

What did he mean by "It's getting daylight?" That he wanted to protect her? Or was he protecting himself?

He wouldn't dare be ashamed of her.

She owned the Bart Ranch.

And then the gray light in her room, his soft footsteps going downstairs (and the awful emptiness beside her) and the click of the back door as he shut it carefully. She always put her hand there on the warmth where he had been.

And what if one night when he went downstairs he decided he didn't love her?

She put her hand there where he had been. She would tell him very soon that she was going to have a baby.

"Eddie, come here." She would say it suddenly, when no one else was around.

He thought slowly, and when she would suddenly shift her thoughts he always stood a moment, puzzled, and somehow his slowness made him seem stronger. "Eddie, come here. Eddie, I'm so happy."

"I'm glad, Lona. Sometimes you don't look so happy."

"Oh, I am. Especially now."

"Now?" That slowness. "Why now?"

"Oh, I'm just happy now." She would smile mysteriously. "Oh, and I love you, Eddie. I love you."

"I love you. I love *you*."

She was thinking of him differently. Was that the baby?

She thought of him working alone, or sitting in his shack, thinking, working out things, planning, living, reading magazines, sweeping the floor.

Now in the early spring (the very signs of spring were frightening, the great hand-shaped bare spots on the foothills) this awareness of Eddie brought others—of her mother, her grandfather, of Clyde.

Like homesickness, her mind prodded at childhood scenes, at a moment in the sun when the sun beat down on the side of the bunkhouse, the anvil rang clearly from the blacksmith shop, and the smoke from the forge. She recalled the pitch of her mother's voice and the look of her mother's hands, the big shadow of her grandfather reading in the living room.

There was a sense of lateness, a terrible lateness.

"I love you. I love *you*."

She couldn't eat, mornings; the handling of frozen chunks of meat, the braising them in the iron pot nauseated her. A book on home doctoring said you could expect that. She had the book in her room. Eddie never questioned it.

Maybe she ought to see a doctor. She had been reading a good deal: Mrs. Dean's *True Story* magazines. There had been a story of a girl going to a doctor, joyous, hopeful. And the husband had been joyous and proud. There was a picture of the doctor, a great kindly man like her grandfather, and the couple. There were plants on the windowsill in the office, and the sun coming through.

There were no green plants in old Walker's drab brown office. Only a fly-specked diploma and a brass spittoon. And going to see him meant leaving the ranch (this room) and having people see you.

And leaving Eddie and Joe Martin alone together.

But Eddie wouldn't leave her. Eddie would fight for her, as the husband in the picture would. Oh, she could stand the chunks of heavy meat if Eddie would stay with her.

She sat in her chair upstairs, on a blanket she could wrap around her legs, looking across the snow-patched fields, across twenty thousand acres, at the willows zigzagging along the creek. Close to the willows you heard the smallest breeze stir the branches.

In two weeks she would have the money from Danny Irwin. She would sign her name to the check for the bank. *Lona Bart Hanson.* Like washing your hands.

She lifted her chin, proud. With those acres, she could face any damn doctor in the world.

"Eddie," she said, "that fence along the east side near the road is in bad shape."

She wouldn't ride now. She wore a housedress, and stood with him in the hall, rubbing her hands with the lotion she used after dishes. "If you'd get some poles from behind the barn and set them, it would help a lot."

"Sure, darling. Right away."

"Darling," she said. "Don't kiss me until this sticky stuff dries."

From upstairs she saw him walk first to the bunkhouse to get two men, then walk with them to the barn. She waited anxiously until she saw Joe Martin ride away from the ranch.

She sat down. Eddie disappeared behind the barn where the poles were.

But suddenly he came back, alone. He walked swiftly toward the house. He stood a moment in the hall. He called, "Lona."

She got up, trembling. Something in his voice. But that was foolish. Some little thing . . .

He stood at the bottom of the stairs, looking up at her.

"Yes, darling. Yes."

His look disturbed her. "Then poles," he said. "Them poles are gone. The ones I cut."

She paused a moment, then came on down. "Gone?" she said. "Gone?" She looked at him.

"All the best ones."

She hesitated. "Maybe Joe took them to fix something."

"Joe?"

"Joe Martin." Offhand.

"No, but—" He had a funny way of turning his head and making a puzzled look. "But if Joe took them, you'd know. You'd know, wouldn't you? He wouldn't go ahead without saying something."

She kept her voice even, amused. "Why," she said, "he might. Sometime—sometime when I wasn't here."

He said suddenly, "Look. Did he ever do it before?"

She smiled. "Do what?"

"Do things—on his own."

"Darling, of course not."

He made that movement of his head. "Then I'd better talk to him. Better have it out." He stood straight.

She controlled her voice. "Eddie," she said softly, "it's nothing."

But his jaw was stubborn. "Well," he said.

She saw him look down at his hand, saw him look at his feet, awkward, about to say something—something she had to stop.

"Come here, Eddie."

But he didn't move. She went to him, felt something rigid about him. "Lona," he said. "Lona, I want to say something."

Her heart began to pound. She spoke to gain time. "You want to say something. Then say it, if you want to say it." Her eyes were wide and innocent, as if everything surprised her.

He said, "It's going to take a little while."

"Take a little while?" Maybe she was going to be sick. If she was going to be sick, he couldn't talk. Suppose she said it suddenly. "Eddie, I'm sick."

He said, "Could we go up to your room and talk?"

She kept her voice matter of fact. Her heart kept pounding. "Why yes, Eddie."

The stairs were long, long.

Get it over. Get it over. Let him speak. Let him say it quickly.

But he wouldn't speak like that. He sat on the bed and looked at his hands again. She looked out the window a moment and then sat down. Still the calm voice. "It's cold in here. I ought to have a fire. It looks like snow."

He looked at his hands. He looked afraid to hurt her. Yet he was going to hurt her. Something about the set of his head and shoulders told her he was going to hurt her, to be selfish, that this was the beginning of something, or the end, that out in the shack he had been thinking.

He blurted out the first words. "You and Joe," he said.

Her patient smile was rigid. "Joe and I?" She rubbed her upper arm.

Blood flooded his face, but his jaw was stubborn. "Before I came back here. Or—" he blurted this—"or any time."

"Eddie," she said, "what in the world are you talking about?"

"I'm sorry," he said. "I'm sorry. Maybe I'm crazy. But I know things. I know—I know sometimes girls want men." His eyes shifted, but came back.

She kept rubbing her upper arm. "I just don't know what you're talking about." Her arm under the cloth was real.

He said, "I'm talking about maybe sometime you—let Joe come up here—right in here—like me." He rubbed his thumb and index finger together. "He's got—he's got a kind of a *look* about him."

She spoke softly. He must see how *small* she was, how alone, how trusting of his love. "Eddie. Oh, Eddie. You know I wouldn't do anything—like that." As if a girl so small, so alone, so trusting . . .

"But did you?" he asked. "Did you ever let—let him?" She saw the scene behind his eyes, the scene that gave his eyes that sudden almost insane look. He was seeing kisses, tenderness, hands cupped over her breasts, a woman lying on her back with gentle eyes, raising her knees. "Did he?"

A cool, cool voice, like a mother's to a child. "No, darling. There was never anything—like that."

His eyes lit up, suspicious. "What do you mean by that? What do you mean, there was never anything *like that*? Was there something else?" He watched her, rigid.

"You—" she began. "You're twisting everything, darling."

"No, but was there anything else? I got to know. A man's got to *know*."

"Darling, of course not. I love *you*. Don't you see?" Her eyes were pathetic. "Don't you—?" A tremulous smile. "I couldn't do anything like *that*."

"And," he said, "and you never wanted to, did you?"

"Oh, darling. My darling."

"You didn't, did you?"

"No, dear. I never did. *Never*."

"Well," he said. "Well, all right."

She got up, went to him. He didn't get up, just kept looking at her. She took him gently by the wrist. "And you won't make a fuss about this, will you?" She sat beside him, and ran her fingers slowly through his hair. "A crazy thing about poles. About some old poles!" She let him see that she could laugh, then, at the word poles.

She knew she would be sick. When he left she was going to have to go down the hall to the bathroom. Not because of what he had said, but because he had a terrible imagination, a monster breathing on her neck. Because now she knew he could leave her.

CHAPTER 38   The sudden breaking and melting of ice in the ditch above the house had brought down high water, a flood moved down and forked around the high ground where the house stood. The dank old cellar was deep in water. She had stood on the steps halfway down, the door opened behind her, and had seen the light reflect on the still black water. The light and the water made her curiously dizzy, apart, not herself.

That was spring—more spring than new buds along the creeks, then shedding horses and sun on the windows. It was a spring that meant a check from Danny Irwin that must come any day, a check that would mean an end to—to what? To sitting upstairs in her room, thinking about being a little girl. Feeling ashamed, feeling your mind prod old ugly things. (And this dizziness, this apartness.)

It was brighter in the living room. There she opened the windows, breathed for the last time the staleness of winter. The new April air was kind and gentle; the sun poured through the open windows.

She got out a bandana, tied it around her head and began to sweep the room—the sun a bright silver blade through the dust. The bandana would please Eddie. She was conscious of stooping to pick up a stubborn bit of lint. Eddie wouldn't have said those things, wouldn't have doubted her, if he'd known about the baby.

She began to hum. Her back ached a little: the book in her room said it would. She felt the small of her back with her hand, and sat down on the old brocaded sofa to smoke a cigarette, watching the smoke curl. She might give up smoking—might at that, for him. He had said something once—

She squinted. This was a day that answered things. You knew, somehow, on such a day that things would be answered, come clear. (No more of that dizziness, that apartness.)

She hummed again, and looked at her hands. You wouldn't have said she'd ever have such smooth hands, would you? But a girl in one of Mrs. Dean's magazines wore cotton gloves at night. The man—the husband—liked the girl to do that.

"That's crazy," Eddie had said. "Gloves in bed."

Her hands were his, she told him. A part of him.

She could hear him now, coming in from the back dining room. He was easy in the living room now, he moved surely, with none of the shyness of other men when they came in here. She patted the place beside her on the sofa. He was part of the room now, his blood flowed with Bart blood. He sat beside her and looked around the room. "Sure looks nice in here," he said. "Bet it took a lot of time to clean this place."

"Not much, Eddie. I like housework. I like fixing up." She looked at her hands. "I never had a chance before you came." She looked soberly at him.

He took her hand and squeezed it. "You poor kid." He settled back on the sofa. They sat a few minutes looking into the bright sunshine. She fixed her eyes on a wavy point in the window where the sun blurred on the glass. Her mind wandered, her fingers explored the back of Eddie's hand, the knuckles and tendons.

Suppose she told him about the baby now, here in this sunny old room? Suppose—but the time was too close to his doubt of her. She could imagine his sitting out there in his shack, thinking.

The telephone rang.

Do you know about country telephones, a party line? It never works just right: somebody's batteries are low, somebody's line is down along sixty miles of thin gray wire. The ring is fuzzy, diffused. You can't tell whether the telephone is ringing one or two rings, or a long and two shorts. But when you live in the country you sense the ring, feel something in your back. You know when somebody wants you.

She kept her eyes on the wavy place on the window. Her fingers stopped on the tendons of his hand.

He was comfortable. He said, "You'd better answer."

She put her head on his shoulder. "Oh, darling," she said, and cleared her throat. "Let them ring again." Now the wavy place had moved an inch. She said, "I was standing on the cellar steps looking at the water."

He looked at her a second. Then, "Oh. There's quite a flood."

"There always was. When I was little, I remember. And the sun's so bright out."

He said, "I saw some killdeers by the creek, cute little fellows. I guess they've got a nest somewheres."

She said, "In some nice safe place away from the water."

"I guess the phone wasn't for here," he said. "They don't ring again."

"No. We could go down and look for the nest," she said. "Why don't we go down now, in the sun?" She stirred.

The phone rang again, insistent, tiny sharp hammer on two nickel bells.

He looked at her. "Eddie," she said, "you answer."

He grinned, and groaned. The sofa creaked under him, and he got up, she watched him stride importantly to the varnished oak box on the wall. He looked stern and important, and winked at her. "Bart Ranch," he said, and waited.

She thought about her hands. What she would do is this: get some of that cuticle stuff (there was an ad in the magazines) and put it on her fingers, soak them first. Her mother used to have that stuff. She would look in her mother's room.

"Yes," Eddie was saying. "Yes." He was not holding the receiver close against his ear, and she could hear the voice, the sound of a voice under water, vague, muffled. (How deep and black the water was in the cellar.)

Eddie turned, holding the receiver near his ear. "Lona," he said, "it's for you."

She shook her head, smiling, whispering. "No. Take the message."

He frowned and spoke again into the mouthpiece. "Will you," he said, "will you give me the message?"

Something came over the wire. (Yes, she would soak her fingers first.)

He turned to her again, holding his palm against the mouthpiece. "Lona," he said, "she wants to talk to you."

She glanced out of the window and spoke a little impatiently. "Eddie, you've got to learn to talk over the telephone here. Tell them—I'm gone."

There was a look about him, a shadow of the stubbornness, of doubt. She braced herself. But he spoke again into the black mouthpiece. "She's gone. She's not here."

Then the voice over the wire, faint, throbbing, drowned.

And Eddie Rohn said softly, "Jesus, I'm sorry. I'm terrible sorry." And put the receiver back on the U-shaped hook. He came back to the couch and sat down. He looked out the window.

She said nothing. She must stop watching her hands, watching them was foolish, tell-tale. She clenched them, looked away from them, thrust them into the pockets of her dress. If she could hide them he wouldn't speak. He wouldn't say anything—frightening.

He said, "It was Mrs. Irwin.'"

It was strange, his saying that, when she'd got her hands in her pockets before he even moved his lips.

"Well?" She was impatient now. "Well—didn't you get the message?" The room was bright, and the sun. The dust danced there. "What did she want?"

He said, "Her husband. He died yesterday." He shook his head slowly.

She watched him: her mind was a thing apart, moving swiftly and surely away from the house, from the dust and the sun and the water in the cellar, and the thing at the end of the flight was Joe Martin.

She heard Eddie say, "You must of loaned her some money, or something." She looked away. "She said she was going to use it to bury Danny, and go away."

CHAPTER 39   Now for the first time she understood Tom Bart.

Here below her was the land he had bought. Not the good land, the greening land along the creek, but the bad land. Here beside her boots were the rough lavalike rocks, porous and dry, here even the sage was stunted, the roots forced deep, seeking a little strength.

But it had been his.

Down there along the dry creek the old cabins straggled, and the Palace Saloon leaned for protection toward the foothills. Tom Bart's hands had lifted those broken doorlatches, his feet had been heavy on those sagging floors.

The April wind brought down the smell of pine trees from the timber line and pushed her hair against her cheek. She made a little clutching motion with her hand and felt the tight leather of her gauntlets press against her knuckles.

Now she understood.

She loved that bad land, loved it because he had loved it, because it had been his and now was hers.

When you lost a part of you were crippled, deformed. You had lost something that wouldn't grow back. Or in its place grew something strange and ugly that you had to hide. She was glad, fiercely glad that he had bought it back.

She had tried to say that he was crazy. Well, maybe she was crazy too. She had sent Eddie off to the funeral. "Be back by three," she told him. "Don't wait around. Come back, Eddie. I'm going to ride."

Suppose she had said, "I want to see that bad land alone. I want to stand on the bluff where I can see it, and then turn and see the good land to the west, down there where the creek bends and the water flows up and eases against the bank. Half of me lives in the bend of that creek. The other half—"

Baldy was hazy and blue in the distance, even the wind flowed blue across the fields.

"The other half of me—"

Tom Bart had had no other half. Now she understood how he had moved and talked and boasted, understood the smile that was not a smile but a sadness. He was half alive. She could see him now, tinkering, building fires, shaving kindling just so. Making the most out of half a life.

But she had Eddie.

She kept her hand clenched, feeling the leather tight across the knuckles. Here at this moment—owning the land and Eddie—she was complete. Complete as the meeting of the sky with the April earth, whole as the lavalike stones at her feet.

She lifted her chin and held her eyes on the peaks. But the fear came back again, the sense of lateness, of loss, that she had felt an hour ago.

"Eddie. Don't wait. Come right back."

She turned then, and her horse's feet struck pebbles rattling into the gully.

The wind whined at her shoulder as she rode.

Eddie Rohn left the Star Garage for the ranch that afternoon at two.

He had sat there in the car near the red gas pump by the curb, and watched the young fellow in tan coveralls fill the tank, check the oil. The young fellow had grinned at him in a friendly way and wiped the windshield with a wad of waste.

"Anything else, sir?"

Sir.

"No, I guess that's all. Charge it to the Bart Ranch."

"O.K., Mr. Rohn."

Mr. Rohn. In twenty-four years it was the first time he had been called Mister. Now he held the big heavy wheel of the soft-purring Pierce and thought. He'd never known people you call Mister. Not even his dad. The only people who called his dad that were peddlers or hide buyers, and if the old man didn't suit them, they dropped the Mister quick enough.

"O.K., Mr. Rohn."

He needed that little prop for his pride. A funny thing had happened. He didn't mind that he had stood in a group of ranchers near the grave, and that none of them had asked him to join them for a drink after. He was prepared for that. He wouldn't have expected it even if they'd known how close he was to Lona. And of course they didn't know.

But he did sort of expect it different from Mrs. Danny Irwin. He understood how she'd be, understood her white face, and even felt he knew about the crying that made her face like that, white and hopeless. That was why he spoke in the first place.

The undertaker was busy rolling up the artificial grass and almost everybody had drifted off toward cars. A few rain clouds were rolling up behind Sentinel and it was getting chilly. Nobody meant it to be that way, but for a moment he saw Mrs. Danny Irwin standing there alone, except for the undertaker.

The Pierce was parked near the grave. He had hesitated there, and then walked suddenly over to Mrs. Irwin. She was just standing there. He didn't know what he was going to say. Something would come.

So far as he could see the old Dodge wasn't parked around, and he thought maybe she would ride with the undertaker. Eddie Rohn didn't want that. It was no time to ride in that big black car of the undertaker's.

So he said, "Mrs. Irwin, would you ride down with me?" He spoke softly, half afraid, because you didn't know how a woman was going to be after her husband died.

The undertaker was still there, rolling up the artificial grass.

She turned, looked first at Eddie Rohn and then over at the Pierce.

She didn't smile. He felt she didn't even see him, only the Pierce. Then she turned away.

He felt a funny thing in his back, driving back to Sentinel to the Star Garage. By the time he asked for gas, he knew the thing he felt was guilt.

There was something in her eyes—like she was judging. He guessed good women were like that. Maybe never in Mrs. Irwin's life had she felt so much love that she would—do anything without being regular married.

Yes, that's what it was. It wasn't all being sad over her husband. It was something else. She knew about him and Lona.

He'd been so careful. He'd been so afraid somebody would find out. He'd worried and worried that one morning early when Joe Martin saw him coming back from the house through the back dining room.

He'd said something to one of the other men right in front of Joe Martin, how he'd gone up early to get a can of 3-in-1 oil. It sounded like the sort of thing a man might want early for some reason.

And then he had glanced at Joe Martin. There was a funny look in Joe's eye.

It was bad, the way he felt. He had no right ever to do anything like that, so that Mrs. Irwin or anybody could look at her that way. She loved him. That's why she let him act like he did. She wouldn't act like that with anybody else. He knew that.

He felt dirty, because he'd questioned her love for him. To do that to a woman, and then ask those dirty questions.

A man gets the most wonderful girl in the world—not like the girls at the Roseland—and then because she does what he wants, he asks her questions and hurts her and makes people turn away.

He began to feel better. He kept calling himself a dirty dog and he felt a big swelling of love inside him, and a terrible tenderness and a deep hatred for anybody who would ever hurt her.

He'd make it all up to her. He'd be—he'd be the best husband. Nobody would ever look at her funny—not at Mrs. Eddie Rohn.

His hands gripped the big walnut wheel.

"O.K., Mr. Rohn."

He drove the old Pierce out from the curb and headed down U.S. Highway 91 for the ranch.

When Lona got back from the gulch she fixed dinner, set it on the back dining room table and rang the bell outside the back door for Joe Martin and the two hired men. Then she went upstairs.

At one o'clock she stood in her window up there and watched the two hired men drive away in a wagon to irrigate. Joe Martin was around somewhere.

She lay on her bed; she kept pulling one leg up and then the other, feeling the spread against her leg. The only real world was this room, these walls, this cold afternoon light. This aloneness. It was not a new feeling. She had felt it in her great-grandfather's room one night, felt it when she married Clyde, felt it yesterday when the telephone rang.

She felt it when she read those *True Detective* magazines. Then only the room and the chair she sat in were real, and the people who moved through the stories.

They had names: Maureen Fauncette. Frank Jordan. They moved in dark tenement halls, used telephones in corner drugstores, sat drinking coffee at midnight in some back booth.

And the trunk in the cellar. Who had scratched up the ground under the elm tree? There were dark streets and the pale flickering of neon signs. A black Cadillac waited under the street lamp. People like Joe Martin. He was like them. Maybe because of the suitcase, the cheap suitcase he kept under his bed. There was a picture of a suitcase like that in one of the stories. In the story they had called the suitcase a clue. A gun was hidden there.

She moved her leg and felt the spread. There was a gun in Joe's suitcase. And a green metal box.

He'd been in trouble—she'd always known it.

The bed squeaked. She stood there in the room. There were the magazines beside her chair. She sat down and picked up the one with the picture in it. This suitcase—see?

Tell Eddie about the bank.

"Well, why not sell it?" he'd say. "It's only one field."

First this field, then another, and then another. She had seen it happen before. Eddie couldn't understand. Eddie never needed a ranch to feel—not ashamed.

This picture, right here. This suitcase. She lifted her head a moment, listening to the silent house.

She hated Joe Martin's walk and his voice and his eyes. He could tell Eddie. But Eddie wouldn't leave her. Couldn't. She was going to have his baby. Eddie's. And Eddie—

Then the thought moved like nausea in her stomach. *What if Eddie asks if the baby's his?*

She stared at the walls of the room, at the bed, at the magazines. In a moment she got up, picked up the magazines, counted them, and put them under the bed.

Joe Martin would go some morning. Ranch work was hard. She didn't pay him much. Suppose she looked up and saw him now, in that tight blue suit, beside the bunkhouse door, ready for town? Standing there as the young fellow who looked like Eddie had stood that time in the snow?

She was breathing hard, fists clenched. Why didn't he go? The work was hard. She didn't pay him much.

And he never went to town.

She couldn't remember when he'd been to town—not since Butte. She remembered him sitting there beside her in the Pierce, maybe thinking—that, planning then to come to her room. The whole thing planned. She'd never have offered to loan him money. Wouldn't have changed that bill for him—that hundred dollar bill.

She had stood on the sidewalk, that bill in her hand. The sun had warmed her neck and glittered on the bright bottle of ink in the show window.

She had said, "This bill is a hundred."

Now she got up suddenly and walked to the window and looked down at the bunkhouse.

She had been drunk in that hotel room. It was all blurred, the mirror and the radiator that banged and the nail file. But there was something that wasn't blurred, something clear and sharp in her mind, as if he was speaking again. He'd said, "I've got more money than you." And she had laughed. But he had said that. There had been a neon sign outside the window. He *had* said that.

In the green box. That's where he had it.

He's just a drifter, a hired man. Suppose there was an accident? Suppose they came running in from the fields some day and said his horse had dragged him and he was dead? That happens. That does happen. Once at the Double-Arrow a man was killed like that. What had they done with the things he had left in the bunk-house? Who owned them? They were nobody, those drifters, had no homes, never got letters. Who put away their socks and ties, their bits of paper and stuff? Who opened their suitcases?

Somebody did.

Did you, Eddie had said, did you ever? Did you?

Oh God, she wished he was dead.

Remember this: nobody ever really kills anybody. Maureen Fauncette (how could that be a real name?) drank. The magazine said they found bottles in her closet. And Frank Jordan took dope. They found the thing he used. There was a picture of it.

Frank Jordan was a real name.

But remember this: nobody you know or ever heard of ever killed anybody. That happens to other people—people in Chicago (in alleys or tenements) or in New York (the Cadillac under the street lamp).

Once she'd known a man named Jordan.

Suppose Joe Martin came up to the house right now? Suppose he came with—with that look? She would have to shoot him. Because look, there were no policemen to call, no neighbors.

She remembered a Mrs. Brunig, a kind of friend of her mother's. Mrs. Brunig had been young. Mrs. Brunig's husband had been out feeding cattle when the man came into her kitchen. There was no gun—no rifle—only the meat knives on the rack over the sink. Her husband found her covered with the man's blood.

Mrs. Brunig lived in Sentinel now, a pretty, comfortable woman with graying curls. She went everywhere, knew everybody.

They understood those things in Sentinel. (The courthouse was yellow brick, and its history was Bert Bart's.) They knew what a woman alone should do. Must do.

But Joe Martin wouldn't come, of course. Not on his own.

Well, suppose she called him. Raised the window, and called

him. But someone might hear. Someone who just happened along might hear—a tramp, or a man hunting a job.

Raise your right hand. Do you solemnly swear . . . ?

Yet it had to happen here, in this bedroom. The bedclothes had to be rumpled, a chair knocked over. They could see how she'd fought.

She'd get him in the office first, looking over a talley sheet. Then she'd slip out, go to her bedroom, and call him. "Joe . . ."

He'd come. He hadn't been to town for a long time. Not since—since Butte.

And then she'd—

Her eyes came back to the room, to the distance between bureau and bed and wall; the Luger would have to be in a safe place, a place Joe couldn't see. Because she'd have to wait for Eddie, so he could hear her scream. She didn't like it that way, but it was better.

There was the little cedar chest on the table beside her bed. If you could fix the padlock so it looked locked, and wasn't—

And you could. She tapped the box and the spring snapped open. She tapped it again. And again.

Tired. She was tired. She sat before her mirror and shrugged her shoulders.

You are twenty-two years old and this is your face. You wouldn't do anything like that. You're Lona Hanson. This morning you put wood in the stove, you can almost feel the roughness of the wood right now. You washed your hands at the kitchen sink and rinsed them in clear water.

The strange things you thought of, and would never do. Didn't have to do. Joe will give you the money. Either he does, or you turn him in.

Before she went to the bunkhouse she stopped in the kitchen and washed her hands. She rinsed them, rubbing the palms and knuckles hard in the cold water, and she dried them hard with a rough towel.

On the path to the bunkhouse there was only the sound of rye-grass—last year's rye-grass rustling in the wind that had sprung up cold in her face. The sun was cold. There wasn't a sound on the ranch she didn't hear.

She heard the click of the latch on the bunkhouse door as she lifted it, and the click when she shut the door behind her. She leaned smiling against it, waiting.

Joe had a habit of braiding things, weaving strands of hair or hide into bands or thongs. He was sitting there exactly as she expected to find him, one leg up on the low windowsill, his fingers moving surely on rawhide. He did not look up at first.

It rather amused her.

"Well, Joe," she said. The words sounded close to her, the beginning of something. "Hat band? Belt?"

He looked up. She had always hated his eyes. Now they recalled every insolence, every plan he'd ever had—here in this chair and in a hundred chairs, rousing to speak when spoken to.

He wouldn't have liked her seeing him as she did—so completely, at bars, and the end of a bar and no one near him. Doing things—reading or braiding in chairs, entering cheap hotels, sitting on a stool in a cheap restaurant watching the waitress, buying a pack of cigarettes and walking to the back of a poolroom. In a hotel hall—

She knew his whole life.

"Joe," she said, "I'm in trouble."

His fingers were still. "Eddie?"

He would think of that. "No. I need money." She came over and sat on the table, legs dangling. She spoke softly. "You've got money, Joe."

Watching her, he worked on the braided thong. "You must of seen it when you sneaked in my stuff that time."

"No. Just the green box. I guessed."

He laughed, but his eyes were cold and hard, like glass in water. "It didn't take much of a guess. Hired hands don't carry hundreds around."

"That's right," she said. (Aware of everything—the table edge against the bend of her knees, the bottle of hair oil on the windowsill, the trademark a transparent rose.) "How much have you got?"

He said, "What do you need?"

She watched his fingers move on the rawhide. "Five thousand."

He kept working; he glanced up. "Why should I give you money?"

She shrugged. "I'll turn you in." She looked at him squarely.

He said, "For what?"

"They've got files. They can find out."

He said, "You've sort of got me, then."

"Yes." And then, "Is the money still under your bed?"

"Right where you sneaked that time."

"Listen," she said, "don't keep saying that—"

"Shut up," he said.

She looked at him, waiting.

He said, "All right. I'll buy in."

Her fingers curled over the table edge. "Buy in?"

"Yeah," he said. "I like it here."

"This is no sale," she told him. "I'll give you a note."

He smiled briefly. "I like it here," he repeated. "I'll like it better up to the shack."

"The shack—" she whispered. "Up to the shack—?"

"Where Eddie is," he said.

She turned away. There was a cobweb on the upper pane of the window. She got up, walked to the window and touched the hair-tonic bottle—a film of oil on the outside made the rose design transparent. Behind her he was saying, "There's no ranch big enough for two men. I don't want him around. I'm going to be big Joe." He coiled the braided thong around his wrist. "Big Joe won't tell about our little party in Butte."

She felt blood in her temples. She said, "Eddie loves me. He wouldn't go. No matter what you said, he wouldn't go." She came back to the table. "Look. You must have loved somebody."

He said easily, "Sure, sure."

She was gentle then, pleading. "Joe, you've always got a place here."

He said, "I know that."

She looked around the room, at the rusty stove, the overalls hung on hooks, the dusty guitar, the boots and shoes drying behind the stove, the battered washtin and a shaving brush fluffed with dried lather. She said, "I know this bunkhouse isn't much. You need a better place, a man like you. Look, Joe, Eddie and I are going to get married. Then you can have the shack. I'll put electric lights out there. You like to read. Maybe running water."

But now she was watching his fingers. He had uncoiled the braided thong from around his wrist. He twisted it around two fingers and slowly drew it tight. He said, "Eddie'll go soon enough when he finds us doing it—up in your room."

The laughter bubbled in her throat. All right, then. She spoke with a strange meekness. "He'll be back in an hour, Joe. If you've got to. Up in my room."

She closed the cedar chest.

When she shot, Eddie would be in the house; he would hear her scream. She would scream with Joe on the other side of the room near the bureau, and shoot him then as if he had his hands on her. Eddie would find her crying, her blouse torn open, ripped. Yes, she would rip it when she screamed.

She looked down at the buttons.

They would believe anything Eddie said. (The yellow-brick courthouse had a smooth green lawn where lazy sprinklers played.)

"I heard her scream," he'd say, and make that movement with his head. "And then I heard a gun and found her all—all—"

The delicate questioning. "Mr. Rohn, did she look as if . . ."

It would come out, the ripped blouse. (Old Simms, the court stenographer, had a scrawny neck and thin wrists and carried an umbrella.)

Well, then Eddie would know that Joe meant nothing to her. She glanced at the little cedar chest by the bed.

She began to file her nails. She heard Joe open the back door; he came right up, his soft steps were sure on the stairs. She wondered if he'd been up before, sneaking, looking over things.

She had her neck bent, looking down at her nails.

He sat on the bed—on her white spread.

She smiled at him, and went on doing her nails.

I was doing my nails. My nails. And suddenly I was aware . . .

He lay back on the bed. She thought of flesh and skin and sweat. She kept filing. (Zip-zip-zip.) In a moment she stopped filing and got up. She felt him watching her. She glanced at the alarm clock.

Two. Eddie would be home by three. She said, "No need for you to come up so early."

He stretched an arm out, lying back. "It's all right here."

She had to move. She had to do something. She turned and went to her closet, a cubicle concealed by a length of cretonne. (How the sun had faded it—that cold sun.) She pushed the cloth aside and shoved clothes and hangers about, as if she looked for some dress.

She felt the cotton cloth in her palm, and heard the bed creak. He was just stretching. She wouldn't look at the chest.

Well. There was lots of time—forty-five minutes. His eyes moved to the clock too. It was as if—as if what moved her eyes moved his.

When she heard the car pull up on the gravel outside, she would tell him to get up and take off some of his clothes—tell him to put them on the bureau. He'd see he must be partly undressed. But he never would be. When he got to the bureau she'd pin him there with the Luger until Eddie came in.

She sat down: the file again. cross. That was the name on the file. She could watch him from the corner of her eye. He suspected nothing. Why should he? She was a Bart.

(Zip-zip-zip.)

She wouldn't sleep in that bed tonight. She'd burn that spread. He had looked, too. She worked feverishly at her nails. Listening, now.

How far away can you hear a car?

Joe yawned. "We got half an hour." And then, "We could really do it. It don't take long."

"No," she said. "I don't want to. Not now."

"It would give you that look," he said. "You got to look that way."

"No," she said. "I told you no."

Of course, Eddie might be late. Her mind followed him. If he bought a pack of cigarettes after the funeral, he might talk a minute with the clerk. (Well, she could file her nails forever.) The clerk might say something, and then Eddie would say something. They'd get talking.

She put her hands up and rubbed the back of her neck, and then her fingers found a thin place on the shoulder of her shirt.

On the right shoulder, a place that would tear and rip under her left hand, and leave the right hand free.

(Old Forbes the coroner limped.)

She mustn't listen for the car. She had never listened for the Pierce before. It had a sound of its own, the Pierce. Eddie would be sitting there, boyish, proud behind the big walnut wheel. Once he had grinned at her. "Say, look at me driving a Pierce-Arrow." It was a long way from a flivver to a Pierce, a long way from a dirt farm to twenty thousand acres. And it hadn't changed him. He was still Eddie in the night club, a white shirt and a fancy tie, flushed with pride, showing off his father's watch.

"She's full of jewels," he'd said.

Well, she was going to change. She was going to be what he wanted. Soon, now. Starting tonight.

That's Mrs. Eddie Rohn.

They would dance together at the Roseland. And after the dance was over (the drive in the dawn, the wet-smelling fields) they would stand together in a room—not this room—remembering the music and the voices.

"I had such fun, Eddie."

"But look—" he'd say. *"We didn't do anything."*

How could she tell him of the music and the wet fields and— him? "Oh, Eddie, I love you."

This thing now had nothing to do with Mrs. Eddie Rohn. She filed. There was a thin spreading line of blood under one nail. Odd, she didn't feel it. And her hands were steady. Only this next twenty minutes (fifteen) she would be Lona Hanson. Then—

. . . Mrs. Eddie Rohn. Had a ranch, but she turned it over to him. She likes to sweep and fix the house and take care of the little boy . . .

She would walk down the street in Idaho Falls, walk in the sun in high-heeled pumps.

Oh, he's up to their ranch. She came down to visit with Eddie Rohn's old man, to bring the little boy down.

"Lona." She started, and was back in the room again. "Lona."

"What?"

"There's ten minutes."

Who was he? Who was she? What did she want from him?

Suppose she said, "Get out of here. I don't want your money. Get off the bed. All I want is Eddie." In a minute she would say that.

But there was the hotel room, and Eddie's eyes.

Joe said, "It don't look much like we did anything. Come here."

"No."

"Your lipstick needs smearing. Put some more on, and I'll smear it."

All right.

She prepared carefully, took up the lipstick called Flame. She leaned forward to look in the mirror. How long did that take? Think about the color. Was this red, or red and yellow? What was there in the past about yellow?

"Hurry up," Joe said.

And when he'd kissed her and smeared the lipstick, she'd tell him to take off his clothes. "Over there by the bureau," she'd say. "It'll look—"

She got up, leaned over him, closed her eyes.

He had one hand on her neck. He took his fingers and rubbed them against her lips, then harder, hard against her teeth.

She tried to pull away. And he did it again. Her breath was high and shallow. She started to speak.

He said, "That's all right." And let her go.

"Well," she said, "finish it. Go on over there. Go on over to the bureau. Make it look right. Get your clothes off. Unbutton—"

He said, "We got time. Get on the bed."

"I—" she said. "Oh, God damn you." High breath in her lungs. Then she heard the car out front. Eddie would call—

He did call. "Lona. Lona, honey." His voice was muffled.

Now. Get Joe over there by the bureau. Get the gun, hold it on him until Eddie got near the stairs, under the portrait, then say those things loud. Then scream.

"There he is," she whispered, desperate. "Get over there. Over there and take your things off." She began to make little motions at her blouse, as if unbuttoning. "Get on over there. Get on—"

"All right," he said. He began to get up, put his hands on the bed and pushed himself up, moved, moved.

And he grabbed her.

He had her arms pinned. Her breath made a sucking sound.

Her arms—she struggled. Got one free. She struggled, her mind a point on the cedar chest. If she could touch it—he was big. If she could touch it—just let her touch it.

She felt the box at the end of her fingers, the cold smooth varnish, and the hump of the hasp under the lock.

He knocked it away. The gun fell free at her feet. He held her quiet a moment, her arms locked. There was nothing but the tick of the clock and the cold light and her breathing. He looked into her eyes. His brain was inside her, feeding on her. He said, "I wondered where you had it."

She screamed then, a sick flat scream that hurt. And Eddie was calling. She heard him on the stairs.

Joe had the gun.

There was Eddie in the doorway, dressed up, blue suit, silk tie. Eddie looked at them.

She began to move, struggling up from the bed, her eyes on the gun. "Gun," she screamed. It came out a whisper.

Eddie moved, lunged. He was beautiful lunging, moving, moving across that cold room—and then he stopped.

He stopped, and a stupid look came over his face, over his eyes. And then his hands—his hands began to move and go up.

She kept her eyes on the gun. It was moving, down a little, down, over and down. The heart, there. To the heart.

The walls bulged with sound.

The silence came from far away, she felt waked by silence. Then she knew that she was breathing, then she knew the room, felt the cold, and saw Eddie on the floor.

She tried to speak, felt a twist in her womb; she tried again because the man who should know her womb was dead. There he was, dead on the floor. The silence then, wave after wave.

She got up then, still watching Eddie, and whispered. "You're going to hang for this."

Joe said nothing.

She said, "I'm going to telephone."

Joe Martin looked up. "All right."

"They'll come get you."

He stepped around—around what was on the floor, stood between her and the door.

He was taking the clip from the Luger. He had a handkerchief in his hand, she watched the white of it in his fingers wiping the butt. He held it out to her.

"Go ahead," he said. "But before you go, put your prints on your gun."

She still saw the white of the handkerchief. She stared at him.

He kept holding out the Luger. "You poor kid," he said. "I heard you scream. Too bad I didn't get here in time." And he smiled then. "You never know, do you?" he said. "These gentle-looking guys."

She whispered. "You're going to hang. They're going to put a black thing over your head."

There was nothing behind his eyes.

She said, "A black thing. They'll have your picture in a magazine, and a picture of your suitcase."

His voice was cold as the late night, as flat as the grayness in the mirror. "You're safe," he said. "You had it all figured out." Then his voice changed. "If they take me, you'll never get that money."

She was afraid to move her eyes from Eddie. If she moved her eyes to that gun—

If she moved her eyes, her mind and body would go with them; nothing was real except where your eyes were. She looked out the window: at four o'clock the smoke from the bunkhouse chimney moved up into the afternoon and faded into evening.

He kept holding the gun out.

Out there the corrals were gaunt and real; she knew how deep the posts were set in the earth, and which ones rotted.

What was strong in her lay there on the floor. Right there. She couldn't see his face, but that face and body were her strength. And always she had loved him. But she couldn't bring him back.

Well.

It was a funny thing to have happened to Mrs. Eddie Rohn.

She stood very tall a moment. In a little while the sun would go down, the room would be colder; she would turn on the light and sit there. It was a funny thing to have happened to Mrs. Eddie Rohn who never wanted anything but to walk down the street sometime in Idaho Falls. But now she raised her eyes to the window again, to the mountains.

High up there on the mountains the shadows were forming, crawling together, and then the shadows began to spill down to drown the canyons, moving like soft dark water over twenty thousand acres.

She guessed it was better than nothing—nothing at all.

The butt of the Luger was still warm from Joe's hand.

THOMAS SAVAGE was born in Salt Lake City in 1915 and spent his youngest years at the sheep and cattle ranch of his maternal grandparents, Thomas and Emma Russell Yearian, in Lemhi, Idaho. His mother, Elizabeth Yearian, divorced his father while Savage was an infant. In 1920 she remarried, this time to Charles Brenner, youngest son of the Brenner ranch family in Horse Prairie, Montana. Savage spent his boyhood between these two ranches, on the west and east side of the Continental Divide, and in Dillon, Montana, where he boarded out for school.

A loner during his school years, Savage—known as Tom Brenner until he published his first novel—graduated from Beaverhead County High School in 1932. He headed for Missoula where, at Montana State College (today The University of Montana), he studied writing under Brassil Fitzgerald. Savage left college for a couple of years, working at a riding academy and a dude ranch in the Pacific Northwest. After he returned to school, he became acquainted with Fitzgerald's daughter, Elizabeth, who had departed for Colby College, in Waterville, Maine. Savage followed her by train, meeting Elizabeth and her mother at the station in Boston.

Both enrolled at Colby College, where they got married in 1939 and graduated the following year. Savage was already at work on what became his first novel, *The Pass*. During the war years, he worked a variety of jobs: the Savages lived briefly in Chicago and returned to Horse Prairie, Montana, to help with the ranch because of the manpower shortage. Two sons, Robert Brassil and Richard Yearian, were born in 1942 and 1943, respectively; in 1949, they were joined by a sister, Elizabeth St. Mark. Savage taught writing at Suffolk University and then worked at Brandeis University for a few years, as a liaison between administration and the public and as a fundraiser. The Savages lived in Waltham, Massachusetts.

In 1955 the Savages had bought a ramshackle house on a rocky point in Georgetown, Maine, and they moved there, husband and wife remaining for the next thirty years. By then, Savage had published his first three novels, the third novel, *A Bargain with God,* proving his biggest commercial success. They took cross-country trips to southwestern Montana and the Lemhi River valley of Idaho to visit family. Tom liked showing off his newest sports car. After 1956, the year his mother died, the trips became much less frequent.

Savage published only one novel between 1953 and 1967, but after *The Power of the Dog* (1967), he published five more novels within a decade. His novelist wife, Betty, published a total of nine novels, eight of them between 1970 and 1980. Savage published his final two novels in 1983 and 1988. Betty died of lung cancer the following year; thereafter, Savage lived in Seattle and San Francisco before settling, in old age, in Virginia Beach, Virginia, near his daughter. He died in the summer of 2003, at age eighty-eight.

O. ALAN WELTZIEN, longtime English professor at The University of Montana Western in Dillon, has pursued Thomas Savage's trail for several years now. He wrote the introduction to Riverbend Publishing/Drumlummon Institute's re-issue of Savage's first novel, *The Pass*, and he is the author of *Savage West: The Life and Fiction of Thomas Savage*, the only biography of Savage.

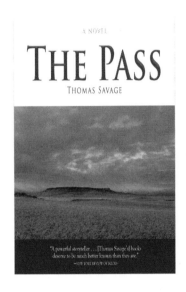

A NOVEL

THE PASS

THOMAS SAVAGE

"A powerful storyteller.... [Thomas Savage's] books
deserve to be much better known than they are."
—NEW YORK REVIEW OF BOOKS